Set in the rural French farm Verdun during World War II, "Eyes for the Allies" is a deftly written and inherently compelling novel by author Chris Santner that is filled with intrigue, action, and romance. While especially recommended for community library General Fiction collections, it should be noted for personal reading lists that "Eyes for the Allies" is also readily available in a hard cover or a soft cover edition as well as a digital book format.

Midwest Book Review

———— ✦✦✦✦✦ ————

Great read! Santner created believable characters amidst historically correct plot lines. Its parallel plot structure kept my attention for the entire book.

A great book full of details describing the super weapons & plans the Germans were cooking up to repel the Allies. It really did take a lot of special forces recon to gather information on what these weapons did and how they might be defeated. This book does a fantastic job showing what goes on to plan and execute an attack on such a prepared enemy. Plenty of action and intrigue as well.

Amazon Books

———— ✦✦✦✦✦ ————

Loved the parallel structure of several plot lines, kept my interest the whole time!

Barnes and Noble

EYES
FOR THE
ALLIES
A NOVEL OF WORLD WAR II
ESPIONAGE IN EASTERN FRANCE

CHRIS SANTNER

LitPrime
"Your story is our priority"

LitPrime Solutions
21250 Hawthorne Blvd
Suite 500, Torrance, CA 90503
www.litprime.com
Phone: 1-800-981-9893

© 2021 Chris Santner. All rights reserved.

No part of this book may be reproduced, stored in a retrieval system, or transmitted by any means without the written permission of the author.

This is a work of fiction. Apart from the well-known and historical people, events, and locales that figure in the narrative, all names, characters, places, and incidents are a product of the author's imagination or are used fictitiously. Any resemblance to current events or locales or persons living or dead is entirely coincidental.

Published by LitPrime Solutions   07/15/2021

ISBN: 978-1-954886-96-4(sc)
ISBN: 978-1-954886-97-1(hc)
ISBN: 978-1-954886-98-8(e)

Library of Congress Control Number: 2021913727

Any people depicted in stock imagery provided by iStock are models, and such images are being used for illustrative purposes only.

Certain stock imagery © iStock.

Because of the dynamic nature of the Internet, any web addresses or links contained in this book may have changed since publication and may no longer be valid. The views expressed in this work are solely those of the author and do not necessarily reflect the views of the publisher, and the publisher hereby disclaims any responsibility for them.

CONTENTS

SUMMARY

Alphonse DeBoy and his three grandchildren, Aurélie, Josette, and Luc, have been busy supporting and supplying food to their American visitor, Major Mark Dornier, for close to a year from their farm just outside Les Petites Islettes, east of Verdun. Major Dornier parachuted into the Forêt Domaniale de Lachalade in October 1943 and has been living in a dugout at an old World War I French artillery camp, complete with connecting tunnels. The British SOE trained a second British officer to join the major, Lieutenant Alex Ryder. And as it happens, Alex is in love with a secretary, Polly Berson, who secretly is more than just a secretary. Having passed the commando school in Achnacarry, Scotland, Polly is a captain in the SOE. She also happens to be the cousin of Aurélie, Josette, and Luc.

As Major Dornier gathers information on German defensive positions, Reich Minister Albert Speer has secretly developed several weapons to slow the Allies when they invade. It falls to the SOE and its operatives throughout eastern France to provide the Allies with an accurate account of these weapons.

Complicating things further, during the months since he arrived, both Josette and Aurélie have developed feelings for Major Dornier.

Now, after almost a year of observing the Germans defenses, General Patton's Third Army approaches the area and requires the information to circumvent the Nazi special weapons. Unexpected events challenge all of their relationships and lives.

Set in the rural French farmland and forest west of Verdun, the story involves the senior war staffs of both the Allies and Germans, the SOE, and provides a tale of intrigue, action, and wartime relationships.

ACKNOWLEDGMENTS

It takes more than an idea to create a book.

Cindy, Gary, Nicolas, and many others, thank you
for encouragement and help, especially my wife
who endured hours alone as I worked.

To all those who sacrificed during World War II

EXPLANATION
OF VARIOUS
TERMS AND
ORGANIZATIONS

OKW or **Oberkommando der Wehrmacht**—High Command group of the German army

Wehrmacht—German army

Schutzstaffel or **SS**—responsible for enforcing the racial policy of Nazi Germany and general policing. It comprised two main sections: the Allgemeine SS (General SS) and Waffen-SS (Armed SS). The Gestapo was a subdivision.

Abwehr—the German military intelligence service

SHAEF or **Supreme Headquarters Allied Expeditionary Force** (the combined Allied Army in Europe)—a command established in late 1943 to coordinate the invasion of northern Europe.

Nikola Tesla—a Serbian-American scientist who worked in electricity and power distribution in the late 1800s.

Heavy water or **deuterium**—water (H2O) with a "heavy" hydrogen atom; the nucleus contains a neutron as well as a proton. Essential in the operation of nuclear reactors.

LST—Landing **S**hip, **T**ank, the naval designation for ships to support amphibious operations by carrying tanks, vehicles, cargo, and landing troops directly onto shore with no docks or piers. The bow of the LST had a large door that would open with a ramp for unloading the vehicles.

E-boat—a German high-speed torpedo boat like the American PT boat.

BIGOT—a special security clearance created for the D-Day invasion that was above top secret.

SOE or **Special Operations Executive**—a group created by Churchill to focus on sabotage in the occupied countries

HE—high-explosive rounds

AP—armor-piercing rounds for use against tanks

Hauptmann—German rank of captain

Feldwebel—German rank of technical sergeant or staff sergeant

Oberleutnant—German rank of first lieutenant

CHARACTERS

―――――――――― ✦✦✦✦✦✦ ――――――――――

Americans

- Major (Lt. Col.) Mark Dornier—born 1905; wife, Joanne, died 1936; married in 1924; two children—William, 1924, and Darlene, 1928
- Awarded: Distinguished Service Cross, Croix de Guerre (France), Military Cross (UK), Purple Heart, WWII Victory, France and Germany Star (UK), European Campaign, American Campaign ribbons
- Colonel Jeremy Walker—head of Planning and Logistics in SHAEF; recruited Mark Dornier
- Major General Brawls—American, but working in a British organization within SHAEF
- Colonel Miller—in charge of coordinating the scientific efforts of the British and Americans
- Sergeant Joe Gillis—M4 Sherman tank commander
- Corporal Gary Elliott—the driver of an M4 Sherman, Thirty-Seventh Tank Battalion, Fourth Armored Division, Combat Command A (CCA)

- Sergeant Mike Lloyd—gunner of the M4 Sherman
- Sergeant Michael Gillett—second M4 Sherman tank commander
- Lt. General George S. Patton—commander of US Third Army
- Col. Carlos Manning—General Patton's chief of staff
- Colonel Koch—General Patton's intelligence officer
- Col. Charles B. Odom—General Patton's personal physician

British

Works for General Brawls

- Lieutenant Alex Ryder
- Captain Polly Berson—secretary to Major General Brawls

Lower Special Surveillance Office 8

- Colonel "Johnny" Gaffney—section head
- Captain Stone
- Lieutenant William Boysden
- Derek from the lab

MI6

- Colonel David Betts

Others

- Lt. William Berson—born 1895; wife, Sophie DeBoy, born 1895 (sister to Olivier); married 1914
- Sebastien Berson—married Aurélie; killed in 1940; born 1914
- Barnes Wallis—British inventor of the Upkeep or Dambuster bomb

Achnacarry

- Lieutenant Colonel Charles Vaughn—commanding officer of the Commando Basic Training Center at Achnacarry Castle
- Sergeant Major at Achnacarry
- Sergeant Aiden Achnacarry—a trainer

French

- Alphonse DeBoy—grandfather (wife, Maria, now dead); two children—Olivier, 1893, and Sophie—born 1895
- Olivier—born 1893; Alphonse's son; wife, Monique, 1895; both declared missing; parents of three boys and two girls; married 1912
- Marc—born 1912; oldest grandson; killed in 1940
- Aurélie—born 1913; oldest granddaughter, married Sebastian Berson (killed in 1940), her cousin, in 1936; no children
- René—born 1915; younger grandson; joined the Resistance and disappeared in 1940
- Josette—born 1918, youngest granddaughter
- Luc—born 1929; youngest grandson; still on the farm
- Henri Benoit—Josette's fiancé; missing since 1941

Germans

- Colonel Franz Dietrich—in charge of construction for several defense sites, including Euskirchen
- Major Schmidt—Colonel Dietrich's adjutant
- Sergeant Alvin Hamming—at Butte de Vauquois
- Harrison, Sander, Zormaan—electricians working for Sergeant Hamming

- Heinrich Kohler—an electrician working on the power corridor
- Private Berne Gerhart—worker on defensive positions around power facilities
- Mess corporal at Vauquois—working for SOE and the Resistance
- Hans—the mess sergeant at Butte de Vauquois site
- Sergeant Havener Varick—in charge of construction of the last BR site at Souhesme La Petite
- Major General Dr. Walter Dornberger—in charge of rocket development until 1942, then antiaircraft rockets Jan. 1944
- Dr. Wernher von Braun—head of rocket development
- Werner Karl Heisenberg—a theoretical physicist and one of the key pioneers of quantum mechanics

Arlon near Euskirchen in Eastern Germany

- Captain Wilhelm Borne—commander of the BR and defensive facilities at Arlon
- Sergeant Wolfgang Fischer—senior NCO at the Arlon site

Butte de Vauquois

- Colonel Borke Fuchs—commander of the Vauquois site

Berlin

- Reich Minister Wilhelm Keitel—head of the OKW
- Generaloberst Alfred Jodl—chief of the operations staff
- Reich Minister Albert Speer—head of industrial production
- Martin Bormann—a prominent official in Nazi Germany and Hitler's private secretary

PROLOGUE

Summer, 1927, on a Farm near the Argonne Forest in Eastern France

A light breeze blew Poddy's hair across her face. Henri was sitting next to her and her cousin Josi. They were on a small rise behind the stone barn, where the rest of her cousins and a few neighbor children were playing. She enjoyed visiting her cousins in France; it was always much different from England. Her aunt and uncle, Olivier and Monique DeBoy, had five children, but Poddy had only one older brother.

The entire area was planted with crops that were soon to be harvested, which created a variety of colors, from golden to deep green, in the fields. The woods on top of the surrounding hills were barely recovering from *Le Grande Guerre*—the Great War. There had been heavy shelling on the ridges surrounding this valley, and most of the trees had been destroyed in the process. It was still not safe to walk in some of the areas around old trenches because of unexploded artillery shells. Even on the farms, occasionally a plow would hit a shell, and the farmer would have to stop and carefully move it to the corner of the field for collection.

Poddy's mother, Sophie, was Olivier's younger sister. Their families got along well, even though they only saw each other every three or four years. Sophie and Olivier's mother, Maria, had died shortly after Sophie was born, which left their father with the daunting challenge of raising a son and daughter in a rural environment by himself.

All the children had given themselves nicknames that sometimes didn't reflect their real names. It was something that Poddy's older brother thought up—he was always the one making up games and stories. He was called Sebby. Her nickname was Poddy. Josi, one of her cousins, was her age, and Josi's older sister was Airi. She was three years older than Josi. They had two brothers, Marc and René. Marc was the oldest and too serious to take a nickname. René, who was almost two years younger than Airi, was the adventurer, exploring anything and everything. Not to be outdone by his older brother, he didn't want a nickname, but Josi named him Problè, short for *problème*, because he was always in trouble. Airi would laugh but tried to refrain from annoying him. Josi didn't mind at all.

Olivier's father, Alphonse, owned the farm that had been built by his grandfather in the late eighteenth century. The barn, made of stone, included a large cellar where the family aged cheese and wine. The children loved to play hide-and-seek in and around the barn because there were so many places to hide.

Henri nudged her. "Here comes Sebby. I'll bet he's looking for Airi." Sure enough, he was looking for his favorite cousin.

Poddy knew he liked Airi, so she delighted in teasing him. "I think she went up on the hill in the forest to get away from you."

Josi and Henri smiled. "She didn't go anywhere. She's down in the kitchen helping *Maman*." They all knew that he would go down and spend the rest of the afternoon talking with her. That's what teenagers did, especially when they liked each other.

Later that evening Sophie and her brother Olivier were out walking, leaving William and Monique in charge of the children. She turned to Olivier. "You realize we're going to have trouble with those two in a couple of years." She was referring to the developing romance between their children.

Olivier nodded. "Probably, but I don't think there is much we can do about it. I say we leave them to find their own path."

Poddy's parents, William and Sophie, brought her brother and her to France seven or eight more times before World War II started and made it too dangerous to travel. She never forgot the good times they all enjoyed but wondered if she would ever be able to see her cousins again.

Late October 1943, over Northeast France in a B-17 Cockpit

On his left, just below the yoke, Major Dornier set the autopilot, unstrapped, and then went back to the bomb bay. He slowly lowered himself into the drop pod. He was still stiff from the recent training in northern Scotland and had wondered if he should've accepted this assignment. He laughed to himself. *It's a little late for that now.* He was trained and well qualified, if not a little old at thirty-eight.

He busied himself with the checklist, making sure the connections to the plane were ready to separate. A look at the timer in the belly of the aircraft indicated he was five minutes from release. He zipped up the insulated liner around his shoulders, lowered his goggles and face mask, and started breathing through the pod's oxygen bottle. He heard the engine's revs decreasing, and then the bomb bay doors opened, revealing a gray, murky cloud layer several thousand feet below. The timer on the pod was showing three minutes. The cold at thirty-four thousand feet, almost 70 degrees below zero, was penetrating the pod and his flight suit. He noticed the airspeed indicator dropping past 155 mph as the plane began to nose over very slightly.

He watched as the timer went below thirty seconds. He pulled the release at zero and an airspeed of 124 mph. The pod dropped, nose-heavy, and the plane disappeared into a cloud above him. The pod's glider wings and stabilizer deployed. It shuttered as the wings stabilized the fall. He turned west to his target in the forest below. Would he be able to see the field to land?

Wow, it's cold!

July 1943, Allied Headquarters in London

Lieutenant Boysden looked at the aerial photos again. He was having a hard time deciphering what he saw between the clouds and the trees. He had a guess, but he had kept it to himself. *No use having the boss ridicule me—no guessing, remember!* Still, he was having a hard time believing it. *The Germans didn't have those kinds of resources—did they?*

April 1943, Oberkommando der Wehrmacht (OKW), German High Command in Berlin

"We need something in this area in case the Allies ever invade the continent."

Jodl quickly replied, "They will not get on the continent, so we don't need to go to this expense."

Everyone in the room, including Generaloberst Alfred Jodl, chief of the operations staff, knew eventually the Allies would attempt to land a force in Europe. However, Jodl was unwavering in his support of the Fuehrer's position. Even though there was sympathy in the room for ideas, no one wanted to risk disagreeing with Hitler. However, after many months of debate, the German High Command finally agreed on a plan to place defensive measures in several areas of eastern France. Thus began an expensive endeavor, concerning money and resources, to ensure the fatherland was protected in case of a breach of the Atlantic wall ... even though no one wanted to admit it.

CHAPTER 1

✦✦✦✦✦

July 1943—Allied Command, War Cabinet Rooms—St. Charles Street, London

Second Lieutenant Alex Ryder was beginning to sweat over the files. He could hear General Brawls in the next room, giving orders to other staff. Ryder wasn't sure why there was so much emphasis on completing this assignment, but it sounded like the general was giving others a similar task. He had been going through the folders for the last twenty-two hours. Yesterday morning he'd been called in and asked to go over a large stack of personnel records, looking for particular skills and personal attributes. It had taken two people to deliver the files to his office. The folders were piled three feet high all around his desk. He had no idea how many files there were, but there were too many, and he was quickly losing patience.

The odd thing about the service records was that they were from several countries: the United Kingdom, United States, Poland, France, the Netherlands, Canada, and even far-off New Zealand. He'd been told to screen potential candidates for piloting skills, knowledge of German and French, a minimum of four years of college, and a high state of physical fitness. Experience and proficiency in small arms were desirable.

This particular set of criteria seemed odd, especially since he had helped pick several people in the past four years for assignments in other countries, most located in France. *Why does it have to be so hot down here?* The ventilation system was off overnight, and the room temperature had risen. His lack of sleep wasn't helping his concentration either.

"How's it going this morning, Lieutenant?" In popped one of the Wrens who worked for the general. Polly seemed never to be bothered by the heat, cold, or even people yelling at her. She was one of those people who always had a smile and a pleasant word.

"Very slowly, and thank you so much for asking," he answered. "And it's *second* lieutenant." Alex liked Polly but found it difficult to focus right now on anything except finishing his task.

She ignored his reply. "Well, you might want to look at the stack next to your file cabinet. I looked through some of the files briefly as I pulled them. I think there are several likely candidates there."

Alex looked up, annoyed, and said, "You might have told me last night before you left."

Polly set a cup of tea on his desk. "No milk again, I'm afraid. I know you like to discover things for yourself, so I thought I'd allow you that freedom, *mon cher*." Turning away, she couldn't stifle a small smile.

He reached over and started combing through several of the service records. It was apparent that several of these individuals were reasonably qualified, but after so many hours of searching, he had only found eight that met all the criteria. They would need at least forty.

He started a new stack containing the records of the highest potential candidates, according to Polly. "Thanks for the tip. You do a good job of sorting files like this."

Polly got up to leave. Then she turned around, smiled, and said, "Next time, just ask."

Alex took a small sip of the tea as it cooled. He didn't mind the lack of milk; he just wanted the lift from the caffeine. Within twenty minutes, he had a stack of sixty-five files that deserved further attention. He made a mental note to thank Polly again. It hadn't been difficult to find people with language skills and college education, but it was a challenge to find any who combined those with a high degree of physical fitness and piloting skills.

He very quickly went through another 150 files and located eleven that he put into his "select" stack. He looked up and saw it was almost one thirty in the afternoon. He decided he would go downstairs to the canteen and get a sandwich. All the secretaries had already left for lunch. He took the stairs down to the subbasement. *At least it's cooler down here.* He selected a sandwich that didn't look very appetizing, but after four years of war, supplies in the UK were limited. He decided he would get a cup of coffee instead of tea and hoped it would keep him alert this afternoon.

As he was climbing the stairs, General Brawls was coming down. "How's the search going?" asked Brawls.

"It was slow at first, but this morning has been more productive. I have another two hundred files to look at, but I've already selected sixty or seventy for further review."

"Splendid, Lieutenant. I won't keep you. Get back to it, then. We need some names this evening."

Alex was trying to look pleasant, but the lack of sleep was starting to make his patience run short. "Yes, sir," he said and continued up the stairs.

Back in his office, all the secretaries had returned, and they nodded at him in cursory recognition. As he passed Polly's desk, she whispered without looking up, "There is a short stack on the left side of your desk you should look at first."

He walked by and silently thanked her. As he started through Polly's stack, he saw that she had found several candidates with piloting skills. In another hour he had a stack of over one hundred to examine more closely. He leaned back and started making a pile that had all of the other attributes, such as the ability to speak French or German, above-average physical dexterity, and even weapons expertise.

He was finally making some progress. Now he had a stack of over fifty that looked reasonable. He decided to make a final cut based on age. Even though no age criteria had been given, he suspected this would be an assignment for younger men. He made a quick decision to eliminate everyone over the age of thirty-five. After he did that, there were twenty-eight files left. He was surprised to notice that one of the records was that of a woman. He reviewed her file carefully again, but she clearly met all the criteria, so he included her in his final cut. There were several well-qualified candidates over thirty-five, so he made a second stack, just in case.

When he finally looked up, he was surprised to see that it was already 6:20 p.m. He decided to visit with the general to review what he had put together. He got up, left his office, and stopped by Polly's desk. "I have some files for the general to look at." Leaning down, he said in a lower voice, "And by the way, thank you again."

"*De rien,* mon cher."

She knew he didn't speak French, and he knew she liked to remind him of that. "If you keep talking like that, you may get selected as one of the candidates for this assignment."

She just smiled. "Let me see if the general is free."

She disappeared into his office and was there only a second before reappearing. "The general will see you." She paused slightly and then said, "And this would be where you say *merci beaucoup.*"

July 1943—Allied Command, War Cabinet Rooms—St. Charles Street, London, Lower Special Surveillance Office Eight

Lieutenant Boysden had a terrible headache. He had been looking at aerial photos for over two weeks and wanted very much to have some time off. He had not been outside for almost three days. Sleeping in the small dormitory in the subbasement was taking its toll. That was where those who had priority assignments lived during the duration of their tasks.

There were times when he wished he hadn't brought the abnormality he'd discovered in the Argonne to anyone's attention. After the initial discovery in the woods north and west of Verdun, there had not been any substantial additions to the structures or the surrounding area. A lab tech brought in a fresh roll of strip photos from this afternoon's flight. "Anything new, Derek?" It had been cloudy most of the period since the initial discovery, and only a few photographs were of any use.

"You wouldn't happen to have anything for a headache, would you?" Boysden inquired.

"Sorry, Lieutenant, no medicine, but I think these new photos should help take your mind off of it," Derek said. "It was clear over the site today, and I think you'll be interested in the changes."

"Let's have them." Boysden sincerely hoped there was something of interest. As he moved his magnifying glass over the new photos, he immediately noticed the changes. There were small black dots scattered roughly in a north-south line approximately one hundred yards apart. On one ridge just to the east of the dots, there was a long, thin structure that was new construction. It appeared to be fifteen to twenty feet in height and perhaps ten feet wide. This was similar to another structure he had located a few miles to the north two weeks ago.

"There look to be vehicle tracks," he said. The dense forest cover made anything definitive elusive.

"Derek, ask the captain to come in here, please."

Captain Stone was Lieutenant Boysden's immediate supervisor in the special aerial surveillance division focusing on eastern France.

"Captain, you should take a look. There have been some additional changes in my area."

As Captain Stone leaned over the photos, William pointed out the new structures.

"Similar to the last set you found two weeks ago. Obviously they're up to something in this area, but our intelligence folks haven't figured out what yet."

Lieutenant Boysden offered a suggestion. "The long structure appears quite substantial and perhaps twenty feet in height. The small black dots may be support structures or defensive positions."

The captain rubbed his forehead and said, "All well and good, but what is in each of these structures? And more important, why are there two of these complexes just four or five miles apart?"

"Whatever they are, they're taking substantial resources to create. One more thing I've noticed: there appear to be new power lines from a nearby hydroelectric facility. I'm not sure what that means."

"Write a report and keep on this," Captain Stone said as he strode out of the room.

Great, thought William. *I may never see the sky again.*

William didn't know that several other divisions like his also had located similar strange activity in this area. These reports had gone up to the Prime Minister himself and had created quite a stir. The British had decided to share this information with SHAEF, and several high-level meetings were held to determine how to move forward. A mission was being organized to learn more about what was happening.

Early July 1943, near Euskirchen in Eastern Germany

Colonel Franz Dietrich was finishing his monthly report. He had placed particular emphasis on the progress of the new project Berlin had requested. Three new hydrogenerators were installed on the Urft Dam, along with a stockpile of steel and wood for construction of additional power lines. The goal was to double the electric output of this dam by the end of the summer. While the colonel realized electric power was needed for the industries in the Ruhr Valley, he was also aware a dam made a very inviting target for bombers.

Regardless of his concerns, Colonel Dietrich didn't intend to ask any questions. Berlin sometimes reacted poorly to such behavior, especially now with the Soviet counterattack at Kursk.

July 1943, Commando Basic Training Center, Achnacarry Castle, Scotland

"Are they out of their bloody minds?" Lieutenant Colonel Charles Vaughn was reading the top-secret dispatch sent from Allied headquarters.

"They must have a good reason, sir. Even the PM knows how

difficult it is to train someone to this level of performance." The sergeant major was looking out the window onto the parade grounds.

"Well, there's nothing to do except prepare. Please see to it, Sergeant Major."

July 1943, Allied Headquarters, Planning and Logistics Office

Colonel Walker strode in. "Mark, please come to my office."

"Yes, sir." Major Dornier got up and followed the colonel.

"Here are the service files of four individuals who have been identified for a potential mission into France or Germany. All four of these individuals work on Ike's staff. Notify each one this afternoon that he is to pack a bag for four nights and report to the officer in charge for orders. They should tell no one that they're leaving or for how long."

"Unusual, but I'll do it immediately. Is that all, sir?"

"Yes, and let me know when they're out the door."

Major Dornier went back to his office to prepare the necessary paperwork, wondering what all this was about. He had seen strange orders before, but this really puzzled him.

Colonel Walker opened up the service records stacked on his desk. The name of the top of the pile was Dornier, Mark—Major. But for now, the major wasn't going anywhere.

Two Days Later, Commando Basic Training Center, Achnacarry Castle, Scotland

Sergeant Aidan watched as the new group went through calisthenics in the early-morning cold. Everyone in this group was struggling, although the sergeant couldn't blame them. How could they have known they would end up in a commando training program in less than twenty-four hours? Yesterday, sixteen men and one woman had arrived, and a sergeant immediately put them on a ten-mile run. He knew it wasn't fair, but the training had to be tough. *Hopefully, we'll have enough time to give them the basics they need to survive.*

He didn't like sending people out with inadequate training. *Suicide, plain and simple, just suicide.*

CHAPTER 2

◆◆◆◆◆

July 1943, Allied Headquarters, London

Churchill, Eisenhower, and several senior advisers were gathered around a table. Colonel Gaffney was briefing them on the situation in eastern France. "While we don't know for sure what the objective of this activity is, we believe it's important to the German defense plan, if for no other reason than the amount of material and the workforce utilized. We have separate confirmation from several sources in France and Belgium that priority has been given to a project in eastern France that involves cement, large amounts of ordnance, electrical equipment, and other supplies."

Colonel Gaffney was the head of several of the new surveillance offices, one of which was where Lieutenant Boysden labored. Three days ago, another set of aerial photos revealed two more installations similar to what they already had identified. This was enough to alert the senior Allied Command and begin the process of gathering more information.

General Montgomery was very curious as to what these installations might do. "I've never seen anything like this. You say the Germans are installing high-voltage lines to this area, originating from some of the dams in eastern Germany?"

"Yes, General, but that's not the only strange thing. While Jerry is apparently laying minefields and building defense bunkers, they are also clearing areas in front of the longer structures. That doesn't appear to make any sense," Gaffney said. "It's all rather odd."

Colonel Betts said, "Three French Resistance groups operate in this general area. Is it possible for us to drop a small team near these installations to learn more about them?"

The British colonel in MI6 was concerned. "Getting them in is easy. How would we get the team out?"

"I have every confidence, Colonel, in your ability to work out a suitable plan. I think it's obvious at this point that we need to find out what is going on as quickly as we can with a minimum number of resources." Churchill re-lit his cigar while looking at Eisenhower.

Ike grinned. "The Prime Minister's confidence can be a dangerous thing sometimes. Isn't that right, Colonel?"

"Yes, sir, but he's right. We do need to find out what's going on and quickly. I'll get back to you tomorrow with a plan for a small group to be inserted, gather the intelligence we need, and get out—or at least have the information transmitted to us before extraction."

"Right. Then we should plan on meeting tomorrow; correct, Prime Minister?" General Montgomery seemed quite anxious to focus the discussion to a point.

General Brawls had been quiet up until this point. "I had anticipated the need for this type of mission and took the liberty to search for individuals with the right skills. Further, we knew they would need some basic commando-type training. We have sixteen men and one woman up at Achnacarry as we speak, beginning their training."

This irritated Colonel Betts. "This could've compromised our situation. You should have gone through channels before sending them up there."

Churchill waved him off. "I approved General Brawls's decision. We all appreciate your concern and share it, but speed is crucial in this particular instance." Pausing briefly, he then said, "I can assure you,

Colonel, that none of this information was compromised in any way. In fact, I can guarantee that the seventeen individuals currently going through training are extremely confused as to why they were removed from their normal lines of duty so rapidly."

A Farm Outside Les Isettes, near Forêt Domaniale de Lachalade in the Argonne, France

Alphonse woke up slowly. *Before Maria died, I didn't need to get out of bed so fast.* It was a cold morning, and his joints were stiff. He walked into the kitchen and stoked the fireplace. He then started a small fire in the stove to heat some water. His two granddaughters would not awake for a few minutes, so he went outside and looked at the forest. He enjoyed early mornings alone, where he could gather his thoughts.

The war had not been easy on his family. His son and daughter-in-law were in the Resistance, but he felt confident they weren't still alive. He had not heard from them for over a year. Their oldest son, Marc, had been killed in 1940 when the Germans invaded France. Their oldest daughter, Aurélie, married a young man who also was killed in 1940. Her younger brother, René, had decided to join the Resistance, and no one had heard from him for three years. Josette was engaged, but again, the war had interfered with these plans as well. Her fiancé had not written in over nine months and was believed to be captured or killed while fighting with the Americans in Italy. Only Alphonse's youngest grandson, Luc, was still with them at the farm.

Alphonse was worried about Aurélie more than the others. She seemed to carry the burden of her parent's disappearance and her husband's death more heavily than her brother and sister. Unfortunately, there was little Alphonse could do. He couldn't make the war or its consequences go away.

He went out the back door toward the barn, going to the far corner, and started gathering eggs. One benefit of living in this part of France was that the Germans had not confiscated much of the produce from the farms. As a result, they had plenty of vegetables, dairy products, eggs, and meat from the farm animals. He stopped by the garden on his way back to the house to pick some fresh herbs. *An omelet might be nice for a change.*

As he was walking back to the house, he noticed a small convoy of German trucks headed north. He made a note of their speed, their number, and the time. His friend in the village, Raoul, would be interested in this information. Alphonse did not know for sure but strongly suspected this information went to the Resistance. He was wise enough to realize that asking questions of this nature could lead to problems.

Josette called to him from her second-floor bedroom window. "How many eggs this morning, *Grand-père?*" She was the curious one, always wanting to know what he was doing.

"Only seven this morning," he replied. "If you can get your brother and sister awake, I thought we would have an omelet this morning— that is, if there's any cheese left."

"I'll get them up, and we'll be down in a few minutes." Josette walked down the hallway to the water closet to make use of it before her brother and sister got up. Aurélie was not a problem with the bathroom; it was Luc who seemed to take all the time. After she washed, she went into Aurélie's room; she was already awake. "Grand-père is going to make an omelet for breakfast, so get up. I'm going to wake Luc in a minute."

Aurélie sighed and sat up. "Let me get to the bathroom first."

Alphonse was cutting bread from the loaf and heating the skillet. He knew it would be several minutes before his grandchildren came down. He started frying thick slabs of ham with some fresh mushrooms. Upstairs, Aurélie had finished in the bathroom, and Luc had taken her place. Luc was only fourteen but was beginning to grow a beard. He didn't like shaving very much, but since he had shaved yesterday, he knew he would not have to do it for another day or two. *Good; less time in front of the mirror,* he thought.

Josette came into the kitchen and started putting plates on the table. "I need to go into town this morning and take some of our milk and cream to trade for flour and salt. I was wondering if I could go over to see Claudine while I was there. They have a new calf." Claudine was Josette's best friend.

Alphonse liked Claudine's family and had known them for many years. Unfortunately, Claudine's mother always wanted to know what was going on, and she was never shy about sharing that information with others in the village. "I suppose, but please be careful what you say about our farm. Sometimes I think a few of our friends may be a little jealous of how much we have."

"We share so much of what we have with others. I would think they would be glad for what we have. But I understand and will be careful."

Aurélie came in. "Be careful of what?"

"Nothing, really; we're just trying to keep gossip down," Josette said as she tried to reach cups on the top cabinet.

Luc walked in. "I'll get them." Even at fourteen, he was taller than either of his sisters.

Alphonse was already thinking about the rest of the day. "Aurélie, would you get my hunting jacket and shotgun from the other room? I need to take a trip through the woods up to the old house. Romain was by there last week and thought that the basement wall might need some work. While I'm going that way, I might see something to shoot for the table." Romain was an old friend who lived outside of Les Islettes and frequently traveled through the woods on his way to the village.

In reality, Alphonse was going up to the old house for an entirely different reason. A man in Lachalade, a village north of their farm, had suggested he needed to go up and "check on the condition of the property." This was a prearranged code that indicated the house might be used as shelter or storage for the Resistance or the Allies. It had been used once briefly in late 1939 by the fledgling Resistance group in the area, but since that time, it had remained idle.

Aurélie went over to her grand-père and stood in front of the stove. "You go sit down and have some coffee, and I'll cook the omelet."

Alphonse kissed his granddaughter on the cheek. "Merci." As he sat down at the table, he turned to Luc. "After your regular chores, would you look at the door hinge on the barn? I think it's going to need some work, and it's better to do it before it breaks." He turned back to Aurélie. "So, Aurélie, do you have plans for today?"

"Tomorrow is our normal wash day, but it might rain the next several days so I thought I would start washing the blankets and heavy clothes today." Washing wasn't one of her favorite chores, but she knew she could do it more efficiently than her sister. Josette was better outside, helping Luc.

Aurélie looked back at Josette. "This is almost ready. You might get the honey out as well."

Josette set the honey on the table next to the butter and poured glasses of milk. Aurélie brought the skillet over to the table and divided up the omelet. Luc brought the platter of ham to the table. As they all sat down, Alphonse realized once again how lucky they all were. He offered a small prayer of thanks, and they began to eat. As Alphonse ate, his mind took account of the supplies hidden in the barn basement. He would need his truck to haul the supplies on his trip into the woods.

Achnacarry Castle, Scotland, Late July 1943

The training for the most recent group had been going on for eight days. Four days ago, three additional people had arrived. Even though Sergeant Aiden was satisfied with everybody's attitude, he was not happy with the progress. Most of the people had been in above-average physical condition when they arrived, but the requirements for commandos were much more demanding, and they were all very sore. The real key to commando training was not necessarily the physical aspects, but the person's mental outlook. They had to want to do this and see that there was no alternative but to finish, realizing that their lives and the lives of their colleagues would be endangered by anything other than their very best efforts.

The sergeant had already picked out six individuals who probably would not make it through the next three days. Tomorrow they would take them out in a truck to the Highlands, where it was partially wooded; drop them off with a fish hook, some rope, a small knife, and no coat; and leave them. They would have to traverse twenty-five miles of rugged country without roads and no compass in twenty-four hours. He was sure that the six individuals would leave the program the following day, and probably another four would leave by the end of the third day. Sergeant Aiden always found it curious that the toughest people were not necessarily the largest or the strongest. It was peculiar how people's minds worked in situations like this. He figured the next three days would eliminate several more, and if not, the fourth and fifth day would certainly eliminate at least three or four. Those were the days scheduled for parachute training. Very few people approached that without a great deal of dread, including the instructors.

The trainees turned the corner and started down the final incline to finish their second ten-mile run of the day. One instructor jogged on either side of the group while the others were bringing up the rear.

"We lost another one on this run," the corporal yelled as they passed the finish line.

The lead trainer stopped and turned around. "End of run! Stand in formation."

Sergeant Aiden yelled, "Left face. Attention to Sergeant Riker. Sergeant Riker will now familiarize you with the fine art of hand-to-hand combat with a knife." He knew there would be even more sore muscles tonight. Looking at the faces of each of the trainees, he tried to discern what they were thinking. It didn't appear as though anyone was anticipating the next four hours.

Outside Euskirchen in Eastern Germany

Colonel Dietrich summoned his adjutant, Major Schmidt. "Major, I have orders to stockpile additional steel, concrete, and electrical wire in a second location about five kilometers from here. We need to have these materials loaded and ready to go on railcars at Euskirchen within five days. We should be receiving the supplies by rail tomorrow night. Please have a work party ready with plans to unload the supplies onto trucks in four hours."

Even though Major Schmidt was surprised, his mind was already working on how many men he would need. "Since this is the second load of construction materials, I was wondering if the colonel could share if there might be additional loads. If so, it might be advantageous to preselect some additional stockpile sites near the rail yards."

Colonel Dietrich didn't like Major Schmidt, but he had to admit the major had a point. "I have no idea about additional loads, but I suspect there will be, so plan on at least two more sites. Also, I have a suspicion that we may be building a high-voltage line from the dam to some site in the Ardennes, but since I have no idea where, we can't preplan."

"I'll start planning on at least two more sites and begin thinking about the logistics necessary to build a high-voltage line. I assume that this is not something to share with anyone outside this room."

"Correct. Please get started, and let me know the progress tomorrow at our status meeting."

Major Schmidt left the colonel's office and walked the short distance across the courtyard to the battalion's supply sergeant. Sergeant Hamming heard the door open and turned around immediately, expecting an officer. "Major, what can we do for you?"

"We need a work party to move construction supplies similar to the first load off a train and onto supply trucks for further transport to our Euskircken railhead. The manpower required will depend on when the train arrives, but plan on unloading it in less than four hours."

"Yes, Major. When does the train arrive?"

"Scheduled time is two o'clock this morning, but with probable delays, who knows? Communicate with Transportation to get updates on the expected arrival time. You should also plan on dealing with two additional loads this size to be transported in the same way to Aachen within the next five days. We're not sure that the supplies will ship, but we should be ready to deal with the situation if it develops."

"We'll be ready, but that is a huge amount of supplies. I'm sure Berlin knows what they're doing, but putting that amount of construction supplies in one area is not a good idea, given the current Allied bombing patterns."

"I'm aware of that, Sergeant, but I'm not finished."

Sergeant Hamming held his breath. *What now?* he thought.

"What I'm about to tell you is not to be shared with anyone. Take a look at a map, and create a possible route for a high-voltage line to go from the dam to the Ardennes. Since I'm not sure of the destination, select three possibilities near our current defensive positions, and come to me for approval."

Sergeant Hamming could barely respond. Running power lines that far was a massive undertaking, and he would need assistance from several of his men. "I request permission to use Harrison, Sander, and Zormaan. Harrison is especially helpful in reading topographical maps. Sander and Zormaan are the experts at picking routes for travel through rough country."

"You have permission, but inform them to keep the information to themselves. After you have briefed your men, make an appointment to see me. I want to talk to all four of you."

"Yes, sir."

"If there are no other questions, you should get started." The major turned and left.

What in the world is going on? Hamming wondered. He had heard of some crazy schemes, especially in the last six months, as Wehrmacht commanders dealt with the deteriorating situation in North Africa and Russia and now the landings on Sicily. This was a great deal of material in an ever-dwindling resource pool. He just hoped somebody on the senior staff knew what he was doing.

He didn't know—nor did the major or even the colonel—that a high-voltage line was already being constructed between Prum, Germany, and Arlon, Belgium. Over fifty men had been working on this for three months. Heinrich Kohler had been there the whole time. Even though he was just a private, he had been a master electrician in Koblenz before the war. While he thought this effort was a waste of time, it kept him out of combat, which was fine by him. The men around him, while not well trained, were hard workers, and this contributed to steady progress. The distance between Prum and Arlon was about one hundred kilometers. There was now a seventy-kilometer leg from Euskircken to Prum and then a final connection from Arlon to the Lachalade area, to be completed later, which was another hundred kilometers.

CHAPTER 3

Achnacarry, Scotland

M ajor Dornier was holding onto the balloon guylines. Four people were crammed into the balloon basket around a large trapdoor in the middle. His stomach was in his throat because they were preparing their third parachute jump of the day. The balloon was stationary at three thousand feet, and the drop would be with a static line. He was even more uncomfortable with the fact that two of the people in the balloon basket were women. No man wanted to appear scared in front of women, but he had put that behind him. They had all trained hard and packed their own parachutes for this exercise. This would be the first jump with their chutes. The last two weeks of training had removed all traces of male ego—or female ego, for that matter. It'd been grueling and fast-paced; hence, there was no place for false pride.

The jumpmaster sat in a chair above them, suspended by the guylines. "Check equipment and hook up." Everyone turned to the right and checked equipment of the person in front of them. Then they turned to the left and did the same, hooking their static line to the balloon anchor at the same time.

"Number one, prepare to jump." Major Dornier moved to the trapdoor and sat down on the edge of the basket. The woman behind him put both feet on either side of his hips to brace him.

"Number one, jump on my command ... number one, jump!"

Major Dornier pushed himself out and started falling. The drop was just beginning as the static line caught and the chute opened. He looked up to check his canopy and then looked down to establish his position. He was drifting slightly to the right, but he would easily land in the clearing, missing the woods. He looked up again and saw the woman, Captain Berson, drifting above and slightly to his front. As he floated down, he thought how attractive she was.

Well, at least I didn't embarrass myself. Major Dornier had a few moments to enjoy the ride down before he prepared for the landing.

He focused on a spot to land, put his feet together, and, as he hit the ground, somersaulted backward to dissipate his momentum. He got up immediately and began to gather his chute. Captain Berson landed twenty feet away and started doing the same. The two others in the balloon landed in quick order, and they all walked to the truck for the return to the gymnasium, where they would repack the chutes.

There was not much talking on the ride back. The trainees were all focused on the jump—what they'd done right or wrong. About halfway back, Captain Berson spoke up. "I would prefer to jump out of a plane than the balloon. I think it's a lot harder and more realistic."

The lady sitting next to her, a British lieutenant, answered, "I haven't jumped before, so having a stationary platform makes it easier."

They both looked over at Major Dornier, as if requesting his opinion. "I'm just glad to get the jumps over. I'm not very experienced either, and the balloon is a good way to get some practice. I guess we'll find out tomorrow because we jump twice from a plane."

Captain Berson smiled. "It's about the same, except for the wind."

"I get the impression you've done this before."

"This is a refresher course for me. I qualified two years ago but haven't jumped much since."

Major Dornier looked at her. *Yeah, I figured you had some jumps in the past. You seemed more confident than the rest of us.*

Captain Berson knew they needed encouragement and said, "You're all doing well. Just remember: keep looking at the horizon, and don't look down."

The truck approached the gymnasium and let them off. As Mark followed the two women into the gymnasium, he began to think back on his journey to this point. Two weeks ago, he was sitting at his desk at Allied headquarters, preparing a training schedule for the Twenty-Ninth Infantry Division. Colonel Walker had asked him to cut orders for four individuals to receive specialized training. The request seemed odd, but in the Planning and Logistics Department, there were always strange requests. A day later, the colonel had called him in and given him a set of identical orders with very little explanation. He did mention that he didn't think Mark would be returning to Planning and Logistics any time soon. After packing and reporting to the train station, he was on his way north, with no idea of what lay ahead.

Mark Dornier was not a stranger to uncertainty. He grew up in Oklahoma, the oldest son of four children. His father worked in the oil industry—in its infancy—and had to travel all over the Midwest. When he was not gone, the family was frequently packing to move to a new location. While it didn't seem to bother his mother, it always made Mark and his sisters uncomfortable to move to a new town. They learned to get used to it, and it probably helped them as adults. Their family life was good, even with their father's frequent absences.

Mark was born in 1905. As he grew up, he played sports and enjoyed athletic endeavors. In his senior year in high school, Mark met a young lady, whom he married a year later. In college, he majored in mechanical engineering and ended up working for a major oil company. They moved from Oklahoma to California, where they started a family. When their son was three years old, they moved from California to Louisiana, where their daughter was born. Several years later, they moved to the Texas Panhandle, hoping this would be the last move for a while.

It was here that Mark's wife, Joanne, found that she had cancer. Initially, the doctors were optimistic, thinking they had discovered it in its early stages. However, it rapidly became evident that the best they could do was slow the progress of the disease. She lived for almost four years before finally succumbing. He was grateful because she was able to run the household and be a mother to their children up until six months before she died. The fact that he had learned to cook from his mother helped a great deal. He and Joanne enjoyed cooking together, experimenting with different recipes. Even though they had time together to prepare, it was still a shock to lose her. She was his best friend as well as a wife and mother. While he didn't mind housework, he appreciated her role as a housekeeper—or more accurately, a homemaker.

So after twelve years of marriage and two children, Mark found himself a widower. His life had a huge hole in the middle of it. At first, it was hard, to be a parent to his two children and work. He also had additional responsibilities because he joined the army in 1935 due to the problems in Europe. His specialty was administration and planning, and the army placed him in a post that was not combat-related. He did most of his work for the army either at his job—his employer was very understanding—or at home. It was all work he could do very quickly, so it didn't interfere much with family life. The army valued his work, and he was promoted twice in six years. He was a captain when the Japanese attacked Pearl Harbor. Because he was a widower and had two children, he had a deferment from active duty. However, once the US entered the war, his workload for the army increased.

In late 1942, the war made him conscious of his need to contribute more. He discussed it with his older sister and finally asked if she and her husband would look after his children, who, at the time, were eighteen and fourteen. They lived in the same town as his sister and her family. While he hated to leave his children at this point in their lives, the war was requiring sacrifices of everyone.

He was sent to Fort Hood to go through the combat infantry officer course and then for additional training on logistics and planning. It was in this course, taught by Colonel Jeremy Walker, that his path in World War II would be forged. Colonel Walker saw Mark's potential and took him under his wing. In early 1943, the army was setting up an expanded command in London. Colonel Walker was assigned to run the Planning and Logistics Department. He wanted Mark to come with him as his assistant. It came with a promotion to major, which was nice but did little to soften the blow of leaving his children.

Things moved rapidly after that. By March, they'd established their office organization and were working on training schedules for all of the men arriving, who would eventually form the basis for the invasion of Europe. They were also busy with the logistics of building the Eighth Air Force into a formidable force. Between the demands of men, equipment, and facilities, their workday averaged twelve hours, six days a week. Even with long hours, Mark enjoyed it because it was something he did well, and he knew it was essential to the war effort. He also enjoyed being in London—very different from the United States, but he liked the difference. He played on a soccer team in his spare time and even tried rugby for a while, before deciding that was a game for people who didn't want to keep their teeth. He was able to keep his physical focus, which helped him destress after the long hours at work. He also developed a liking for British bitter at the local pubs.

Mark's routine continued until Colonel Walker called him into his office and told him to pack a bag, retrieve his orders, and get to the train station immediately. So now, two weeks later, after the most rigorous physical program he'd ever been put through, together with weapons, navigation, and survival training, he was walking into the gymnasium to repack his parachute before another five-mile run. His life had changed drastically in fourteen days.

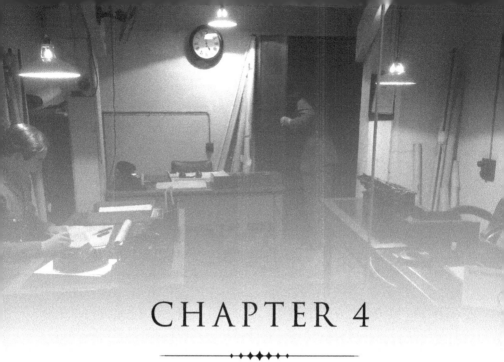

CHAPTER 4

+ + + ◆ + + +

**Early August 1943, Allied Command; War Cabinet
Rooms, St. Charles Street, London**

Lieutenant Ryder was going through another stack of files for a third group to receive specialized training. It seemed there was just one mission after another to Europe that required staffing. General Brawls was driving his staff hard. To make matters more difficult, Polly had been absent for almost two weeks, and the other secretaries were not as efficient as she was. They tried, but between the additional workload and their lower efficiency, it was stressful on all of the officers to keep the administration work adequately organized.

Linda stuck her head in his office. "Going to the commissary to get something to eat. Do you want to go with us, or should we bring you something?"

Alex sighed. "I'll come with you. I'm tired of sitting at this desk."

Alex and three secretaries walked to the commissary and selected some sandwiches. As they sat down, Linda said, "I'll be glad when Polly returns, and I'll bet you guys will be also. She works so quickly; it seems like the workload has increased since she left."

Alex was glad they recognized her efficiency as well. "I will be. General Brawls doesn't want to say when she might come back. I'm not sure what she's doing, but you're right; we could use her here."

Early August 1943, the Ardennes near Arlon, Belgium

Heinrich was dangling from his safety belt atop the last tower, connecting the main cables. This would be the last of this project until supplies arrived for the next section. Most of the crew of over fifty were cleaning up and preparing to leave the site. He would have his connections completed within the hour, and then he could go back into town and celebrate with everyone. They had managed to run power cables almost one hundred kilometers in six weeks, an almost impossible feat. Berlin was delighted and wanted this crew to work on the next two segments. He wasn't very interested in continuing this work, but it kept him out of combat. The war with Russia was not going well, so the battlefield was definitely a place to avoid. He wasn't very interested in helping to build the Atlantic wall either because most of the people working there were prisoners of war or workers from various occupied countries. Nothing sounded very inviting, so putting up power lines wasn't bad in comparison.

I wonder when the supplies for the next segment will get here, he mused. Inwardly, he hoped that the Belgium and French Resistance would slow delivery for several weeks. *I could get shot if I said that out loud.*

Fifty kilometers to the south, a company of Wehrmacht was working on several defensive positions near a large, newly constructed building. This particular position included a main control bunker with four machine-gun positions and mortar pits to the rear. Together with the ammunition dump and the supply bunker, it was a major undertaking, even for a full company.

Today's full company is a joke, thought Private Gerhart. *We barely have 120 men, but at least we're not in combat.* He watched as a supply truck pulled up, and a work party began to unload mortar shells. *At least the Reich still has plenty of ammunition, if not men.* He wondered what this facility was supposed to accomplish. It was evident that it was a defensive line of some kind, but apart from the weapons they were installing to protect the large building, it was not clear what defensive measures would be installed.

Mid-August 1943, Allied Command; War Cabinet Rooms, St. Charles Street, London; Lower Special Surveillance Office 8

Lieutenant Boysden was finishing his latest report. The weather had cleared over the last few weeks, and several photographic missions had been flown. There were quite a few areas of high activity along the Meuse River or in the forest to the east. All the regions indicated a similar pattern of construction. There would be a large building approximately twenty feet high, ten feet wide, and fifty to sixty feet long. Around this building would be smaller structures that appeared to be defensive positions. This was the sixth location he had seen. The intelligence section had not been able to figure out what the structures were or—more important—what their purpose was. Since it was evident that the Germans were preparing these sites quickly and wanted to defend them, it was essential to figure out what was going on.

This latest site was north of Verdun in an area named Beaumont-en-Verdunois. Through the small clearing in heavy forest cover, apparent signs of recent construction appeared daily. Stacks of supplies would change locations, and additional tracks would appear with smaller spots, possibly indicating workers.

His report was due within the hour to Captain Stone. William had come up with several ideas and wanted to discuss them with the captain.

So at four o'clock, Lieutenant Boysden walked into Captain Stone's office. The captain looked up. "Give me a summary."

"An additional site similar to the others is being constructed north of Verdun in an area called Beaumont-en-Verdunois. That makes six sites that I'm aware of, and I would be surprised if there weren't additional sites up and down a defensive line from the Argonne to the Ardennes.

I have no idea what the larger structures house, but it's obvious that it's important to the Germans. They're going to great effort to build defensive positions around them. I recommend that you consider taking this to the colonel, and coordinate the reports from other areas."

Captain Stone flipped through the report quickly. The small amount he scanned, together with the lieutenant's verbal summary, worried him. He knew enough about some of the other areas to know that there were at least fifteen sites similar to this. If intelligence couldn't figure out what was going on, they would run the risk of unpleasant surprises if Allied troops ever got that far.

"Lieutenant, this is good work. I can see what you mean, and I'll bring this up at the staff meeting this evening. I can't tell you much, but I haven't heard of much progress on figuring out the purposes of the sites. Let me read this and get ready for the meeting, and I'll get back to you later."

Daily Staff Meeting, Allied Headquarters

Colonel Gaffney briefed the committee on the latest photographic evidence of activity in the Argonne and Ardennes. He and Colonel Betts were the senior officers present tonight. The Prime Minister and most of the higher-level generals were busy with another issue.

Colonel Gaffney concluded, "So we have twenty sites, all of similar patterns, all having been constructed in the last two months. We don't know the purpose of the sites but have concluded the larger building in each of the sites probably houses equipment or weapons that are important to the Germans' defensive plan. Also, they are placing this along a defensive line in anticipation of an Allied invasion getting to the western border of Germany. Colonel Betts, do your people have any idea as to what the sites are for?"

"We have some guesses, but I'm not satisfied with them. We are certain that the larger building is going to house something that requires a huge amount of electrical power because it appears as though the Germans are building a dedicated power line from the dam near

Euskircken to connect each of these sites. We think they have completed a one-hundred-kilometer segment between Prum and Arlon, Belgium. They are stockpiling supplies along railheads parallel to the sites and will probably start construction on the remaining segments soon. Further, evidence as to their importance comes from the fact that Resistance reports in the area indicate a large number of Wehrmacht soldiers—many with special skills, such as electricians and instrument engineers—are involved in the work parties."

Captain Stone and his counterpart in a similar division spoke almost simultaneously. "As we know, this has been going on for several months. If we're not able to figure out what the sites are for, we may have a serious issue later in the war."

Colonel Betts was somewhat annoyed. "Thank you, gentlemen, for your opinions, which we already have discussed at length within MI6. We're making plans to increase our efforts to discover what the Germans are up to."

"My apologies, Colonel. I was pointing out the obvious. If I might add one more thing, however—all of these installations are near roadways or areas that would support off-road vehicles. One conclusion would be that the Germans will use these to stop any mechanized advance. Unfortunately, that still leaves us where we are now, not knowing the true purpose. So with that comment, I will refrain from further outbursts." Captain Stone knew when to keep quiet.

However, Colonel Gaffney wanted to make Betts commit to sharing the opinions of MI6. "Colonel Betts, can we plan on having your recommendations to the senior committee tomorrow?" Colonel Gaffney wanted to get something in front of the senior command quickly. The training at Achnacarry was going well, and a team likely would be ready by the end of August. While additional mission-specific training would be necessary, they likely would insert a group in the areas in question before the end of September.

"Let me confirm the timing, but I believe our recommendations will be ready by 1900 tomorrow. Will that be satisfactory?"

Colonel Gaffney was relieved because Betts could be difficult. "Thank you, Colonel. Please let me know if there are any changes to that schedule. I will set up a meeting with the senior committee tomorrow evening." As he dismissed the meeting, he was hopeful that the commando training would provide them the resources to obtain the intelligence they needed.

CHAPTER 5

End of August, German High Command in Berlin
Oberkommando der Wehrmacht (OKW)

The daily staff meeting reviewing the status of the various fronts in Sicily and Russia was about to conclude. While Jodl ran the session, Wilhelm Keitel was the head of OKW. They didn't always agree, and as a result, there was usually tension between them. In theory, the OKW reported directly to Hitler. But politics being what they were at that level of the military, many of the generals, including Jodl, had access to Hitler and could influence decisions.

"Gentlemen, the next item for discussion is the activity in eastern France and Belgium," Jodl said; he wanted to make certain he was in control—and not just of the meeting. This particular activity was Jodl's personal project, and the reports were sent directly through his organization. "The activity is on schedule and perhaps slightly ahead of schedule. One-third of the power system has been finished, and the second segment is well underway. Supplies for the third segment will be stockpiled next month. Construction of the generator buildings is almost complete, but the internal wiring and the actual generators themselves won't arrive until October. The defensive positions should be complete by mid-October. There have been minor interruptions from attacks by Resistance groups in the area but nothing serious. Furthermore, from the interrogation of several captured Resistance personnel, it is apparent that the Allies have not yet figured out what we are doing. We have one more test of the device scheduled next week, and that should allow us to make final adjustments on the generators and the targeting devices. Are there any questions?"

"Have you been watching the budget?" Keitel inquired. "This device is still somewhat experimental and is costing a lot, with regard to money and resources. We want to make sure it will work."

The head of the ordnance section replied, "You're correct; it is experimental. I have seen several of the tests myself, however, and the results are impressive."

Jodl added a final comment. "One of the things about this particular device is that while it needs a great deal of electrical power, it is basically quite simple, so there is little to malfunction. My staff and the project leaders are very confident in its effectiveness."

Due to the competition within the German military, however, to impress both the High Command and Hitler, they were unaware of the development and testing of an entirely different experimental weapon … but they soon would be.

First Week of September, Western Germany, near Saarburg

The British Mosquito was on a heading just north of due west, cruising at about 320 knots. They were returning from a bombing mission in central Germany, where they had been the marking plane for the bomber string that dropped flares to mark the target. Flight Officer Chaplin was looking forward to getting back to their base. It was already two o'clock in the morning, and he and his exhausted crew had flown four missions in a row.

Besides carrying flares, marker planes always carried high-resolution cameras in case there was a need for photographs. Chaplin didn't realize he would have an opportunity to use the cameras in a couple of minutes.

Chaplin turned on the intercom. "See anything down there worth investigating?" He hoped the answer would be no because he didn't want the delay.

The bomb-aimer came back. "No, sir, just a bunch of dark."

The navigator's voice came through the intercom. "Turn right, heading 310 in sixty seconds."

Chaplin turned the plane to 310 degrees and checked the altitude—7,150 feet. At this altitude and airspeed, there was little chance of running into night fighters. They usually went for the slower bombers.

There was a sudden bright burst just a few degrees to the left of their new course. It expanded rapidly in both intensity and size and covered a large area of the forest below.

"Charlie, do you see that?"

The bomb-aimer replied quickly, "It's kind of hard not to see it, and it's ruined my night vision. I've got the cameras going; although all we were going to get is large, bright blobs."

"Pilot to navigator, I'm altering course to 307 degrees to fly over it." The plane swung to the left slightly and started traversing directly overhead. The light had expanded in a few seconds to approximately the size of a four-hundred-yard square. Even though the light was diminishing in intensity, secondary fires were spreading all over the area.

"Whatever that was, it was the biggest flash bomb I've ever seen. I hope we don't run into any fighters tonight because my night vision is gone."

On the ground, in a small bunker approximately two thousand meters east of the light, several German officers and scientists were recording data and congratulating themselves.

The senior German officer smiled. "Heisenberg will be pleased."

One of the scientists replied nervously, "No, he won't. This is a fizzle, not a complete merge."

"It's not his place to complain, just to produce."

The First Week of September, Achnacarry Castle, Scotland

Lieutenant Colonel Vaughn and the sergeant major were finalizing the rosters for the various mission teams. There were four separate missions to staff. The two most important would take place in the area around Saint-Mihiel and another location just west of Verdun. The mission east of Saint-Mihiel involved attacking a German observation post on top of a butte that rose several hundred feet above the plane—a critical position in World War I. While important, this was more of a diversion for the real focus of that mission, which was to drop one man in the woods west of Verdun.

The mission, planned for several weeks, had a cover story about a small bombing raid near a facility outside of Munich that made ball bearings and explosives for artillery shells. Ball bearings were critical to the German war machine, as they were for any mechanized army. The explosives being produced in a small factory nearby added an additional incentive.

The mission called for three B-17s to fly and deliver a custom bomb load on the target. Two of the B-17s would carry twelve five-hundred-pound bombs and one thousand pounds of ten-pound incendiary bombs. The third B-17 would be fitted with a new type of engine and additional fuel and would carry one thousand pounds of incendiary bombs. British Mosquito bombers would mark the target by dropping flares. The first two B-17s would return to England, while the third B-17 would turn west. It would be carrying a crew of ten highly trained commandos. This B-17 would be equipped with a new autopilot system, operated with mechanical cams that would allow the plane to fly on after the crew bailed out.

All of the crew except the pilot would position themselves in the bomb bay area and the front hatch and jump together with two five-hundred-pound supply bundles. The crew expected the pilot to drop out of the front hatch after they had safely left the plane. Once on the ground, the group would attack and destroy the German observation post at Montsec. They didn't realize, however, that the pilot had an entirely different mission. As soon as the crew left the plane, he would turn northwest and fly for another fifteen minutes before bailing out over the forest near Lachalade. The pilot would be Major Mark Dornier.

The sergeant major completed the rosters and presented them to the colonel. "I still can't believe we were able to train this many so quickly. I still think their training is thin, but they are as dedicated a bunch as I've ever seen."

"We haven't trained many Americans here, but if the rest of them are as good as this group, they'll do fine."

A woman's voice rang out as the colonel's office door opened. "I want to thank both of you gentlemen for your cooperation and focus. Not only General Brawls but the PM himself wanted this to be an American mission, if at all possible. Your efforts have made it possible." Captain Berson walked over and took the sergeant major's salute before saluting the colonel.

"Please sit down, and thank you, Polly, for all of your assistance. You helped us pick a good group of candidates."

"Well, if my contribution is complete, I will return to my duties in London. I think there may be a young man in my office who is curious as to my whereabouts." Polly Berson had been one of the first women to complete commando training two years earlier and had helped headquarters pick additional people to receive training.

"Return with my blessings, and tell the general the mission training starts this evening."

The Second Week of September 1943, Allied Command; War Cabinet Rooms, St. Charles Street, London; Lower Special Surveillance Office 8

For almost a week after the Mosquito bomber returned from photographing the flash of light, MI6 struggled to understand what they had seen. It'd been considered important enough to bring to the Prime Minister's attention, and he had contacted President Roosevelt. While several possibilities as to the origin of the light existed, one idea had to do with an American secret project that very few people in Britain were aware of. Manhattan was the code name, and its focus was to make an extremely powerful bomb, harnessing the power of the atom.

Two scientists from the United States had been flown to London to confer with the flight crew and MI6. For two days, they interviewed everyone associated with the flight and studied the photographs. They then requested a meeting with the Prime Minister and two other high-level generals—one American and one British.

The scientists prepared a brief presentation to explain their thoughts. While far from being entirely certain, their conclusion was the light had very likely been a test of a nuclear device. Making a successful atomic bomb was simple in theory but extremely difficult in reality. It involved slamming two noncritical pieces of nuclear material together to initiate a chain reaction to release the energy contained within the atoms. The process required delicate precision to start the chain reaction. Otherwise, the bomb would release energy in the form of heat and light but then fizzle out with only a small explosion. The heat would be enough to scorch the earth and start secondary fires similar to those witnessed by the bomber crew.

Churchill was adamant. "We need to find out what they are doing—*now!*"

The next day, plans were made to accelerate the schedule for raiding a select list of specialized German facilities that might be associated with their nuclear program. At the same time, the possibility existed that this weapon would be deployed along with the other mystery devices that were being installed in eastern France. Major Dornier's mission schedule was moved up by ten days.

Last Week of September, Lieutenant Colonel Vaughn's Office, Achnacarry Castle, Scotland

Four missions were scheduled to take place in the next month, associated with the German defensive construction in eastern France and the enormous flash of light in western Germany. Two of these missions involved insertion of teams near facilities suspected of being involved in atomic research. The other two missions focused on the construction and observation sites in eastern France. Until recently, the men involved in these missions were under the impression that it was only one mission.

The mission-specific training for all four teams had started ten days ago. The mission concerning the construction in eastern France would involve three B-17s on a diversion bombing raid in southern Germany. Two of the B-17 crews knew nothing about the goal of the third. They were training separately with the British at a base near Norfolk. These two B-17s would lead the raid, and Major Dornier's B-17 would follow, dropping incendiaries. This crew was training to destroy the observation site at Montsec and then to investigate the latest construction site southeast of Verdun on the west bank of the Meuse River. Up until two days ago, Major Dornier was training with them and was under the impression he would lead the mission. Then he'd been called into Lieutenant Colonel Vaughn's office and been given sealed orders to be read in the colonel's office and then destroyed. Vaughn was aware of the overall mission but not all the details.

Major Dornier opened his orders:

His B-17 would participate in the small bombing raid on the Karlsfeld facility just outside Munich. Once completed, his plane would separate from the other two, as planned, and fly northwest to the general area of Verdun. He would then position the B-17 southeast of Verdun at twenty-eight thousand feet and have the crew bail out with their supply pods.

After the crew had left the plane, the plan took a sharp change—he would turn and fly northwest to an area south of Aubréville, climbing to thirty-four thousand feet. There, he would place the plane on autopilot and drop out of the bomb-bay doors in a uniquely designed pod that would act as a glider. While it was experimental, it had been tested many times in the last year. It could achieve a glide ratio of just shy of two to one, which meant he should be able to travel approximately ten or eleven miles from the drop point—critical factor in disguising his landing point.

As soon as he was clear of the plane, the autopilot would execute a ninety-degree turn to the left, putting the bomber on a course to eventually fly near the French town of Nantes. After clearing the French coast, the autodestruct mechanism would then destroy the engines and allow the fuselage to crash with its remaining explosives, located to ensure the plane and its specialized equipment were utterly destroyed.

Major Dornier would pilot the glider pod to a small field two hundred yards wide and nine hundred yards long. If needed, emergency parachutes in the pod could bring it to a safe landing; the landing field, however, would be prepared to allow the glider pod to land safely. The pod would have a small two-cycle engine, together with an undercarriage, to enable it to travel at five miles an hour with a maximum speed of twelve to fifteen miles an hour. He would proceed using the road at the end of the field, approximately one mile to an old World War I French trench system and artillery base. One of the command dugouts had been prepared to house him in the tunnel system below it. While he would be bringing food, ammunition, clothing, and medical supplies, the dugout would be supplied with additional food and supplies. His contact would be a member of the Resistance living in the nearby area.

Major Dornier's purpose was to observe multiple construction sites along a German defensive line east and north of his position. He would delay any action for a week after arrival to ensure the Germans were not aware of his presence. He was to avoid contact with any Germans and only communicate as needed with his Resistance contact. In other words, he was to be invisible.

There was a small map of the area that he was to take with him. He looked up at the colonel. "I assume you know nothing of what is in this envelope."

"I know little of your specific orders, but I have been given sealed orders as to your specific training, which will begin tomorrow morning. I'm not sure why, but several hours of each day will involve removing you from your crew's training so you can train on gliders."

"So I shouldn't say anything about this to anyone?"

"Correct. Wait until one of the instructors comes for you."

Mid-October, Les Islettes, near Forêt Domaniale de Lachalade in the Argonne, France

Aurélie had ridden her bicycle into the small village. As she passed in front of the church, she noticed several old wooden buckets placed around the old well. She recalled her grand-père had told her to be on guard for any unusual things she might see in the village.

After she went to the market, she started back for the farm. She put the food in the kitchen and then walked out to the barn, thinking her grand-père would probably be there.

Alphonse came to the door as she approached. "Did you get everything?"

Aurélie nodded. "Remember you asked us to be on the lookout for any unusual activity or signs in the village? I noticed there were several old wooden buckets placed around the well in front of the church."

"Oh, I wonder if the people brought the buckets to the well and then went to church to pray for water." He paused. "It must be old Pierre. He is the only one dumb enough to try to get water out of that old dry well."

Aurélie shrugged. "I'll start preparing dinner. Do you know where Josette is?"

"She may be out back. Do you remember how many buckets were at the well?"

"At least five or six, maybe more."

Alphonse went back into the barn to think. He had been waiting for a sign to prepare the dugouts and the old farmhouse. The number of buckets indicated everything was to be ready within seven to ten days. He would make his first trip to the dugout tomorrow, midmorning, after his chores. He didn't understand what could be so crucial in this particular area, but then, it was better not to know these things.

Mid-October, a Remote Glider Strip, Northern Scotland

Mark Dornier was sitting in the pilot seat of the glider pod, getting ready to drop on his seventh test flight. The last two weeks had been very intense, not only training with his bomber crew but also receiving additional training about how to pilot this new type of glider. He was going through the final checks before his release in the bomb bay of a B-17, on loan from the Eighth Air Force.

His instructor was seated just above him, observing as he went through the checklist. "Be sure not to lose control in the first few seconds." Last time, Mark had pulled back on the release, and the nose came up too high. "You don't want to hit the plane."

Mark was nervous, but the cold at thirty-four thousand feet and his checklist gave him plenty to keep focused. Piloting this pod was like trying to fly a locomotive with a pair of short, stubby wings. It just wanted to go one direction—straight down.

Last night, the training with the bomber crew at Achnacarry had been completed, and he was taken to a glider strip forty miles away for this training. He'd been working with the replica of the pod during the noon hour, away from his crew. Today's session would provide him ten test flights, which was all he would get before the actual mission.

Mark looked up at his instructor, who was holding the checklist card and signaling a thumbs-up. "I'm ready for the sixty-second countdown," Mark said into the intercom.

The instructor nodded and told the pilot to slow to 155 knots. The instructor reached up and opened the bomb-bay doors. The cold was numbing, even through the thick layers of the flight suits they were wearing. The airspeed indicator showed 165 knots and dropping. When it passed 155 knots, he started the timer, counting backward from sixty. "Make sure you get the stabilizer up before you extend the wings."

Mark nodded and prepared for release. Only three more tests after this one, and he could get warm again. At 121 knots, the pod dropped away.

Late October, Allied Command; War Cabinet Rooms, St. Charles Street, London

"You still haven't answered any of my questions about where you were at last month." Alex Ryder had been more than curious when Polly returned. "I'm glad you're back, but I would've liked to—"

"Lieutenant"—Polly cut him off—"I told you all that information is on a need-to-know basis, and besides, how do you know I didn't go see an old boyfriend?" Polly enjoyed the back-and-forth with Alex and could see he was jealous. Seeing the chagrin on his face, she couldn't help smiling. "No, I didn't go see a boyfriend, old or new. I had some business connected to the war effort. And yes, I will go to a movie with you this weekend." She knew he would ask. "So can we talk about something else?"

Alex just looked at her for a few seconds. "There is something you are keeping from me."

She sighed. "You know my brother was killed several years ago in Belgium, so the war effort is something that's personal to me. Perhaps if we go out a few times, you'll understand." She smiled and turned to go back to her desk.

She needed to help General Brawls prepare for the transition of the newly created Allied command—Supreme Headquarters Allied Expeditionary Force, or SHAEF for short.

CHAPTER 6

✦✦✦✦✦

October 28, 1943, Eighth Air Force Base, Polebrook, England

The three B-17 crews had finished their final briefing and were checking their planes. Take off would be single file at 11:10 p.m., followed by a five-hour flight to their target outside Munich.

Major Dornier's bombardier was coming back from checking the bomb load. "Major, we have a large supply pod in the middle of the bomb bay. I thought we were just going to carry two pods."

"This afternoon I heard we would carry an additional pod that has some special equipment we'll need when we get to our target area. No information on what is in it or how much it weighs. I hope Operations computed the weight and fuel correctly."

The navigator overheard and said, "The wheel weights look right, and we have the extra fuel. We'll be okay as long as we don't run into strong headwinds."

"It looks like we have additional carrier pigeons as well. I suppose it never hurts to have multiple ways to communicate." The bombardier turned as the copilot walked up.

Major Dornier knew, of course, that the extra pod was his glider, but he was not at liberty to say anything. Changing the subject, he asked his copilot, "Did you check the autopilot equipment this afternoon?"

"Everything looks like it works, but what a contraption! I'm glad we're going to be leaving the plane before that gets turned on. There's no telling what it'll do."

The major laughed. "That's easy for you to say because I have to turn it on before I can jump."

Polebrook's ops officer walked in. "All right, gentlemen; it's time to go to the planes. Here's the radio code for rendezvousing with the RAF pilot plane." He handed a small envelope to each of the three pilots. Only plane one would send the code, but as a backup, they all got a copy.

At 10:50 p.m., the three planes started their engines and began their warm-up and final checklist. At 11:00 p.m., three planes taxied out single file and held at the end of the five-thousand-foot runway. All radio communications between the three planes ceased, and from that point forward, they would use only hand-light semaphore signals.

At 11:07 p.m., a white flare was shot over the control tower as the first plane revved its engines up to full power and started its takeoff roll. Fifty seconds later the second plane followed, and fifty seconds after that, Major Dornier started his B-17 down the runway. The copilot called off the airspeed as it slowly increased. As it reached 130 knots, both pilots slowly pulled back on the yoke. The plane responded, climbing off the tarmac. They were on their way.

The ops officer informed his CO that the planes were off. The CO picked up the phone on his desk and made a call to a small bedroom within the War Cabinet rooms. "Sir, the planes are off. He should be down in about seven hours."

"Thank you, Colonel. Go get some rest." The Prime Minister picked up the crystal brandy decanter next to his bed and poured another drink. He was going to bed early so he would be awake when the bombers got to Munich.

1:15 a.m., October 29, 1943, Twenty-Eight Thousand Feet over Western Germany

"Pilot to top turret, see anything?"

The navigator's voice came over the intercom. "Nothing—nice and lonely here. I'm coming down to recheck our position. We should be somewhere between Strasbourg and Karlsruhe."

Five minutes later, the navigator came on. "We're about ten minutes ahead of schedule. That front must've provided more tailwind than we thought. That should be Stuttgart off to the left."

Major Dornier had noticed a few lights off to the left already. *Sloppy. Even with no bombers out tonight they should keep the lights off.* "Thanks. Let me know when we need to turn to the south for our approach."

"Roger. Should be in about fifteen minutes."

Each man was deep in his own thoughts. Even with all their training, dropping into enemy territory with little or no light was never an easy task. The flight was the easy part of the mission because it was not likely the Germans would send up night fighters for three planes, especially since they weren't making a direct line toward any large military target. The closer they got to the Munich area, the more likely it was that resistance would increase.

Major Dornier turned to his copilot. "You think we'll see any night fighters?"

Captain Fordyce shook his head. "I doubt if they'll send anything up until after the bombs hit, and by that time, we should be gone."

"You're probably right. I hope the marker plane is accurate. There's a lot of civilian housing around the target. Even though it's for factory workers, I'd still rather not bomb housing if we can avoid it."

"The British have been doing this for four years now, and they're pretty good at it. The marker plane flies over at a low level to confirm landmarks aligning with the target."

"Navigator to pilot, prepare to turn to a heading of one seven zero in sixty seconds, on my mark." The navigator kept his eye on the plane just above him to his left. They would start turning only when the lead plane sent its signal with the light semaphore.

Right on schedule, the lead plane signaled, and the navigator notified the major.

A few seconds later, three B-17s turned slowly to the right from east southeast to a more southerly direction. The new course would give a better approach to the target, as well as avoid several known flak sites. They flew on this heading for another forty minutes before turning toward the east for the final seventy minutes of the flight.

3:55 a.m., October 29, 1943, British Mosquito Bomber over Eching, Northeast of Munich

Flight Officer Blissett was preparing to mark the target site. Thirty minutes earlier, they had flown over the target twice at one thousand feet, and his bombardier and belly gunner both confirmed the landmarks required to mark the target. They had pulled up abruptly while dropping four small incendiary bombs with time fuses. Then they left the area to buzz other sites to confuse the Germans. They had also marked four different locations around the factories north of Regensburg.

As they approached Dachau, Blissett would execute a 100-degree turn to the south and drop his altitude from ten thousand feet to six thousand feet. They had already received the signal from the lead B-17, indicating they were ten minutes away.

It was always tricky business to mark a site because it required close coordination between the lead bombing elements and the marker plane. Obviously, the flares had to be dropped over the target, but they also needed to be released so they would be between twelve hundred and six hundred feet above the target when the bombers were overhead.

Flight Officer Blissett turned to his copilot and nodded. "Turn left to 080 degrees. Reduce speed to two hundred miles an hour and reduce altitude to one thousand feet a minute." The copilot nodded and executed the turn. "Charles, get ready with the flares. I think I see our incendiary markers ahead. Can you see them?"

"Got them, and I've armed the marker flares."

The markers were ten-pound flares attached to a parachute that would slow its descent. Tonight they would drop six flares. The first two were white; the second two, green; and the last two, marking the end of the target area, were red.

"Bomb-aimer to pilot, thirty seconds. Final clearance?"

"Navigator to pilot, received final clearance from the lead bomber."

Blissett took a deep breath. "Pilot to bomb-aimer—clear to drop."

Blissett took over the controls, preparing to turn northeast and then gain altitude, increasing their airspeed. They didn't want to be anywhere near the target in two minutes. The Mosquito shuddered as the bomb-bay doors opened. A few seconds later, the flares left the plane. Blissett immediately rammed the power to full throttle and put the aircraft in a 90-degree turn to the left.

4:12 a.m., Five Miles West Northwest of Karlsfeld

Major Dornier's bombardier was opening the bomb-bay doors following the signals of the two planes in front. The two lead planes were flying abreast, approximately three miles ahead. Their bomb load was mainly incendiaries. The lead planes' bombs would break up the target structures, which would allow the incendiaries to be more effective.

Major Dornier turned the aircraft control over to the bombardier. They could see the flares in the distance and the lead planes flying abreast about sixty feet apart. At a little past 4:15 a.m., the lead planes turned sharply to the left and signaled back to Dornier's plane that they had released their bombs. It would take a little less than a minute to reach the bomb-release point.

"I have the flares, and we're right on target. Preparing to drop." The bombardier reached for the toggle switch to his left.

There was no flak, and so far they had not seen any night-fighters. They would be over the target and release their bombs before the lead planes' bombs detonated. This would increase the chances for all the aircraft to get away from the area before the Germans could take any defensive action.

They were very close to the flares now. Major Dornier prepared for the 90-degree turn to the right as soon as the bombardier returned control of the plane to him.

The bombardier made final adjustments on the bomb site. "Almost there … I've got the middle of the flare stream … bombs away." The plane lifted as it released its cargo. "Closing bomb-bay doors; returning control to pilot."

"Roger, pilot has control. Turning right. Everyone keep their eyes on the target. We want to know if we've hit anything."

Just then the lead planes' bombs impacted and walked across the target area, followed by their incendiaries.

"Ball turret to pilot, all bombs hit." Just then there was a large fireball from the target. "And evidently they were on target," he added, referring to the blast.

Major Dornier kept his eye on the compass as the plane swung around to a heading of 270 degrees. He began a slow climb to go from the bombing altitude of twenty-eight thousand feet to thirty-two thousand feet. Just as they settled on their new course, their incendiary bombs added to the dots of light. There had been several secondary explosions, and fires were breaking out over the target area.

"Tail gunner to pilot, Charlie put his bombs right on top of theirs." Again, several large explosions occurred, indicating they'd hit the munitions factory.

The ball-turret gunner, who had the best view, added, "It looks like a good drop. Whatever they were making down there clearly doesn't like fire."

"Pilot to navigator, send the success signal." The prearranged short transmission would inform their base not only of the success of the mission but also that they were on the first leg away from the target area. As soon as they sent it, he would turn the plane slightly north to a heading of 285 degrees for the flight to the Montsec area.

As the plane settled on the new heading, Major Dornier turned on the intercom. "Good job, everyone. Start preparing for the drop. It's approximately an hour and ten minutes away. Check your chutes, and get into your camouflage. Charlie, go back and check the supply pods."

The plane droned on, slowly gaining altitude. Their B-17 was now at 31,200 feet. Even with the electrically heated flight suits, the cold was an issue. They would all be glad to get down on the ground, even though jumping over enemy territory at night wasn't anyone's first choice. Once the equipment check was complete, everyone settled back for the remaining flight. Their preparations and training had brought them this far, and now there was nothing left to do except wait.

6:10 a.m., East of Strasbourg, France

"Okay, guys, we have approximately ten minutes of flying left. Go to your drop hatch."

The bombardier, navigator, and front gunner moved to the nose hatch. The copilot would join them five minutes before the drop. The tail gunner, ball-turret gunner, and waist gunners went to the bomb bay. They all went through a final equipment check. To the southeast, the sky was starting to lighten, even though the sun would not be up for another two hours. Ahead, the Moselle River crisscrossed the landscape like a silver ribbon. It would be seven minutes from that point to the drop.

"It looks like we're right on course, so why don't you go ahead and get set up," Dornier said to the copilot. He started unbuckling and moved back down to the nose hatch area. As the plane flew over the river, he switched on the intercom. "That's the Moselle down there, so we have a little more than six minutes left."

Three minutes later, Major Dornier pulled the throttles back, causing the plane to slow to a speed safe for the drop. "Preparing to open the bomb-bay doors. Open the nose hatch. Call out the final check."

Each of the crew called out. Major Dornier flipped the switch to open the bomb-bay doors and released the safety for the supply pods. "All safeties are off; pods ready to drop. Sixty seconds."

The plane was slowing to 120 miles per hour. Major Dornier could barely make out the Montsec butte off to the right about eight miles. They were over the wooded area, with several clearings that would serve as the drop zone.

"Okay, gentlemen, prepare to jump on my signal—and Godspeed." Ten seconds later, he gave the order to jump and released the supply pods. Everyone went out fast and started the long drop to the five-thousand-foot level, where they would open their chutes. The fall to five thousand feet would take about two and a half minutes.

Mark wondered how long it would be before they figured out he wasn't following them. As soon as they were out, he shut the bomb-bay doors and increased speed as he turned to a heading of 305 degrees. It would be another thirteen minutes to Aubréville and his drop zone. He busied himself doing the checks in the cockpit. After he was satisfied everything was operating correctly, and he set the explosive charges, he moved back down to the bomb-bay area. He strapped on his parachute and slowly lowered himself into the drop pod. He was still stiff from the recent training in northern England. *What have I gotten myself into?* The display just above him had a control panel for the plane and a countdown timer for his drop.

He started through the checklist, which helped him bury his doubts. A glance at the timer in the belly of the plane showed he was five minutes from release. He zipped up the insulated liner around his shoulders and lowered his goggles and face mask as he started breathing through the pod's oxygen bottle. He heard the engines start to slow down, and the bomb-bay doors opened, revealing a gray, murky cloud layer several thousand feet below. The timer on the pod indicated three minutes. The cold at thirty-four thousand feet, almost 70 degrees below zero, cut into the pod and his flight suit. He saw the airspeed indicator dropping through 150 knots as the plane began to nose over slightly. He watched as the timer went below thirty seconds.

6:35 a.m., over Aubréville France, Northwest of Verdun

He pulled the release as the timer went to zero; the plane was flying at 124 miles per hour. The pod dropped, nose-heavy, as the aircraft fell away above him. The stabilizer deployed, followed by the glider wings. It shuddered as the wings stabilized the fall. As soon as they locked, he began gliding, turning west to his target in the forest below. Would he be able to see the field to land? He heard the plane increase the engine power and turn to the southwest. *At least the autopilot is working.*

The clouds enveloped him, and he flew by compass and altimeter for several minutes. He didn't notice the cold as he concentrated on maintaining control. After gliding for three minutes west, he turned 90 degrees to the north. He would continue on this heading for another three minutes. He would then turn west again at an altitude of ten thousand feet, and hopefully, by then, he would be able to locate his landing site.

At fifteen thousand feet, clouds broke, and the landscape came into view. It took him a few seconds to recognize landmarks. He realized he needed to correct to the north slightly to line up on his landing site. As he started to correct, the rudder on the stabilizer jammed and wouldn't go back to the neutral position. He pumped the rudder pedals, and it finally released, but now he was too far north and had to fly south for the approach. This unfortunately used up precious height, and by the time he was lined up, his altitude was six thousand feet instead of eight thousand. *This is going to be tight.* He relied on his training, forcing the panic out of his mind, and he pulled back on the elevator control to slow his descent. He mentally calculated that he would be able to make it to the clearing but only by a slim margin.

The sky was much lighter now, and the landscape features were becoming clear. He saw the landing field ahead and made some small adjustments, pushing the nose down to lose altitude rapidly. So far he had not seen any movement on the ground. All he noticed were a couple of small herds of cattle.

He passed over a small farm and made his final approach to the clearing. He was at one thousand feet, flying ninety miles an hour. He pushed the nose further over as the field began to rush up to meet him. He passed over the last of the trees at ninety feet and pulled up to slow his speed. He was over the last of the brush in the clearing as the airspeed dropped to sixty miles an hour. At forty feet, he descended slightly and then pulled up again to reduce his speed. He just hoped that the intelligence on the field was correct, and there weren't any obstacles.

He impacted the field and bounced slightly. The undercarriage held, and as he hit the second time, the pod stayed on the ground. He was going approximately forty-five miles an hour, but the friction of the field grass quickly slowed him. He steered to the right slightly toward a break in the trees, where he thought there should be a path for him to maneuver onto a dirt road.

As the pod slowly rolled to a stop, he did a quick check of the instruments. He breathed a sigh of relief and quietly said a prayer. *Thank you, Lord. I'm not ever doing that again!* He just sat there for a few seconds, taking in the silence and the smells of the country. He heard no one, not any sounds of life, for that matter, which was good. His next task was to open an access cover on the back of the pod, crank the main wings back into the sides, and open the container that housed the homing pigeons. The pigeons were moving around slowly but didn't appear to be any worse for wear after their ten-hour journey.

Next, he got underneath and hooked up the belt drive from the small engine that would propel the pod—slow, but it was better than trying to move the pod himself. He pulled out his Sten gun; then removed the two reserve chutes and stowed them. Parachutes were useful for any number of things on the ground.

CHAPTER 7

———— ✦✦✦✦✦ ————

Forêt Domaniale de Lachalade

M ark steered the pod toward the edge of the field where the path started. The belt drive had been slow to engage initially, but it seemed to be working now. The maximum speed was just over twelve miles per hour, but on a path like this he was only going two to three miles per hour—walking speed. As he left the field, the forest closed in on both sides, leaving only the narrow path going forward. One of the reasons they selected this time of day was that it was improbable that anyone would be on the road.

Up ahead, the path divided; the left fork led to the country road, and the other continued into the forest. Both would take Mark to the dugouts, but it was safer to stay in the woods and off the road. Fortunately, the terrain was relatively flat, so once the pod was moving, the belt drive worked just fine, although going up a steep incline would've been impossible.

"I could walk this fast," he said under his breath but knew he had to have patience. The pod weighed almost fifteen hundred pounds, and it obviously would've been impossible for him to have moved it, even on wheels, without some method of propulsion.

He relaxed slightly for the first time in several days, breathing in the fresh air of the forest. He could smell the leaves, the trees, and other forest scents. He always liked being outside in a variety of climates and locations, but this was especially pleasant, as he knew no one else was around—or at least he hoped that was the case.

The path turned slightly to the right, taking him farther away from the country road that would help mask sounds. He reached down for his canteen and took a couple of swallows. As he relaxed, he heard his stomach growl and realized he hadn't eaten anything for almost twelve hours. He reached into one of his pockets and pulled out a pemmican bar.

The path widened out, and the forest thinned slightly. There was a small stream about two feet across. *Shouldn't be a problem.* Just to be sure, however, Mark stopped the pod about fifty feet before the stream and walked up to inspect. The water was only a couple of inches deep, and medium-size gravel covered the bottom. He looked down the stream both ways and again listened very intently for any sounds of life. While he could hear birds, there were no other sounds. As he turned to walk back to the pod, he caught a glimpse of movement off to his left in a small clearing. He stopped immediately and slowly reached into his shoulder holster for his silenced .22 caliber pistol.

He stood there for perhaps sixty seconds and realized that whatever it was, it hadn't detected his presence yet. He kept his ears open for sounds behind him and on both sides, but he kept his focus on where he first noticed the movement. Just then, a large stag took two steps from behind the bushes and looked around. He was a magnificent specimen with a large rack. He looked around for a few more seconds, with his nose high in the air, before turning and walking away.

Mark wondered how many deer there were in this forest. If he had been there longer, he would've chanced a shot. Since he had only been on the ground for a little over an hour, he wasn't about to make any loud noises or create extra work.

He climbed back into the pod, started the engine, and moved

the lever forward to engage the belt. The pod scooter started forward slowly. One of the significant disadvantages of belt drive was the lack of gears, which meant getting the pod to move from a dead-stop was slow. Nevertheless, he gained speed as he drove toward the stream.

After splashing through the stream, the path went through a small clearing and then back into the forest. As the forest closed in again, it had a comforting effect. Mark followed the trail for another forty minutes before it turned sharply to the left. He stopped the pod about thirty feet before the turn because the path led directly to the country road. He wanted to make sure there was no local traffic before he attempted to cross.

He unholstered his .22 caliber pistol and proceeded down the path to a point where it intersected the road. The trail crossed the road and went into a small clearing and then resumed its journey through the forest. The dugouts were only about three hundred yards into the forest. He stood on the road and listened again very carefully but didn't detect any signs of human life. He walked back to the pod and started forward. As he approached the road, he increased the speed as much as possible to minimize the amount of time he would be exposed on the road and in the small clearing.

After crossing the road, the path narrowed and entered the forest. It turned slightly left and started down a gentle incline. In a few minutes, Mark saw his home for the next several months off to the right. He was impressed with how well it blended into the forest. This location had been chosen for its proximity to several German activities of interest and because the encampment was deserted after the war. It had been forgotten, and since there had been several accidents in the woods from the unexploded World War I ordnance, most of the locals avoided the forest. As he approached, he kept looking in all directions for any unusual movement.

There was a row of four timber and earth-covered shelters; the larger, second one was his final destination. He was impressed with the layout, but since this had been an artillery headquarters, it was only natural that they would've provided for reasonable access and storage of supplies.

He pulled up beside his new home and killed the engine. With his

Sten gun out, he started a slow walk around the dugout, looking for any signs of life and also familiarizing himself with the area. He took his time because he knew this initial introduction to the woods was significant. He walked in ever-widening circles and eventually came to a series of old trenches about fifty yards to the east. There were larger depressions at regular intervals, which probably housed the artillery pieces. He walked down into the ditch; the walls were eroded to a gentle forty-five-degree angle; the trench itself was only about four feet deep. The elements had worked to conceal the man-made scars.

He had been on the ground for about three hours and was satisfied there was no one in the immediate area. After inspecting the woods around the bunkers out to one hundred yards, he decided it was time to go inside. The doorway to his dugout was only five feet high, and the interior was approximately six feet wide and about ten feet deep. The walls were lined with sturdy wood planks and appeared to be no worse for wear. He went to the back left-hand corner, looking carefully for any signs of recent activity but didn't see anything unusual. He started gently tapping around on the dirt floor until he heard a hollow sound. He reached down, moving the dirt away, and found the handle for the trapdoor. He took out his flashlight and illuminated the cellar. He listened carefully for any signs of life, taking in the slightly musty odor associated with all basements.

He went down the access ladder slowly, moving his flashlight back and forth. He saw what looked like a light switch and turned it on. Amazingly, the cellar was illuminated by four electric lights. Even though he had been told the French had run electricity to these dugouts during the war, he was surprised that the transmission lines were still intact. The main overhead lines ran east and west through the forest to connect Lachalade with the power system on the west side of the woods. From one of the lines, the French had dropped a power cable down one of the poles and into the ground, so it wasn't obvious. While it had been damaged several times because of shelling, the French were always able to make repairs. The line was buried almost five feet deep. The electric power it provided gave them an advantage over the Germans, who, at that time had trenches only three hundred yards to the north.

Mark was impressed with the cellar. There was a bunk with a straw mattress and a sink with open cabinets above it for storing food. There was a small stall that would allow him to shower. He looked over and noticed the well that would supply fresh water, including a fifty-five-gallon holding tank, located above the shower stall. The propane stove was next to an old pot-bellied stove, clearly from World War I, and offered another source of heat and cooking.

The most impressive thing, however, was an electric freezer and a cold box. They looked in good shape. *Where in the world did they obtain something like this, and how did they get it down here?* The cold box contained a small selection of fresh vegetables—carrots, cabbage, several tomatoes, some onions, and green beans. Hanging from the ceiling next to these two appliances, surrounded by a wooden frame covered with metal-screen material, were two smoked hams and a chicken. Over in a corner by the shower stall was a wooden crate with wine bottles in it. On top of the bottles was a small card with BIENVENUE! written in block letters.

Welcome, indeed! Mark was flabbergasted at the conveniences someone had worked so hard to provide. He was painfully aware of the sacrifice several people in the area would've accepted to prepare this location and maintain the supplies. There was even a handmade chair and an old cable spool set next to it as an end table. He had to try the bed. As he lay back, he was surprised at the comfort and the support the mattress provided. *I hope the mission is worth the cost.*

Enough relaxation. He got up and went out to the pod again, visually checking the area for any signs of life. Nothing looked suspicious, so he began to unload some of his supplies. It was now ten thirty in the morning.

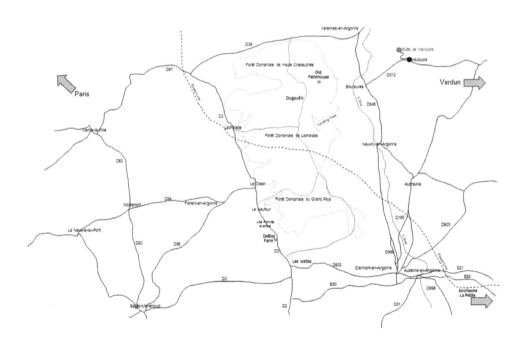

CHAPTER 8

10:30 a.m., October 29, Alphonse's Farm, North of Les Islettes

Alphonse and Luc were in the field behind the barn. They were loading wheat straw bales onto a low wagon to move into the barn. The wheat was harvested at the end of September, and the straw was a component in the winter feed for the dairy cattle.

Aurélie walked toward them with a small package and a container of water. "Are we going to have enough feed this winter?"

"I need to get the load of grain that Xavier promised me, but other than that, we'll have plenty." Their dairy cattle and the milk products that came from them were an essential part of their income. While most people in the area had some dairy cattle, Alphonse had six, and they were all very productive. It kept them busy, separating cream and making butter and different kinds of cheeses. The Germans tried to confiscate their produce, but they had no accurate way of knowing how much they made. As a result, Alphonse had plenty to use as bartering income.

"What are we having for lunch?" Luc was always more interested in eating than working.

"Ham, potatoes, and green beans." Then Aurélie turned to her grand-père. "By the way, when I went to the cellar, I noticed two hams were missing. Did you take them into town?"

Alphonse had been prepared for this inquiry ever since he had taken the hams and a few other supplies to the dugout. "Well, actually, I took some stuff over to Xavier's to help remind him about the grain."

That evening Aurélie asked Josette to go down to the house cellar to get a wedge of cheese. When she returned, she commented, "I thought we had more cheese down there than we do. Did you take some into town for barter?"

"No. I think we had twenty or more rounds of cheese."

"Well, we don't have twenty now. You don't think Luc is involved in the black market, do you?" Going around the Germans by trading produce on the black market was dangerous. While they knew their grandfather did it sometimes, they didn't want their younger brother involved in that kind of activity.

"We'll just keep a better record of things in the future." Aurélie had a suspicion that their grandfather was involved, but she kept it to herself.

12:15 p.m., the Dugout, Forêt Domaniale de Lachalade

Mark had removed the ammunition and the extra weapons and divided everything between his dugout and a bunker about fifty yards away. He had been provided a German 50 mm mortar and ten rounds, which he put just inside the shelter. After dealing with most of the weapons, he started unloading his medical and food supplies. He'd had two weeks of canned food and considerable medical supplies, including anesthetics and morphine. He would divide some of his canned goods and medical supplies into a parcel that he assumed would be collected at some point by his local French contact.

After working a few hours, he sat down outside the dugout and ate some K rations. He was amazed at how quiet it was. While he knew a solitary existence would get old after a while, he was enjoying being alone for the time being.

He got up and went down to the cellar and tested the stove and then the water supply. Everything seemed to work fine, even though the water tasted slightly of iron. The remedy was to use water directly from the well instead of the fifty-five-gallon drum.

He took his lantern and decided to explore the tunnel that exited the back of the small cellar. The shaft was almost seven feet in height and four feet wide, plenty of room for a man to move through it quickly. It traveled back about twenty feet before it forked into two branches, one branch turning left sharply and the other bending slightly to the right. Both branches had old, rusty steel doors that squeaked and groaned as he opened them. He walked down to the left to a point where the tunnel stopped. This was one of two escape routes. The small makeshift ladder would allow him to dig his way up to the surface.

The right branch went back several hundred yards, with two side tunnels, neither of which went very far. At the end, the tunnel turned to the right again until it stopped. An iron ladder led upward to a trapdoor that opened inward. There was supposedly nine or ten inches of dirt and grass above the door, which would make it easy to escape, if it became necessary.

He spent the next several hours getting his living area arranged and then started thinking about what he would eat for supper. After he had made preparations for his meal, he decided to go for a walk. He reached for his Sten gun and put on his supply belt, along with his emergency pack. He had been told not to leave the dugout area without weapons and supplies. His emergency pack had enough dried food for three days, simple medical supplies, water purification tablets, extra clothes, and a shelter half. The Sten gun had a silencer, as did his .22 pistol. He didn't want to use either, but at least he wouldn't make loud noises if he had to shoot.

He walked out into the forest and down the small trail to the road. He turned east and kept walking. In World War I, the Germans had positions just several hundred yards away that spanned across the same road. Farther past their forward positions were the remains of a German supply depot, complete with a tunnel that ran through the ridge, with a miniature railway to move supplies. *The Kaiser Tunnel. Everyone lived underground and in trenches during that war. Glad I wasn't here then.*

Sunset was approaching, and he was curious as to what it would be like out there in the dark. Still, although he had his flashlight with him, he had no intention of using it.

Suddenly off to the right, there was a loud snort and the dry rattle of brush. He shouldered the Sten gun toward the noise. He was wondering if it might be another deer, but it was a wild boar—considerably more dangerous. The boar looked at him for a few seconds and then turned and retreated. Mark drew in a huge breath of relief. At least he would have a choice of wild meat during his stay.

An hour later, he returned to the dugout and prepared his supper, convinced there was little, if any, human activity in the area. He had moved the pod inside the first dugout, and he shut the trapdoor for the evening. He checked on the homing pigeons, giving them both water and some seed. He would be sending the first pigeon off early in the morning to signal his arrival. He then heated water to wash up and clean his mess kit.

5:00 p.m., Butte de Vauquois, Eight Miles to the Northeast

The work crew and three trucks of supplies were pulling through Vauquois. Sergeant Hamming was in the lead truck with Heinrich Kohler. "I wish that they would make up their minds on these facilities. We can't string power lines over all over eastern France." Berlin had contacted Colonel Dietrich two days ago and ordered him to prepare a position on the Butte de Vauquois for one of the new weapons. *I've heard all about their Wunderwaffe—wonder weapons—but orders are orders.* The Butte had been used as a lookout point by both the French and Germans in World War I and was still considered a useful observation post.

Major Schmidt was in the second truck and had decided to accompany the work crew to make sure the effort got started well.

Trucks passed through the small village of Vauquois and over L'Aire River. They turned right and started up an incline that passed by a World War I French cemetery. From here the road climbed steeper into the forest until it reached the top of the Butte. The summit was coveredby huge artillery craters, as this area had been shelled heavily by both sides.

Sergeant Hamming told the driver to stop in the middle of a large, flat area. Ahead about one hundred meters was the drop-off that allowed observation of the valley below. He went back to check with Major Schmidt. "We can set up camp here until we can start construction."

Darkness was rapidly settling in, and Major Schmidt was in no mood to sleep in the truck. "Agreed, so get them started. The sooner we get set up, the sooner we can get some rest."

CHAPTER 9

◆ ◆ ◆ ◆ ◆ ◆

The Dugout, Early Morning, October 30

Mark got up at four in the morning, as he had several things to accomplish. After making coffee, he sorted through his message file and found the preprinted message that would announce his arrival. It was a simple note, written in code on thin tissue paper. The block letters were written in red ink: BVBX. The color of the ink and the last letter was the key to the message. Mark had several prewritten messages like this to report activity, divorced from any code, thus making them unbreakable.

He checked on the pigeons again. After feeding them, he took the one with a red mark on his foot and attached the message. He didn't know that this pigeon would fly directly to a farm outside Lachalade, where the farmer there would collect the message and radio it to London. Xavier was part of the Resistance.

The remaining pigeons, when released over the next few weeks, would fly to the north coast of France to a farm outside the small fishing village of Isigny-sur-Mer. From there, the messages would be transferred to other pigeons that would be taken three miles offshore in a fishing boat and released to ensure the Germans couldn't intercept them. The Germans had discovered that homing pigeons were one of the methods the Resistance used to get messages back to England. So they stationed sharpshooters all along the coast to shoot any birds that remotely looked like pigeons.

At seven that morning, Mark took the pigeon outside and released it. The pigeon flew up between the trees, cleared the forest canopy, and began to circle as the sky started to lighten in the southeast. He went back in and ate breakfast, treating himself to a couple of the eggs and cold sausage and bread. After cleaning up, he put on his equipment to begin walking down the small trail in front of the dugouts.

Today he planned to explore west to the edge of the forest that overlooked Lachalade. He was also going to set up his first of three survival stations along the way. Each station was a twenty-pound pack with one liter of water, .22 caliber barrel extension with one hundred rounds, a shelter half, an extra coat, underwear, socks, a shirt, and hat. It also had enough food for five days, simple medical supplies, fishing line, and a knife. It was just enough to keep him going for a short period if, for some reason, he couldn't return to the dugout.

He set out down the small path, going mostly south. It descended gently until it leveled off and turned to the west. He estimated that would be approximately one and a half miles to the edge of the forest above Lachalade. Actually, the forest had three names—Forêt Domaniale de Haute Chevauchée, to the north; Forêt Domaniale de Lachalade, slightly south where the dugout was located; and Forêt Domaniale du Grand Pays, which was the southern portion of the forest, north of the village Les Islettes.

As he walked, he kept his eyes moving. Even though the forest was fairly thick at this point, he was taking no chances of being surprised by someone. While the path did not look like it had been used in some time, he was careful about leaving as little evidence of his presence as possible.

At about nine thirty, he was approaching the edge of the tree line. He slowed and became more vigilant as he approached. As he stood behind thick brush, he looked out across the field in front of him. It was a pasture with several cattle grazing. The ground gently sloped down to cultivated farmland and then down to a road running approximately north and south. *That should be the D2 that runs south all the way to Lisle-en-Barrois passing through Les Islettes.*

He crawled the last five yards to a comfortable observation spot, where he could see a small amount of activity in Lachalade and the several farms sprinkled around the village. He was carrying the Springfield bolt action 30–06 with a sniper scope. He began to scan the area. There was a farmer in a field on the other side of Lachalade, plowing behind a horse. As he continued to study the country, he realized he'd only seen one automobile moving. *No fuel, no spare parts—better in the US.*

He continued watching for another thirty minutes, made some notes, and slowly retreated into the forest. He decided to go south and parallel the D2 toward Les Islettes, which he figured to be approximately three miles. He stayed on guard as he walked through the forest, not on a path. He kept his eye on the open ground about twenty-five yards to his right. As he got even with Le Neufour, he moved carefully to the edge of the woods, repeating his observation and making notes.

Continuing for another hour, he passed Les Petites Islettes—just a few houses. He moved to the edge of the forest and scanned the open ground. There were more farms and several people working in the fields. Two people were walking on the D2.

He moved back into the forest a short distance and decided to take a break and eat. He'd brought a small amount of bread with him from England and found some dried sausage in the cellar. This, some cheese, and dried apples made up his lunch. As he ate, he continued scanning the valley. He was particularly interested in how the French farms were constructed and was amazed at the amount of stonework. Most of the buildings he was looking were at least two hundred years old.

One farm, in particular, caught his eye, due to the size of the barn. It was taller and larger than the other barns, and the farm itself had more outbuildings. He spotted an older gentleman hauling hay bales into the barn from the field, with a younger boy helping. As he looked over toward the farmhouse, he caught sight of two ladies outside, apparently doing the family wash. From this distance, he could not hear anything, but he could see the two women were talking to each other. It made him want to go down and introduce himself, but he reminded himself he was here for a purpose and had to stay out of sight.

After he finished lunch, he got up and went back into the forest. He kept an eye out for an acceptable location to hide the survival pack. He walked east for approximately a mile and then, checking his compass, turned north back toward the dugout. It was almost two o'clock when he came upon the small road that ran past his original landing site. He decided to parallel the road and was surprised a few minutes later when he came upon a small French cemetery from World War I. He passed the cemetery and continued in the woods, parallel to the road, until he came to a stream. He turned and went to the road so he could cross at the bridge. As he got on the road, he spotted a large tree about thirty yards in the woods, with three branches forming a fork about ten feet above the ground. *That's a good place to hide the pack. I can use the bridge as a landmark.*

After securing the pack in the tree and camouflaging it, he continued his hike. He followed the road for approximately another mile and then turned west into the forest again, hoping to cross the path that he had taken earlier that morning. He wanted to explore as much of the area as possible and also find out if there were any hidden secrets in the surrounding forest he needed to discover.

In a few minutes, he crossed the path he'd taken that morning and turned to go back to the dugout. He carefully studied the trail to see if there was any evidence of other people in the area. *None.*

It was close to four o'clock when he came in sight of his dugout. Suddenly, a movement to the left caught his attention, and he froze. There was a large crater on the near side of his shelter approximately two hundred yards away. He could see a large, dark animal, probably a wild boar, moving around the edge of it. He remembered that there were some berry bushes near the hole and figured the animal was feeding.

He slowly moved off the path behind a large tree and brought the Springfield to his shoulder. He reached back to the side pocket of his backpack and retrieved the silencer. He braced the rifle against the tree and carefully scanned the area with the scope. The boar came into sight.

It looked very similar to the one he'd seen the day before. It didn't seem very concerned. Mark checked the wind, which was coming from the east. *It won't catch my scent.*

He slowly scanned the area behind and in front of the dugout for signs of additional life After satisfying himself that there was no one around, he took the rifle off safety and put the crosshairs right behind the animal's front shoulder. It kicked as he shot, but the report was reduced by the sound suppressor to the sound of a small firecracker. The boar jerked and fell over without any additional noise. Mark remained where he was for several minutes to ensure the noise had not stirred up anything or anyone else in the area. Only when he was sure did he walk over to the boar and inspect it.

It had been feeding about twenty yards from the dugout, which made it very convenient. It was a relatively large animal that probably would yield almost two hundred pounds of meat. This was much more than he needed, but he wasn't going to waste anything since he had a freezer. He walked back to the dugout, carefully inspecting the area for any activity. He went down into the cellar to get his set of butchering knives. He found several gunnysacks to bring the meat back. He also turned on the water heater so that he would be able to clean up later.

He returned to the boar and dug a hole about four feet deep next to it. He cut the belly and removed the internal organs. He retrieved the liver and heart and discarded the rest into the hole. He used his saw to take the head off, throwing it in the hole as well. He put a rope over a tree limb about twenty-five feet high and tied the rear hooves. He raised the carcass, with great effort, about four feet off the ground, which made it easier to skin and section. He paused every five minutes or so and checked the area for activity or noise.

With his saw and knives, he cut the carcass into manageable pieces. After removing the hide, hooves, and some other unusable parts, he threw some lime in the hole and filled it in. He carved a roast from the loin and cut the backstrap into smaller pieces to use as tenderloin. He carried the meat into the cellar, where he began washing the portion he was going to freeze. He also took ten pounds from the shoulder and cut it into small, thin strips to smoke for jerky later. *Now I'll have to build a drying rack.*

By then it was approaching seven o'clock and was dark outside. He sliced some potatoes and carrots and added a little onion and garlic. He used a generous slab of butter in the skillet to fry one of the back-strap steaks. Before cooking, he went back up and checked the area one more time. The temperature was dropping, and the wind had picked up. He smoothed over any signs of his activity as well as he could in the dark and then went back to the dugout, closing the trapdoor.

Although he took off most of his equipment, he left the pistol on. The one bad thing about this assignment was that he probably could never remove all his weapons. He put the meat away and started cooking the potatoes and carrots in a pot. After letting them boil for several minutes, he heated the skillet and fried the meat. After eating, he cleaned up and decided to take a shower. He had several listening tubes that would allow him to hear noises from four different directions, and he checked those before taking his clothes off. He got in the shower when it was warm, quickly rinsed off, applied soap, and rinsed again. *No time for a long shower now.*

He put on fresh clothes, and noting it was past ten o'clock, he decided to turn in. It'd been a good day. He'd explored the woods and was tired. Two more days of exploring, and he could begin his mission. As he lay down, he decided that he would move northeast tomorrow. Sleep came quickly.

Three Days Later, Butte de Vauquois

Sergeant Alvin Hamming walked through the camp toward the mess tent. This was their third morning. They had organized their encampment and began to position construction supplies. It was still early morning and barely light, but a significant number of the crew was already awake and getting dressed. The aroma of breakfast was beginning to drift over the camp, including the scent of coffee. One very distinct advantage to working on the projects like this was real coffee, not the ersatz coffee the rest of the army had to put up with.

He walked through the tent entrance and went over to the large pot of coffee. "Good morning, Hans. What's for breakfast today?"

"You're not supposed to have coffee until we open the mess line, and what do you think we'd have? Same old gruel."

Alvin took a sip of coffee, savoring it. The first coffee in the morning was always the best. "Gruel—a lot better than hard biscuits and cold beans, and besides, you make the best gruel in the Wehrmacht."

The mess sergeant turned to one of the cooks. "Sergeant Hamming thinks we make good gruel. I think the sergeant needs to finish his coffee before saying anything else." The cook smiled and continued stirring the gruel. "So where is the rest of your material and equipment? Don't tell me the Reich is running short on construction supplies."

Sergeant Hamming had noticed the variety of materials that were arriving and especially the small amount of concrete. While he had not heard anything to the contrary, he suspected this site was going to be different from the others. "We're supposed to receive more material before noon. I believe there's a convoy of trucks coming in. I think we may be building something a little different this time."

"Where's all the concrete? And the heavy equipment to prepare the foundations?"

"Listen, Hans, I don't design these facilities. I just try to make sure we build them properly. I don't have any idea yet what we're doing because I haven't seen any plans. Besides, if I had, I wouldn't be telling you. Everyone knows you can't trust the cook!" Alvin liked to harass Hans. They both joined the German defensive force in the early 1920s and had served together most of the time from that point forward. "Just hurry up and get breakfast. The men are getting up, and I have a meeting with Major Schmidt in thirty minutes."

Hans chuckled and went back to supervise his cooks. The corporal who was standing next to Hans, stirring the gruel, had a strange look on his face—one of concentration.

Late Morning, November 2

The supply convoy had arrived and was being unloaded. Sergeant Hamming was even more confused as he supervised staging the materials. Some additional concrete had come but not enough to begin to build something similar to the previous facility. Materials for the high-voltage power line were included but only enough to run a few miles of line. His meeting with Major Schmidt had confirmed that the facility would not be like the others, but he was not told anything more. The strangest part of the supplies arrived in a large flatbed truck. There were four pieces of pipe approximately three meters long and over three hundred millimeters in diameter. The wall thickness was over twenty millimeters, and they were made of high-quality steel. There were also several large round plates that were at least fifty millimeters thick.

Along with this truck, a crew of four men arrived with welding equipment. There was another meeting with Major Schmidt and one of the civilian contractors at three o'clock that afternoon. He suspected the major would reveal more detail, as they wanted to start construction that afternoon.

After the Evening Meal

Everyone at the site worked hard because they enjoyed better living conditions than those in the rest of the army. When they were given free time each day for their own activities, some read, some exercised, and some liked taking walks alone. The mess corporal made a habit of taking walks through the woods in the evening, away from the camp. This time, however, it was more than just a walk. He had been told of a message drop site about a mile from the summit of the Butte. He was carrying a note detailing the supplies delivered that day and the number of men in the group. This information would be picked up and passed to at least two others before being sent to a member of the Resistance. From there, it would be delivered to an SOE agent, who would radio the information back to London.

CHAPTER 10

———— ✦✦✦✦✦ ————

Forty-Eight Hours Later, November 4, War Cabinet Rooms, St. Charles Street, London

T he daily cabinet meeting had been going on since seven o'clock that evening, and it was now close to ten o'clock. The agenda had several standing items, reviewing the status of the war in Europe, on the Eastern Front, and in the Pacific. Two American staff officers attended the meetings, since most of the activity in the Pacific was led by American forces.

The agenda had a section of special items. Churchill was glad they had worked through the routine stuff in the last three hours. The current focus had to do with SOE activities, which he found much more interesting and, in his opinion, critical to the war effort.

"On to the two projects in eastern France. Colonel Betts will now update us on the status."

The colonel cleared his throat. "We only have a little information as of this evening. We received messages from both teams that they arrived safely. Team One lost a man on the jump and another man in a brief firefight. Unfortunately, this alerted Germans to their presence, and the team left the area to allow things to cool down. They will use one of their alternate plans and send two men to observe while the remainder of the team remains undercover."

General Brawls seemed annoyed. "I thought they had clear instructions to avoid all contact until they had studied their targets and were prepared to act."

"Yes, sir, that's correct. We don't have details at this time, but it is likely this encounter was simply bad luck."

"We are supposed to make our own luck, Colonel."

Churchill interrupted. "General, I think we should let the colonel complete his report."

Colonel Betts nodded to the Prime Minister and turned to the general. "I share your concern, and we *will* find out what happened. In the meantime, I have positive news to report from Team Two— the single-man team. He successfully arrived at his position and reconnoitered the immediate area. He'll make contact late tomorrow evening with the Resistance. They will travel through the night to the facility near Thionville. It appears the Germans have taken advantage of the old Fort de Koenigsmacker and constructed one of the sites, requiring high-voltage lines near the fort. Our agent and his Resistance colleagues will scout the fort under the cover of darkness, remain in hiding the following day, and returning that evening. We should have a report on that facility in about two to three days."

Now was Churchill's turn to look annoyed. "I should like to emphasize that we do not have excess time regarding these facilities. When we receive more accurate information, I suspect it will take weeks to discern what the Germans are doing and longer to counteract them."

"With respect, Prime Minister, this agent is on schedule. And we'll be training two members of the Resistance on this trip, so we'll have three trained observers to send to other sites. These two additional observers are stationed in the Argonne and the Ardennes so that we can have quicker access in the next ten days to the other facilities."

"Excellent. What else do you have?"

Betts turned to Colonel Gaffney. "I believe the colonel would like to report on information he received late this afternoon. Colonel Gaffney?"

"Thank you, colonel. Gentlemen, ma'am, we received a radio message from one of our SOE agents concerning a new facility, evidently in the early stages of construction at the Butte de Vauquois. For those of you familiar with the area around Verdun, this butte overlooks a valley and was an observation and defensive position for both the French and Germans in the Great War. We have someone in the area who has been making notes on the construction activities. We also have a list of supplies and materials and the size of the construction crew."

Colonel Gaffney turned to the woman sitting behind General Brawls. Polly handed him copies of the two-page report. "General Brawls was kind enough to loan me the services of his secretary to prepare this brief report." He divided the stack of reports in half, gave one to the persons on either side of him, and watched as the report made its way around the room.

When everybody had received a copy, Colonel Gaffney continued. "The list of supplies on the left is an approximation of the required materials for the previous twelve facilities in the Ardennes and the Argonne. The column on the right is a list from the agent's report, detailing what is on-site. We think this is substantially complete because, again, according to the report, construction has already started. Two things make this facility unique. The first is the small amount of concrete and the lack of heavy equipment to prepare foundations for bunkers. The second is the delivery of four pipes and a specialized team of welders. Each of the pipes is approximately ten feet in length and six inches in diameter, and at this time we do not know their purpose. We will be sending a special reconnaissance plane first thing in the morning for photos, and then we will divert a squadron of Lancasters, returning from a raid in Germany, to fly over the site early the next morning."

"Are they attempting to camouflage the site in any way?"

"We have seen no signs of attempted concealment at this time. In and of itself, that is strange because the Butte is a substantial geographic feature, and the camp they have set up is out in the open. It's almost like they want us to know they're there."

"Or they don't care," Churchill added.

"If I may, Prime Minister," Colonel Betts suggested, "this site is only a little more than seven miles northeast of Team Two's base. We might want to change our agent's schedule in the next several days to allow him to observe and report."

Gaffney countered. "Let's wait and see what the photographs tell us and then decide. In the meantime, we can keep Team Two focused on the other facilities."

"Done. Next item: progress at Station X."

CHAPTER 11

11:00 p.m., November 5, Three Miles Northeast of Thionville

It'd taken three hours to travel 130 kilometers from his pickup point to an area near Cattenom, just east of the D1. The facility they were to investigate was on the other side of the Moselle River, next to Fort de Kœnigsmacker. Concealed with camouflage netting on the high ground, its field of fire could cover the D56, D654, and a considerable stretch of the Moselle.

Major Dornier had met his two French colleagues two miles past his dugout. They had an old French farm truck with cabbage in the back that was supposed to be delivered in the area. They traveled on back roads and only encountered one German checkpoint. Major Dornier's clothes and his knowledge of French had not caused any suspicion. His two French allies were impressed.

The major was sitting between the two Frenchmen. "Usually the SOE agents they send do not speak French well enough, and it gets them—and us—into trouble."

"Merci." Mark did not add anything to the conversation because it was better not to get to know people.

When they arrived, the man driving took them onto a small road in the woods, where they backed the truck into an area with thick brush. They walked the next mile and positioned themselves near the bank of the river. In this area, the river meandered west and was well on its way to creating an oxbow lake—a curved section of the river that becomes isolated from the main river when erosion cuts a direct path. They were going to cross the oxbow and then the primary channel at this location because both streams were smaller here and not near any farms where they might be detected.

They found the small canoe concealed near the bank where it was supposed to be and slipped it into the water. Once they reached the other side, they carried the canoe to the second crossing—the main channel. They arrived on the east bank undetected. Now they had to go east through the village of Kœnigsmacker and up to the high ground for about a half mile.

While they were driving, Mark had instructed both Frenchmen on what they should look for and how to make notes that could be easily converted into a coded radio message. They wanted to notice the defensive perimeter, including the patterns for guards and machine-gun positions. They would count the number of vehicles around the facility as well and make a note of any personnel outside the buildings. They were going to estimate the size and construction of each of the buildings, as well as the electric lines.

They arrived without incident in a small copse of trees north of the facility next to the fort, only sixty yards away. Mark motioned to the man on his left to work his way around to the other side of the facility; he gave the same motion to the man on his right. Mark would concentrate on the main structure in the middle of the facility. It was a concrete rectangle approximately twenty feet tall and around twelve feet wide. It was very similar to what he'd seen in photographs back at Achnacarry. There appeared to be entrance doors on either of the small ends of the rectangle, with wide double doors to accommodate trucks and heavy equipment at one end of the long side. Mark immediately noticed a black turret-like structure on the roof. It was difficult to tell without proper lighting, but it appeared there might be an embrasure in the turret, indicating the presence of an observation port or weapon. That made sense, as there would be no reason to build a facility such as this without weapons trained on the river, road intersections, and approaches.

Strangely, there were few guards; Mark could see only two on the perimeter, but they were stationary. There was a small concrete fortification that probably housed a machine gun at one end of the facility. There appeared to be another concrete fortification on the right side that probably housed either another machine gun or mortar. He waited for his French colleagues to return with their reports.

The unique element of the facility was the number of high-voltage lines and transformer stations. It was much larger than anything he had seen, even in a city. It was obvious that whatever was in the building required a significant amount of electrical power.

Two hours passed as three vehicles pulled into the parking lot. One was a troop carrier. Mark counted nine men exiting the truck, but they didn't look like soldiers. For starters, they were not carrying any weapons, only briefcases. An officer walked around the main structure to greet them. *Probably the CO of the facility.* He saluted a man who appeared to be the senior officer of the group and ushered them into the main building.

At about two in the morning, the men who had been riding in the truck left the main building and walked out into the field to Mark's right. They spaced themselves approximately one hundred yards apart, leaving about two hundred yards between them. They removed things from their briefcases; it looked as though they were setting up instruments of some kind. Mark continued to take notes, as he suspected a test was imminent.

He hoped his two French allies had seen this as well and were remaining alert. About thirty minutes later, a flashing light came from the door of the main building, which was a signal to the men in the field. He heard a low mechanical rumbling and noticed the turret structure turning slightly to the right. It looked like it might be aligning the embrasure with the two-hundred-yard-wide path between the instruments. As soon as the turret stopped, another type of sound began to grow at a very low frequency. As it increased, Mark could tell it was coming from the main building. The few outside lights started to dim, and the sound increased rapidly in pitch and vibration.

Mark had been taking photographs but doubted that much information could be obtained at night. He decided to take a picture of the turret. As he pointed the camera, the noise inside the building stopped and was replaced by a higher-pitched hum in the turret, followed by a yellow glow. In just a few seconds, the hum increased, and the yellow glow flashed into an intense orange that shot out of the embrasure through the instruments. The flash of light was concentrated on a small structure about four hundred yards from the turret. The structure immediately began to glow and then caught fire as it collapsed.

All of the noise and light was replaced by the muffled sounds of the men gathering around the instruments. Several people came out of the main building to observe the structure as it burned to the ground. While Mark had no idea what he had just seen, he knew the facility housed a powerful weapon. He also surmised that the Germans were still perfecting how to use it, as evidenced by the large number of instruments.

It was about three thirty in the morning when the German team drove off.

Mark's two French friends returned several minutes later. He could read the confusion and fear in their faces.

"What was that?" one of them asked.

Mark shook his head. "Obviously a weapon, but I have no idea what kind, other than it's very potent." Mark looked at his notes and asked his two companions, "Did you take good notes?"

They both nodded, and then one said, "We should go back toward the truck and wait for a couple of hours before we move away from here. We'll pull off into some woods about ten kilometers from where we parked and spend the daylight hours."

Mark spent the next day in the back of the truck, compiling the notes into a summary form suitable for a radio message. It was difficult to describe in a few words what they had seen. He had two rolls of film that needed to go back as well. He would have to rely on the Resistance for the task. His French colleagues had already anticipated this and had prepared two separate drops for each of the rolls of film on the way back the next evening. They also passed the notes to a contact who would give them to a radio operator.

Midnight, November 7, War Cabinet Rooms

The radio operator immediately took the message to cryptology to have it decoded and then woke up Colonel Gaffney. As soon as the colonel read the report, he called Churchill's assistant and woke her up.

"I've just received a message that the Prime Minister needs to see immediately."

"You're lucky this evening, Colonel; he's still awake. I'll ring you through."

Colonel Gaffney briefed Churchill on the tests. Churchill requested a copy of the message, so the colonel brought it up to his small room, adjacent to his office. Churchill was sitting at his desk, working on some other papers.

After reading the message for the second time, he sat back. "What are these people doing? What in the world is this device?"

"I've never heard of anything like this. Right now, I think the best thing to do would be to get these details to several scientists for their thoughts and then wait for the film to arrive."

Churchill looked down at the floor. "I'll get this into the right hands first thing in the morning. You make sure the film receives priority handling. I'm not sure how much use the photos will be since it was night, but you never can tell. Check with Operations on any bomber flights that might be going by this area, and see if they might be equipped to take nighttime reconnaissance photos."

"I'll check, but I doubt that any of our bombers carry the strobe necessary for nighttime photos. It might also be wise to wait and send a plane over to take photos early tomorrow morning. Night photos with strobes, even if we could get them, would alert the Germans that we suspect something."

"You're right. See about putting on a flight for tomorrow morning. We'll have that film and the major's film about the same time."

Churchill got up, walked over to the stand by his bed, and poured himself a whiskey. "Would you care for one, Colonel? I think this information is certainly worth a small libation."

"Thank you, sir; that would be nice."

"Well, between this development and the report on the new facility, your Major Dornier may be very busy over the next week or so. Let's see what the photos show us tomorrow and get the scientists' feedback. Then we can decide where to send him next."

2:00 p.m., November 8, a Government Building on the Mall, London

Major Dornier's film and the morning's reconnaissance flight photos all arrived about the same time; copies were sent to the War Cabinet rooms and to an office on the Mall. A committee of scientists, who had rapidly assembled, were herded into the session shortly before eight o'clock that morning to discuss the information in the message. Major Dornier's photos were, as was expected, not very clear, but one picture showed the intense glow shooting from the turret structure. Another showed the resulting fire.

The morning reconnaissance photos revealed more information but failed to clarify the situation. There were three black marks on the landscape that appeared to be long scorched areas. Colonel Gaffney's team had indicated distances of each from the turret. One was approximately four hundred yards; this was likely a result of the test last night. One was only one hundred yards, and one was about six hundred yards. It appeared that these two marks were part of the tests that didn't yield the same destructive power as the previous evening's test.

The head of the committee paced in front of the conference table.

"So, gentlemen, what we have is evidence of a device that can emit some form of destructive energy. Furthermore, it looks like—at least from this location—the Germans are still in the testing phase. However, since there appear to be similar structures already completed and many still under construction, they must have confidence this device can inflict significant damage.

"We also know that these facilities require a great deal of electrical power, as evidenced by the new high-voltage lines in the area. It is likely that there are large generators of some type concealed in the long concrete structure. The Germans feel these are valuable enough to expend the money to protect them. Finally, it looks like they are anticipating additional tests because there are several small black dots that appear to be structures similar to what was destroyed last night at different distances from this device. One troubling issue is that one of the structures is almost five miles away, which would make this device quite formidable. Any thoughts as to what type of weapon this is?"

One of the scientists spoke up. "A professor at London College phoned me with a thought. Strangely, he was a fan of the 1920s science fiction character Buck Rogers and said this sounded a lot like an ion cannon or some sort of power ray. We performed some basic research into this in the late 1920s but abandoned it ten years ago because of other priorities. We aren't sure if such a device is even feasible or, if it is, how effective it might be. However, right now, it might be prudent to keep this on the list of possibilities."

One of his colleagues added, "I am somewhat familiar with the research into this area. What we concluded was that while it could be possible to build a device like this, the physical size would be prohibitive, not to mention the immense power requirement."

Another scientist added, "There are ways to reduce the power requirements by building transformers that multiply the electrical energy and focus it more effectively."

The committee chairman wanted to get other ideas on the table. "Let's consider additional options as well, as we need to brief the Prime Minister and general staff at five this afternoon."

War Cabinet Rooms, St. Charles Street, London; Lower Special Surveillance Office 8

Lieutenant Boysden had been busy since nine o'clock, analyzing the newest photos. More black marks meant additional activity, but he still had no idea what the Germans were doing. Colonel Gaffney had asked for additional reconnaissance flights over eight other installations, and they would be taking off about right now. It meant another long night, since the film would not be back and developed until ten o'clock. Captain Stone was not in a better mood either. At least something was happening, and eventually, they would figure out what it was.

The photos of the new facility at the Butte, along with the note concerning surrounding activities, had thrown a new twist into this mystery. There was considerably less material at the site, and apparently, it would not be as large. While some excavation had begun, it was too early to determine its purpose. The four "pipes" were still the biggest mystery.

CHAPTER 12

--- ◆◆◆◆◆ ---

4:00 p.m., November 8, the Dugout

Major Dornier had gone out to the road to listen for his contact. This was his tenth day at the site, and he was supposed to receive additional food and fuel. He had returned from his excursion to Kœnigsmacker yesterday and was resting. He had gone out earlier and put the last of his three survival packs about four miles to the northeast. He had not noticed any traffic on this road since arriving and, apart from his trip two nights ago, had not talked to anyone.

He heard a vehicle moving up the road slowly from the south. He checked his Sten gun and lay down in the thick brush about twenty feet from the road. An old truck with high sides on the bed, possibly of German manufacture, rolled by him and toward the path to the dugout. It stopped, and an old man got out, looking around. It did not appear as though he had a weapon, but he clearly knew about the dugout. Mark stayed in his position for a few more minutes, listening to make sure no other vehicles were approaching. After satisfying himself that the truck hadn't been followed, he decided that this was as good a time as any. He cupped his hands and yelled, "Brooklyn."

The old man immediately turned around and looked in the direction of his voice. "Lachalade."

Mark got up, keeping his Sten gun focused on the man, and walked over. His instructions were to keep communications to a minimum and not to use any names. When he got within six feet, he stopped and nodded toward the truck. "Supplies?"

"*Oui*, some food, vegetables, and a few other things. How are the accommodations?" The man clearly had a sense of humor.

"Excellent, much better than I had anticipated."

"There is no meat this time. I have to be careful that things do not disappear too fast."

"I shot a boar last week and still have some of the original supplies that were left."

"Be careful with any shooting. The Germans only come into this general area once or twice a month, but many of the residents will be curious about hearing shots in these woods. Very few people come up here because of unexploded shells from the Great War."

"Let's get the supplies unloaded so you can leave."

It only took ten minutes to put the supplies in the dugout. Mark would move them down as soon as the man left. He noticed the two fresh loaves of bread; he would enjoy those.

Alphonse was impressed with the man. He seemed polite and appreciative of what they had done. Mark just hoped that nothing would go wrong and, in particular, that somebody in the area would not betray him. As long as he operated without being seen or heard, apart from contacts for missions, he would probably be fine.

1:00 a.m., November 9, SHAEF Headquarters, London

The briefing by the scientific committee at five o'clock yielded several possible ideas as to what the German device was. The photos taken of the other installations in the afternoon had revealed additional black marks, indicating continued testing. These revelations were sufficient to cause Churchill to ask Eisenhower to convene the Allied staff for a meeting on an emergency basis.

Churchill personally led the briefing, going over the original reconnaissance photos taken in September that showed the start of construction along a defensive line in eastern France. He also went over the latest information and pictures concerning the test witnessed by Major Dornier and the two French Resistance fighters. Then he outlined the facts about the fizzled mystery explosion in western Germany two months previous. Since that time, several photographs of the area had revealed the forest and vegetation in a half-mile diameter had been burned, in some places down to bare ground. There were still several structures standing, which indicated that the blast effect was minimal. He then went into a list of possibilities of the purpose for the facilities the Germans were building.

Questions started immediately and interrupted Churchill's discourse. The most significant issues focused on determining the purpose of these mystery facilities. The list of possibilities wasn't very encouraging, as most of them pointed toward a new technology that hadn't previously been developed for military weaponry. The intelligence people were still struggling with the possibilities and didn't have a good handle on a specific answer—and might not for several weeks.

Then the question of the fizzled explosion was discussed. It almost certainly was a test of a small nuclear explosive device that somehow had not been able to initiate the type of chain reaction necessary to cause an explosion. However, the destructive force, even without the explosive effects, was impressive. If one of these devices were dropped on any metropolitan area, it would result in tremendous damage, just from the heat and fires.

As the initial excitement wore off and the questions slowed, Churchill announced there was another piece of information that might or might not be connected. He turned to the last folder and took everyone through an explanation of the facility at Butte de Vauquois. The recent photos didn't reveal much of what the Germans were doing at this location, but it seemed evident it was a different type of facility, which led to the conclusion it was a different type of weapon.

After approximately two and a half hours, Eisenhower closed the meeting to allow everyone to get some sleep. He and Churchill walked out to the street, where the Prime Minister's car was waiting. Eisenhower turned to him. "So we have a line of facilities in eastern France that might have a Buck Rogers death-ray weapon. The Germans are testing nuclear explosives, despite the fact we destroyed their heavy water facilities in Norway.[1] And they are building another facility with a commanding view of the surrounding countryside, and we have no idea what their purpose is. Are you sure you don't have any more good news?"

Churchill took his cigar out of his mouth. "It's obviously not good, but we'll get to the bottom of this; we must." He turned and got into the car, rolled down the window, and looked out. "Ike, we *will* figure this out and solve it. You cannot imagine how glad I am that you are in charge and that the United States is with us."

Eisenhower smiled and saluted the PM and then went back upstairs to lie down on the cot he used in a side office when he didn't want to go back to his quarters.

---

1. Operation Freshman in 1942 and Operation Gunnerside in 1943.

CHAPTER 13

$\leftrightarrow\leftrightarrow\blacklozenge\leftrightarrow\leftrightarrow$

November 9, German OKW Headquarters in Berlin

The development committee had met yesterday to analyze the results of the test near Kœnigsmacker. Albert Speer was pleased as he listened to the preliminary results from the field team.

The major in charge of the field team was leading the briefing. "The weapon charged 30 percent faster with the new transformers, but the power level fell short of the target value. Nevertheless, the weapon destroyed the test structure at four hundred meters. The instrument readings we took indicated we could improve the power discharge of the stream by changing the focal length in the weapon's core. Another test employing these improvements in the Ardennes was successful out to nine hundred meters. We think this weapon can be effective at least out to five thousand meters and perhaps beyond. We should be ready for additional tests in two weeks."

Good news, indeed, but the Reich Minister knew that more would be demanded, so he was already thinking of a strategy that would put more of a positive spin on this report. *Politics*, he lamented mentally, *are always the enemy of scientific development.* However, if this weapon proved successful, the Reich would be forever in Mr. Tesla's[2] debt.

Now if he could just figure out how to push the nuclear program forward. They didn't need much to produce small-size shells.

November 16, the Dugout

Mark opened his eyes slowly; where was he? It was pitch-black. Then he remembered—of course it would be dark; he was in a cellar in the middle of a forest. He didn't move. He remembered his training and wondered what had caused him to wake up. And then he heard it— scurrying sounds about seven or eight feet away. It was probably mice or rats coming to explore for food. He thought about getting up and turning on the lights, but that would only scare them off. Whatever they were, he would listen and remember where they were so he could put out traps tomorrow. Anyway, the food was secure from pests.

As he lay there, his mind wandered to the recent activity. In the last week, they had observed three different sites. He liked the fact he was busy, but it did stretch his endurance. They had visited two more sites similar to Kœnigsmacker but had not observed any activity as they'd seen on the first visit. They'd probably just been lucky. Then there was the old man's visit three days ago, when he handed Mark a sealed envelope. It confused him because there was not supposed to be any exchange of messages in this manner.

Nonetheless, the old man had left some additional supplies. This time Mark gave him a couple of sacks with wild boar and venison. At first, the old man didn't want to accept it and muttered something about not being able to explain it. But he looked at it, and in the end, he thanked Mark and left.

The message had directed Mark to visit the site at Butte de Vauquois as soon as possible. After determining the location, he realized it was only

---

2. Nikola Tesla was an inventor, electrical engineer, mechanical engineer, and physicist who was best known for his contributions in AC electrical power generation. He also experimented with a particle beam.

three or four miles away. He planned to leave tomorrow morning and then do his reconnaissance in the evening after dark. It was intriguing, as the site was completely different from the others he had visited. Apart from the construction crew and a few defensive positions, the main focus seemed to be around a central excavation site connected somehow to the four large pipes he'd seen. He had photographed everything that he could before sunset and then retreated into the forest and left, arriving at the dugout around three in the morning. He worked the remaining few hours of darkness, preparing his report and film.

His thoughts came back to the darkness that enveloped him. This was something he hadn't thought through when he first accepted the assignment. Being alone—completely alone—sleeping in a pitch-black hole, and hearing strange sounds didn't necessarily engender a sense of calm. He'd always enjoyed being alone, but this was pushing it.

Needing to change his focus, he thought back to his wife and family. It saddened him to remember that Joanne's life had been cut short. She'd seemed so perfect for him. He missed her greatly—just being around her and hearing her voice. As the knot started forming in his stomach, he forced himself back to the present. The small scurrying noises finally went away. *I guess they found what they were looking for.*

Midmorning, November 18, the German Position at Butte de Vauquois

Sergeant Hamming was not happy. Major Schmidt had just told him to get the four large pipes loaded on the flatbed trucks that had arrived about thirty minutes earlier. They had been delivered less than two weeks ago, and now they were being removed. He put together a small work party and moved the pipes back onto the trucks. Major Schmidt didn't seem very happy about it either. It didn't matter; orders were orders.

All through the morning they labored with loading the pipes. They almost finished by lunch but stopped to eat. As they went to the mess tent, one of the servers casually asked what was going on.

"I don't have any idea. We were just told the pipes and most of the steel that came with them are going back."

The corporal made a note of this, and later that evening, he took another long walk. *Another message for the drop point.*

Near Arlon, Belgium

Berne Gerhart was one of several in a small work party that the sergeant had organized.

"We're going to be receiving another part of our facility late tomorrow, and we need to prepare for it."

"Any idea what we're supposed to do?" joked one of the men.

"You are supposed to shut up and do what I tell you." The sergeant didn't have much patience with stupid questions. "An excavator will arrive later today, and we are to dig a pit approximately four meters deep and several meters wide. We need to prepare to lay a footing around the pit. The lieutenant has the plans, and I'll get them in about an hour. Just report with shovels over by the stakes in an hour."

Private Berne Gerhart thought, *Here we go again. Get one thing started, and they reverse it on us—but it's still better than the Eastern Front.*

The same scenario was playing out at three other similar facilities. The pipes were being moved to the sites with the beam weapon—but none of the people involved knew this.

CHAPTER 14

———— ◆◆◆◆◆ ————

November 20, the Dugout

M ark was rested and had started ten-mile runs to retain his conditioning. The days were getting shorter. It was beginning to get dark by five o'clock in the afternoon, especially in the forest. The weather had changed as well, being overcast more often than not. After getting up this morning, he checked the smoking rack he'd made to see if any adjustments were needed. He'd been lucky enough to shoot a large stag early in the morning before a reconnaissance mission last week. He was thankful for the suppressor. Unwieldy as it was, it significantly reduced the rifle report. He decided to smoke a large portion of the meat, including some roasts and jerky. At first, he worried the smoke might draw attention to his location, but the weather cooperated, and the smoke wasn't noticeable.

He had built the racks in another dugout about two hundred yards away. It served his purpose well, as it was small and enclosed. He checked on the fire and added wood. Once completed, he went back and dressed for his morning run. He wore his twenty-pound emergency pack, pistol, rifle, and ammunition, even though he didn't want to. He rotated his three pairs of boots every day. He decided to jog west toward the village of Le Claon and then move south and go by Le Nefour and Les Petites Islettes; he would remain in the forest and out of sight.

He left the dugout in midmorning and turned west, and he broke into a slow jog. He set approximately a ten-minute-per-mile pace. He left the path about three hundred yards from the dugout, going due east. The vegetation was still damp from the light rain during the night. In about fifteen minutes, he could see open ground between the trees as he reached the eastern edge of the woods. He stopped briefly and listened carefully, crawling a short distance so that he could look over the small valley. Nothing appeared out of place. One farmer was in the field on the far side of the valley, and there was smoke coming out of several of the houses in Le Claon. Satisfied there were no threats here, he moved back into the woods and resumed his run, turning south, keeping the edge of the trees about fifty yards to his right.

He continued his jog for another fifty minutes, approaching the southern edge of the woods where he could look over Les Petites Islettes. Repeating his routine, he lay down behind cover and began to look out over the open ground. He used his binoculars to study some of the details of the farms. Les Petites Islettes was nothing more than a few buildings along the D2 Road. Just as he was getting up, he saw a truck coming southward on the road from Les Islettes. As he brought up his binoculars, he could see that it was a German army truck. It slowed as it approached the farm he'd observed when he first arrived, the one with the large barn and farmhouse.

The truck turned in to the farmyard and pulled up to the house. A couple of soldiers jumped out the back and helped a small man out. Another soldier got out of the passenger side and escorted the man to the house. A couple of women came outside to meet them, and there was an exchange of words; then soldiers returned to the truck.

Mark chuckled to himself. "Since when does the Wehrmacht run a taxi service for French men?" Just then, another man came out of the barn and walked over to the smaller man. The men exchanged words, and the second man seemed agitated, likely irritated with the shorter man. Mark looked again at the women, who were turning to go back into the house, leaving the two men to their discussion. It was then he recognized the coat worn by the second man; it was very similar to the one worn by the older gentleman who delivered his food. He wondered if they were one and the same.

He pulled back into the forest to continue his run northeast. He would turn east shortly, cross the small country road that went by the cemetery and his original landing field, and then follow that road back to the dugout. He wanted to get back before one in the afternoon because he was expecting the old man to bring supplies before dark.

The run back was quiet except for a wild boar that he startled. He had plenty of meat, so he had no reason to shoot. As he approached the dugout, he slowed about two hundred yards away, listening carefully for any sounds of life, as well trying to catch the scent from his smoking hut. No noise and no smell. He turned west and walked down the small path until he reached the road that ran by all of the artillery dugouts. Maintaining his cover and stopping every fifty yards to listen and observe, he arrived at his dugout shortly after one o'clock.

As he went into the shelter, he could tell that nothing had been disturbed, so he went downstairs and started removing his equipment. He was interested in checking on the stew that he had begun that morning. He'd put several large chunks of venison in a pot with potatoes, carrots, beets, and onions. It had been on the stove at low heat for about eight hours. As he smelled the aroma, he realized how lucky he was to have had a mother who taught him the basics of cooking. He often would cook when Joanne was tired, and he enjoyed it. It made him homesick to think of her again, but he was grateful for the memories.

After cleaning up, he tested the stew and then ate a bowl. *It could use a little more garlic but not bad, all things considered.* He made a mental note to talk out loud more, even though no one was around. It was good to hear his voice. He focused on some routine chores in the afternoon and found himself looking forward to the possibility of talking, however briefly, to the old man, should he show up that evening.

4:00 p.m., November 20, Allied Headquarters

General Walter Bedell "Beetle" Smith, Eisenhower's chief of staff, was chairing a meeting in Ike's absence. Ike was meeting with Churchill and other Allied leaders concerning the formation of a new Allied command organization named Supreme Headquarters Allied Expeditionary Force, or SHEAF. Attending this meeting were General Brawls, Colonel Gaffney, Colonel Walker, Colonel Miller, Colonel Betts, Captain Stone, Captain Berson, Lieutenant Boysden, and several civilian scientists. Several additional military and scientific personnel were in the outer room, waiting for their time to report.

Quite a bit of information had flowed into the Allies' hands in the past six days concerning the activity in eastern France. Major Dornier's visits with his two French colleagues to the sites with the long concrete structures had yielded some interesting facts. The sites were almost identical, differing only in the location and type of the defensive positions; additional visits to eleven of the fifteen known sites by other teams yielded similar facts. Reconnaissance planes flew over several of the sites, and the photos revealed additional scorch marks, indicating continued testing.

General Smith turned to Colonel Gaffney. "What have your people dug up in the last couple of days?"

"Jerry is still busy finalizing the defensive positions around all of the BRs." *BR* was short for Buck Rogers; not Churchill's first choice, but it had been proposed as a code word for the facilities they were studying. It stuck before he could change it. "Our teams in eastern France have sent back photographs and layouts of all of the BR sites they visited. Most have the equipment already installed, but there are two things still being revised. The first is additional electrical equipment, probably specialized transformers. Evidently, these are a late modification because at two of the sites visited recently, there were additional burn marks, indicating testing shortly after installation."

"If I may add, Colonel," Captain Stone interjected, "it is highly likely that the additional equipment is an advanced transformer that has increased the range and power of this weapon. Based on the photographs taken on the ground and from the air, we would estimate that this weapon can reach a target two miles away with enough power to significantly damage a structure."

General Brawls asked, "Define *significantly*, and what type of structure?"

"One test was on a cinder block structure approximately twenty-by-twenty feet, and three of the four walls came down. Of course, we don't yet have enough information to accurately estimate the power of this weapon or exactly how it projects its force. Obviously, if it also generates significant heat, then it can disable armored vehicles by heating them to the point that the crews inside would be disabled or killed outright."

Brawls turned to Captain Stone. "Out to two miles! My God, what have they created?"

Colonel Gaffney continued. "We're going to hear a briefing from our scientific team that's working on this later in this meeting, but suffice it to say, this is something we need to understand better before we get anywhere close to these areas." The colonel turned the page of his briefing book to announce yet another fact. "We think six out of fifteen known sites are operational. Three have added the additional electrical equipment—transformers, if you like—and the other nine are still waiting for additional high-voltage lines to reach their location. We think that another five sites out of this nine will have the upgraded electrical equipment within the next couple of months. Is that accurate, Colonel Betts?"

"Based on the information we've received through the Resistance, that's a good estimation. One of the French workers handling the transformers saw one fall off a truck. The crate split open, and the transformer casing came apart. The worker helped put the pieces back in the crate and guard it until its removal. In that time, he was able to photograph it from several angles, and our electrical experts have come to the conclusion that the transformers concentrate, or 'step up,' the voltage. While these devices are very efficient, they require specialized metallurgy for the connections and shielding. These materials are in short supply in Germany; hence, it's probably going to be a few months before they can fabricate enough for all the sites. Colonel Miller and his scientific team can explain this in more detail, if required."

"Are we taking care to schedule the reconnaissance flights over these areas with the same frequency that we do any facility?" General Smith wasn't interested in tipping off the Germans about their interest in the sites.

"We increased reconnaissance over several areas; some of which we know the Germans are not installing new weapons but are creating the impression they are. We are allowing them to think we're duped in those areas. Be assured; we are monitoring the frequency of flights very carefully."

General Smith turned to Colonel Walker. "Based on what you've heard, how quickly would we be able to manufacture these transformers, either in the UK or in the US?"

"We could manufacture this equipment in a month on a crash basis, assuming the materials were available. They are not available in the UK right now and are also in short supply in the US. We estimate that the Germans will not be able to manufacture and transport this equipment to all of the sites before late March of next year."

"Please communicate to Marshal Tedder what targets we deem a priority to slow the manufacturing schedule even further. Then we need to work that into the overall strategic bombing planning."

Colonel Gaffney cleared his throat. "General, if I may, I would like also to discuss briefly the recent information received concerning the facility at Butte de Vauquois."

"Certainly. Proceed."

"As most of us know, we have a team only seven miles from the Butte, and we asked them to visit this site in daylight. They did an excellent job in providing both photographs and sketches of the facilities. This report corroborates the aerial photos taken of the site, indicating that the four large pipes are probably some kind of cannon or artillery. Our people have not been able to figure out exactly what they may be. As we said earlier, the pipes are approximately three hundred millimeters in diameter and three meters in length, which would not be long enough for a proper artillery barrel and too long for any sort of mortar."

Colonel Miller added, "The big mystery is that they are building this in plain sight and not attempting to camouflage it. It makes us believe they may not be serious about any large artillery position, but then, with the shortage of supplies in Germany, it doesn't make sense for them to waste resources on a project this large if it's simply a diversion."

"That's not the only mystery. I believe Captain Stone and Lieutenant Boysden have some information to share with us." Colonel Gaffney nodded at Stone.

Captain Stone stood and began. "The team visited the site on November 14. We had a reconnaissance plane take photos five days later. So while the team saw supplies on the ground at that time, the situation changed substantially in those five days. The four pipes and all the steel had disappeared. The excavation is continuing, but we have no idea where the pipes and steel went."

"Lieutenant Ryder and I have gone over these photographs in detail. We even ordered some stereo photos taken, and it appears as though the pipes and steel were trucked away," Lieutenant Boysden reported.

Colonel Gaffney looked up. "Lieutenant Boysden is correct. We have received a report from someone at the facility that, indeed, this is precisely what happened. It caused a great deal of confusion with the construction crew there. Further, there is an unconfirmed report from the same source that other pipes and materials will be delivered to the site soon."

There was murmuring around the room as many wondered out loud what all this meant. General Smith took control and silenced them. "Well, it's likely that we will need additional attention on this site in the coming days." He then turned to Colonel Gaffney. "But I want to make sure that it's accomplished in a measured way. I don't think anything significant is going to happen at this site for several weeks, so I don't want to draw undue attention to it."

"I agree, General, and I think the best thing we could do would be to ask our agent near Lachalade to visit the location in a few days."

Polly looked down and then over to General Brawls. She knew Major Dornier was going to be busy for the next several weeks.

CHAPTER 15

◆◆◆◆◆

5:25 p.m., November 20, the Dugout

A drizzle was falling, increasing the gloom and chill. Mark had
moved across to the other side of the road, where he would have a
good view of anyone approaching the dugout from either direction. He
was beginning to wonder if the old man would make it this evening.
While he didn't require much resupply, it would be nice to have some
additional vegetables and seasoning. Mark had been told that the French
would estimate his needs and provide what they could.

The low rumble of an engine filtered through the trees and down
the road. Mark crouched in the cover and flipped off the safety of his
Sten gun. As the sound increased, he relaxed, recognizing the engine
noise as the old man's truck. Still, he held his weapon at the ready and
stayed behind cover. *Be alert.*

In less than a minute, the old truck appeared around the bend in the
road and rolled to a slow stop on the side. The old man looked around,
got down out of the cab, and stood in the middle of the road, listening.
Mark was about one hundred feet from the truck, so he yelled out the

challenge and relaxed when the old man returned the countersign. He turned around and watched as Mark emerged from his cover.

"I wasn't sure that you were going to make it this evening. It's not the best weather." He was referring to the rain and overcast sky. There wasn't much light left.

The old man smiled slightly as Mark approached and then led him around to the back of the truck. There were several wooden boxes full of various supplies—surprisingly, more than Mark had expected. "I had some work at the farm to complete today, and we had an unexpected visit by the Germans earlier in the day, which disrupted our activities."

"I hope the German visit wasn't anything serious." Mark carried one of the crates toward the dugout. "I wouldn't like to think you would get in trouble because of me."

The old man chuckled. "Monsieur, you are not the trouble. The Germans started the war, and we'll do what we can to beat them. Really, you're no trouble at all."

They deposited the boxes in the dugout and returned to the truck for more. Mark saw a container with a bottle of milk and another box full of dairy products. He picked it up, and as he did, he jostled another one, which produced clinking noises. He looked over and saw that it was full of wine bottles. "Are you sure you can spare all of this extra food and especially the wine? Haven't you heard there is a war on?"

The old man looked up, realizing Mark was joking. "We have plenty on the farm. My only concern is to mask the disappearance of some of this so that my family doesn't get suspicious. I have a granddaughter who likes to count everything, and she's already noticed a few things missing." The old man stopped talking as he realized he should not have revealed anything about his family, particularly his granddaughter. He looked over at Mark. "Perhaps you should forget that last comment."

Mark turned his head as they walked toward the dugout. "I discovered something today I probably should share with you. I went on a reconnaissance hike earlier in the morning to the western edge of the woods and watched the activity with my binoculars. Then I went down south past Les Petites Islettes and observed that part of the valley as well. There is a farm with a large barn just south of the village.

While I was watching the area, I noticed a German army truck coming north on the D2. It deposited a young man at the farm. I also saw two women come out of the house. Then I saw a man leave the barn; he was wearing a coat exactly like the one you're wearing now. While I don't know your name and shouldn't, I unfortunately now know where you live. I also know there are women in your house, as well as a young man. I suspect that they are your grandchildren."

They reached the dugout and stacked the boxes, returning to the truck for more. "The barn was built first in 1805 by my *arrière arrière grand-père*. His family lived in the barn while they finished the house and the other structures. It's been in my family ever since."

"From what I could see, it's a beautiful place. You're lucky in that regard."

"Luck, yes—some good and some bad. I can tell you a few things at this point without jeopardizing either you or my family. My wife, Maria, and I had two children, Olivier and Sophie. Olivier married a girl named Monique. They had five children; the oldest was Marc, then Aurélie, René, Josette, and Luc."

Mark flinched and looked down as he heard the French version of his name.

"Marc was killed when the Germans invaded in 1940. Aurélie married a young man by the name of Sebastian, who was also killed about the same time. René joined the resistance in 1941, and we have not heard from him for over a year. Josette became engaged to a young man in 1939, and we have not heard from him for two years. Luc, the man you saw returned to us this afternoon, wants to join the Resistance also, but I have so far been able to keep him from doing that. Olivier and Monique also joined the Resistance right after the invasion, and they too have disappeared. So you see, while I still feel blessed to have my three grandchildren with me, it's not been without loss."

Even though Mark knew the people in Europe, particularly those in the occupied countries, had paid a great price, it was different somehow to hear it from the mouth of a man who was living it. Since the war started, most Americans knew little of these hardships, and being isolated by two oceans made it difficult for them to comprehend fully.

"You and your family have courage—to have these losses and continue to hope and resist. Americans know about some of these hardships, but it's just through news stories and letters. It's different when you're here, and you see it."

"Thank you, but most people in Europe are doing the same as we are under much more difficult circumstances. At least our family hasn't been rounded up and taken back to Germany for God knows what. We have the farm, a comfortable home, food to eat, each other, and our health."

They returned to the truck for the final trip. As Mark picked up the wine, he felt he should invite the old man down to the cellar briefly. "Thank you for the wine. Would you like to help me unload this into the cellar? I have made some coffee, and I also have something to give you."

The man looked at the sky, noting that the light had almost completely faded. "I should be getting back, but I can spend a few minutes."

Alphonse motioned for Mark to go down the ladder and then he began to hand him crates. After all the crates were in the cellar, Mark motioned for him to come down. Mark turned the lights on and began to unpack the supplies, noting that there were vegetables as well as additional flour and salt. As Mark put things up, he said, "I was married for twelve years and have two children, a son and a daughter. My wife died of cancer, and I left my children in the care of my sister and her husband. Now I find myself in the middle of France, far away from my home, sometimes wondering how it happened."

Mark poured two cups of coffee and offered one to the old man. They sat down at the table and looked at each other.

"Did you fix this place?" Mark asked, indicating the cellar.

Alphonse shook his head slightly., "I had help. I knew this place from World War I and knew of the many tunnels running underneath."

"I'm not sure exactly what my mission is here, and of course I couldn't tell you if I did, but this is a comfortable place to stay, if not a bit unusual."

Alphonse finished his coffee got up. "I need to get back."

Mark went over to the cabinet and pulled a can of coffee and several cans of fruit and put them in one of the crates. "I wanted to share some of the things that I brought with me. You'll need to make up a story about how you found them—perhaps a lost parachute drop or something from the Resistance." Mark carried the crate up the stairs.

"Merci. It will be nice to drink real coffee for a while, and the girls will enjoy the fruit."

It was still drizzling, and full dark had fallen. Mark walked the old man back to his truck. "While it can be lonely, it is also very peaceful here, especially at night. No lights, no other people—if you don't mind being alone."

The old man nodded as he climbed in the cab. "I forgot to tell you that our alternate supply point is an old farmhouse about a mile and a half from here. If, for any reason, it's not safe to stop here and unload, I will place the supplies in the cellar of that house. Enter from the rear as the stairs inside the house are not stable anymore. There is a trail marker—a pile of stones over there." He pointed to where the trail into the woods started.

"I've seen it."

"Normally, there is a round rock on the top. If you see that there is a flat rock, go to the farmhouse for the supplies. Do you know it?"

Mark nodded. "It was included in my training." He backed up, and Alphonse started the engine and slowly drove off. Mark went back to the dugout. He was deeply impressed with the old man and his family.

As he went back to the cellar, he started thinking about Thanksgiving. *I guess I'll have to skip the turkey this year.* He wasn't upset, though, as he had plenty of food.

CHAPTER 16

---◆◆◆◆◆---

November 26, about Halfway between Arlon
Belgium and Lachalade

The weather had been miserable for a week, which slowed progress. Kohler and his team had been moved from the Butte de Vauquois, north to this area, where more of the high-voltage towers were being constructed. While there were still some final connections to be made in the Ardennes, the line had was complete twenty miles south of Arlon. Tower construction slowed because of the lack of concrete and structural steel. Several supply trains had been ambushed in Belgium and France, delaying materials.

Kohler and his team were living in small tents on the ground and weren't comfortable. It was cold and wet, and the food wasn't particularly good. Kohler again wondered what all was going on, but one didn't ask questions like that unless he wanted to visit the Eastern Front. There was even more reason to avoid that after the disaster at Kursk.

Colonel Dietrich himself had visited their area three days ago and was less than impressed with the progress he saw. The entire construction crew was told to work seven days a week, twelve hours a day, in an attempt to get things back on schedule. When the officer in charge mentioned the shortages, Colonel Dietrich informed him that he was getting replacement materials on a priority basis. He was also told to quit complaining and accomplish what he could with the supplies already on-site.

December 1, German OKW Headquarters in Berlin

Speer was pacing in his office. The latest report on material supply for the high-voltage lines was discouraging. The design of the new transformers was successful; unfortunately, obtaining enough specific metal for fabrication was a significant problem. Without transformers, they would not have the facilities operational in January. It looked as though it might be into late spring before this would be a reality. With the Allied invasion expected sometime in April or May, this was unacceptable. Finally, the nuclear program had run into a serious obstacle. They discovered the uranium used to fuel a nuclear explosion had not been appropriately refined. As a result, there was only enough material to build ten or fifteen small artillery shells. It would take three months to create a new refining facility underground and another three months for the refining process itself. The shell-casing fabrication process was going fairly quickly, and now he was contemplating shortcuts in the refining process that could be fatal to the workers involved.

Walking out to the secretary, he looked around and saw the gentleman responsible for supplying concrete for the construction of the high-voltage lines. "Major Bader, please come in." This was the first of eight meetings for the Reich Minister today in an attempt to get these programs back on schedule. He wanted to get things better organized this week. When he reported to the general staff, he needed something positive to report. He was a master at solving logistics issues, but this war was putting pressure on him.

December 8, the Dugout

It had rained almost every day for the last two weeks. Mark and his French colleagues had visited sites during that time; one of them was Kœnigsmacker. They were shocked at the changes in that facility and the evidence of additional longer-range testing. It appeared the weapon could destroy any kind of structure except a concrete pillbox out to three miles or more. It didn't take much in the way of imagination to realize a weapon like that would also disable any armored vehicle.

He'd also twice visited the site at Butte de Vauquois. The Germans seemed somewhat confused and had redone some of the excavation and structures. He'd gotten close enough twice to listen to some of the conversations among the workers, and they seemed annoyed that they were redoing some of their work. The last visit was three days ago. Now, he noticed four more pipes along with the associated steel. He had no idea what was going on, but he took photos, made sketches, and passed those along in his report. The old man had established a second message drop site two miles from the dugout, where he could leave his messages and photos for pickup. It was evident London was interested in the facility, just from the requests they made to visit it. He was currently scheduled to visit once a week for the next three weeks. He doubted that London had figured out what was going, simply because he was not asked to provide information on specific parts of the site, just the general progress.

He had taken the pod out for short excursions on several occasions to make sure it was in good running condition. Unloaded, it could go about fifteen miles an hour. On the next visit to the Butte, he was planning on driving it to within two miles. Up until now, he had used those visits for part of his training runs, but the bad weather had made that less desirable. The pod had a simple frame that sat over the cockpit, so he could drape a poncho and keep most of the rain off.

After finishing breakfast, he stood in the dugout, drinking coffee and watching the storm. It had been raining off and on all night, and now it was coming down in sheets, with the wind driving it sideways. He liked weather like this, even better when he had a dry place like the dugout to stay. He had finished smoking the venison last week and had one ham, about forty pounds of beef, and sixty pounds of pork. The old man had brought two dozen small smoked sausages that Mark had found very tasty. He had plenty of meat.

The old man also told him about a garden behind the old farmhouse in the woods nearby. It was located in a clearing about seventy-five yards off the road to the right at the end of a narrow path. There were still some potatoes, carrots, and beets in the ground, which Mark harvested and put in his cellar. He had a couple of half barrels full of dry sand to store the root vegetables. While the farmhouse was old and had been vacant for many years, it was still structurally sound. It wouldn't take much to make it ready to live in—a few boards, a lot of cleaning and clearing the brush. The garden itself was in excellent shape.

Because of the weather, he decided to make some chili out of the beef and wild boar. He took a scoop from his dried beans and started preparing the chili. He had so much food that he began to wonder how long he was expected to stay. It wasn't hard to guess that the invasion would take place sometime before the end of June, but he suspected that it would be several months after that before the Allies arrived at this location.

He was grateful that the French had included a decent drainage system for the tunnels. The small amount of water leaking into the tunnels found its way into pipes that took it downhill to some unknown location, probably a small stream.

He trimmed the fat off the beef and the wild boar and cubed it into small pieces. He had decided to make enough for several days since he had a way to keep it cool. He chuckled to himself. *I hardly need a refrigeration system in this weather—never gets above fifty degrees. Thank God for the small heater.* As he cut up onions, he started soaking the beans. He would get this on the stove by eight thirty and let it cook all day.

He was looking forward to another visit from the old man; it would either be today or tomorrow. The trail marker indicated he would come here, so Mark would be sure to have a few things for him to take back to the farm. They had talked again the last time he was here, and Mark was looking forward to seeing him. He seemed like a dependable person and a competent farmer. Mark was sure he was also a loving grandfather and probably worried a lot about Luc.

Mark awoke at four in the morning and ran six miles before it started raining again. He thought about lying down and resting after a quick lunch and maybe catch up on some reading. He'd brought several novels with him, some in German and some in French.

As he was checking the chili, he felt a vibration and thought he heard the rumble of the vehicle. He went over to his listening pipes and discerned the vehicle was approaching from the south. He quickly put on his field jacket and slipped into his emergency pack. He buckled the ammunition belt and his shoulder holsters. He grabbed his Sten gun and moved up to the dugout, staying low. A few seconds later, a German army truck rumbled down the road, taking the curve left, and disappeared, going toward the Kaiser tunnel. It didn't slow down at all, and he suspected they were on an errand. They might have been on the way to the Butte, and then there was a German garrison about thirty miles to the south in Bar-le-Duc.

He stayed upstairs for another twenty minutes, listening, without picking up any more signs of life. *So the first contact with the Germans has finally occurred.* He was glad his morning run had been in the woods—no footprints.

CHAPTER 17

Noon, Same Day, Butte de Vauquois

Alvin Hamming walked into the mess tent to get out of the rain. As he shook off his poncho, he walked over to the coffeepot on the fire. "So, Hans, what's for lunch?"

"Did I invite you in for a cup of coffee? You might want to go out and make sure that your crew is making some progress. I heard that Colonel Dietrich visited a site up north in Belgium and was unhappy with the lack of progress there, despite the confusion he caused."

Sergeant Hamming just looked at his old friend and smiled. "I invited myself in for coffee because I'm tired of being out there in the cold rain. Besides, I wanted to find out what you've made for lunch so I can go back to my guys with some good news. Please tell me its soup or stew. Nothing else in this climate will do."

Hans bent over and poured a large bucket full of celery and onions into one of the pots. "It's a thick soup or thin stew. We had some leftover pork and plenty of beans, so I made something out of thin air." He went back to stirring.

Sergeant Hamming rolled his eyes. "Great. Recipes that you've never made before. I'm sure it will be delicious." He turned and went back to the worksite. Hans just shook his head.

Sergeant Hamming had redone the main excavation site last week. A larger and much longer tube had been delivered and was placed in the ground vertically, with a cover on top. It was made of lighter material than the first tubes. Its function was anybody's guess. The rest of the crews had dug four more individual pits about six meters deep and two meters wide. There were trenches to run communication and electrical cable; again, the purpose of the electrical wire was not clear. Major Schmidt had been in a horrible mood since the rain had slowed progress.

At least Sergeant Hamming had been able to get Zormaan and Sander back, which made up for the loss of Kohler. Even though their electrical skills were needed, their leadership was more important. He could trust them to supervise five or six men each. As he approached the site, the crew, which numbered approximately twenty-one, was struggling in the mud and clearly not in a good mood.

Zormaan approached the sergeant. "It's difficult to keep the runoff out of these holes when it rains hard like it did this morning. We get the water out, and the rain fills it back up again."

"I know, but we have orders to work, regardless of the weather. It doesn't make sense, but I'm not arguing with the major, and I doubt he's going to argue with the colonel. Anyway, tell your guys to stop and clean up for lunch. I'll go tell the others." He wanted them to get warm before they ate. He decided he might let them stay in the tent a little longer today since he could see a rainstorm moving in their direction across the valley. *One heck of an observation point, but what does that have to do with our job?* He remembered looking at the new blueprints calling for thirty pits approximately three meters apart, with tubes installed at angles from forty to seventy-five degrees. *Maybe some sort of mortar, but what kind of mortar is buried in the ground? More than likely it's some sort of new rocket weapon.* It didn't matter, as it wouldn't change the amount of work required. One thing for sure was that a crew of twenty-one would not be able to finish this on schedule.

Same Day, Early Afternoon, War Cabinet Rooms, St. Charles Street, London; Lower Special Surveillance Office 8

Lieutenant Boysden was studying the latest surveillance photos of the various sites from the past two days. They also had diverted a flight of Lancasters returning from a raid near Munich to fly near the Butte de Vauquois at sunrise. One of the planes had was fitted with special stereo photographic equipment.

Colonel Gaffney had decided that the reports and photos should be shared with the photographic division to help with interpretation. It had been Lieutenant Boysden's idea, and Captain Stone had enthusiastically supported it.

It was apparent that additional tests had occurred at several BR sites and that the range of the weapon had increased. In one case, it looked like it might have destroyed a structure five miles from the facility. He and his team had been working since early this morning to put together a report for Churchill and the Allied Supreme Command.

Derek came in from the lab with an envelope. "We just got new photographs of the Butte, taken three days ago. A report accompanied them."

William looked up. "Thanks. Leave it, and I'll look at it in a second."

Derek hesitated. "Don't expect too much. The guys at the lab said there didn't appear to be much to conclude."

"Well, let me take a look at it. Sometimes conclusions are drawn from small details accumulated over a long period."

Captain Stone walked in, curious as to Boysden's progress. "Anything interesting in today's information, William?"

Boysden answered, "Not so far, sir. Indications are that the additional testing is increasing the range of the BRs; I don't know about the Butte yet. That information just came in."

Captain Stone looked annoyed, but he knew the lieutenant was doing his best. Neither of them knew that the mess corporal at the Butte had overheard Major Schmidt talking on the field telephone. It'd been enlightening, and he was anxious to pass it along. However, this time he felt that it would be better to delay and continue gathering information, at least for today. It would look suspicious, going out in this weather to leave another message.

One floor above the Special Surveillance Office 8, Lieutenant Alex Ryder was called into General Brawls's office. Polly smiled at him as she showed him in. The general appeared in a bad mood as he asked Ryder to sit down.

"Alex, I want to send you down to work for Captain Stone for a few weeks. They need some help, and while you don't have much experience in studying photographs, he thinks because of your background, you can be of some assistance. I'm also going to send one of the ladies down to help them organize things a little better. It's getting to the point that we need to speed up the turnaround of the information."

Alex got a knot in his stomach. It would mean not working around Polly for a while. Even though they hardly did anything more than exchange pleasantries, he still looked forward to seeing her every day. Her organization and background knowledge had proved to be an enormous help to him over the past several months.

"Yes, sir; as you say, I don't have much experience, but I'll be glad to help in any way I can. Besides, I know William Boysden from school. I think we'll get along fine."

"Glad to hear it. Polly will give you your orders as you leave. Go ahead and plan on reporting to Captain Stone this afternoon. You can leave most of your things here, as they'll have a desk for you down there."

Alex got up to leave, but the general said, "By the way, it says in your service folder that you indicated an interest in Special Forces at one time. Is that true?"

"Yes, sir, but it never went anywhere. I was nabbed for desk duty before that request could develop."

"Well, don't read anything into this; I'm just thinking ahead. We may need to insert some additional people into France at some point. If that is the case, would you be interested? It would involve six weeks of training at Achnacarry and another week of specialized training. It wouldn't be easy, but it definitely wouldn't be boring either."

"I'd be interested sir." Alex turned to leave. "If that's all, sir, I'll get ready to go see Captain Stone."

Alex left the general's office and walked to Polly's desk. She looked up at him, seeming amused. "So I hear you're going downstairs to help look at pictures of naked women."

Alex blushed. "I don't look at pictures of naked women; in fact, I don't look at *any* pictures of women, and you know it."

"Why, Lieutenant Ryder, I do believe you're blushing!" She gave him one of her smiles. "Don't worry; I'm just teasing. By the way, here are your orders."

Alex hesitated; he wanted to say something to her but didn't know what. "I guess we won't see each other very much for a while. I just wanted you to know I appreciate your efficiency and help. And …" He paused, wanting to say that he just wanted to be around her.

She stood up, handed him the orders, and smiled again. "I like being around you too, and I wouldn't worry much about our not seeing each other. General Brawls has assigned me to go down with you to help Lieutenant Boysden and Captain Stone. It won't be today, though, because I have some things to get ready for the general. He has a meeting with the PM and Ike this evening. It seems as though they're very concerned about what's going on in France. I also know that you expressed interest in Special Forces at one time." She looked him directly in the eye. "Be careful what you wish for." Polly turned and went into the general's office.

CHAPTER 18

✦✦✦✦✦

Early Morning, December 9, the Dugout

Mark went up to the dugout after breakfast to finish his coffee. The old man had not shown up last night, which worried him, but it was probably due to the weather. It had rained hard during the afternoon and evening, and it would've been difficult to bring supplies. It was okay, since it gave him some time to make stew in addition to the chili. He probably would offer some to the old man to take back.

He knew he shouldn't be sending them food, but they were doing so much for him, and besides, he suspected the two granddaughters thought something might be going on. He'd go out later and confirm that the trail marker had not changed and then await the arrival of the supplies.

In the meantime, he went back downstairs and did some general housekeeping chores. He put on his backpack and grabbed his Sten gun. He was going to check the exit point of one of the tunnels. This one terminated in another dugout on the other side of the small ridge, west and slightly south of his location. He wanted to ensure the exit was clear and well camouflaged. He was also going to check the other tunnels.

A few feet in, he noticed rainwater accumulating in a low place. It took a while, but he discovered a clogged drain, just a badly rusted grate. He knocked some holes in it, and the water started draining.

He walked the other tunnel as well. The tunnel exit was camouflaged but required some work on the door and rear of that dugout. There was a considerable amount of brush piled over the dugout, evidently accumulated over the years since the last war. *Good camouflage.*

A few hours later, he was finishing lunch when he heard the rumble of the vehicle. He went up the stairs quickly and saw the old man's truck pulling up. He was early, but maybe that was due to the weather. Mark just hoped there would not be any German army trucks today.

Mark looked carefully in all directions, as he always did, to make sure the old man wasn't followed. He was surprised to see a woman get out of the cab. He was immediately suspicious, and while she was on the other side of the truck, unloading supplies, he snuck out of the dugout and circled so he could see what she was doing. She took the supplies, just as the old man did, placed them in the dugout, and returned to the truck for another box. She looked around but did not appear concerned.

Mark put his hands around his mouth and yelled, "Brooklyn!"

The woman stopped, turned in the direction of the voice, and yelled back, "Lachalade."

Mark moved from behind the tree so she could see him. He kept his Sten gun leveled but not pointed at her. "Where is the old man?"

She stared. "Ill. The rain and the damp."

Even though he had a good idea who she was, he asked anyway. "Who are you, and who told you about this place?"

"My grand-père—" She caught herself, realizing she should not have revealed that. She looked down, obviously annoyed. "This would go faster if you would help. And I would also appreciate it if you'd put your weapon away. I'm not dangerous," she snapped.

Mark stared at her for a few seconds before deciding she was probably telling the truth. He moved down the incline toward her, still keeping a sharp eye for anything that looked suspicious. She was wearing a heavy work coat over her dress. Her work boots were worn but functional. The dress looked like it had been mended several times and was faded. However, as he approached her, he noticed her eyes—*sky blue, just like the old man's.* Even though she had a scowl on her face, she was clearly very pretty. "I'll help," he said, and he took the box of supplies from her. "Let me put them in the dugout, and I'll come back and help you with anything else."

She just stood there, staring as he walked back to the dugout. When he returned, they both walked to the truck. There were three more crates to unload. He handed one to her and noticed she was strong. She was also still scowling at him. It became evident that, for some reason, she didn't want to be here or had taken an instant dislike to him.

Regardless, he attempted a little conversation. "Your grandfather and I talked the last time he was here. By chance, when I was scouting the area a few days ago, I came upon a farm and happened to see your brother Luc getting out of a German truck. I recognized your grandfather in his coat, coming out of your barn."

She stopped and stared. "How could you have done that?"

"I move around in the forest a good bit to see if anyone else is here—necessary for my privacy. I was at the edge of the woods, just northeast of your farm. While I was looking over the valley, the German truck came up from the south. I saw two women, you and your sister, come out of the house."

"That information could put my family at risk." The tone of her voice indicated she was getting more annoyed.

"It's possible, but it was all accidental. I mentioned your grandfather's coat to him last time, and he explained a bit about your family. I'm guessing that you are Aurélie."

"You should mind your own business."

"Your parents have disappeared along with one of your brothers. I also know that your husband was killed in 1940, and I'm very sorry."

This time she stopped in midstride and turned to face Mark. "I'm here to deliver supplies; that's all!"

They walked to the dugout in silence as it started to rain. "Why don't you stay here and let me go back for the last box," Mark said. "I think my coat is better in the rain than yours." When she didn't respond, he turned and left, half expecting her to follow. As he got the last crate, he noticed that her right front tire was almost flat. He placed the box on the hood, and when he knelt beside the car, he could hear the air leaking from around the stem. It looked like the inner tube had rotted from age and had cracked around the stem. Mark picked up the box and returned to the dugout, knowing that this was not going to improve her mood.

He entered the dugout and set the box down. "Bad news, I'm afraid. Your right front tire has a leak in the tube around the stem. Would you happen to have a spare tube and tools in your truck?"

The look on her face confirmed what he thought, but there was something else there—a sadness, almost like she wanted to cry. "I think we do. It's happened before. The tubes and tires are old and crack from time to time, so we have to change them out and repair the old ones. It's not like America, where you go down to the market and buy something new whenever you want."

Mark ignored the jab because she was right; even with rationing, Americans were so much better off. He went back out to the truck as it began to rain harder. He found a replacement tube with a jack and tire tools, but it was raining too hard to attempt a repair.

Returning to the dugout, he put the tools and tube in the corner and started unloading the supplies down into the cellar. Aurélie continued to stare at him with her arms crossed; now obviously fighting back tears. Mark went down the stairs, not sure what to say. As he put the supplies away, he realized that she would probably have to stay here until the rain subsided, and they could repair the tire. He put the coffeepot on the stove and turned it on. *At least we can be warm while we wait.*

Mark went back upstairs for another load. Aurélie was holding a box and handed it to him; then she picked up another box and followed him back down the stairs.

"The washing and bathroom supplies go in that cabinet," he said, indicating behind the shower. They continued bringing supplies down, and she helped to put them away.

She suddenly started talking. "We used to come up here for picnics when I was a young girl. Maman was always afraid of unexploded shells from the war, but *Père* said it was all right if we stayed on the main paths. René and I discovered this tunnel entrance by chance one day, but we were too scared to come down."

"Someone did a lot of work to fix this up. It is a very comfortable place, and I'm grateful. I'm grateful for not only the place but for your grandfather's support."

He noticed a tear start down one cheek. She reached up to wipe it away quickly. "Aurélie, I didn't mean to upset you. I realize …" He stopped to collect his thoughts. *There is no way that I can understand what their family has been through.* "I'm sorry about the losses your family has endured, and all I can do is thank you for the support."

She didn't reply; she just kept staring. Obviously, something was bothering her, so Mark searched for a less painful way to break the news that she wouldn't be able to return immediately. As he prepared to tell her that, she spoke again.

"Grand-père is quite ill. His lungs are not strong, and he has heavy congestion in his chest. He is also running a fever. Luc is trying to keep up with the chores, but it really requires two men. Josette, my sister, worries a lot about him, especially since her fiancé disappeared." She took a deep breath and composed herself.

"You've been through a lot." Mark paused a moment and then said, "Maybe I can help with some medicine. I have plenty—a large supply of aspirin and even some new stuff called penicillin. When we get the tire fixed, I'll send you back with some and instructions on what to do."

She looked at Mark and stopped scowling. "Thank you," she said softly. "How long will it take to fix the tire?"

Encouraged by her change of demeanor, Mark smiled and said, "Depends on the rain. The actual work will take only an hour, but we have to have a solid place to put the jack." She nodded. "In the meantime, we can have some coffee, or I could make some cocoa, if you'd like."

Her eyes widened. "You have cocoa?"

Mark looked down, smiling. "I guess they thought I would need some luxuries before I would say yes to this mission." He set the coffee aside and heated milk, motioning for her to sit at the table. He glanced her way, realizing that she might not have eaten lunch. "Would you like something to eat?" Trying to lighten the mood, he added, "I have *your* bread, *your* cheese, *your* sausage, *my* stew, and *my* chili—even though *my* stew and chili have a lot of *your* vegetables and seasoning."

She smiled slightly. "I … I … yes, merci. I would like something, if it's not too much trouble."

"I think the chili is still warm. I had it for lunch. I'll reheat some, and you can have some bread and cheese, and then we will have our cocoa."

As Mark put the food on the stove, he heard the rain pick up and went up the stairs to check. It was raining very hard now, with a strong wind from the north. The temperature was dropping from forty degrees. He was concerned about having the truck sit out, even though it was off the road and was not immediately visible. However, the rain lessened his concern; it was unlikely anyone would be out in this weather.

As he came back down the stairs, he could see Aurélie looking around his quarters. For a moment, she reminded him of Joanne, inspecting his room the first time he had brought her to meet his parents. It put a knot in Mark's stomach. He missed his wife.

He went to the stove and checked on the chili and milk. Turning the milk off, he stirred the chili. They were both quiet for several minutes.

Aurélie broke the silence. "Grandfather did most of this work himself. It's quite nice." She looked away momentarily and then asked, "If you don't mind, what were you just thinking about?"

Mark kept looking at the chili and thought about how to answer. "You reminded me of my wife, the first time I brought her home and showed her my room. She was inspecting as well." He quickly added, "She died seven years ago of cancer." As he composed himself, he searched for something to say. "I think the chili is ready."

Aurélie's face turned soft, and she quietly offered, "Now it's my turn to say I'm sorry."

Mark set the bowl in front of her, together with a loaf of bread and some cheese. "Would you like some coffee as well?"

She nodded as she started eating. After he got her coffee, Mark sat down across from her. She ate quickly, obviously hungry. "This is very good. Where did you learn to cook?"

"My mother. And then my wife and I used to cook together quite a bit. I also learned a few more things in my training."

She stopped eating suddenly. "I almost forgot. I am to give this to you." She pulled the envelope out of an inside pocket of her coat. He took it and put it in one of his pockets.

By the time she finished, she had eaten a second bowl. They talked some but mostly sat in silence, listening to the rain above. Checking his watch, Mark could see that it was about 3:45, and he began to lose hope that he would be able to fix the tire before it turned dark. That would leave them in a bit of an awkward position, as she would have to stay the night or risk pneumonia walking home in the rain.

He put a cup of cocoa in front of her. She drank it slowly, savoring it. "I don't think I've had cocoa since 1938. Maman used to make it for us on Saturday evenings in the winter, if we were good." She stared into the cup and looked back at the stove. "It's going to be dark soon, and I don't hear the rain letting up. What do we …?"

Mark could tell she was not enthralled with the possibility of spending the night away from her family, particularly in a cellar with a strange man, but he wasn't sure there was a good alternative.

"Well, there aren't many options. Walking home in this weather wouldn't be a good idea. And obviously, we can't fix the tire now. You could stay here. I have an extra bedroll that I can use on the floor, and you can take the bed."

Aurélie's eyes narrowed. Mark could tell she was getting annoyed again. "I can sleep up in the dugout," she announced stiffly.

"If you like, but it will be more comfortable down here. I give you my word that nothing is going to happen to you."

She continued drinking her cocoa, weighing the different options.

"I suppose I should stay down here. With Grand-père being ill, I should be careful not to get sick as well. If we're going to sleep in the same cellar, I should at least know your name."

Mark hesitated, not wanting to appear rude but not sure that he should give that information. When he looked at her, he decided against holding that information back. "My first name is Mark. I think that I probably shouldn't say more than that. It should be obvious that I'm in the US Army and that I like camping out in the woods." While he was trying to be humorous, he could see that she had reacted to his name.

"My oldest brother was named Marc."

"Your grandfather told me he was killed when the Germans invaded. I'm sorry."

She looked up from her cocoa with an amused expression. "What don't you know about our family?"

Mark ate some chili and then began to lay out his bedroll. "You can wash up there. If you would like, I can go up to the dugout."

She shook her head. "I trust you, and besides, we should keep the trapdoor shut; it's freezing."

Mark added wood to the stove. *Save the propane, but I don't want my first guest to complain about the cold.*

Later that evening, Mark opened the envelope and decoded the message. He was to go back to the site at Kœnigsmacker and specifically look for evidence of longer-range tests. Further, he was to tell no one and to do this entirely on his own.

Strange—did they not trust the two Frenchmen?

9:00 p.m., Same Day, War Cabinet Rooms, London

The information from the mess corporal at Vauquois arrived earlier in the morning. It indicated that the Germans had abruptly removed the main steel tubes and replaced them with material of inferior quality. Their instructions were to continue creating a site that would have the tubes entrenched in the ground, with the ability to change their aim up to thirty degrees. The consensus was that the tubes were some sort of large but crude mortar. There'd also been a rumor the shells were of unique design.

Churchill was not in a good mood. "Is this site something about which we should be concerned? And where did the first set of pipes go?"

Colonel Gaffney knew the question was coming but didn't have an answer. "Prime Minister, the only thing we know right now is that the original pipes were removed and replaced. The people at the site are not being told much either. It's evidently being kept very secret."

"Colonel Betts, what is the status of our information on the German development of atomic explosives?"

"Prime Minister, that program is proceeding, although somewhat behind schedule. The American scientists estimate there might be enough atomic material to make a small bomb or perhaps a dozen artillery shells, obviously of smaller size. However, all this is still speculation. Refining uranium for a bomb is a very time-consuming effort, requiring a huge facility. We aren't certain the Germans have such a facility."

General Brawls spoke up. "One explanation could be these pipes are indeed some crude mortar that would use shells from this particular program. Colonel Betts will know better in several days, but it appears the purpose for this site was revised, possibly because of its exposure. There are several other possible locations for a similar mortar position within five to ten miles. We need to have a few people scout the area but very carefully. We don't want Jerry to think we're interested."

Eisenhower had just returned from the Mediterranean theater and was sitting next to Churchill. He leaned over and whispered something to the Prime Minister, who then replied, "Well, go ahead and suggest it."

Ike looked surprised but said, "One way to possibly get a better idea as to alternate sites would be to review the rough plans that we have for proceeding through France into Germany after the invasion. These plans are top secret and very preliminary, but they would give us an idea of where the Germans might want to set up a strong defensive position with this type of weapon."

Colonel Betts offered, "Perhaps we could set up a small subcommittee that can interface with SHAEF planning and review our plans?" SHEAF was in the process of being organized, and it was likely Ike would be the boss.

General Brawls interupted, "Colonel Walker, will you get with General Smith and see what we can do about setting up a small-group meeting tomorrow morning?"

The Prime Minister was still not satisfied. "And in the meantime, I think that we should have our resources in the area make a visit to the Butte and several of the other facilities. We need more information."

Major Dornier was going to be busy the next several days.

Early Morning, December 10, the Dugout

Mark woke up at five o'clock and stuck his head up into the dugout. The rain had stopped, although it was still misting and foggy. It was too dark to do anything at present, but he wanted to get ready to fix the tire as soon as possible. Aurélie was still sleeping, quite soundly for someone concerned about being away from home.

He quietly washed and shaved and put a pot of coffee on the stove. He cut several slabs of bacon and started frying them. The smell caused Aurélie to open her eyes. "I'm sorry I slept so long. I'm normally the first one awake."

"No problem; you wouldn't know where things were anyway. The rain has stopped, but we will have to wait for it to get light. We should get out there soon so we get it fixed before someone comes by."

"I need to use the toilet." She got up and moved around Mark.

"I'll turn away, but I need to keep cooking the bacon."

Aurélie did not seem overly modest and went through her morning routine rapidly. They had a breakfast of bacon, potatoes, and bread. By the time they finished and had cleaned up, it was beginning to get light. Mark went up to the dugout and arranged the tools. Aurélie finished dressing and joined him. There was a light breeze blowing the mist through the trees, and it had warmed up slightly overnight to about forty-seven degrees.

They went out to the truck, and Mark asked Aurélie to hold his flashlight while he set up the jack. Once the truck tire was off the ground, it was a relatively simple matter to remove the tire and replace the tube. The hard part was going to be inflating the tire with the hand pump.

Two hours later, the truck was back on all four tires, and the tools were back in the truck bed. They walked back to the dugout to warm up with a last cup of coffee. Aurélie was getting ready to leave when Mark reminded her, "I need to give you the medicine for your grandfather. Come back down."

Once in the cellar, he gave her a small package with two syringes and a vial of penicillin. "Use the alcohol with these swabs and clean the area around the back of his arm. When you insert the needle, push it in about two centimeters and then slowly inject the medicine. It would be best if you did this every third day for a total of three times. That should help him get better; bed rest for at least a week after that would be advisable."

Aurélie was grateful but wasn't sure how to express it. While she was thinking about that, Mark filled two containers with food—one with chili and one with some venison stew. "This should help, especially the stew. It can be thinned down into soup for him, if necessary. Plenty of fluids and rest."

"Thank you, but are you sure you can spare these things? You're here for a reason, and you must not let anything get in the way of your mission."

"I won't. Some of the things that I brought with me are extra. And remember, it's also in my best interest that your grandfather gets better as well."

They both went up the ladder to the dugout and walked to the truck. "Are you sure you understand the instructions for the medicine?"

"Yes, monsieur, and merci."

"If he does not get better within a week, you should come back, and I can provide some other type of medication. Tell him hello for me."

Aurélie nodded and started the engine. She pulled away slowly in order not to create tracks. Mark watched the truck disappear around the curve, wondering about her. She was also thinking about the last eighteen hours. After her initial annoyance, the American seemed to be a warm and kind man. She had not been around someone like that for several years.

As soon as she was out of sight, he went back and started preparing for his trip to Kœnigsmacker. He would need to check out the pod scooter since he would have to provide his own transportation. With the round trip of 130 miles, he would need at least five gallons of gasoline and oil from his reserve. He wasn't looking forward to the trip at all because, at a sustained speed of six or seven miles an hour, it would take almost eleven hours to get there.

As he went through his preparation checklist, he planned for a departure at one o'clock the next morning. He would try to get into position near the site to get the necessary information before sunset and then leave early in the morning of the next day. It would require a stopover somewhere on the way, which he wasn't pleased about either. After looking at a map, he decided to take the back roads and use Forêt Domaniale de Verdun, just west of the Ornes, as one of his intermediate points. With his pod scooter, he would have to stick to the back roads, but that was okay since he couldn't travel fast.

He ate an early lunch and continued his preparations. He would try to go to sleep at five o'clock that evening, since the next few days would be busy. Besides his standard forty-pound pack, he would also take four small mines and the large tent, in case of bad weather. He chuckled as he thought about the weather. *All the weather at this time of year is miserable!*

What could the Germans have done in a few days to warrant another trip—and without his French friends?

December 11, German OKW Headquarters in Berlin

Spear was aggravated. He had been to meetings almost nonstop for the last few days with little to show for it other than bureaucratic complaining. *Well,* he thought, *I shouldn't have expected anything different. That's why the alternative-weapon program was kept secret. No use feeding the bureaucrats with more things for them to slow down. Fuel—always in short supply but perhaps with some luck …*

Same Day, War Cabinet Rooms, St. Charles Street, London; Lower Special Surveillance Office 8

Lieutenant Ryder settled into his new role quickly. Three other officers were helping as well as Polly. She'd helped immensely in organizing the new group. Alex appreciated her talents even more in this new role.

They had received additional aerial photos of the Butte de Vauquois area over the past couple of days, but the images still didn't lead to any solid conclusions. Also, other photographs of six BR sites continued to show activity. Photos and reports from the French Resistance indicated the Germans were still actively running power lines to these sites.

As dinnertime approached, Alex decided to ask Polly and two of the other ladies to accompany him to the cafeteria. There had been little time for anything other than a quick hello between them the last few days. Polly and the other women accepted, but several of the other officers decided that they were also invited, much to Alex's chagrin. Polly seemed to sense this and walked over to his side, looping her arm around his. "Well, at least you can escort me. It's not a formal five-course meal, but we can pretend." She looked up and smiled at him as she gave his arm a light squeeze.

CHAPTER 19

⋅⋆✦⋆⋅

December 11, 11:00 p.m., Outside Kœnigsmacker

Mark arrived near the site in the early afternoon and spent the rest of the day setting up a small camp on the west side of the Moselle and planning his approach. Even on this side of the river, there were several additional burn marks on hills. There was also evidence of other equipment, newly installed. There was a great deal of activity around the site all afternoon and into the evening.

Mark used his telescopic lens to take several photos, but from the outside, there didn't appear to be much in the way of change. He decided to cross the river. He found the canoe again and started across, slightly to the south of the first crossing.

The activity had slowed the last several hours. Most of the people had moved to what he thought was the mess hall. He approached the site, concealing himself in the copse of trees to the north. He had decided before he left that if the opportunity presented itself, he was going to try to get inside the facility to take a few photos. Realizing this could mean capture or death, he had left a message for Alphonse in the emergency drop location, describing his actions and indicating that he was probably in German hands if he didn't return.

He dropped all of his equipment except for his camera and moved slowly toward the door in the rear of the main blockhouse. The Germans still had not erected any fence or barrier, evidently not wanting to advertise to the locals the importance of the facility. As he arrived at the door, he cracked it open and was surprised to hear nothing but the hum of equipment. *Could they have left this facility completely unguarded?*

He proceeded inside and found himself in a large room with electrical switching gear and control panels. At the far end, there was a line of what appeared to be generators running. He counted twelve generators, with space for at least another six. Heavy conduit ran between the generators and the switching gear. He began taking photographs as soon as he got inside. He slowly looked around to make sure no one was in the room. As he walked between the generators, he looked up to the second floor and could see a closed-in office with the light on. It was evident someone was in there because of the moving shadows, but it would be difficult at this angle for them to see him on the floor.

Mark proceeded through the doorway into another room that was much smaller but extended to the end of the blockhouse. In the center were a series of large cylindrical objects, approximately four feet in diameter and ten feet long. There were three of these spaced about two feet apart, with a connection that was curved like a venturi pipe, roughly one foot in diameter. He continued to take photographs as he got to the end of the room.

Suddenly, the door on the right side of the room opened, and several officers entered. Someone, who evidently was a technician, was explaining to the officers about a modification to the venturi-type connections. Mark risked a few pictures as he crouched behind some equipment in the corner. He realized there was a door about eight feet behind him that he could exit undetected. Now that Mark had gathered information, he felt it was time to leave. He decided to risk moving in that direction.

He was back across the river at his camp a little after three o'clock in the morning. He loaded his camera with fresh film and got ready to observe what he felt would be a test very soon.

Mosquito Reconnaissance Plane, Five Thousand Feet above Bar-le-Duc

The pilot had been circling for about ten minutes at the lowest power setting he could risk, keeping the engine noise from attracting attention. They had been out here last night as well and had orders to begin flying over the Kœnigsmacker area, with cameras rolling, starting slightly after two o'clock every night.

"I wish I knew what we were looking for because it's dark down there," the pilot commented into the intercom.

The navigator, who was also running the cameras, chuckled, "We're not supposed to *know*; we're just *to do or die*. If they're interested in pictures of black, then that's what they'll get."

"Well, take us over Kœnigsmacker, and we'll make several passes." The pilot steered the heading the navigator gave him and started the descent to two thousand feet; another long evening for nothing.

December 12, 3:10 a.m., German BR Site Outside Kœnigsmacker

Major Dornier could hear the hum of the equipment increase, so he trained his binoculars on the turret on top of the blockhouse. Earlier in the day, he had made a note on his map of several wooden and cinder block structures built north and west of the facility. They were probably test structures for the weapon. They were at least seven or eight miles from the facility, however, and that bothered Mark.

The hum of the equipment increased suddenly, and there was a small red glow, quickly followed by a yellow light that flashed into an intense orange, just as he had witnessed over a month ago. There was a brief high-pitched sound as a beam shot out of the embrasure, and then the hum of the equipment abruptly dropped. There was a small red glow off to the north, indicating the termination of the beam.

Mark had set the camera for rapid photographs but was not sure how well they would turn out; for that matter, he wasn't sure how his first set had turned out. This time, however, he had back-up, although he didn't know it. The Mosquito bomber above had managed to catch ten images right at the moment the beam left the turret.

6:00 a.m., on a Small Road Outside of Maucourt-sur-Orne

It was raining, sleeting, and downright miserable. Mark had left the site about 3:45 a.m., after which the test was completed. He estimated the target had been approximately nine miles away, which was clearly an increase in range by over 100 percent. He left quickly and carefully because he wanted to make sure that he got his report and the film back to London as soon as possible.

He had encountered only one truck outside Hayange on a small back road. Luckily, he had been on a relatively flat piece of ground and had been able to pull off the road where he was concealed. He had traveled only the on small back roads, some of which were not even numbered. As Mark approached Maucourt, he knew he would need to get back onto the D Road, which was why he had increased his speed. He wanted to get through Ornes and into Forêt Domaniale de Verdun before first light.

As he drove, he wondered if Aurélie had been able to help her grandfather with the medicine. He knew from experience that illnesses in this kind of weather, particularly with the elderly, could lead to pneumonia and serious complications. His father almost had died of pneumonia when Mark was a young child. He also wondered if Aurélie would be the one to visit with supplies next time. He knew he shouldn't be thinking of her this much, but what could it hurt since there was no opportunity to develop a relationship?

As he approached the intersection near Maucourt, he scanned the countryside as best he could in the darkness and rain. He could see no signs of activity, so he turned right onto the road and increased his speed to the maximum. Within a short time, he was at the top of a small rise just outside of Ornes. He shut the engine off and listened carefully. Ornes was a group of five structures near to the road at the edge of the woods. He saw no lights or indication of activity, so he revved up the engine and started down the slope toward town. Halfway down, he cut the engine and coasted. As he rolled through the village, he went across an intersection and then took a small dirt trail into the forest. He had to start the engine again, but this time he kept the speed low to keep the engine noise at a minimum.

After about thirty minutes, he was north of the village of Douaumont, traveling on a small road that traversed a large hill. Continuing northbound, he looked for a place to turn off. He passed up several old logging roads until finally, he found what he was looking for—a narrow path hemmed in on both sides by trees and brush. Turning off the road onto what amounted to a path, he continued slowly into the forest until he found a thicket protected on one side by a ravine and a steep rise on the other. This was an ideal place to stop. He began to set up poles that would support his camouflage netting and tarp. Since the pod was over eight feet long, he could lie down inside next to his supplies and stay relatively warm and dry. He set up the platform at the rear of the pod that supported a small cookstove and heated some of the venison stew he had brought with him.

As he ate, he recounted what he had seen last night, and he was convinced that the Germans had successfully developed some kind of a weapon that concentrated a beam of light capable of reaching out perhaps as far as ten miles. While this was troublesome, the positive part of his discovery was that it took a great deal of electrical power to be effective. He would let the experts in London evaluate things, but he didn't think they would be able to shoot a beam more than once every three or four minutes—maybe longer. If true, that would limit the effectiveness of the weapon.

He noticed it getting light. He intended to prepare his report next, place it and the film in the containers provided, and then get some sleep. He finished up before ten in the morning and then sat quietly listening for any sounds of activity. He walked along the road he had traveled for a few hours, looking to see if there were signs of his passage. The rain and sleet, while light, were enough to mask his tracks. After he was convinced no one was around and wouldn't be able to see any tread marks, he lay down in the pod to sleep. Unfortunately, try as he might, he was not able to put Aurélie's visit out of his mind.

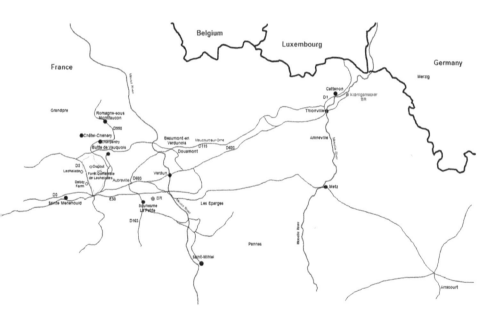

CHAPTER 20

+‧+‧◆◆‧+‧+

10:00 a.m., December 15, Lower Special Surveillance Office 8

Lieutenant Boysden woke at four in the morning with the news of the latest report and photographs of the BR site near Kœnigsmacker. It took another three hours to have the pictures processed. He awoke Lieutenant Ryder and one other officer at five o'clock to start working on the report. They needed to assimilate and compare it with past reports so that an accurate picture could be presented from this latest set of facts. It was evident to William that whoever had gathered this information had taken significant risks in doing so. It was also apparent that the information could push the understanding of the BR mystery much farther along.

A little past six o'clock, the phone rang. The sergeant from Flight Operations was on the line. "Sir, I was just informed that we had a reconnaissance aircraft over the Kœnigsmacker BR site on December 12. For some reason, the report did not make it through as it should have. Apparently, there is a series of fascinating photographs that we'll be sending over immediately. I wanted to make you aware so that you can watch for a package that should arrive before eight this morning."

"Thank you. It doesn't appear the delay caused any damage, but make sure those photographs get here quickly." William hung up the phone and turned to talk with Alex. *More information. Always a good thing but confusing.*

Ryder looked up as Lieutenant Boysden approached. It was clear from his demeanor that something serious was on his mind. "Alex, we're getting another set of photographs taken by a reconnaissance aircraft that should arrive in a couple of hours. I want you to organize the staff to look at this carefully. I think we may need to bring in some scientists as well, but we'll let Colonel Gaffney decide that later. I suspect we'll need to brief him before noon."

"Yes, sir, and we just received a packet of photographs taken from the ground that has both external photos of the site and others taken from inside the structures." He spread the photographs out on a drafting table. It showed the various stages of the beam as well as the target impact. More important, the internal photos showed the extensive electrical equipment that was involved.

"What are they doing? I've never seen anything like this."

Neither of the men noticed Polly standing behind them. "I don't think we've ever heard of anything remotely similar to this kind of a weapon. I'll get the staff organized at once, as I suspect we'll be typing up reports quickly this morning."

Alex and Lieutenant Boysden turned around and looked at her. "Thanks, Polly. As soon as we get this information assimilated, we *will* need a quick turnaround of the report." Lieutenant Boysden turned and walked away. Alex looked at Polly, and she pointed over in the corner. "I made a fresh pot with a small supply of some real coffee. Help yourself." She turned and walked away to get the secretaries organized. Alex sat there wondering how she found a coffeepot and real coffee. If anyone could, Polly would be the one.

Midmorning, December 15, Butte de Vauquois

Sergeant Hamming was in Major Schmidt's office. "The schedule cannot be met with only twenty workers. I need at least ten or twelve more. After all, the original plans were for only one hole, and now they are asking for thirty."

"I know, and I've already brought it up with the colonel. He has placed a requisition for additional workers, but I don't know when they're going to arrive. I suspect it will be a few weeks, at least. In the meantime, do your best to keep things moving."

"I can have the surveyors lay out the markers for the additional holes and the supply lines. I was thinking about starting all of the holes at the same time, with two-man teams on each hole. They could dig and bail water as needed. That's about as fast as we can go, particularly in this weather."

Major Schmidt sighed. "Do what you can, but make sure we have camouflage netting over any new areas. Intelligence has reported increased reconnaissance flights all over eastern France. We don't want the Allies to detect this new expansion."

Sergeant Hamming left the office and found Zormaan at the worksite. As they stood under a work tent used for a field office, he explained the plans. Zormaan was not sure that they would be able to camouflage all of the additional holes because of a lack of netting.

The surveyors struggled through the rest of the morning, marking the new sites. Shortly past noon, Sergeant Hamming came out and told Zormaan to have the crew go to lunch. The men were glad to get out of the weather and into the mess tent. While they all griped about the food, they knew that the mess sergeant kept them well fed. They could be wet, miserable, and worked hard, but as long as there was good, hot food, it was tolerable.

The men disbursed after getting their food, as they usually did, to seek out their friends. They began discussing what they were doing but not in much detail. The whole camp knew they were digging holes, and it was somewhat of a joke. *Digging holes—to collect all the rainwater so the rest of the camp won't be muddy.* The corporal made note of all of the comments, and after cleaning up in the afternoon, he added them to his report. He would wait for a few more days before submitting this information.

9:00 p.m., SHAEF Headquarters, London

The senior staff met at Eisenhower's request. Churchill was also in attendance. The report that Major Dornier had submitted, along with his photographs and the photographs taken by the reconnaissance aircraft, was a focus of concern, not only in the intelligence sector but also with the SHAEF staff. They had submitted all of this information to the scientists who had evaluated the blast in November. The data didn't get to the scientists until two o'clock that afternoon, and it had taken until five o'clock for them to assemble and begin to discuss it. Naturally, in this small amount of time, no firm conclusions could be drawn. It was decided to meet the next day again, once everyone had enough time to digest the new information.

Two of the scientists, whose expertise was in electromagnetic physics, had made a couple of troubling observations. Even though the other scientists did not agree, as they argued, the name Nikola Tesla kept coming up.

December 17, the Dugout

Mark was busy cleaning and repairing all of his gear. The trip to Kœnigsmacker, while successful, had been very tiring. He had pushed the scooter to the point where one of the two cylinders lost compression. Luckily, he had spare parts with him and was able to make the necessary repairs. However, the amount of work involved took its toll on Mark. He spent the entire next day working on the scooter.

Early that morning when he went up to the dugout, he saw a deer only fifty yards away. He slowly retrieved his rifle from the cellar and shot it. It took four hours to butcher the animal, and bury all the remains to assure his presence would remain undetected. He had also started smoking a large amount of the meat to preserve it.

He walked around to the outside water drums to check their level and ensure they were clear of debris. Earlier he'd set up a system of collection hoses in different locations to drain the rainwater into fifty-five-gallon drums. Each of the hoses had a triple filtration system to eliminate debris; he handled bacteria with purification pills. He used the outside water mainly for washing and maintenance. The drinking water drums were filled with the external drums periodically and treated with a small amount of disinfectant. The recent wet weather ensured that all of his storage was full.

He'd used the pod yesterday to retrieve a message at one of several drop points. It'd been a test run for the newly repaired scooter, and it performed well. Unfortunately, the note indicated he was to visit the Butte de Vauquois as soon as possible. *They sure are keeping me busy.* He wasn't interested in another excursion, but he made plans to leave about three o'clock the following morning. Since it was only four miles away, he would do it on foot. *It's a good thing I have several pairs of boots and good socks. They warned me about the walking, but I didn't think it would be this intense,* he mused as he unloaded one set of pistol magazines and loaded another set.

He had left a message at the drop yesterday, requesting additional gasoline, film canisters, and medical supplies. He had not heard from Alphonse or Aurélie since he had sent the antibiotics home with her. He hoped that the old man was recovering and would be able to visit him again soon. He missed the conversations with him, even if they were short.

CHAPTER 21

✦✦✦✦✦

6:00 a.m., December 20, Stuggart Luftwaffe Airbase

The Junker's tri-motor dipped its right wing as it lost altitude into a cloud bank. Reich Minister Speer was busy going over the latest status reports from the Reich's nuclear program. The nuclear program at Haigerloch was not well known in the Nazi organization because it supposedly had been disbanded a few months after Germany invaded Poland in 1939. A supply of heavy water had been transferred from Norway to the facility at Haigerloch before the British tried to destroy that facility. Haigerloch had been in secret but continuous operation since the end of 1939 and had produced minimal amounts of uranium-235.

Speer had been interested in this program from its inception and had convinced Hitler not to cancel the program in a private meeting that was known only to Bormann. The failed test explosion in early September had used a batch of uranium-235 that was not adequately purified. The scientists had warned that it might not create the kind of explosion everyone expected, and indeed, it hadn't. Nevertheless, it did show that the facility was on the right track, and they continued their efforts with the purification.

Because of the secrecy, Speer had awakened early and left at four o'clock in the morning to avoid attention. The two-hour flight had given him an opportunity to look at the status and be prepared to offer suggestions on how to increase production. He had to admit that the Haigerloch staff had been quite efficient in organizing and focusing the small amount of resources they controlled. The director of the Reichsforschungsrat (the Reich Research Council, or RFR, set up in 1936 to centralize planning for all basic and applied research in Germany) had been careful to segregate the nuclear efforts from the other research and development going on in Germany. Kurt Diebner, the head of the Reichsforschungsrat (RFR) nuclear physics experimental site at Stadtilm in Thuringia, had been transferred, under secrecy, to the Haigerloch site in early 1940.

Diebner was especially adept at getting the most from his staff. Last year he had proposed the construction of a new nuclear reactor at Haigerloch that might produce three times the amount of U-235. This new facility would be run by skilled operators selected from the prisoner ranks in the various concentration camps across the Reich. The controversial part of his project was that the cost and schedule of the new reactor had been greatly reduced by not providing the operators with the correct amount of shielding. The German scientists were in the control room, monitoring the work behind adequate protection, but this meant the operators had a limited amount of time before becoming sick from radiation poisoning. Instead of hiding this fact from the operators, they had told them upfront about the dangers and had offered them the same quarters and food as the German workers. As an additional incentive, they had collected all of their surviving family members and placed them in a camp nearby. As long as the workers produced results, they and their family members would be treated well.

The JU-52 landed and taxied to an empty hangar, where a car was waiting for the Reich Minister. He transferred to a vehicle for the forty-minute drive to the facility. *It's convenient to have a Luftwaffe base near. I hope that doesn't make it a target someday.*

When he arrived, Diebner greeted him and took him to a conference room with two other senior scientists. Speer was given a quick update on the current status and projections for the raw materials destined for the small explosive containers. No one in the room, except Speer, realized the explosive containers would be artillery shells. Further, only a separate group of scientists outside Berlin, under Speers direct control, knew how much material was required for each shell.

"The new reactor went online last month with only minor delays. The new operator program appears to be working well, and the initial uranium-235 production has approached almost twice the amount produced in the old reactor. Purification is still an issue, but we have perfected a pilot-scale test unit that we believe will decrease the time for purification."

"When do you think we will be able to ship the uranium in usable quantities?"

Diebner looked at the scientists before answering. "We should be able to ship about ten kilograms in approximately ten weeks, roughly by the end of February."

Speer showed no emotion, but he was disappointed. His scientists had indicated each shell would need approximately 0.3 kilograms of uranium, so this first shipment would only result in perhaps thirty shells. He also knew that there would be inevitable delays in the estimated schedule. "Diebner, you and your team have done well. Keep the pressure on because we need as much of the material as you can make. Most of you are aware that there will be an Allied invasion sometime in 1944, probably in the spring. When that happens, we are going to need all of the new weapons the Reich can produce." Speer got up and walked to the door. "Shall we take a tour? I would like to see the facility myself."

Diebner and his team gave Speer a thorough tour and made careful notes of his suggestions. Diebner was surprised at Speer's insight into this complex scientific issue and even more surprised at his recommendations for increasing production. He might be able to increase output by as much as 15 percent or 20 percent if Diebner could implement all of the ideas. Speer was satisfied that the facility was in good hands and decided to leave right after lunch.

As Speer boarded the plane back to Berlin, he did some quick calculations. Unfortunately, he would not be able to create the nuclear "wall" that he had planned with the shells, but he could still slow the Allied advance considerably. The key would be the placement of the firing facilities. He was glad that he had developed an alternative use for the tubes. It was amazing to realize all of the wisdom that could come from reading the history of the Great War.[3]

Noon, Christmas Day 1943, Lower Special Surveillance Office 8, London

The entire group was celebrating with a special Christmas dinner that included turkey and ham with many accompaniments that hadn't been around for years. There were undoubtedly advantages in having the Americans as allies. Captain Stone went to Colonel Gaffney to pull some strings to get food and wine. He had successfully argued that if they gave the group a few hours off on Christmas with a nice meal, it would keep productivity and morale high. As he looked across the group, he knew his efforts had paid off.

Lieutenant Ryder was sitting between Colonel Gaffney and Polly. General Brawls was across the table with Captain Stone and many of the lab personnel. All of the staff officers and secretaries were present as well. Colonel Gaffney leaned over to Alex. "How are conditions here?"

Alex thought before he replied. "Well, it beats a foxhole in this weather. It's hard work and very intense, but we all realize the information that we develop is important."

"This information is helping a great deal, and we all appreciate your effort." With a small pause and a smile, Colonel Gaffney added, "And I've been in a foxhole in this kind of weather, and inside *is* much better."

Polly elbowed Alex and shot him a look that said, *Be careful*. Alex smiled back at her. They had managed to have a couple of hours together

---

3. World War I saw the use of large caliber, short-range mortars, sometimes called Minenwerfer ("mine launcher").

to talk over the last week, and it was apparent Polly was a special woman. He just hoped that she felt the same way about him.

General Brawls leaned over and addressed Alex. "I need to see you after dinner."

Alex nodded, but for some reason, he developed a knot in his stomach. Polly leaned up against him and looked him directly in the eyes. "Could we take a walk after you talk with the general?"

Alex again nodded, pleased that he would have some time with Polly, but he suspected that the talk and walk might be connected.

Dinner went on for another hour, and everyone thoroughly enjoyed themselves. As the conversation died, people started going back to their quarters. Alex looked over to the general, and he nodded toward the cafeteria exit. As they stood up Alex commented to the general, "I'm glad that we could do this with the entire group. Captain Stone did an excellent job. I know it will help with morale ." They walked the rest of the way in silence to the general's office.

When they got there, General Brawls indicated that Alex should sit at the conference table. Brawls sat across from him and opened a folder, which he turned around without saying a word and pushed it in front of Alex.

Alex took the folder and saw that it was orders for him. He was to report to Achnacarry on January 3 to begin commando training. The knot in his stomach grew.

"This is not a random assignment, Alex. You have acquired a great deal of valuable experience analyzing the information we've received. We need to have someone in the field who can help us this spring. As you can tell, a lot is going on, and experienced men and women in the field are invaluable at focusing on the most productive areas of reconnaissance."

"I'll be sad to leave the group, but I realized this had to come at some point. I hope I can handle the training. I know it's very tough."

"I have every confidence that you can, although there will be times when you'll want to quit." General Brawls looked him in the eyes. "Please don't. To help you prepare mentally, I'm going to reveal something to you that is top secret. One of the people you work with has been through the training and will help you prepare, but the identity of that person is top secret. Do you understand?"

"Yes, sir."

"I'm referring to Polly Berson. She qualified several years ago and does refresher training occasionally."

Alex could not hide his surprise, and the general saw it. He smiled. "We will arrange for you to have a little more time together to discuss the training … and whatever else you want to discuss."

"If I could ask, how long is the training?"

"Normally twelve weeks; in your case, six. If I were you, I would begin exercising immediately, and Polly can help you with that as well." The general got up and indicated that Alex could return to the party.

Alex turned around. "Thank you for your confidence; I won't let you down." He walked down the hallway and took the stairs back to the cafeteria in a daze. He entered the room and saw Polly with several secretaries, talking in a corner. As he approached her, she looked at him and took his arm, walking him out of the cafeteria.

"It's going to be hard, but I know you can do it."

He whipered as they walked. "You knew, didn't you?"

"Only last week. The General asked my opinion. I think several other people were asked as well. You're smart and quick, and you're in reasonably good shape, so you should be able to make it through." She squeezed his arm slightly and smiled. "But believe me, there will be times when you won't be able to go on. That's when you learn to take the next step. Just remember, this is training, and when you're in the field facing the enemy, you'll have no choice except to continue or be killed or captured."

"When did you get involved? When did you go for training initially?"

"The summer of 1941. I've gone back every six to nine months for refresher courses, especially parachute training."

Alex twitched at the mention of a parachute; he did not like heights.

Polly read his mind. "The key is not to look down. It's never easy the first few times, and some people never get used to it. Listen to the instructors carefully, and when you get to the door the first time, look at the horizon. Gravity takes care of the rest."

"It's the gravity part that bothers me. So when you disappeared in August, were you up there?"

"Yes." She wanted to move on to other things. "So, if we could talk about something else, General Brawls gave me a bottle of a single-malt whiskey from the Achnacarry region. Why don't we go back to the guest quarters, and I can begin telling you what you need to prepare for—and maybe a few other things."

Alex wasn't sure where this was leading, but he knew he was glad Polly was on his arm.

December 27, in the Air over Southeast Germany

Reich Minister Speer was on the second leg of his trip to Ploesti. He wanted to visit with the production manager in the R&D facility outside the refinery. Most of the damage from the large bomber raid earlier in the year had been repaired, and new air defenses had been implemented to discourage the Allies, but so far, it hadn't.

The refinery manager and the head of the R&D facility both met the plane at the air base outside Bucharest. Speer was taken directly to the R&D facility. The refinery manager briefed Speer on the production figures of the refinery and the activities of the R&D facility. After the briefing, Speer made his request.

"Gentleman, the Reich is in need of 5.7 million liters of gasoline. We require the first shipment of one million liters in four weeks."

The request shocked everyone in the room because the request was almost two full weeks of gasoline production. The issue wasn't just producing the volume of gasoline; it was also the problem of enough railcars to transport it. The refinery manager finally replied, "Herr Reich Minister, naturally we will do whatever is necessary. However, that amount of gasoline will place a burden on the refinery to produce it, not to mention the disruption of supplies to both fronts. Also, as I'm sure you are aware, railcars are in extremely short supply."

"First of all, the gasoline will be going to the R&D facility here, where a special formulation will be prepared and then placed into canisters before shipping. That should address your concern about railcars. As far as the disruption of supplies to the front, let me worry about that. I will provide you with paperwork absolving the refinery of any responsibility. Once we have received the gasoline, your normal distribution will resume."

Speer then looked at the manager of the R&D facility. "I assume there are no issues with your facility to produce the special blend?"

"The production facility will be ready to begin formulation in two days, Reich Minister."

"And the facility to place it into canisters?"

"The facility is ready now, but we are short of steel to make the required number of canisters. An air raid destroyed a supply train last week, and we have not been able to requisition more steel."

Speer flipped several pages in his folder until he found the quantity of steel required. While substantial, he knew how to get the steel to Ploesti in four days. "The steel will arrive in several days. Make certain you are ready. Immediately after this meeting, I will make a call to ensure the delivery. Are there any other concerns?"

He looked around the room and saw worried looks on everyone's face, but no one said anything. He smiled slightly. "Take heart. I have confidence in your abilities. Let me know if any other shortages occur. Now, if that's all, could I find a phone with a line to Berlin?" Speer got up and left the room, with the R&D manager trailing behind.

January 29, 1944, Forêt Domaniale de Lachalade

The weather had cleared up over the last several days, although it remained cold. In the mornings, there was ice on some of the streams. Mark was again grateful that he had a warm, dry place out of the weather. He had visited the Butte de Vauquois three times in the past couple of weeks and photographed the additional excavation points. He had continued to estimate sizes and distances, make sketches, and take photos, but he still had no idea what they were doing. New tubes had arrived about two weeks ago and appeared to be longer than the original tubes. There were also additional excavations, with berms built up around them, almost like ammunition storage sites. It made sense that the Germans would attempt to put some type of artillery at this position because of its height. What didn't make sense, however, was that it was a relatively easy site to bomb.

He'd also visited two other BR sites nearby since December. One of them showed considerable activity, similar to that of the facility outside Kœnigsmacker. The defensive facilities around each site continued to be developed and were reaching a point where it would be difficult to approach the sites without detection. He'd attempted to get inside one of the facilities but had almost been discovered when a sentry came back, looking for a set of keys. He hoped that the information and photographs he supplied made it back safely and were helping the scientists to figure out what the Germans were doing.

Mark was walking west through the woods toward Lachalade. He hadn't accomplished any area reconnaissance in almost a month and wanted to make sure there were no changes. As he approached the edge of the forest, he got down and slowly crawled the last fifty yards to a point where he was shielded by brush. He had a good view of the shallow valley below. It was midmorning, and the sun was out, illuminating the valley. He could see some activity in Lachalade, as well around one of the farms on the side of the village.

Satisfied, he moved slowly back into the forest and headed south. Alphonse had finally shown up the first week of January, almost three weeks after Aurélie had visited. He had thanked Mark for the medicine and the extra food. His fever had left him three or four days after Aurélie's visit, but it took him a couple of weeks to get his strength back. He indicated Aurélie was not willing to return, and Mark didn't press the issue. Somehow, it disappointed Mark that Aurélie did not want to come back, but he took it in stride.

About halfway to the southern edge of the forest, Mark stopped to eat some lunch. He had packed sausage, cheese, and bread—big surprise. He also brought an apple with him. Alphonse had somehow found apples and had provided Mark with several. As he sat on a log, he listened to the silence of the forest. There was a slight breeze that made a humming noise in the tops of the trees. Every once in a while, there would be the rustle of a small animal moving around, but by and large, there was not much in the way of noise. Even though Mark missed talking with people, he still enjoyed being out there alone.

When he finished eating, he continued on his track south. After another forty-five minutes, he saw the edge of the trees and crept slowly toward the clearing. He could see the village of Les Islettes in the distance to the south, and Alphonse's farm north of the village. Through the binoculars, he could see that Luc was moving around in the yard between the barn and the house. He could also see a woman going out to a small building that probably housed chickens, but it was not Aurélie. He assumed it must be Josette.

He set the binolars down and enjoyed the view. While concealed behind the brush and small trees, he was also in a patch of sunshine, and it warmed him Suddenly, off to the right, he heard movement. He slowly sank to his belly, raising his rifle in the direction of the noise. He could now hear talking, both a man and woman. As they came around a dense clump of trees, he was surprised to see Alphonse and Aurélie. He knew that this was not their land, but Alphonse had mentioned that he sometimes paid his neighbor for the extra grazing space.

They were coming within fifty feet of his position, but it looked like they were content to walk at the edge of the forest. He was tempted to reveal himself, but then he thought better of it. If he allowed them to get this close undetected, there could be others, and there was no purpose in it. So he let them keep walking. When they were out of earshot, he slowly got up and carefully moved back into the forest to the north. *I would have liked to have said hello.*

CHAPTER 22

◆◆◆◆◆

February 4, 1944, Commando Training Center, Achnacarry, Scotland

It was late afternoon, and Alex's training group was not looking forward to the all-night survival exercise. The groups of three were let out twenty miles from the base with one pocketknife, thirty feet of rope, three feet of ten-gauge wire, and one match each. They had to find their way back to the training center before noon the next day.

Lieutenant Alex Ryder was cold, sore, and running a slight fever. His two companions were only in slightly better condition. The training had been tough, but he had kept up—but barely. Last week he successfully finished three parachute jumps, which had lifted his spirits. The first jump was difficult, but subsequent jumps were easier. Polly had been right—trust the instructors, and look at the horizon. Sergeant Aiden was a great example of this. While he was tough on the trainees, he was always careful to evaluate their actions and point out deficiencies in a manner that encouraged them.

He had another ten days of training and was determined to finish. His group included a very large American lieutenant and an Australian captain. He was impressed with the quality of the people at Achnacarry, the staff as well as the trainees. Everyone was motivated and, for the most part, in good physical shape.

Alex's group was climbing a steep hill in a wooded area. As they got to the top, they were disappointed to see a steep ravine with a broad stream at the bottom, about fifty feet below them. The side of the gorge was extremely steep and covered with vegetation that was damp and slick. They couldn't just climb down.

The Australian captain immediately started evaluating options. As his companions were studying how they might cross the ravine, Alex suddenly hit on an idea. They could take their knife and make stakes to drive into the ravine wall. The wall looked like it had plenty of soil between the rock outcrops. There were plenty of rocks around as a way to drive the stakes into the wall. Then they could use the rope to secure two people together. One could navigate down while the other was his anchor. When both were at the halfway point, the line could be thrown back up for the third person to navigate down. Intermediate anchor points would ensure that if the third person slipped, he would not fall past the other two at the midway point.

They discussed their options quickly, as it was almost dark. "We need to get branches about an inch in diameter, cut the side branches off, and leave about two inches to form a hook; if we fall, the rope won't slip completely off." The American captain volunteered to go down first, allowing Alex and the Australian to be the anchor at the top. The Australian was large and strong enough to support the other two as they descended later.

The Australian looked at the sky and his watch. "It's going to be dark in about two hours, and I don't think we'll be able to complete this before dark. Let's concentrate on gathering the branches, making the anchors, and gathering firewood. One of us can look for something to eat, while the other two make the anchors."

Alex didn't like the idea. "That means we'll have to stay here all night and lose time. We'll probably have to jog most of the way tomorrow, assuming we get across quickly."

The American lieutenant thought for a moment then suggested an idea. "I think we can try it in the dark as long as we go slowly. We just need to make sure we don't get disoriented after crossing. Remember we have to go southeast to get back to the castle."

After additional discussion, they agreed to push forward for a crossing in the dark. They immediately began looking for branches, and after finding solid pieces of wood, the Australian sat down to prepare the anchors. While he was doing that, Alex continued to gather firewood, and the American looked for a possible food source.

Alex prepared the firewood and placed some dry moss at the bottom of the pile. He had been lucky enough to find an old hollow log that had both moss and leaves inside, relatively dry. To that small pile of tinder, he added some of the shavings from the Australian's efforts at shaping the branches into anchors. They had found a small piece of wood and a piece of flat driftwood to use as a fire starter. They still had one match but did not want to use it because they might need it the following day.

The Australian was quite adept at whittling and already had eight stakes prepared. Alex set about the task of creating an ember from his "fire-starter kit." He rubbed the stick between his hands, rotating it in the hole, heating both the bottom of the stick and the driftwood. After five minutes, he added a few small pieces of wood shavings and leaves and continued his efforts. Just about the time the Australian finished the last stake, he saw a small ember and quickly added some moss and additional leaves. The ember took, and he carefully transferred it to the pile of tinder, blowing gently to keep it alive. In less than a minute, he had a flame that they carefully nursed into a campfire.

Just then, the American came over the ridge. "Look what I found." He was carrying a small rabbit and a small bird.

"How did you get that?"

He held up a makeshift slingshot. "I was pretty good with a slingshot back home, so I made one out of my boot laces and a piece of my shirt. I just barely got the rabbit, and the bird is half crushed, but beggars can't be choosers."

He set about cleaning both the rabbit and the bird. They put together a makeshift rack to roast the meat. Within an hour, they were eating their small feast and warming themselves next to the fire. The whole effort had taken about two and a half hours. The last little bit of daylight was fading fast.

Alex got up and looked down the ravine. "I guess we better get going."

They set about creating a solid anchor around a tree at the edge of the ravine, and the American slowly lowered himself down about fifteen feet, placing anchors every three or four feet. By the time he had run the rope out to its limit, he had descended approximately twenty-five feet. The Australian went next and was down in a few minutes. Alex undid the rope after the American secured it on a tree growing out of the ravine. They had acquired a stone that would allow them to throw the line up, but it still took several attempts.

Eventually, Alex was able to get the rope and tie a slipknot around the tree. This was going to be the tricky part because if the slipknot let go, Alex would fall. On the other hand, if the slipknot didn't free up after he was at the midpoint, he wouldn't have a rope for the final descent. Alex looped the rope around each of the anchors as he went down to give him some level of security, undoing the upper anchor as he reached a new lower anchor point.

Finally, at the midpoint, Alex secured the rope to the double stakes located there and wrapped it around himself. Then he shook the line to loosen the slipknot. Try as he might, the slipknot did not appear as though it was going to cooperate.

"Keep snapping it, mate; try sideways as well. It will give way eventually." His two colleagues continued encouragement over the next fifteen minutes. Alex was getting to the point that he thought that he might try the descent without the rope. Finally, however, it gave way, and Alex threw it down to the bottom.

"I'm tying another slipknot on the anchor tree here and starting down."

"Be careful. About halfway down there's a sharp outcrop that you can stand on, but it's very slick."

Alex shimmied down about four feet to the first anchor. He looped the rope around the anchor and then disengaged the slipknot from the tree. He began working himself down the way he had done in the top part of his descent. When he got to the bottom, they all congratulated each other. The Australian brought them back to reality. "All right, chaps; now we have to get across the stream without getting wet and catching pneumonia."

After gauging the stream, it appeared perhaps chest deep. With few options available, they decided to strip down, hold their clothes above their heads, and wade across. After putting their clothes back on, they decided to keep moving, mainly to fight off the cold. The whole effort had taken about five hours. They took turns in the lead and kept a close eye on their bearings. When Alex was not in the lead, he allowed himself to think about Polly. Just ten more days, and then what? *Straight to Europe or perhaps some time off before the assignment?*

CHAPTER 23

◆ ◆ ◆ ◆ ◆

March 31, 1944, SHEAF Headquarters

The weekly progress meeting with the entire senior staff had been in progress for over two hours. Most of the discussion focused on the invasion planning and logistics. While the staff was in favor of a May invasion, Eisenhower wasn't convinced. There had been the inevitable problems with stockpiling supplies and equipment. As an example, they hadn't anticipated how much space was required to stage all of the material. They were using ditches covered by corrugated metal to store bombs, and farm fields to locate the larger equipment. Just about every large structure available was a makeshift warehouse. And southern England was full. They were simply running out of space to store their supplies. They were also running out of places to billet the soldiers, and then there was the landing-craft shortage. *Any good news?*

General Montgomery had become annoyed with the Planning and Logistics staff for not anticipating these issues. "I find it extremely difficult to believe that we overlooked the need for storage space. Apart from putting people on the ground, the most important thing is to stage supplies and equipment so that they can be moved to the front quickly."

"General, I agree with your opinion, but now is not the time to lament this particular oversight. We need solutions." Churchill did not want the meeting to spiral out of control into "name and blame."

"Planning and Logistics are already working on alternative plans and will report tomorrow at noon. Please include General Bradley in this meeting." Ike didn't want Montgomery making this decision alone. He slipped a sideways glance at the PM and noticed a slight nod.

The most significant issue on Ike's mind was the landing craft. Latest report indicated they only had approximately 85 percent of what they needed. If this trend continued, an early May invasion would be impossible. The planning and logistics difficulties could get worse, or the extra time might allow for solutions. *Nothing to do now but keep buggering on, or KBO, as the PM likes to say.* Ike smiled.

As Eisenhower was thinking, he could see the Prime Minister tapping on his cigar, a sure sign he had something on his mind. He knew Churchill was interested in a quick report about the activities along the eastern border of France. Turning to him, he said, "Prime Minister, you seem to have something you want to say."

"Yes, General, if possible, I would like to have Colonel Betts give us all a short briefing on the situation in eastern France and any progress we may have made toward figuring out what the BR sites are about."

The attention turned to Colonel Betts, and he reached into a folder to retrieve his report. "As you know, we received a report complete with both external and internal photographs of the Kœnigsmacker BR site about two months ago. This report gave us our first insight about the weapon's construction. We also received a series of photographs of tests performed that night, including a series of photos from a reconnaissance plane at two thousand feet." He turned to his assistant. "If we could pass out the copies now."

Betts waited until everyone had their copy before continuing. The report had a copy of the photographs and a summary of Major Dornier's input. "As you can see, the external photographs of the test are very similar to those that were taken last November, except for the higher intensity of the colors. This, along with the longer range, indicates a higher energy output. The ground images correspond well with the aerial photographs. You'll note that one of these photographs shows a stream of energy, which is the dark-orange streak across photograph fourteen. This streak is approximately nine hundred yards long. The target structure, shown in photograph seventeen, was hit and is glowing red. Further analyses of these photographs indicate that another structure was totally destroyed. The target was approximately eight to ten miles from the BR facility, which means the Germans have been able almost to double the effective striking distance."

Eisenhower looked over at General Brawls. "What confidence level do your people place in their analysis?"

"Very high, General, particularly with the aerial photographs. They are high resolution, and it was not difficult to estimate the distances. We're convinced this weapon has been upgraded significantly."

Eisenhower looked at Churchill and then at Montgomery. Even though this weapon wouldn't be active for many months, and problems with the invasion planning would need to be solved first, they all knew their forces would eventually come up against this weapon sometime before the end of the year.

"What exactly are we facing here?" Churchill inquired.

Colonel Betts directed them to the report again. "If you turn to the last page, there is a summary of an invention disclosed by Nikola Tesla around 1900, concerning what he called a particle-beam weapon. It requires high-level energy focused into a narrow beam, which basically can go through almost anything within its range. After our scientists evaluated the interior pictures, it took a while before they were able to draw this conclusion, but now they are all in agreement that somehow the Germans have found a way to construct a particle-beam weapon similar to Tesla's design."

"What does this mean for a modern army, specifically for an armored division?"

"General Bradley, our scientists are now conferring with General Montgomery's staff and yours to understand the destructive potential. It is clear that this beam will reach out and destroy structures and armored vehicles at the range we witnessed in the December test. Further, we assume the Germans will continue to improve this weapon. The one current weakness is that we think it will take eight to ten minutes to power up, which suggests its destructive potential may be limited."

Montgomery leaned back in his chair. "You mean we have a death-ray weapon that can reach out to perhaps ten miles every eight to ten minutes?"

Betts groaned inwardly. Monty was good at repeating things, just to hear his voice. "Yes, sir, but recent reconnaissance of several other sites indicates that the Germans are adding additional generators to all of their BR sites. We don't know exactly how the weapon will use these, but we can estimate that if the Germans are satisfied with the range, it's possible the additional generators could be used to increase the frequency of firing."

Bradley looked at Montgomery and then interrupted him. "So how fast, based on current information, could these weapons fire with the additional generators?"

"Using the information we gathered from tests witnessed in November and early in December, and estimating the number of generators in each facility, we think it is possible the Germans could fire these weapons every sixty seconds, particularly if they are willing to shorten the range to five miles."

There were several mumbled comments around the room as people assimilated this information.

"So we're facing a potentially powerful weapon when we get to eastern France and Belgium?" Eisenhower lit another cigarette and continued. "So we have a plan to neutralize the sites?" He looked to Field Marshal Tedder in charge of the Allied Air Force.

"My staff is also working with scientists as we speak to understand the situation better. We can bomb the sites, but we would have to utilize either small twin-engine bombers or single-engine dive bombers. Neither appears very desirable. We can also interrupt their power supply by cutting the high-voltage lines to the sites. That would more likely be an action for special forces on the ground."

"Colonel Betts, what is MI6's position?"

"Luckily, we don't have to react quickly, so we have time to review our options. Our thoughts now are that interrupting the power supply likely will be the most effective way to reduce the sites' potential. For example, we don't have to interrupt the entire electrical supply, just cut it in half and each of the sites will become much less potent—and it appears as though their defensive positions would not stand up to an armored assault."

"Colonel, please continue working on this in conjunction with General Montgomery's and General Bradley's staffs, and keep Field Marshal Tedder's staff informed." Eisenhower's finger went down the agenda to the next item. "Colonel Betts, the next item is also yours. Any additional intel on the September explosion in eastern Germany?"

"The American scientists have confirmed it was almost certainly a failed nuclear test and most likely a result of impure radioactive material. We thought the Germans had been deprived of all the heavy water after we sunk the ferry in Norway.[4] However, information has come to our attention in the last month that they had already stockpiled a large supply prior to the sinking. We also know that in 1939, they started up a reactor to make the raw materials to create a nuclear explosion but were struggling with the purification processes. The Americans have confirmed that this is one of the most critical aspects in the manufacture of the raw material."

Churchill relit his cigar. "What do we know now about their abilities to purify the material?"

"Unfortunately, not much. We don't even know if the Germans have a nuclear reactor in operation, although we assume they do somewhere. We estimate they could be close to making enough material for a small atomic explosion, but it's unlikely Jerry would be able to manufacture enough to build a more destructive bomb. We also think it would be difficult for them to have mastered the critical purification step in such a short time. So we feel it's highly unlikely they will be able to fabricate any significant weapons fueled with nuclear material."

---

4. In February 1943, a team of SOE-trained Norwegian commandos succeeded in destroying the heavy-water production facility in Norway. As a result, the Germans elected to cease operation and remove the remaining heavy water to Germany. Norwegian resistance forces sank the ferry, SF *Hydro*, on Lake Tinn, preventing the heavy water from being removed.

"Thank you, Colonel, but I'd feel a lot better if we had some backup information. The Tesla beam weapon is enough of a surprise; I don't want to see additional surprises." As soon as Churchill spoke, he realized the Allies lacked the resources to obtain this information. Besides, no one in the room knew anything of Reich Minister Speer's other project.

Mid-April 1944, Lower Special Surveillance Office 8, London

Colonel Gaffney's group had grown by almost another 50 percent since the first of the year. Reports arrived regularly on all fifteen of the BR sites as well as several other areas of high activity along a north-south line through the Ardennes, down south of Verdun.

Alex Ryder had returned the last week of February—now a full lieutenant—after finishing his training at Achnacarry. He had mixed feelings about his assignment, since he had assumed he would be going to Europe immediately following his instruction. However, his orders were to return to his old job. The time in London allowed him and Polly to know each other better, and their feelings had begun to flourish. He had to admit, however, working in this group gave him access to an enormous amount of information others would not typically have. He had pressed Lieutenant Boysden about additional information on the various sites they were studying. Captain Stone and Colonel Gaffney had received it as well.

The entire team had learned to work smoothly over the last six months and was becoming one of the best groups in MI6, although they weren't aware of that. However, General Brawls was aware, and that meant Polly knew. Polly was proud of Alex.

Near Arlon, Belgium

Sergeant Wolfgang Fischer asked the typist to leave the office. He had served with Captain Wilhelm Borne since 1939, the most recent service being on the Eastern Front. He respected the captain but also knew he had a wild temper. The captain was engaged in a phone conversation, probably with someone in OKW, and his voice was growing louder.

"I realize supplies and workforce are inadequate, but do you realize, Colonel, that we have nothing to defend this site with at all? The bunkers are complete, but we have only one MG 42, two mortars, and three men, each with a total of one thousand rounds. This is insane! We were promised—" He abruptly stopped talking to listen. The sergeant could hear him pacing even faster. "Colonel, I'm only informing you of the facts. If you are diverting the supplies and manpower to another site, that is your decision. We will do our best here, but a squad of old women armed with single-shot rifles could take this site!" And with that, he slammed the phone down.

Sergeant Fisher waited to a count of ten before slowly opening the door. The captain was standing, facing his office window, twiddling his hands behind him—a sure sign of irritation. The sergeant stepped inside and softly closed the door behind him.

Captain Borne slowly turned around. "So, Wolfgang, as I'm sure you've heard, the platoon of men, along with the armament and supplies promised, will not be arriving next week. Plans have changed, and everything is going to another facility south of here. The High Command, in all their radiant glory, has decreed that we can hold this site with our existing resources."

The sergeant knew better than to criticize superiors, but even he was shocked. "I suppose we have to trust they have a better understanding of the overall situation, but this borders on desertion by negligence."

"Sergeant, that statement borders on insubordination, and you know it." With a slight pause, he continued. "But you're correct. However, we'll do the best we can with the situation. I believe we have three electricians left that the colonel forgot about. Please dispense the remaining rifles and side arms as you see fit, and begin training everyone, including the secretary."

Sergeant Fisher turned toward the door but then stopped abruptly. "Captain, remember that 'requisition trip' I mentioned a few months back?"

"What about it?"

"Well, I believe we have some additional armament, although completely unofficial."

Captain Borne looked at Fisher closely. "Do I want to ask where you got this material?"

"It would probably be better if you didn't. I can tell you we have one additional MG 42, three thousand rounds for each MG 42, an additional 82 mm mortar with three hundred rounds for each tube, twenty-five antitank Teller mines, and one hundred small anti-personnel mines."

The captain smiled. "What would I do without you, Wolfgang? Continue with training and prepare a plan for a minefield. I'd like to review it in a few days."

"At once, sir."

"Oh, and would you please organize a work party to load all of the steel tubes and their associated equipment on trucks. They'll be arriving in two hours. At least this site will not be used as an experimental proving ground, once we get rid of all that steel."

"That's good news. May I ask where they are sending it?"

"For your ears only, Wolfgang—somewhere outside of Echternach. I guess they want it closer to Germany."

Captain Borne paused and lowered his voice. "You may have noticed a small box, heavy for its size, that arrived last week." The sergeant nodded. "Have it placed in a secure area. I don't want it damaged in any way, and it's not to be opened without my express permission."

The sergeant looked at Borne. "I will see to it myself. Anything I should know about it?"

Borne shook his head slightly. "I was told that it's some kind of new shell that creates a large explosion. It's experimental, which probably means it's not going to work. We need to keep it out of sight for now."

Borne wasn't aware, however—nor was anyone else—that Haigerloch had managed to produce a small sample of U-235, and four shells were fabricated from a preliminary design. Arlon received one of them, and the Butte de Vauquois had received one.

Mid-Afternoon, Same Day, Butte de Vauquois

They had finished the thirty holes and began installing the tubes. Electrical lines and other support equipment still needed to be set in their holes. One of the original pipes had been sent back with no explanation. The corporal made a note.

Without the daily rain, the workers made good progress on all of the excavation, including communication trenches and the larger shallow depressions surrounded by berms. Sergeant Hamming had been able to keep the morale of his platoon up until a second platoon, if you could call it that, arrived in early March. The extra men numbered eighteen, less than half a platoon, but beggars couldn't be choosers. Sergeant Hamming realized the Allies were preparing for an invasion that could happen any day, and he wanted to be ready.

Colonel Dietrich had been traveling extensively during the first four months of 1944. Hamming had overheard enough to realize that there were other sites in eastern France similar to the Vauquois site. Evidently, some of the locations were designed for different weapons, but that didn't concern him. Major Schmidt had disappeared for about ten days in February, probably also traveling to other facilities, and he returned in an extremely foul mood. However, there had been no significant changes to the design of the site work, other than the return of one of the original steel tubes. Shortly after Major Schmidt returned, he was promoted to lieutenant colonel, but it did little to improve his attitude.

Zormaan was down in one of the trenches, checking the measurements, as Hamming walked up. "When are you going to be ready to bury the cables?"

"I have Harrison over at the storage yard with a work party bringing cable back." He looked up at the clouds forming in the northwest. "We have all the trenching and digging done, but we need to get the cable in the ground before any additional heavy rains."

Looking at the steel tubes, Hamming asked, "Are the tube bases installed yet?"

"The concrete should be cured enough to begin installing the tubes tomorrow. We just need the electricians to make sure the connections are completed properly." Zormaan looked up at Sergeant Hamming. "This is a strange device, setting these tubes at different angles and then having electrical connections wired through the base. They almost look like the old mortars that were used in World War I, but they were flexible, and these aren't."

Sergeant Hamming had served with Zormaan for several years and knew him to be not only a loyal German but also an excellent soldier. "I have no knowledge of their purpose, but I agree with you that they look like mortars. These new tubes are much longer than the original ones, and large trench mortars typically don't have to be very accurate, so why the extra length?"

Zormaan continued working. "Regardless, given decent weather, we should have these tubes functional in four weeks."

CHAPTER 24

------- ◆•◆◆◆•◆ -------

April 28, SHEAF Headquarters, London

The conference room was more crowded than usual that morning. The emergency meeting had been called for seven o'clock. The reports of the disaster had first reached Churchill, Eisenhower, and senior staff members at approximately 1:30 a.m. from the command ships via coded radio messages.

There'd been a series of exercises of various sizes, held all over the UK, to practice the tactics needed during the upcoming invasion. One of the largest of these was codenamed Operation Tiger. It involved elements of the Fourth Infantry Division landing from LSTs and other landing craft at Slapton Sands—a beach very similar to Utah Beach in Normandy, where they were scheduled to land in the invasion. Details were unclear, but at least one German E-boat had stumbled across the flotilla of LSTs and had torpedoed an unknown number of ships.

"Admiral, what is the latest status of damaged ships?"

Admiral Ramsey sighed as he looked down at his report. "Right now, at least one LST was seriously damaged and sunk. It appears additional LSTs have also been damaged. An unknown number of naval and army personnel are missing, some presumed dead. The initial estimates are over five hundred."

Churchill immediately asked the question on everyone's mind. "Do we know how many BIGOTS are missing?"

"One lieutenant colonel and one full colonel are not accounted for; they had the BIGOT classification."

Eisenhower took a draw on his cigarette. "Apart from rescuing and tending to the wounded, our highest priority is to determine how many BIGOTS are missing and then determine what paperwork they had on them."

Then he turned to the senior intelligence officer. "I know we were watching the E-boat base at Le Havre. How many boats left that base last night, and how many boats do you estimate were in the channel?"

"Activity around Le Havre was normal. There were three sorties; two of those returned before this incident. There were five sorties the night before, and four returned by dawn. So it is possible that two E-boats were involved."

"Is there any possibility that this was the result of a U-boat?"

"While possible, it's not probable. The explosions were too close together, and there are reports of the sounds and wakes of fast boats in the area."

Admiral Ramsey nodded. "Gentlemen, as silly as this may seem, it may very well be that this is the result of terrible luck. This E-boat may have just blundered into this flotilla. Luckily, it happened in the dark. While I'm sure the German crew is being debriefed as we speak, it's possible the Germans will consider this nothing more than a training exercise of unknown size for the invasion that they are expecting this spring."

Churchill put out his cigar and looked at Ike. "Let's think how we can play this to our network so that we can minimize our damage and maximize Jerry's confusion." Churchill was referring to the Nazi spy network working in the UK that had been completely turned by MI6 two years prior.

"I want all resources possible on identifying the missing BIGOTS and any paperwork they might have had on them. I also want to find the bodies." Eisenhower didn't want to be morbid, but they had to be positive that no critical invasion information had fallen into German hands.

April 30, near Souhesme La Petite, about Eight Miles Southeast of Forêt Domaniale de Lachalade

Colonel Dietrich and Lieutenant Colonel Schmidt were looking at the blueprints of the facility with three engineers from the Todt Organization. Sergeant Havener Varick was studying the prints as well, as he was in charge of this new site. The success of the other fifteen weapons sites had encouraged Berlin to invest in one at the southern end of their defenses. The group had driven out into the field east of the D163.

Earth-moving equipment had been staged at the location the day before. The plans called for the dirt work to begin immediately and to be completed in two days—ambitious but necessary to keep overall construction time to a minimum.

Behind this group huddled around the hood of the vehicle, the surveyors were already completing the layout. The site would be identical to the other weapons sites, except it would incorporate all of the improvements developed over the last eight months.

One of the Todt engineers explained the need for high-voltage lines. "The original plan was to build a site near Lachalade, and the towers have already been erected to support that facility. Moving to this location means we'll have to build additional towers through Forêt Domaniale de Lachalade."

Sergeant Varick had a concerned look on his face that Lieutenant Colonel Schmidt noticed. "Do you have something you want to tell us?"

"Yes, sir. What is the schedule for the voltage lines to arrive here?"

The Todt engineer looked over to one of his assistants. "The line should be here in three weeks, assuming that we finish with the Lachalade terminal in the next three days."

"And the construction of the site should take a little over five weeks, so the line should be here prior to completion."

Colonel Dietrich looked up. "The equipment including the transformers and generators should begin arriving in two and a half weeks, so installation can begin as soon as the buildings are complete."

High-voltage lines would run through Forêt Domaniale de Lachalade, very near the dugout.

They didn't notice the old farm truck on the road on its way to Clermont-en-Argonne.

CHAPTER 25

+ ✦✦✦✦ +

May 1, the Dugout

Major Dornier was lying on his bed, staring at the ceiling—or
more correctly, staring into the dark. Only a small amount of
light filtered in from the ventilation openings. He had been out in the
forest doing reconnaissance the last two days and had decided to run
some evacuation drills since he'd been busy with missions the previous
several weeks. He knew that Alphonse or perhaps Aurélie was scheduled
to show up today with supplies, and he wanted to make sure there was
no sign of German activity. No one had been by for a long time, and
Aurélie hadn't been back at all.

He wanted to run an evacuation drill now since he had not done
one in the dark for over two months. Even though he wasn't looking
forward to the sudden physical exertion, he knew he needed to stay
sharp.

He grasped his flashlight and turned on a stopwatch to time himself.
He went over to the rack where his emergency pack was, slipped his
arms through the shoulder loops, and secured it. He pulled his trousers

on and laced up his boots. He grabbed his rifle and weapons belt and then secured the trapdoor that led up to the dugout.

He looked down at the watch and noted a little over two and a half minutes had passed. He picked up his hat and walked to the back of the cellar, moving through the old World War I steel doors that led to the tunnel network. He closed the doors and rapidly walked straight back in the main tunnel until he reached the junction. He went left and continued for approximately two hundred yards, where it terminated near a ladder. He climbed the ladder, pushed open the trapdoor, and stepped out in the woods. A total of a little over five minutes had elapsed. *Too slow.* He would have to come up with ways to cut at least two minutes off.

He slowly closed the trapdoor again, carefully rearranging the camouflaging vegetation, and secured it behind him as he went down the ladder. He would come back later to ensure the vegetation was correctly arranged.

After removing his equipment and making sure everything was ready again for evacuation, he began washing up. He had turned the water heater off around midnight, so the water was only warm, but that was okay; at least he was not outside in a foxhole with no water to shave. He ran his hand through his hair and made a mental note to ask Alphonse to cut his hair the next time he showed up. He had been cutting it himself and was not pleased with the results.

He prepared a breakfast of potatoes, bacon, and an egg; he decided to splurge this morning as a reward for the evacuation drill. After finishing, he took a cup of coffee up to the dugout and enjoyed the early morning sounds and smells of the forest. This was his favorite time of the day. Everything was peaceful; he could sense the potential of the coming day.

As he was finishing his coffee, he heard the sound of a truck approaching. Even though he recognized the sound as Alphonse's truck, he went down to retrieve his Sten gun and emergency pack. Returning up through the dugout, he moved directly across the forest to a small clump of brush, just as the truck pulled up and stopped. When Alphonse stepped out, he felt a slight jab of disappointment that it was not Aurélie. However, he enjoyed Alphonse's company, and this meant he was better.

Mark cupped his hands and yelled, "Brooklyn."

Alphonse turned in his direction. "Lachalade."

Mark approached, with his Sten gun still leveled but not pointed at the old man. Sadly, in this war, no one could not trust any situation completely. "It is good to see you."

"Bonjour. It is good to be here on such a beautiful morning."

Both men moved to the back of the truck and began unloading the crates and continued until all the supplies were in the dugout. Alphonse offered to help Mark moved the supplies from the dugout into the cellar. Then Alphonse came down, as was his practice, for coffee.

As Mark worked putting the supplies up, Alphonse enjoyed his coffee. "German activity has increased in our area, but we expected that, with the coming invasion."

"I think it will come this month, assuming the Allies have accumulated enough supplies. I guess you can never tell about things like that."

"Luc is becoming more of a problem and has gone out with some local groups in the last month. I have asked him not to become involved with the Resistance, but he is young and thinks he knows best. I finally slowed him down last week, telling him I would approve of him joining a group but only after we've confirmed that the invasion and the Allied advance is moving our way."

"Good point." Mark wondered if he should ask the next question but did anyway. "I assume you will have a way to find out about the invasion status."

Alphonse just looked at him. "I will find out—and will share any information when I get it."

Mark decided to change the subject. "How are the girls doing?"

"Aurélie is fine, but she became ill right after I got better. Being younger, she was able to get well quickly. Josette is our happy girl, but lately, she has been thinking about her fiancé. It's hard on both of the girls to be without the men they loved."

"How long ago did Josette's fiancé disappear?"

"It was the spring of 1941, a Resistance mission that ran across a German patrol. We know that two of the group were captured and executed, but we don't know for sure what happened to Henri."

"The uncertainty can be worse sometimes than anything. I hope she'll keep focusing on the good in the world. This war will be over someday, and while I don't know her, I'm sure she has a great deal to offer."

"And how is your world, monsieur? Do you think our effort to have you here has been worth it?"

Mark thought for a second because he was not allowed to reveal any details. "Yes, and you and your family have been a big part of that."

Alphonse reached into his jacket. "I almost forgot—a message for you."

Mark took the envelope and decided to open it. As he'd expected, it was in code, so he would have to decode it later. He was sure it was another mission to some of the sites he'd already visited.

Alphonse seemed to read his mind. "I have some news that could affect you and this location."

Mark folded the message and looked at Alphonse.

"A friend of mine observed a construction crew in a field east of Souhesme La Petite, southeast of here. After inquiring discreetly, we found out that they have hired some locals to build a facility that apparently will house a group of weapons. They also require high-voltage electricity to this new site. We don't know why, but we do know they will be completing high-voltage lines running from Belgium to just outside Lachalade in the next few days. We'll monitor this carefully, but it is likely they will run the electric lines from there down to this construction site. That means they'll come right through the Forêt Domaniale de Lachalade, probably very near the dugout."

This was not good news, and both men knew it. "Has this been reported back to England yet?"

"I doubt it. While I don't know the schedule for messages, I don't think it'll go back for another day or two."

Mark thought carefully. He wondered if the decoded message would shed some light on this, or if it was merely a request for more information on old sites. He decided he would decrypt the message now, while Alphonse was here, even though the additional time would mean the Germans could spot the truck. "Alphonse, please go up to the dugout and take my rifle. Watch the truck and let me know if anyone comes around. Don't leave the dugout."

As soon as Alphonse was gone, Mark got the codebook and began working on the message. Five minutes later, it was decoded. It was a request for more information from the Butte de Vauquois site. It would require an overnight visit. They also wanted another visit to the Kœnigsmacker site—two more sleepless nights. He thought about what Alphonse had just told him and the orders he held in his hand.

"Come back down."

"No activity or sounds, but I probably should be leaving soon."

"Don't share this with anyone, but can you point out the location of this new construction site?" Mark unrolled a detailed map of the area, and Alphonse pointed to the location. "And you say that it appeared that they would begin construction immediately?"

"Oui, and our information was that construction would be completed as quickly as possible."

"I'm going to visit this new site today and then prepare a report that I want to get back to London. It'll be at the drop point by nine o'clock tonight. I think it's important to get this to London quickly."

Alphonse nodded and started to leave. He turned around at the base of the ladder. "We will also look into their plans for the power lines from Lachalade. If it turns out they are going to come through this area, we will try to bring additional supplies tonight or tomorrow, sometime before their activity could threaten us."

Mark nodded again. "If you come tonight, make it after ten o'clock, and pull the cord that's in the first dugout. That will signal me."

Alphonse nodded and started up the ladder. Mark yelled after him, "Tell Aurélie I hope she is well." Alphonse nodded again and continued up the ladder.

Mark immediately went back to the map and began to plan his approach to this new site. He had to find out if it appeared to be another site similar to Kœnigsmacker or even Vauquois.

The Same Day, East of Souhesme La Petite

The equipment operators were working rapidly to level the construction sites. The surveyors were even helping with the small shovel work. It was apparent that Berlin wanted this site completed quickly, if for no other reason than the fact that Allied planes could see it very clearly from the air.

Sergeant Varick had already requested camouflage netting and the necessary equipment to erect it. Colonel Dietrich had approved and promised to call in the request as soon as he got to a phone that day. Varick knew that this was not a perfect solution, but it would help. The tracks of the heavy equipment in the field would be difficult to hide completely.

Varick also had a squad to defend the site, which he would deploy after sunset, but that would not provide much protection because only two soldiers could be on watch at a given time. His only advantage was that the site was in the middle of relatively flat land with little cover.

2:00 p.m., Same Day, in the Woods East of Brocourt-en-Argonne, near the Intersection of D603 and D163A

Mark was crouched at the southern edge of a small group of trees. He was approximately one mile north of the construction site but was still not close enough to determine what was going on. It'd taken him longer than he thought to move the thirteen miles because he had to traverse open ground in between small wooded areas. He was planning to move south into the trees, just to the east of the D163A. The only dangerous part of his approach would be crossing the A50, a major east-west highway.

After taking a few notes, he started moving south. It was not as bad as he thought because there was little traffic, and when he had to, he could find concealment. When he reached the A50, he sat in the ditch for five or six minutes, listening for traffic patterns. Again, this road wasn't heavily traveled. He checked in all directions for any human activity, and when he was satisfied, he moved across the highway quickly and melted into the woods on the other side.

From that point, he moved east to a small hedgerow that would allow him to get within three hundred yards of the site. It took another hour to maneuver into a good position, and by that time, it was past five o'clock. As he observed the site, he noticed the workers moving toward a portable field kitchen for their evening meal. He took out his telephoto lens and began snapping pictures of the construction crew and heavy equipment. His position was slightly higher than the construction site, so he was able to get an idea of the potential buildings from the cleared land. As he made several sketches, he was careful to estimate distances. It was past six o'clock when he slowly started back up to the hedgerow. He would be late for his nine o'clock report drop.

11:00 p.m., Same Day, the Dugout

Mark finished his report and started toward the drop point. He knew it might not get sent out this evening. It had taken a lot longer to get to the new location than anticipated. As he started to leave the dugout, he heard a truck approaching. He put the report behind a tree and knelt in the dugout. It sounded like Alphonse, but he wanted to be sure.

The truck pulled up and parked, and he could hear someone walking to the first dugout. He pulled the cord, and the signal sounded in the cellar. Mark got up and gave the challenge quietly but loud enough to be heard. A woman's voice returned with the countersign, "Lachalade." It was not Aurélie.

The woman approached, and Mark stayed behind cover in the dugout with his Sten gun leveled at her. As she got closer, he could see she was of similar build and size as Aurélie. "Who are you? Don't move until I can identify you."

"I am Josette, granddaughter of Alphonse and sister of Aurélie."

Mark got up and walked toward her, still keeping the Sten gun on her. "Why are you here?"

Even though he was curt, the woman did not seem upset. "I bring you supplies. Grand-père could not come tonight, and neither could my sister."

Mark felt relieved but remained cautious. "So is Josette single or married?"

"Single, monsieur. I will need your assistance in unloading the supplies. We must do it quickly because there is a German patrol in Les Islettes that we think could come into the woods."

Mark approached her so he could see her better in the dark. She had similar features to Aurélie but light-brown hair as opposed to Aurélie's black hair. "You bear a resemblance to your family. Let's get the supplies in."

They worked quickly over the next fifteen minutes and stacked the supplies in the dugout. Mark opened the trap door and began to move the supplies into the cellar. Without being asked, Josette handed him the crates at the top of the ladder. When they finished, Mark asked her if she would like anything to eat or drink.

"Aurélie said you had hot chocolate." Her eyes were staring at him, but it was obvious she was uncomfortable with the statement.

He tried not to laugh, but couldn't help himself. "Yes, ma'am, and you're welcome to a cup if you would like. You could stay up here or come down in the cellar—your choice." She didn't reply, but she moved toward the ladder.

Mark moved over to the stove and began heating some milk. He poured himself a glass of wine and drank it in one gulp. It'd been a long day.

"You should learn how to appreciate wine rather than drinking it like that."

"You're right; I've had a lot to do today. By the way, thank you for the supplies, and be sure to thank your grandfather as well." Mark indicated for her to sit at the small table.

"Grand-père says you can be trusted. He is one who doesn't trust people easily, so take that as a compliment. My sister said the same thing."

He wanted to ask about Aurélie but somehow didn't think it was a good idea. "Since I just saw your grandfather this morning, I know that everything is okay at your house, except Luc seems to want to fight the Germans before his time."

Josette smiled. "He's young and thinks nothing can happen to him." Then the smile disappeared. "Things happen to everybody in this war."

Mark poured another glass of wine, and this time sipped it slowly. "It's sad. Your grandfather told me your fiancé disappeared three years ago. I'm very sorry. I know that you've lost your brother and your parents, and Aurélie lost her husband. I lost my wife a few years ago, and there's still a hole in my life."

"We go on and try to focus on the good, although the longer the war goes on, the less good there is to focus on."

Mark made the hot chocolate and set the mug in front of Josette. She took a sip, and her face lit up. "It's been so long."

"I believe Aurélie said your mother used to make it for you on cold days."

She looked at him thoughtfully. "It reminds me of happier times."

"Well, perhaps if this war would end, we could all spend some happy time together."

They continued to talk for another thirty minutes, and Mark was surprised at how easy it was to speak with this young woman he had only just met. As they finished their drinks, Josette went up the ladder, and Mark followed her to the truck. He retrieved the report on the way.

"Would you give this to your grandfather when you return, and ask him if it can be transmitted as soon as possible?"

Josette held out her hand and took the report, and then she reached for his hand and squeezed it. "Please be careful. There may be more German activity in these woods soon."

Mark watched as she got in the truck and then left. It was past midnight, and he was drained, but for some reason, he felt a new energy inside. He would have to plan his next trip to the Butte and Kœnigsmacker quickly. Hopefully, Alphonse could find out about the route of the new power lines soon.

CHAPTER 26

+ ◆◆◆ +

May 5, SHEAF Headquarters

Eisenhower was splitting his time between London and the new invasion headquarters at Southwick House in Portsmouth. While most of the time he journeyed back and forth in a car, he had taken a small plane today. Earlier, after a meeting with his top advisers and staff, he made yet another difficult decision. The Allies would not invade France in May, despite the favorable weather. There were several reasons for the delay, but the overriding factor was to give Higgins more time for fabricating invasion craft.[5] The Allies' success in the Pacific had placed heavy pressure on the allocation of craft suitable to bring troops and equipment onto a beach. Finally, Operation Fortitude, which was an effort to make the Germans believe that Patton would lead the invasion at Calais, so far was working very well. *I hope George can keep his mouth shut.*

Also on his mind were the BR sites. Even though it was clear they housed a new type of beam weapon, they still hadn't figured out the

---

5. The landing craft, or Higgins boat, was used extensively in amphibious landings in World War II. The craft was designed by Andrew Higgins in Louisiana.

best way to neutralize them. The Germans had selected their locations well, and they were going to be in the path of the Allied advance into Germany. Something would have to be done—and quickly. Even though the projections showed that the Allied armies would reach these locations ten to twelve weeks after the invasion, Ike knew those projections were optimistic. However, he knew a practical plan for neutralization of these sites was required soon so that the necessary resources to execute it could be assigned.

The BR sites and the nuclear threat—I wonder how many other unknown threats the Germans have up their sleeves?

May 11, near Butte de Vauquois

Just as Alphonse and Josette had warned, German activity in the area had increased dramatically over the past week. The electrical line the Germans were constructing between Lachalade and the new BR site just east of Souhesme La Petite was cutting through the forest about one mile southwest of Mark's location. He had been careful not to have any fires or engage in any activity that might reveal his presence. This also restricted the use of any equipment in the dugout that emitted noise or fumes. He did his cooking only after a quick reconnaissance of the area, and even then, it was just a couple of times a week. He was still relatively comfortable because he could reheat food using sterno in the cellar.

He had left the dugout late last night, traveling to the Butte. He arrived around four in the morning, just before it started getting light. While England was on double summer time, France and all of Europe weren't.

Mark had managed to move close to the construction area. The Germans had placed a few guards around the perimeter but were clearly not expecting anyone to pry. Mark continued to scan the location with his binoculars, making notes of the tube placement as well as the support equipment.

Looking at his watch, he saw that it was just past four thirty, and he knew from past practice that the guards would congregate near the field stove for coffee just after sunrise.

Sure enough, shortly before five o'clock, the two guards started walking toward the field stove, which was two hundred yards away. As they left, Mark slowly approached the site, moving to one of the tubes. His curiosity of what these tubes were for was just as great as London's. He could see from his position that there were over twenty-five, and they were buried in the ground at different angles. The tubes protruded above ground approximately two feet, which meant they were at least ten feet below ground.

As he slowly crawled toward one of the tubes, he began taking photographs while making a note of the trenches and other support equipment. Ten meters away from the pipe he was approaching, he came across a noticeable depression about three and a half feet deep, with a thick berm around the edge. *Ammunition storage*, he thought and snapped a picture. When he reached the tube, he took a quick measurement of the diameter and thickness of the metal. With the help of his flashlight, he looked down the pipe and could see contacts at the bottom. What could they be? Perhaps an ignition system for shells or rockets? He snapped pictures of the interior of the tube, using his flashlight to illuminate the inside of the tube, always looking toward the field tent to make sure he wasn't discovered.

He visited two more tubes, documenting the different angles and the support facilities. One of the pipes was only a few feet from two large trees, which afforded him cover. He took advantage of this location to complete his notes and recheck the figures he had collected. After that, he slowly stood up and took four photos, overlapping them to make a panoramic view. Looking at his watch, he saw it was a few minutes before six o'clock. It was time for him to leave. Work parties would be arriving in a few minutes. He slowly crawled back approximately one hundred yards into some trees before he felt it was safe to walk.

As he started the seven-mile hike back to the dugout, his mind went over what he had seen. Even though it didn't make any sense, he thought this site was going to support large-diameter mortars of some type. Large-diameter siege mortars had been used in World War I but were not popular now because of their weight and lack of mobility. While it still might make sense for defensive positions, why put them on a ridge like this? It would be an easy target for an air attack, especially with smaller bombers.

A little over three hours later, he was moving through the southern part of Forêt Domaniale de Haute Chevauchée. The last part of his journey would be slower because of the recent German activity. Even though the route of the power lines was about a mile south of his position, the Germans had extended patrols throughout both Forêt Domaniale de Haute Chevauchée and Forêt Domaniale de Lachalade. He had encountered a German vehicle as he was crossing the L'Aire River, which reminded him that he needed to be more alert. He followed one of the small tributaries east that led into the forest, the Ravin de Cheppe. While there were no paths to follow, the ravine would provide more cover and get him within a quarter mile of the dugout.

A little past noon, he chose a spot with good cover and decided to have something to eat. He went over his report again, making small corrections and preparing it for packaging and transmittal. That done, he leaned back on the incline and listened to the sounds of the forest. So far, this had been a lonely assignment, but he enjoyed the countryside— up to a point. Each time he stopped to appreciate the sights and smells of the forest, however, he was glad that he had accepted the assignment. His thoughts drifted briefly to Alphonse and his family, particularly Josette and Aurélie. Their lives were easier than for most in France but still hard, even compared to his existence. At least he did not own a home in danger, nor did he have any family that could be threatened.

He got up and began the last part of his walk. He wanted to put the report and film in the drop location this afternoon and then prepare for his next trip to the Thionville- Kœnigsmacker area. He needed to check out the pod to make sure it was ready for the trip. He wasn't looking forward to going back, but he knew any additional information he could obtain would be valuable. It would be another two sleepless nights. At least he had a shelter in which to return, and sleeping in the pod was better than sleeping on the ground, particularly since he was expecting rain over the next several days.

CHAPTER 27

<hr>

Mid-May, Lower Special Surveillance Office 8, London

Captain Stone had called a staff meeting earlier in the morning to discuss the overall situation and how all the new reports related to each other, especially at the Butte de Vauquois. Over the past few days, they had received new aerial reconnaissance photos indicating the progress of the construction sites. They revealed that thirty tubes were buried and that the support structures for them were very close to completion. Also confirmed by a report from the mess corporal was that the site was almost operational. He reported the tubes looked as though they were a mortar weapon. He had witnessed a test a few days earlier. His report had suggested that the range of the mortars was anywhere from one mile up to eight miles. The description of the shell impact, however, was confusing. He had described a midair explosion that had evidently dispersed fuel, perhaps gasoline, and then ignited the mixture. The resulting explosion was not very loud, but it created a giant fireball.

Major Dornier's report had been received early yesterday and confirmed that there were indeed approximately thirty tubes, all buried at different angles. It was also clear from his photographs and notes that the tubes were a mortar weapon. What was unclear was how the shells would be loaded and detonated. The construction of the pipes, especially the metal thickness, meant that the mortars would have a limited life before the pipe would crack.

Lieutenant Boysden was talking with Lieutenant Ryder to get his opinion on the facts they had to this point. "What I don't understand is why the Germans would invest this much effort in a static defense position when clearly they need a mobile defensive line."

Alex thought for a minute and then offered a thought. "Some of the communications we've intercepted indicate that Hitler may be influencing some of these decisions. For example, we know that he has issued 'no retreat or withdrawal' orders several times in the war, particularly on the Eastern Front. These kinds of installations may reflect that kind of thinking."

"We know of at least ten similar sites."

"We should ask the Resistance to gather more information about all of the sites. One concern is that while they are trying to camouflage the sites, they're not doing an effective job hiding the construction from us. This means they have to realize that the sites will be easy targets from the air."

Captain Stone walked in. "I have to brief Colonel Gaffney in two hours. What do you have for me?"

Boysden handed him a folder. "This is what we have right now, but we will have a more thorough summary in about an hour, complete with photographs."

Stone opened the folder and perused it quickly. "So the obvious question is, why are they building this in plain sight? At least several of these facilities are contructed that way. It just doesn't make sense." He paused for a second, thinking. "It worries me because I think we're missing something."

Alex handed Captain Stone a second folder. "This is a summary of the BR sites. Most of them appear to be very close to operational. A senior German officer has been seen at several of the sites in the last three weeks, possibly a general. We've also documented the presence of a Colonel Dietrich at the sites. He's been put in charge of this effort, as opposed to the 'tube' sites."

"Interesting. None of these facilities seems capable of seriously slowing any broad front advance, but they certainly can inflict quite a bit of damage."

"Yes, sir, and we also know that Reich Minister Albert Speer seems to be heavily involved in the BR program."

"Boysden, did Major Dornier's visit to Thionville a few days ago yield any additional useful information?"

"The visit occurred when the site was completely inactive. There was little additional information, other than that an unidentified major was interested in the defense measures around the site."

"A shame. We could use more information, but we need to be careful about how many visits we make. We don't want to raise suspicions. Keep working on the summaries, and I'll be back in about an hour."

Captain Stone was correct about the tube sites. He didn't realize, however, that production failures in Germany had caused one program to be refocused, and that affected the other sites. While it was understandable, their attention to this detail had caused him to overlook the important fact that one of the tubes in each of these sites had been built to the original specifications—to handle a much more substantial weapon.

May 18, Forêt Domaniale de Lachalade and the Dugout

It was a beautiful morning. Mark rose before sunrise to do an equipment check and run an evacuation drill. He knew that he would be able to escape using the tunnel system; the only unknown was diverting dogs, should the Germans decide to use them. He didn't think that was probable unless he gave the Germans hard evidence of his presence. Before he left England, SOE had prepared several small rockets similar to US commercial fireworks containing sealed liquid vials and scraps of old clothing that he had worn. The vials had a combination of sweat and urine. The rockets would be fired in different directions—their range was only a quarter mile to a half mile. They would distribute his scent in different areas while he stayed stationary, hopefully confusing the dogs.

He also had the emergency packs he'd placed in the forest that would give him additional food, ammunition, and medical supplies should he ever be separated from the dugout.

He was drinking coffee in the dugout when he heard a truck approach. The Germans had driven by this location several days earlier, but this didn't sound like one of their trucks; it sounded like Alphonse. But what was he doing in the forest with this much German activity?

Sure enough, it was Alphonse's truck, only this time it pulled off the road and into a clump of brush. He and Alphonse had prepared this area to hide the truck. He kept his Sten gun leveled until the driver got out. It was Josette. He waited while she unloaded a crate and started toward the dugout. He called out the challenge, and she responded correctly. He went over to help her. He was worried. "What are you doing here? With all the German activity, this is not a good idea."

"Grand-père said the same thing, but Aurélie and I felt it was necessary."

"Let's get the things unloaded quickly."

It only took a few minutes to unload the rest of the crates. Once they had moved containers into the cellar, Josette moved to the ladder and then paused. "Luc and Aurélie went out early this morning and saw German patrols well south of here. They won't be back in this area today." She continued to look at him, apparently hoping for some response.

Mark was a little confused, but he had to admit that visits from this family had become an essential part of his life. "Don't get me wrong; I enjoy each of the visits that your grandfather, Aurélie, and you have made—not just the supplies but the visit itself. However, it's becoming increasingly risky."

She looked down at the floor with a slightly amused expression. "Could I have some chocolate? The trips may be risky, but the chocolate makes it worthwhile."

Only Josette. "Josette DeBoy! You risk coming here for hot chocolate?"

She sat down at the table, looking at him. "Not just for the hot chocolate but the visit." She clearly wanted to talk. "Please let me stay for a while."

Something in the way she acted tugged at him, which caused him to go against his better judgment. He turned around and began to heat some milk while putting up the rest of the supplies.

"I just want to be around someone outside my family. Don't misunderstand; I love them, but sometimes I tire of their company."

Mark stopped working for a second and turned. "I know the feeling. I love being out here in the forest, but sometimes it's nice to talk to someone"—he faced her, smiling—"even if it's against my better judgment."

She smiled and watched as he continued organizing the supplies. She walked over to the stove and stirred the milk.

Mark brought the empty crates over to the base of the ladder so they could be loaded back on the truck later. He included some canned food and some other basic medical supplies that he knew they would not be able to obtain. He also added a small packet of cocoa and sugar, but he didn't tell Josette.

As he worked, he looked over at her. "Do you know about the old farmhouse near here with the garden?"

"Naturally. It's our main garden plot."

"The house looks in good shape; it's just old. Who used to live there?"

"It's where my parents first lived and started their family."

He was just about to ask more when he looked over at the stove. "The milk is about ready."

Mark went over to the shelf with the cocoa and sugar, but Josette reached up and took it down herself. It caught Mark off guard, and he bumped into her. It was only a small bump, but he had not been that close to a woman in several years.

Josette turned to face him. "I know how to make hot chocolate; in fact, I think the French invented it."

Mark could not help but laugh at her sense of humor. "I'm sure they did. They invented almost everything that tastes or smells good."

Josette started making the cocoa and then continued about the old farmhouse. "So when the threat of war became strong, and Mère and Père were killed, we moved down to the farmhouse with Grand-père. He was living there alone and needed the help." She sipped her chocolate. "We closed up the house and tried to make sure that it didn't deteriorate too much over time. We thought that one of us would move back someday after marriage. We have a lot of good memories there."

They talked into the early afternoon. Mark heated some pork, and Josette insisted on frying some potatoes and cooking string beans. They enjoyed a nice lunch, which included a bottle of Alphonse's red wine. When it came time for her to leave, he carried the containers back to the truck and then insisted on a couple of minutes of silence to ensure there was no activity nearby. After Mark listened, he satisfied himself they were alone. He wanted to make sure it was safe. He turned around to find her standing immediately in front of him, looking up.

"I enjoyed our visit, and I'm glad I took the risk." She looked at him as if expecting some response.

It threw Mark off guard. He had not felt this way in a long time. "I ... enjoyed it also, but I wouldn't want anything to happen to you or your family. Please be careful in the future."

She seemed happy he had enjoyed her company; in fact, more than happy. "Thank you, monsieur. I will be careful, but I will also come to visit again." She smiled and got in the truck. He helped guide her as she backed out of the brush and went out on the road, and he watched the truck disappear around the bend.

Why did he feel like this? Now he missed not only Aurélie but her sister as well. *I've been up here too long.*

CHAPTER 28

─── ✦✦✦✦ ───

May 20, Haigerloch Nuclear Reactor

Albert Speer finished reviewing the latest production report for Haigerloch as his car pulled through the front gate of the reactor complex. Kurt Diebner had alerted him to the problems a week ago. Production of U-235 material had fallen sharply since early February. While the measures Diebner instituted had initially increased production, the removal of the safety protocols had resulted in the workers getting sick at a faster rate than they had initially projected. He had tried several different approaches, even shutting the reactor down at the end of March to install additional shielding. This helped considerably, and production figures began to rise. However, it was evident that the production of U-235 was going to be much lower than initially projected.

Diebner walked out to greet Speer as his car pulled in. "Welcome, Herr Reich Minister. I assume you would like an immediate briefing?"

"Let's go to your office."

Diebner led the way with Speer by his side. As they entered his office, Speer closed the door and took a seat at the small table. Diebner had laid a folder on the table with the latest report from the day's production.

Speer opened the folder and reviewed the figures. "So the shielding is helping, but the efficiency hasn't recovered to its January levels?"

"No, sir, and after troubleshooting the last several weeks, it appears that the installation of the shielding may be interfering with the reactor. While we can remedy that, it would mean another three to four weeks of lost time. My recommendation would be to continue at the lower efficiency."

"I see that you have 2.1 kilograms of material produced and purified. This is at 92 percent; is that correct?"

"Yes, the improvement in the purification process has greatly enhanced our ability to purify the material. Of course, that means a higher yield from any weapon."

"So you are projecting now the end of September before we could have ten kilograms of material?"

"Yes, sir." He pulled out a chart from his desk. "Here is an updated estimate for production over the next three months. You will see that we could meet our target by the middle of August, but that assumes no additional problems. In my frank opinion, Reich Minster, it would not be wise to base production figures on that assumption."

Speer closed the folder and looked at Diebner. "There may be a shift in our projected use for this material. You are to say nothing about this conversation to anyone. Is that clear?"

Diebner nodded. "Absolutely."

"Because of issues in other areas of our weapons program, I think this material might be better used in smaller quantities for antiaircraft rockets. I have a team working on the design of a warhead, but I will need to involve the rocket boys to see if it's feasible to place a small warhead on a rocket and send it up approximately eleven thousand meters."

Diebner looked at Speer and considered what he had just said. "I assume you would use much less material in that type of warhead. It certainly would stretch the material that we can make to maximum efficiency, assuming a rocket can be fabricated to deliver it."

"These are the preliminary plans for the warhead." Speer took a folder out of his briefcase and handed it to Diebner. "I want you to put your team on this, and I expect your comments on the design in a week. If this is to be successful, we need to start fabricating parts of the warhead immediately. Of particular importance is its total weight and shape. When I return to Berlin today, I will meet with the head of the rocket program for antiaircraft weaponry." Speer paused. "Do you know of Major General Dr. Walter Dornberger?"

"Herr Reich Minister, I've heard the name, but I didn't realize we had an antiaircraft rocket program."

"The Führer just created one in January and placed General Dornberger in charge. So, do you see a problem in reviewing the design and producing your comments in a week?"

"I will place Friede and Korner in charge as soon as you leave. They are not only my best, but they are also quite practical and work together well. Korner's engineering ability complements Friede's scientific expertise. We'll have comments for you within the week."

"Excellent. And now I must return to Berlin. I would like to stay for lunch, but there is no time." Speer got up and, after taking Diebner's salute, went out to his car. He would get back to Berlin in midafternoon and go directly to see General Dornberger.

May 22, Ploesti R&D Facility, Romania

The refinery manager and the head of the R&D facility were sitting across from Speer, along with the production manager for this program.

"Gentlemen, I'm glad to see the production is ahead of schedule and that we have finally delivered all the raw materials that you require. Are there any other issues you need to bring to my attention?"

The production manager referred to the production chart. "No sir, as you can see, we're approximately 20 percent ahead of schedule."

Speer smiled and looked at the refinery manager. "In that case, can we divert another one million liters of gasoline to this program?"

The refinery manager tensed, giving thought to his reply. "We can do another 250,000 liters. One million would cause shortages in the strategic fuel supply unless we delayed the additional 750,000 until early August."

"I appreciate your candor and cooperation, Ernst. I believe that the casing production will approximately parallel that schedule." He looked at the production manager. "Is that accurate?"

"Reich Minister, we can keep that schedule."

"Excellent. I want your engineers to review these plans for a different type of casing and have your comments back to me in two days." Speer passed a folder across the table that had the external dimensions and specs for the proposed nuclear rocket warhead. "Those are for your eyes only and those of your team. Please restrict access to this material."

With that, Speer stood up. "Gentlemen, thank you for your service. I appreciate your efficiency." Speer walked out of the office to return to Berlin. With the mortar sites complete and the potential additional fuel shells, this part of the program might prove more beneficial than he had anticipated. Now, if he could get a decent design for the nuclear warhead, he might be able to integrate these two weapon systems with the Tesla sites. His earlier meeting with General Dornberger had gone well, and Werner von Braun was in charge of creating a preliminary rocket design for the warhead by as early as tomorrow.

CHAPTER 29

✦ ✦ ✦ ✦ ✦

June 3, Southwick House, Invasion Headquarters

General Eisenhower was walking from his trailer that served as his personal quarters into Southwick House for another meeting with the invasion staff. Everyone, including Ike, was remembering the summerlike weather in May and comparing it with the current stormy weather. An earlier discussion with Captain Stagg indicated that an invasion date of June 5 might not be feasible.

As he walked the short distance to the house, he felt the wind gusts and knew that, unless they subsided quickly, sending the fleet across the channel would be foolhardy. General Omar Bradley joined him, and the two men continued in silence, both realizing that the weather appeared to be conspiring against them.

They entered Southwick House and went to the conference room, where people were starting to gather. Admiral Ramsey walked up to Eisenhower and asked to speak with him privately.

"Ike, it doesn't appear very positive, but we'll listen to what Captain Stagg's team has to tell us. I've had reports from three craft in the channel, and it appears as though both the wind and the seas are getting worse."

Eisenhower listened and nodded quietly. "Let's see what the meteorologists have to tell us."

June 4, the Dugout

Major Dornier carefully made his way to the area with the new high-voltage lines. He'd received several supply drops in this area and wanted to be positive there was no evidence left for the Germans to find.

The Germans had made rapid progress through the woods, being careful not to remove many trees. A quick visit toward the new BR site near Souhesme La Petite last week had confirmed that the power lines had reached that facility and were apparently energized. They had been very careful to keep the towers crossing open areas, next to regular power lines, making them less conspicuous. This was a bit of risk because the wires were not elevated as much as they should have been, but the positive was that from the air it would be difficult to differentiate them from regular power lines.

As he walked along the corridor for the new power lines, he realized they would be completely hidden from the air. The Germans had trimmed a few branches along the route, gambling that the trees would not interfere with the lines. He made a note to send a report that evening with the sketch he made of the completed corridor.

Satisfied that the Germans had left the area—for the time being—he returned to the dugout. Alphonse was due to come back this evening for resupply, and he wanted to have his report ready at the drop point before he arrived. Remembering the feeding point he had created about a quarter mile west, he turned to check it. *Might as well see if I've snagged anything.*

He had also set out traps and snares. As he approached the area, he saw that he had snared two rabbits and trapped several squirrels. There was no large game in the area now, but it was apparent that one of the boars had developed an interest in the feed. He threw out some additional food scraps and started back to the dugout with the rabbit and squirrel; he was thinking about making a stew. It would go well with the cooler weather that had blown in last night. He wondered briefly what the weather would be like over the channel, but he had no way of knowing. He knew, however, the invasion could not be far off.

As he approached the dugout, he took his standard precautions, circling carefully about a quarter mile away, looking for any sign of human activity. After seeing nothing, he decided to get inside; it had started drizzling. The heavy, overcast sky in the late afternoon had created a damp and gloomy atmosphere.

Mark cleaned the game and prepared it for cooking. He disposed of the carcasses in a waste hole about two hundred yards from the dugout. Then he browned the meat and started the stew in a large pot. It would take another two hours to cook, so he started to lie down; then he realized he should clean up. It'd been two days since his last opportunity to bathe. *It is nice to have a shower.*

Mark was cleaning the sniper rifle when he heard the truck approaching. He went up quickly to listen and relaxed when he realized it was the sound of Alphonse's truck. Always on alert, however, he put on his emergency pack and had his Sten gun at the ready. The vehicle immediately pulled off the road and into the concealment area. He had moved thirty yards east of the dugout when he saw Josette get out. He smiled to himself, realizing that he wanted to see Aurélie or her rather than their grandfather.

He shouted the challenge, and she yelled back the countersign. He came out and walked down to the truck to help her unload. It was still drizzling, so they worked quickly. It was after seven o'clock when they got everything into the cellar.

"Would you like to stay and eat before you go back?"

"It smells good. What is it?" She moved over to the stove and took the lid off. "Rabbit and …"

"A little squirrel; it makes for a change. So?"

She smiled. "Yes."

She sat down, and Mark put a bowl of stew in front of each of them and then opened a bottle of wine. "Would you like some water as well?"

She nodded, and they ate their stew in relative silence.

When Mark looked up, she was staring at him. "Is there something wrong with the stew?"

She shook her head. "I was just wondering what causes a man to accept an assignment like this."

Mark just looked at her for a minute, wondering why she had asked. "Well … I guess it just happened. I was doing another job in London, and before I knew it I'd been selected for training and then offered this mission. I suppose like everyone in this war, I felt like I should do what I could, but I will admit that I had some doubts about something this intense."

She continued to stare. "But you didn't have to come. We have no choice here; this is our country, but you had a choice."

He exhaled slowly. "You should understand that there is a great concern in the free world for what is happening in Europe. You don't get an opportunity to hear all that happens, but I can tell you that the Allies—particularly England and America—want the Nazis out of the occupied countries. While it's true we could ignore this, all we would do is delay the inevitable. We know that they won't stop until they have occupied the rest of the world."

"I don't know what you do here, and you shouldn't explain it, but it seems that having one person out here alone for so long is not a good thing."

"I suppose it could look that way, but there was quite a bit of talk about the conditions of the mission before the final selection. I admit sometimes I get lonely, but most of the time I don't mind being alone. I think I mentioned that I lost my wife several years ago, and that changed my perspective on life. It made me realize bad things can happen and that I should try to contribute what I could while I'm able."

Josette continued eating. Mark got up and brought a wedge of cheese over and poured more wine. As she ate the cheese, she looked over at him, watching him clean the bowls at the sink. "Did you enjoy being married?"

Mark wondered why all the questions. "Joanne was my best friend, and yes, I enjoyed all of the time we had together. We also enjoyed raising our children."

Mark finished cleaning up and returned to the table. He cut off a piece of cheese, and he drank a glass of wine—slowly—and smiled. "See? I remembered your admonishment from last time. You're right; wine is almost like a living person, something to be enjoyed slowly."

She leaned forward and smiled. "That sounds more like a Frenchman than an American."

"Learning a language helps you understand the culture, and the French have developed a unique viewpoint on living. It should be shared with more people"—he smiled briefly—"which is one of the reasons I accepted this mission."

"Monsieur, I think you're making fun of me now."

He shook his head. "I hope you won't mind the comparison, but you and your sister share many physical traits. You both have beautiful smiles, but you have a disposition that makes it easy to talk with you."

While Josette did not particularly want to hear a reference about Aurélie right then, she could not suppress another smile. Mark looked directly at her and smiled as well. They continue talking until it was almost dark. It was still drizzling and overcast when they walked back to the truck. Mark had given her the rest of the stew to take back. She had brought him a bottle of French liquor made from apples. He opened the door of the truck and helped her in. She leaned out of the window and quickly kissed him on the cheek. "Take care, Mr. Mark. I enjoy our conversations."

Mark nodded and helped her back out and get on the road. He watched the truck go around the bend. As soon as the vehicle disappeared, he turned back to the dugout but couldn't deny a feeling of loneliness.

CHAPTER 30

June 6, Berlin OKW Headquarters

Jodl was pacing back and forth. Several of the senior generals were insisting that he inform the Führer of the Allied landings.[6]

"The Führer is sleeping and has left strict instructions not to be disturbed. He was up late last night."

Several of the staff turned away and rolled their eyes. Someone in the back of the room stated what everyone was thinking. "The Allies are in Europe, and we're giving the Führer a couple more hours of sleep! That doesn't seem wise."

Jodl turned and confronted the group. "You are more than welcome to wake him if you'd like." He walked out of the room without addressing anyone else.

Albert Speer was just as upset as everyone else in the room, but for a different reason. The Führer should know of all of the developments of the past several hours, and the army should be responding, even now. This, however, was not his primary concern. As armament minister, he needed to make sure that all of the manufacturing locations in the Reich

---

6. The Allies landed at Normandy on June 6.

were secure and well defended. Luckily, he had gone over several of his programs just last week, and most of them were progressing nicely. The nuclear program was the only exception, and it worried him because it was an essential part of the overall defense of the fatherland. He made a note to visit all of the Tesla sites, beginning tomorrow.

June 7, the Dugout

Mark was returning from a quick excursion to the eastern part of the forest. The late-morning sun filtered through the trees, giving the woods a mottled appearance. He had just dropped into the old World War I trench about a hundred yards from his dugout when he caught a glimpse of motion through the trees. It looked like something was on the road, but he wasn't sure. He moved behind a tree, knelt down, and carefully looked around, listening and watching for any additional movement.

He could hear faint noises along the road. He thought about where he was in relation to the dugout and what he had on him in the way of supplies and ammunition. He was carrying his sniper rifle instead of the Sten gun, which he regretted. If somehow the Germans were coming to challenge his position, he would have preferred to have the Sten gun, but he had to work with what he had.

A female voice drifted through the trees: "Lachalade." Mark froze; it sounded like Josette, but she was not to use that challenge without a follow-up within thirty seconds. He waited until he heard *"Apremont"*; he relaxed momentarily, as that was the sign that she was not under duress. He had a good view through the brush of the dugout and saw Josette approaching it. She disappeared inside and then momentarily came back out, looking around.

He decided to wait a few minutes and see what developed. He wasn't sure how she had arrived because he hadn't heard the truck. He slowly moved to within twenty-five yards of the dugout and watched her as she walked down the road to the south. He was convinced she was alone, but why she decided to show up unannounced was a concern.

He yelled out the challenge, and she returned with the countersign. He came walking down the slope behind the dugout toward her.

"Why didn't you answer earlier?" There was palpable tension in her voice.

"Josette, you know I have to be careful, and you aren't supposed to be here. What's wrong?" He could see she was keyed up about something.

She strolled toward him and then ran and threw her arms around him tightly. "We heard this morning that the Allies have landed in northern France." She looked up at him. "They have finally come back."

He could feel her shaking with emotion and put his arms around her as well, even though he was confused as to why they were in this embrace. She stepped back and that's when he noticed she was wearing a dress. "Why in the world are you dressed like that?"

Her face fell. "I thought it was appropriate, given the circumstances." She hesitated for just a second and then added, "And I wanted to wear it for you."

Mark was taken aback and didn't know how to respond. "You look very nice. I apologize. It's been a long time since I've seen a woman in a dress." He motioned for them to go back to the dugout. "How did you get here," he asked quietly.

"I rode our bicycle. Luc has the truck in the village."

"Did you see any German activity on the way here?"

"Nothing. Grand-père was in the village last night, and the talk was that most of the Germans moved to the camp at Sainte-Menehould. I think they are trying to organize their efforts in response to the Allied landings."

They started walking toward the dugout, and Mark caught a whiff of perfume. "You smell good. Perfume?"

She looked down and then turned to him. "Aurélie and I saved a small amount from before the war. Do you like it?"

Mark just smiled and decided it would be better to remain quiet at this point. When they got to the dugout, he invited her down to the cellar for some coffee. "I think you should go down first with the dress."

He set the coffee on the table after wiping down one of the stools.

She was carrying a large bag, and she reached in brought out an envelope. "This message came last night. It probably has to do with the landings."

He reached over, opening the envelope carefully, noting that it not been tampered with. He saw no reason to delay decrypting, and he retrieved his decoding book. Josette sipped her coffee as he worked on the message, which took about ten minutes to decode. There was no mention of the landings, but there was a code phrase indicating that the landings would be imminent. Not surprisingly, it was a request to visit several of the weapons sites and gather more information. The first mission was to go to the BR site east of Souhesme La Petite. Then he was to recheck Koenigsmacker, followed by Butte de Vauquois. He was to pay special attention to any of the tubes that looked different, including their installation. This would be a hectic week, but at least he was permitted to use the French Resistance fighters to go to Thionville.

"More work for me, but I guess it's better than just sitting around."

"When do you think we will be liberated?"

Mark smiled because he knew it would be many months before the Allies would be able to fight their way across France. "I think it'll be a while. The Germans have built up a considerable defense system, especially in northern France, and I think it will take a huge effort to get this far east."

"Do you think there will be many battles in this area? I only ask because I don't want to see our country torn apart."

Mark knew little about strategy and tactics, other than what he could deduce from common sense. He knew that battles would be fought around high points and road junctions, but the general area surrounding Lachalade did not seem to hold many vital positions, except for BR sites like the one east of Souhesme La Petite. He suspected if the high-voltage power supply to that site could be interrupted, it would not be much of a defense point. As he looked at Josette, he realized he needed to look at the towers and come up with a plan to bring some of them down.

"I think the armies will fight around important points, like hills and major road junctions. It's hard to say, but I suspect that there may be fighting northwest of here and further east but perhaps not large battles in this valley."

Josette looked down at her bag and then up at Mark. "I brought some bread and a little of Grand-père's special cheese. If you want, we could go down the road to a little clearing in front of some of the tunnel entrances and have a small picnic."

Mark was surprised but somehow wanted to do as she asked. "I'm not sure that's a good idea. This message is asking me to gather additional information, which will take several days. I probably should begin preparations immediately."

As soon as he said it, he could tell Josette was disappointed. She looked at him and said in a hushed voice, "I'd like to do it if you could spare a couple of hours."

Mark thought for a minute. He would have liked to spend more time with Josette, but somehow he felt a little uncomfortable. However, in the final analysis, another few hours wouldn't make any difference. "I can. I've always had a hard time saying no to a pretty woman."

Josette could tell he wanted to spend time with her, and she struggled to tone down her response. "Perhaps we could use some of your sausage and smoked meats?"

"And of course, a bottle of wine." Mark couldn't help smiling at her.

Mark showed Josette where the food was. While she was loading her bag, he laid out some of his equipment and ammunition, careful not to bring out the cameras. *No sense exposing her to information that could be dangerous.*

Josette went back up to retrieve something from her bicycle. Mark finished his preliminary equipment check and started up the ladder, just as she was coming down.

Mark looked up just in time and started back down. "Sorry. I was thinking about something else."

Josette looked down, which caused her to miss a step. "Oh! Mark!" she squealed. As she started to fall, Mark reached up to catch her. He had both hands on her waist, but unfortunately, one of his hands was under her dress. As soon as she was stable, he realized where his hand was and quickly removed it.

"Why don't you come on up and bring the bag?"

Mark went up the ladder to the dugout, clearly embarrassed. "Forgive me. I didn't mean to … I mean … I was just trying to keep you from falling."

Josette laughed and grabbed his free arm. "Mr. Mark, I know you're a gentleman." She looked up at him and smiled. "And besides, it wasn't unpleasant."

Mark thought it best if they started down the road. Why was he always caught off guard with her?

Josette had linked her arm inside his as they walked. He could feel her up against him and smelled her perfume.

"I haven't been on a picnic in years," she said as they went down the old road. "Thank you for taking me on one. Let's promise not to talk about the war for the next hour or so—just our families and ourselves."

They stopped in front of a small structure, which was the entrance to the lower tunnel system. This originally had been constructed by the Germans with wooden walls and concrete reinforcement. There was a small clearing in front with several tree stumps to use as stools. Josette started unpacking the food, while Mark moved on down the path to listen for any activity. It was a beautiful day, slightly cool, very few clouds, and no wind. He had to admit that eating outside was a nice change.

Satisfied that there was no immediate threat in the area, he returned to where Josette had the picnic laid out on a blanket. "This was a good idea, and it's certainly perfect weather."

"Our family used to do this often. I remember that our English cousins would join us when I was much younger. When they came, Père would bring us up here, and we would spend the day exploring."

"Do you know what happened to your older brothers?"

Josette looked up. "No unpleasant talk. Remember the rules?"

Mark nodded. "Sorry. Tell me about your cousins. Isn't it rather unusual for a French family to have English cousins?"

"Not really. Our grandparents had two children, Oliver and Sophia. Oliver was our papa. Sophia met an English officer who was attached to the French army in 1913. They fell in love and got married—over the objections of Grand-père and Grand-mère."

"Was it because she was marrying an Englishman or because marrying a soldier with the possibility of a war was not a good thing?"

"I'm not sure, but they were not going to be denied, and they married that fall. Sebastian was born the next year, just after the start of the war. Uncle Bill sent Sophia and Sebastian back to England for their safety while the war dragged on for over four long years."

"Sebastian? Wasn't Aurélie's husband named Sebastian also?"

Josette sipped her wine and ate some cheese. "It was the same Sebastian—and yes, they were first cousins, which is not normal. However, they were like Uncle Bill and Aunt Sophia and weren't going to let anything stand in their way. They were married in 1936 but had no children, possibly by choice because of the close family relation."

Josette moved the meat and bread toward Mark. "The bread is fresh today, and I think *your* meat is good too."

Mark started eating as Josette continued. "Uncle Bill and Aunt Sophia had Polly in 1918. They would come over and visit us for several weeks at a time but never often enough. Our two families got along very well, especially Aurélie and Sebastian, even as young teenagers. Several of our friends in the area joined us when we played together." Josette stared up the path as her mind drifted back almost twenty years. "We all looked forward to the visits and never forgot those times."

Mark was finally beginning to relax. Listening to Josette's voice was soothing. He hadn't had an opportunity to talk with a woman like this for a long time.

"We all had nicknames for each other. I was Josi, Aurélie was Airi, Sebastian was Sebby, and Polly was Poddy. It was also when Henri and I played together."

"Polly is a nice name. I met a Polly Berson during some of my training, just before this mission. She seemed very smart. What was your cousin Polly like?"

Josette's attitude changed when he mentioned Polly. "You met Polly Berson?"

Mark could tell that she was surprised. "Yes, I can't tell you where or when."

Josette looked away in thought. "Polly Berson is my cousin. Sebastian's and Polly's father was William Berson." Josette seemed anxious. "Was she okay? We have not heard from her since 1939."

"Polly is fine. I don't know where she works, exactly, but I suspect London or somewhere in the south of England. As I said, she's a smart woman." He hesitated briefly before adding, "And very attractive. She's one of those people that others enjoy being around."

"I'll tell Grand-père and Aurélie; they'll be surprised and happy." Josette looked at Mark while he took some bread and meat. "What type of people do you like to be around?"

He chuckled. "It's hard to define specific personality traits, but a person who is happy, interested in others, and makes the time you spend with them seem special."

"I thought men were more interested in how a woman looks."

Mark chuckled again. "I guess that's part of it, but when you get right down to it, if you're not a good person inside, outward beauty—physical beauty—doesn't mean much." He looked up as he took a sip of wine. "I'm not sure that makes sense, but I was attracted to Joanne initially because she was kind to others. As I got to know her, her appearance attracted me as well, but I think without her kindness and goodwill, we wouldn't have developed a relationship."

"If you don't mind my saying so, I think you have that type of kindness as well."

He reached for a piece of cheese. "Thanks. We don't know each other that well, but I think you and your family have that type of kindness also. I was impressed with your grandfather the first time I met him and the same with your sister, even though I will admit she seemed a bit standoffish." Realizing Josette might not understand the term, he added, "Standoffish is similar to being aloof or uninterested in a person."

She nodded. "Aurélie was hurt when Sebastian was killed, and I think she tries to guard her heart closely." Josette changed the subject and asked, "What about your family? Brothers? Sisters?"

They continued eating and talking. Time passed very quickly as they talked about different subjects, not always agreeing but somehow enjoying each other's opinion. As Mark studied her, he realized he hadn't enjoyed being with a woman in years, and as she had said, it wasn't unpleasant.

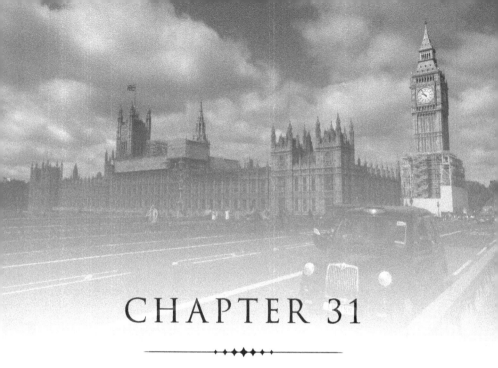

CHAPTER 31

June 24, SHAEF Headquarters, London

Two weeks had brought successes and disappointments. The landings had been successful, and supplies were coming in regularly, despite the violent channel storm that wrecked the Mulberry Port at Vierville-sur-Mer. One of the main issues challenging the Allies was the way the French countryside in Normandy had been divided into small fields by hedgerows. Even though the UK had hedgerows, their significance had not been appreciated by the Allied planners. The French had named this area the *bocage*.

A major disappointment was the lack of progress to take Caen. Montgomery had promised to capture the city the day after the invasion, but German resistance in the area had proved to be extremely stiff. That area of Normandy had considerably less of the bocage-type countryside, but the Germans had prepared their defenses well.

The hedgerows were a significant defensive resource for the Germans, and they planned well to extract the maximum benefit. Each of the fields was typically small, perhaps one hundred by three hundred yards. The Germans had set machine-gun positions at strategic points to cover any paths the Allies might use in their advance. In addition, they placed mortars two or three fields to the rear. The result was that each time the Allies captured one of the small fields, they were immediately met with well-placed firepower that increased casualties, resulting in slow progress.

The Germans also had been successful at reestablishing much of the communications and transportation links cut by preinvasion bombing and sabotage. Clearly, the Allies needed to focus more on this.

As a result, Colonel Betts was tasked by SHAEF to put together a plan that would focus on additional tactical bombing and increasing activity by the Resistance to take out communications and transportation. The easy part was developing a plan for tactical bombing. The more difficult task was to plan sabotage activities. These needed to be carefully coordinated with the actual troop advance, remaining as plans only until the Allies were close; otherwise, the Germans would repair the damage before the infantry could attack. Colonel Betts knew he needed to send additional agents into France to determine primary targets, while assisting the various Resistance groups.

He picked up his phone and called Colonel Gaffney. "Johnny, this is David. I may need to borrow some of your staff for missions into France." Without giving Gaffney time to object, he asked, "Realizing you can't spare anyone, tell me who I can have."

"God, David, we just put our new staff together a few weeks ago. Surely you can find other candidates."

"I need people familiar with the area and who know the difference between low- and high-value targets—and their vulnerabilities. Unfortunately, that's your people."

There was a silence at the other end. Gaffney knew Betts was correct. "All right. I'll have a list to you in two hours."

"I knew I could count on you."

"You realize that if we don't have trained intelligence officers here, other things are going to suffer as well. I'll get that list to you."

An hour later, Gaffney was looking at a short list of three names that he didn't want to lose. Lieutenant Alex Ryder was the first name on the list, along with Lieutenant William Boysen. *They'd better come back in one piece.*

June 26, East of Souhesme La Petite

I'm getting tired of coming down here. It had taken Mark over four hours to maneuver to where he could take pictures. This was his third visit in two weeks, but it was better than going to the Thionville area with his pod. At least he could get back to the dugout on the same day.

It was apparent that construction had not proceeded at the same rapid pace he'd observed in May. The main buildings were complete, and one small defensive pillbox looked ready for action. The power lines extended all the way to the main bunker. He had noted on his last visit that normal-sized power poles had supported the power lines. He suspected that while it would cause trouble long-term, it might reflect the Germans' realization that the line supports wouldn't be required for long.

It was half past twelve, and the workers slowed for lunch. He carefully took photos and counted the workers. In his recent visits, they had upwards of forty people working on this site; at least half appeared to be locals. Now it seemed that the majority of laborers were German, with only a few local Frenchmen—probably an indication that the hard labor was complete.

Mark noted the equipment covered by a tarp next to the main bunker. *Most likely electrical gear.* He made notes of the estimated size. *If they have the right people working on this, they'll have it hooked up and ready to run in two or three weeks.* He continued to make notes and take photos. He made sure his notes included the lifting equipment that had already been staged next to the electrical gear under the tarps. As he continued making notes, he heard a low rumble from the horizon. He decided to withdraw to a small copse of trees three hundred yards to the rear.

By the time he arrived there, safely concealed, a small flight of medium bombers flew overhead. He didn't know, however, that one of the planes was equipped with photography equipment. His reports, along with several Resistance reports, had alerted London as to the operational potential of this site. For the last four weeks, they had followed the construction progress with great interest.

Mark waited for the planes to pass, and after a small amount of activity at the site as a result of the flyover, he began to move up the hedgerow and across the main road. He hugged the hedgerow until he got back into the Forêt Domaniale du Grand Pays.

Early Morning, June 27, Lower Special Surveillance Office 8, London

Colonel Gaffney walked into the room and went directly to Lieutenant Boysen's desk. Alex looked over as the colonel bent down and said something. Boysen got up, and the colonel walked over to Alex's desk. "Would you please come to my office?" A knot immediately formed in his stomach because Colonel Gaffney very seldom addressed people in this manner.

When both William and Alex were in Colonel Gaffney's office, he closed the door and motioned for them to sit. He held two envelopes in his hand. "An assignment has come up for the two of you, similar in nature but in different locations. Normally, we do not allow agents we insert to know anything about the other missions, but in this case, I felt it was important for both of you to know."

William and Alex were surprised and realized if the colonel was using terms such as *agents* or *missions*, it meant they were going behind enemy lines. Alex was surprised because he was unaware that William had gone through the same training as he had six months prior. Most of the staff working for Colonel Gaffney had gone through the training so that they would understand what agents had to endure.

Colonel Gaffney gave both men their envelopes. "When you open it, you will see that we're asking you both to drop into France in different areas for specific reasons. Neither of you should know the reasons for the other's mission, but you both need to know that you have been selected because of your knowledge of the intelligence we've gathered to date and the type of information we require going forward. Open this in the privacy of your quarters, memorize it, and bring the orders back to me."

Lieutenant Boysden asked permission to speak. "How soon will we be required to go?"

"In two days. Now, if that's all, you should go read your orders and start your preparations. The sergeant major can assist you with any supplies or equipment."

William and Alex got up, saluted, and left the colonel's office. They briefly glanced at each other with a confused look and proceeded to their quarters. Lieutenant Boysden was going to drop into an area north of Evercy, southwest of Caen, several miles ahead of the British Second Army. Alex was to jump into a field just east of Marigny and south of Bergerie. Lieutenant Boysden would help the local Resistance groups to find access roads to the high points that overlooked Caen. Alex would assist in confirming German unit positions, in an effort to determine the best targets for the carpet bombing.

Both men went back to their quarters and began packing their belongings. The orders indicated that they would return to these quarters, which meant they didn't need to vacate their rooms. A couple of hours later, both men went back to the office to make sure their current work would be picked up by another member of the staff. As Alex sorted through his papers, he made notes as to who would be best to follow up on the different areas he was assigned. As he concentrated, he noticed movement, and a note appeared. Not looking up, he opened it.

Meet me in the cafeteria for lunch.
P.

Alex knew better than to look up, but he looked at his watch. Another thirty minutes before lunch.

Alex sighed and said, "I'm sorry, Polly. Something has come up, and I may be out of the office for a while."

Polly was busy with some papers. Looking down, she said quietly. "I know. I work for a general, remember?"

Alex still had the knot in his stomach, and so did Polly. General Brawls had briefed her about his mission. She didn't want him to go but knew that gathering this type of information was very important.

"I have the rest of the afternoon off. Do you have anything you have to do?"

Alex shook his head. "I've packed a few things, and the sergeant major said my kit would be packed and ready for me to inspect tomorrow morning."

"General Brawls was able to get two small steaks and some other things from the Americans' mess. I can cook them this evening." Before Alex could comment that Polly didn't have a place to cook, she smiled. "The general was able to find an empty flat about two blocks from here. Evidently, they put visiting officers in it, so it's fully stocked."

Alex looked at her and realized how much he was going to miss being around her. "What time should I come over?"

"How about right now?"

"It's only a quarter of two; it's a little early for dinner, don't you think?"

Polly put her foot on top of Alex's beneath the table and pressed down and then reached over and took his hand. "You can't be that stupid, Lieutenant. Please finish your work, and let's go to the apartment."

It was a pleasant day outside, and the walk along St. James Park, especially with the spring flowers, added beauty to the day. Since Polly was not in uniform, she took his hand and then put her arm into his.

"It's a beautiful day; it's such a shame that we have this ugly war."

As they walked along, Alex felt like he was the luckiest man in the world; in fact, he felt it so strongly that he turned to Polly and whispered precisely that.

They had a nice dinner—a dinner that very few folks in the UK had enjoyed in the last several years. It wasn't anything fancy by prewar standards but was certainly special for them. Alex realized just recently that he was in love with Polly and wanted to spend the rest of his life with her. Polly had already come to that decision but waited for Alex to work it out for himself.

The next morning, Polly made a full English breakfast, which very few people in England had experienced in the last five years. After shaving, Alex walked into the small kitchen area and slipped his arms around Polly from behind. After kissing her, he whispered, "If I live to be one hundred, I'll never forget last night."

Polly was tempted to stop cooking, but she didn't want to waste the food the general had provided. Besides, she felt warm and content—no, it was beyond that; she felt loved.

Lieutenant Boysden and Lieutenant Ryder left thirty-six hours later on different Lysander flights from different airports. Their adventure was only beginning.

July 4, in the Bocage, South of D900 on the D29, South of Montreuil-sur-Lozon

Jacques motioned for Lieutenant Ryder to stay where he was. Jacques and the other two Frenchmen were spread out behind the hedgerow in the next field. It was one thirty in the morning, and they had traveled several miles from a small farmhouse near La Fossairie to the west. Alex had dropped in a little field several miles south. The three Frenchmen were there to greet him, and then they went to a small, deserted barn just to the west of Marigny. They rested there for the remainder of the night and then went to a nearby farmhouse for food at midday.

Jacques showed Alex a map of the area, which had the main German troop dispositions marked. Alex marveled at the resources the Germans had pulled together. That night as they moved through the countryside, he saw hundreds of Panzer V 'Panther' tanks and thousands of troops. Jacques and his friends pointed out to him the intricate detail of the German defensive positions. They had used the hedgerows to their maximum advantage, and it was obvious that frontal assaults would be disastrous.

Jacques turned around and motioned for Alex to come across the field to their hedgerow. He moved quickly, stumbling twice as he stepped into mud holes. *Some of that 'mud' comes from the cows. Well, I've been in worse.*

As Alex leaned up against the hedgerow bank next to Jacques, he motioned for quiet. Removing his hat, Jacques slowly put his head above the top of the bank and motioned for Alex to do the same. In the darkness, they could make out tanks and men spread out across the unusually large field. They all began making notes, counting as best they could in the dark. When finished with that position, they moved a half mile to the south and repeated the process several times. Afterward, they slowly retreated across some smaller fields until they were confident they could talk.

The three Frenchmen and Alex sat in a small circle behind two hedgerows. Jacques was the first to speak. "The last couple of fields housed a battalion from the Panzer Lehr division. That was probably sixty heavy tanks with lighter reconnaissance armored vehicles, perhaps as many as eight hundred men."

Alex was trying to make sense of his notes, but it was difficult in the darkness. He knew any one of the German tanks could knock out a Sherman easily. "I count perhaps two full regiments concentrated in this area. What reports do you have east of Marigny?"

One of the Frenchmen whispered, "About the same in terms of armor. They are positioned just outside Marigny, going southeast to Canisy."

"And reports from other groups indicate the same, all in this area. I think it is suicide to try to attack here. I would recommend you tell London to consider another location."

Alex knew that Montgomery was having problems approaching Caen and that both the British and American armies needed to advance together or risk creating a gap in their lines that the Germans could exploit. "I think we have enough information between what you've shown me and the reports from the other groups. We should go back, consolidate our information, and get it back to London."

The group found their way back to the farmhouse outside La Fossairie, where they got some food and rest. They spent the morning compiling their information. Jacques sent one of his men to arrange for a Lysander pickup that evening.

Fourteen hours later, in a field south of the farmhouse, a Lysander landed and picked up Alex. It flew northwest at treetop level for thirty minutes before climbing to three thousand feet to cross the coastline. Even with careful planning, they encountered flak as they left France, but it wasn't significant. However, it was Alex's first experience with being shot at, and it left him quite unnerved. He would be glad to get back to London—and Polly.

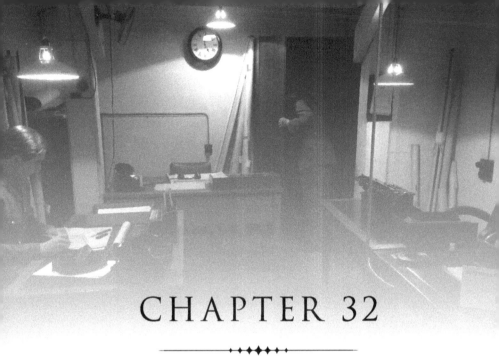

CHAPTER 32

Midday, July 6, Lower Special Surveillance Office 8, London

"This report fits with the others. It's good we gathered this information because clearly, we have seriously underestimated the Germans' defensive posture." Colonel Betts was addressing a group that included Colonel Gaffney; Lieutenant Boysden, just recently back from his excursion; newly promoted Lieutenant Ryder; and the rest of the senior surveillance staff. Also present were General Brawls, General Bradley, Field Marshal Montgomery, and several of the senior SHAEF staff.

"These two recent missions, as well as the three earlier ones, confirmed that continuing to attack conventionally is going to be very costly. Operations have started working on several possibilities. General Bradley suggested a concentrated carpet-bombing operation to pulverize an area, followed by a rapid attack. Field Marshal Montgomery has suggested a similar type of operation around Caen. We cannot carry out both of these operations simultaneously—not enough aircraft and munitions to support both."

General Brawls interjected his opinion. "We should give the planning folks a couple of days to work out the pros and cons of different approaches and then get back together to discuss it."

Brawls turned to Boysden and Ryder. "I think you both did well, particularly for your first mission. You got the information, and most important, you came back alive—always a factor in a successful mission." Polly had entered the room as the meeting broke up. Turning to Lieutenant Boysden, she said, "I prepared the annex to your report, and it's on your desk."

Boysden nodded and then looked at Alex and then to her, smiling. "I suppose I need to proofread the annex. You never can tell what errors will creep into these reports." Polly gave him a mock scowl.

The meeting broke up, and Alex went up to William. They had not talked since returning. "What do you think of field missions? Are you ready to join the infantry?"

"Interesting, but I would just as soon stay in the office for the rest of the war, thank you."

Alex moved over to Polly and took her elbow. "How is your time for the rest of the day?"

Polly sighed. "Unfortunately, I'll be working late. We have several other things going on, now that you two heroes are back from the field."

Alex was disappointed, but he'd thought this might be the case. "I have a forty-eight-hour pass, so if you get some free time, let me know."

"I said I had to work late. I didn't say I wouldn't see you. I have the flat for forty-eight hours. I should be there by ten o'clock." She handed him the keys.

July 10, the DeBoy Farm and the Dugout

Luc was helping Josette and their grand-père load supplies into the truck. Alphonse had not been feeling well again and had asked Aurélie or Josette to deliver supplies to Major Dornier. Aurélie had asked Josette to do it, even though she had made him a meat pie. As Josette got in the truck, her grand-père reminded her to be careful.

"Remember to take the road out of Le Neufour. Once you get in the trees, pull over and stop the engine for ten minutes at least. A German motorcycle went up the road two days ago." He hadn't mentioned to anyone the small, single-engine German reconnaissance plane that had been flying over the area the past ten days or so, but it worried him.

Josette pulled out of the farm and onto the D2, north toward Le Neufour. While she listened carefully to everything her grandfather said, sometimes she felt he was too cautious. Nonetheless, she would do as he asked. She was looking forward to seeing Mark again, and she hoped to convince him to go on another picnic. She had mentioned this to her sister. *Possibly that's why she made the meat pie.*

Josette could not figure out Aurélie when it came to Mark. She hadn't mentioned his name, and she didn't react when Josette mentioned him. Still, there was something about her sister's behavior that made her sense Aurélie was guarding something. She knew her sister had been hurt when Sebastian died, but Josette had suffered as well. Her fiancé had been missing for several years, with no information. Josette had mourned for over a year before she finally decided that she had to put it behind her.

As she turned onto the small road leading up the hill into the woods, she waved at a mother and her daughter in their garden. The Germans didn't demand the French turnover all their produce, so all of the farms and even the houses in the small villages had gardens. The Deboy's had one at their farm and of course the one in the woods which they canned most of the produce.

The road took a turn to the right and then veered north about two kilometers from the village. Josette picked a large tree, pulled the truck underneath, and turned the motor off. As she sat there listening to the quiet of the woods, she wondered what Mark was doing just then. He had mentioned the sounds and the smells of the forest several times, and it was clear he enjoyed them. She did as well but all the more so when they were together. In the few times they had been together, it was obvious they liked each other. Of course, with Mark, it might be simply loneliness. But somehow, she didn't think that—at least she didn't want to.

The low hum of an engine intruded on her thoughts. She listened carefully and could tell it was a small plane of some kind. She got out of the truck with binoculars, making sure to stay under cover. The engine noise grew. It was obvious the plane was going to pass close overhead. She recalled that the new high-voltage lines the Germans had installed from Lachalade ran through the forest less than half a kilometer from where she was. She would pass underneath them when she took the road north at the intersection.

Josette saw the plane through the trees and looked at it through the binoculars. It was a small single-engine plane that seemed to have a pilot and observer. It was low enough that she could see the markings. It was flying over the power lines, which made sense. She wondered if any of the Resistance groups would attempt to sabotage the lines. Then, with a start, she realized that Mark might be ordered to do it. That would cause the Germans almost certainly to discover his hiding place.

She looked around and listened carefully, as Mark had taught her. The plane's engine noise was diminishing, and she was reasonably sure there were no other vehicles around. She started the engine and pulled out to continue when she suddenly realized that the plane might return in a few minutes. She backed the truck under the tree again and decided to wait.

After twenty minutes, she was confident the plane would not return, so she continued. When she got to the intersection with the road to the dugout, she turned the engine off again to listen and then turned north, increasing her speed so that she would pass through the open areas quickly. She also was in a hurry to get to the dugout.

Mark looked at his watch, noting it was a little past ten thirty. He wondered when someone would show up. *Probably before noon. I wonder who it will be this time.* While he wanted to talk with Alphonse, he couldn't help but think about Josette. About that time, he heard a vehicle approaching from the south. Since the high-voltage lines were in that direction, he decided to move away from the dugout and get closer to the road. He had set up a series of booby traps—really just sixty millimeter mortar shells buried in the road—that could easily disable a troop truck. There was a convenient clump of brush only thirty feet from the road, well hidden in the trees. From this point, he could see down the road and decide about disabling the truck, if it was necessary. He knew if he did, he'd have to leave the area, so he was cautious.

He breathed a sigh of relief as Alphonse's truck came into sight. He disconnected one contact, put the detonator back underneath a log, and settled back to see who was driving. As the truck went by, he could see it was Josette. She went up to the bend in the road and then put the truck underneath the trees that helped conceal it. Mark listened carefully for any sounds of additional activity and then started walking toward the truck. When he was about a hundred and fifty feet away, he called out the challenge, and she yelled back. He walked over as she was beginning to unload the crates.

"Why did you take the road from the south?"

"Grand-père suggested it. There've been a few German motorcycles on the road the past several days."

Mark noticed Josette was wearing a dress again, and while he appreciated seeing her dressed like that, he wasn't sure it was a good idea for errands such as this. "Your grandfather was right; you need to take different routes." He reached over and unloaded a crate. "Here, let me help you."

As she gave him a box, he caught a whiff of her perfume. He could not resist teasing, at least a little. "I see that you must have a date after this stop."

She blushed slightly. "No, Mr. Mark, I did it for you, hoping that we could go on another picnic. Aurélie made a meat pie for us, and I think it would be nice to share it."

"There's been more German activity in the last two weeks. It might not be a good idea to be outside."

"I saw a small patrol plane flying over the new electric lines about an hour ago. So maybe we could have our picnic in the dugout and then take a short walk."

Mark shrugged as he continued unloading supplies. "Perhaps if we stay in the dugout, at least we could escape to the tunnels if needed."

Josette helped to move the supplies into the cellar. As they put the containers in the small space where the dry supplies were kept, they kept bumping into each other until Josette started giggling.

Mark was hard-pressed not to smile. "It's a good thing we like each other; otherwise, this wouldn't be very much fun."

Josette stopped and turned around, standing only a few inches away. Looking up into his eyes, she asked, "Do you like me?" Mark looked down, and this time it was his turn to blush. Josette smiled and said, "Never mind; I can see your answer." She reached up and touched his hair, "I think you need a haircut. When was the last time?"

"About two months ago. Your grand-père."

"I wish I'd thought about it because Aurélie and I share the haircutting chores in our family. We have scissors and clippers."

"Well, I have similar equipment here. The clippers were modified so that I could do a basic trim myself. They weren't sure, when planning the mission, if I would have the opportunity to have someone else cut it." He started to move out of the storage area and across to the cabinet, but Josette was standing in his way with her hand in his hair. He put his hands on her shoulders and gently moved her. As he did, she stood on her toes, gently leaned in to him, and kissed his cheek. Mark paused and then put his arms around her and hugged her before he even realized what he was doing. He let her go and looked gently at her. "I'm sorry. It's been a long time since I've held a beautiful woman. However, I promised your grandfather that I would look after you, Luc, and Aurélie when you are here."

Josette just stood in front of him, smiling. "You have nothing to be sorry for. It was just a small kiss and hug, and besides, I know you're a gentleman." She turned around and walked over to the table. "So where do you want the haircut—down here or outside?"

Mark walked over and pulled the clippers from the cabinet shelf. "Let's go outside, but we'll need to be careful and not make much noise." He picked up his pack and grabbed his Sten gun. Smiling, he turned around. "This time I'll go up the ladder first. I don't want to ruin your impression of me as a gentleman."

They walked east to the old World War I trench system. Mark thought they would be out of sight. He had scattered several stumps around the area to use as a seat, so he set one up as his barber chair. Josette put a sheet around him to catch the hair and began by combing his hair with her fingers. As she arranged his hair, he closed his eyes enjoying the sensation. *I need to stop feeling like this.*

She began cutting his hair. "I will make it fairly short, but still long enough for you to comb. Aurélie or I can do this every month, if you like." She moved his head to different angles as she cut his hair, enjoying the closeness.

For his part, Mark was happy having her close to him. Several times he would move his head, and she had to lean over to reposition him. Feeling her lean against him was not doing much for his concentration. Josette didn't necessarily have to be as close as she was, but she wanted him to know she enjoyed being near him.

As she was finishing up, she moved in front of him to trim his eyebrows. "Let me stand between your legs so that I can do this right." Once she finished trimming his bushy eyebrows, she took a brush and began to brush out the loose hair as she gently blew on his head. Again, before even realizing it, Mark placed his hands on her hips and looked up. As she looked down, she put a hand on his cheek, and they kissed. This time neither pulled away, and in fact, Mark pulled her closer to him. They both looked at each other for a few moments before Josette smiled and finished his hair.

"Let's get this stuff back into the cellar," Mark said. "Do we need to heat the meat pie?"

Josette looped her arms around his free arm. "We could eat it cold, but it's probably better warm."

They returned to the cellar and lit the oven. Josette had brought a small salad with turnips and fresh vegetables. Mark grabbed a half a bottle of wine and some water and took it up to the dugout. He brought in some stumps to use as a table and chairs. Mark looked down and could hear her humming a tune. He dismissed a quick thought to go down and wrap his arms around her.

She turned around and caught him staring at her. "Yes?"

"Nothing. It's nice to have you here. If the pie's ready, I can take it up."

After he set the food on the makeshift table in the dugout, he walked out to look around. *The picnic is great, but if we get caught, it could endanger the entire family.* They ate quietly and then took the dishes down below. Josette walked behind the dugout toward the old trench. "Could we walk this way for a while?"

Mark nodded and caught up with her. "If you look closely, you can see a faint trail. This is one of the paths I take to check the east side of the forest."

"I think you know these woods better than I do."

They walked in silence for several minutes before she took his arm and faced him. "I would like to hear what you think of me."

Mark tensed, and Josette squeezed his hand. "You're very nice, and I enjoy being with you, and I think about you when you're not here."

"However? There's something else, isn't there?"

"I don't know. Perhaps I'm unsure because it's been so many years since I've been around a woman like you. You do realize, don't you, that I'm much older."

"The age difference is not important to me, and I don't want it to be important to you. Since Henri disappeared, I have not met anyone I cared about"—she moved closer to him—"until you."

Mark put his arms around her and kissed her. It felt nice, but there was something in the back of his mind that wouldn't go away. They looked at each other for several minutes and hugged again. "I think we should start back now." He took her hand and led her back toward the dugout. He was enjoying this, but something told him it wasn't for the best.

CHAPTER 33

✦✦✦✦✦

July 15, German Rocket Test Facilities at Peenemünde on the North Sea Coast

Speer had traveled by auto to Peenemünde after Dr. von Braun called to announce the scheduled test of his small rocket. Von Braun's team had worked quickly to finalize the design and had made several prototypes as soon as possible.

Speer was standing next to von Braun in the blockhouse, located a considerable distance from the launchpad. The separation was necessary when testing the V2 rocket but not for this smaller rocket. Still, the scientists and engineers at the facility had insisted on using the main launchpad because of the existing controls.

"This rocket is programmed to ten thousand meters. When it reaches that height, the engine will cut off. The instruments will record all the necessary data, and it should be returned just offshore with a parachute."

"Have you solved the issue of how to detonate at a specific altitude?"

Von Braun looked at one of the senior members of his team. "Ludvig, would you share some of your ideas with the Reich Minister."

"The Americans have developed a fuse for their artillery shells and their bombs that works off either a timing device or barometric pressure. We've been trying to obtain a sample for months without success. However, last month one of our retreating infantry units came across an unexploded shell, and it turned out to be armed with such a fuse. They removed the fuse in the field and sent it back to our lab, and we are in the process of duplicating it. The second test today will have a small explosive device in the warhead with such a fuse."

Speer nodded. "I saw the report several weeks ago. I understand that the soldier who found the shell and removed the fuse was killed later when the shell exploded. I recommended the Führer award him the Iron Cross. Obtaining the fuse was a fortunate piece of luck for us. However, the manufacture of this fuse appears difficult. I doubt we'll be able to use it for our artillery shells, but we can use it on these rockets."

Von Braun motioned to the viewing window. "Reich Minister, if you're ready, we can proceed." Speer nodded, and von Braun instructed the technicians to begin the countdown. Seconds later, the small rocket, three hundred millimeters in diameter and two meters high, leaped off the launchpad and climbed into the sky. "It should take approximately forty seconds to reach ten thousand meters." Several seconds later, the rocket engine cut off, and the instrument package contained in the nose separated, a parachute deployed, and it began floating back to the North Sea.

The technicians carefully evaluated the small amount of data they had received while the retrieval boats left to retrieve the nosecone. A few hours later, they completed a preliminary analysis and decided to proceed with a second test. The second rocket was fueled and ready on an alternate launchpad.

"So this rocket will explode at ten thousand meters?"

"Yes, sir, if everything works properly. We also have a small instrument package in the rocket body itself that will help us evaluate the results. Our radar and rangefinders will also check the terminal altitude."

Just like the first rocket, this one shot up into the sky rapidly, and in less than a minute, there was a small explosion with four red flares that would be visible from the ground. Speer turned to von Braun and extended his hand. "Please extend my gratitude to your team especially the speed at which they developed this. I'll be reporting to the Führer tonight." Speer and his aide walked out past the offices to his waiting car and began the three-hour drive back to Berlin.

July 20, Approaching the Ploesti Refinery

The B-24 Liberators had taken off at three in the morning from Benghazi, Libya, part of the 376th Bombardment Group. It'd taken almost eight hours to approach Ploesti; most of the trip was flown at altitudes below ten thousand feet. It made for a long and tedious flight, especially for the pilots. This raid was much smaller than the previous ones, particularly the one in August 1943. There were only thirty B-24s in this group, as it was expected a smaller precision raid could be more effective without risking so many men and planes. As they approached the refinery from the southeast and east, they split into two groups and dropped to fifteen hundred feet.

The lead pilot switched on his radio and said, "Follow the rising sun," which was the code phrase to proceed.

"Pilot to bombardier, get ready; we're about three minutes out."

The bombardier checked his bombsight; they were using a different sight on this mission because of the low altitude. Since they were carrying four thousand pounds of incendiaries, precision wasn't as critical as it usually would've been.

"Bombardier to pilot, I'm ready to take control."

"You've got it." The pilot flipped the toggle switch and transferred the control of the plane to the bombardier. "Pilot to crew, be ready with the cameras."

A moment later, the bombardier released the first group of incendiaries over the eastern edge of the refinery and then released the second group a split second later. He held the last set for the buildings and warehouses on the western side of the refinery.

Incendiaries did their damage, but particularly unfortunate for

Albert Speer's project was the damage the third group did to the R&D facility and the warehouse storage. Even though the R&D facility and manufacturing plant were ahead of schedule, only about 30 percent of the fuel shells had left the facility. After the incendiaries hit the warehouse, the fuel-shell inventory exploded into a firestorm. The small number of shells that left the refinery was all they had until more could be manufactured. That, however, would be difficult since the second group of fifteen planes had dropped their incendiaries smack in the middle of the storage and refining area, destroying not only the raw materials but the manufacturing equipment as well. Germany would have to defend its western border with a few hundred fuel shells.

July 11, the DeBoy Farm

Alphonse opened the door. He looked up at the sky as dawn began to drive back the darkness. He turned toward the barn to perform the daily milking chores. He saw a small envelope leaning up against the side door of the barn. He picked it up and opened it, noticing there was another sealed envelope inside. It had a single mark across the upper right-hand corner, which meant it was a message for Major Dornier. He put the note in his pocket and went on to the barn. As he milked the cows, he thought about his two daughters. He realized that Josette was likely becoming attached to the major, but he suspected that Aurélie had feelings for him as well. Both his health and responsibilities around the farm had kept him from going to the dugout for almost two months. He had tried to get Aurélie interested in taking supplies, but she always had a reason not to go. This time he would insist. Major Dornier needed to have the message today, and Josette had to go into the village with Luc this morning.

Alphonse moved the milk down to the cool barn cellar, and then went back into the house. The sun was up, and everyone would soon be awake. He went to the kitchen to make some coffee—or at least to make a hot drink that passed for coffee.

He heard the stairs creaking and turned to see Luc coming into the kitchen. "I thought it was my turn to do the milking today."

Alphonse sipped his coffee and shrugged. "Sometimes I wake up early, so I thought I'd go ahead and get it done. The milk is down in the cellar, but it still needs to be separated."

Luc nodded and went out the door toward the barn. Alphonse reflected on the fact that even though their family had experienced loss in the last few years, they still had each other, which was more than many families. He stood in the doorway, watching Luc heading to the barn.

The stairs creaked again. "If you want to get up this early, you're welcome to wake me up, and I can fix you some breakfast."

Alphonse turned around to see Aurélie going to the stove in her housecoat. He started to say something and then realized how much she looked like her mother; for that matter, she acted like his Maria. He smiled. "I thought you didn't like getting up early."

"Sometimes but not always." She poured a cup of ersatz coffee and sat down at the table. "I wish we could get more coffee from our visitor in the forest."

Alphonse knew that she had something on her mind. "What is it, *chéri*?"

Aurélie looked up. "Sometimes I feel that I'm missing things in life."

"Well, I guess we're all missing some things as a result of this war. You miss Sebastian, don't you?"

She held her cup with both hands and stared out the window. "Yes, but I think it's more than just that. When we found out he had been killed, I thought I would never get over it. I never wanted to go through that kind of pain again, but in the last year or so, it seems like life is somehow … empty or not as full."

"Losing your husband is something that never goes away. When your grandmother died, I felt like I had a hole in my life, and in many ways, I still feel that way. However, I realized I had a family to raise, and I didn't have time to dwell on those feelings. I felt like finding another wife a few times, but somehow it didn't seem the right thing to do. I guess I was lucky that when your grandmother died, I was older.

While love doesn't have an age limit, age at least has the advantage of experience and wisdom, so I was able to go on."

Aurélie looked up at her grandfather with sad eyes. "I think I'm lonely, and I know that's a selfish thing to say because I have you, Josette, and Luc, but I feel that way at times."

"Aurélie, you cannot command your feelings. I've watched you over the last year or so, and I've been worried about you. I'm worried about Luc and Josette also, but Josette is different. She is somehow able to put her sorrow behind her. Luc is still young, and if we get him to the end of the war alive, he'll be okay. You're more like me, and it's hard for you to put your memories away. And it should be harder because you're still young and have your whole life ahead of you."

"I feel confused at times, and I feel trapped in this country, without the possibility of ever meeting someone and starting a family." She stood up and started back up the stairs. "Foolishness. I need to get dressed and start breakfast."

Alphonse remembered the message. "Aurélie, you're neither foolish nor stupid." He paused and then said, "I need for you to run an errand today." He took the envelope from his pocket. "This is for our special visitor in the woods. Would you take it to him this morning?"

Aurélie turned around on the stairs. "Why can't you or Josette take it?"

"I'd like for you to take it … please." He walked over and gave her the envelope. "And wake your sister because she and Luc need to go to the village this morning. I have a meeting at noon in Lachalade about our chickens."

Aurélie had forgotten about the trip to the village and her grandfather's trip to Lachalade. Somehow, she sensed that her grandfather wanted her to deliver the message. As she took the envelope, she realized, with surprise, that she was looking forward to seeing Major Dornier again.

Midmorning, the Dugout

Aurélie had taken the road north out of the village and then turned onto the road leading into the forest. Her grandfather wanted her to approach from the west, since Josette had used other routes for the last two visits. She checked to be sure she had the challenge and password. Even though supplies were not due for another week, her grandfather had insisted she take some milk, wine, and some of their old cheese. He had remarked, "It never hurts to have good cheese around, particularly if you have wine."

As she came around the bend, she saw the small intersection and the shelter to the right for the truck. She slowed and carefully moved the vehicle into the brush. *They've improved with this cover.*

As she got out of the truck and moved to the back, she paused to take in the sounds of the forest. She had remembered that Major Dornier had mentioned the smells and sounds the last time she had been here. That seemed like a long time ago.

"Brooklyn!" It seemed to come from in front of the truck, but it was difficult to tell with all the trees.

Aurélie replied, "Lachalade." When there was no further reply or sounds, she decided to take a crate out of the truck and start toward the dugout. She got about halfway there when she saw him standing next to a tree.

"I'm glad to see you again, but I hope it doesn't mean that your grandfather or sister aren't well."

Aurélie stopped and faced him. "They are quite well, monsieur. They had other errands."

"No one was supposed to show up today—or for that matter, for at least a week. Why are you here?"

For some reason, this annoyed Aurélie. "We come when we have a reason, and not just to visit. A message was left for you last night, and my grand-père thought since we were making the trip that you might enjoy some cheese and milk. However, if it's too much of an inconvenience, I'll take them back."

Mark didn't want to argue. As he saw Aurélie get out of the truck, he realized that his feelings for Josette were more superficial, and he understood better what was bothering him each time she visited. "I apologize, madame, and I forget my manners. Let me help you with that." He walked over and took the crate, and they walked toward the dugout.

"Josette and Luc had to go into the village this morning, and my grand-père had to see another farmer about some chickens. It left me to deliver the message."

"I'm glad to see you again." He turned to look at her as they walked. "Please come down and have some coffee. In fact, I can give you some extra to take back." He could see her reaction and also the question that was forming. "You're not supposed to know where I get this, but it should be obvious that they come either from another supplier in the area or are dropped by parachute. Don't worry, though; I have plenty."

Aurélie was feeling more comfortable with him and smiled ever so slightly. "You don't look like you have missed many meals, and you also look like you have a good … how do you say in English? A barber."

"I don't miss meals because of your family, and Josette cut my hair last time she was here. She mentioned that you are good at that as well."

Somehow the mention of Josette didn't bother her, nor did the fact that her sister had been bringing supplies for the past several months. Aurélie was just glad to be here now.

She helped pass the milk and cheese down the ladder to him and then came down into the cellar as he was putting up the supplies. He turned around and smiled, remembering the hot chocolate from last time. "I wonder, instead of coffee, if you would like some hot chocolate?" As she started to object, he said, "It seems like I've just received a fresh supply of milk, and it would be a shame not to share it."

They stared at each other for a few seconds. "I'd like some hot chocolate. May I sit down?"

He nodded toward the table and turned to start heating some milk. As the milk warmed, he decrypted the message and saw that he was being asked to return to the Butte de Vauquois as soon as possible. He wasn't surprised, but for some reason, he wasn't enthusiastic about going. At least that area was close enough for him to go on foot.

Aurélie looked around at the cellar. Her grand-père had done a first-rate job fixing it up. She also took note of the stack of parachute material in the back. She walked over and picked some up. "You should be careful with this, monsieur. The material is greatly sought after here."

Mark looked up. "Take some, if you'd like, but be very careful. If the Germans find you with it, there could be questions." He went back to decoding, while Aurélie selected two chutes.

He stood up, and she noticed the change in his demeanor. "I hope it's not bad news."

"Not bad news, just something else to do. I guess there is a price to be paid for living in all this luxury." He smiled at her/ "Really, I'm fortunate to have a place like this. I often think about all the hard work your grandfather did to prepare this place. He is a good man."

She studied him as he spoke, realizing he had a kind face and an inviting smile. He continued to move some of his equipment around as she sat and watched. "If you would like, I can leave if there is something you need to do quickly."

Mark glanced at her as if that was the last thing he wanted. "Please stay for a while. It's nice to have someone here. I have to get some things ready for an errand I'll need to complete later."

Later, Aurélie would wonder why she'd said it, but at the time, it came out before she realized it. "Do you ever get lonely? I mean, you're out here by yourself; it must be difficult."

"When I accepted this mission, I was told plainly what the conditions were going to be. Yes, I get lonely, but I don't mind being alone." He paused for a second as he remembered having similar conversations with Alphonse and Josette. Smiling, he looked directly into her eyes. "I just realized that your grandfather and sister asked the same thing, and I gave them the same answer. I think that's why I like your family. You care about other people."

Again, Aurélie didn't mind the reference to Josette, even though she suspected that they had spent quite a bit of time together over the last couple of months during her visits. She was aware that Josette had come up a couple of times in a dress, which certainly wasn't required for delivering supplies. Aurélie didn't know why she said what followed, but it also came out before she realized it. "Do you care for Josette?"

Mark was leaning over, putting some ammunition into his belt, when her question hit him. Somehow, he knew it was coming, but he had wanted to address that subject in his way. Nevertheless, Aurélie seemed like the type who appreciated a frank conversation. Turning back, he glanced at her and then went over to the stove to pour the hot chocolate. He took her cup over and sat down. He put his elbows on the table, resting his head in his hands as he looked at her. "You are much like her and also much like your grandfather." He paused for a second, looking at his mug. "Yes, I care about Josette. On the last couple of visits, she's made it quite obvious that she cares about me."

Aurélie just kept looking at him, letting him finish.

"There is something, however, that doesn't seem right about my feelings for her. I think it's more than just our age difference." He paused and looked up. "Can I ask you something about Josette and Henri?" Mark thought he saw the shadow of a smile cross her face as she nodded. "How much in love were they?"

This time there was a flicker of light in her eyes. She took a moment to compose her thoughts. "They had known each other since early childhood. The Benoit farm is very near ours, so our families were very close. At first, we thought that they were more like best friends—brother and sister—but as they grew up, it was clear there were other feelings, very strong feelings." She paused to see if Mark understood.

"That makes sense, but she seldom mentions his name. Your grandfather told me what had happened."

Aurélie continued. "Sebastian and I were married in 1936, and very soon after that, Henri asked Josette. Both sets of parents wouldn't allow marriage because of their young ages, but they were allowed to become engaged. Then the Germans invaded, and Sebastian was killed fairly soon after that, and shortly after that, Renée was also killed. Within a month, Henri was reported as missing, and since he was in the same general area as Renée, everyone assumed he probably was killed also. It was tough on all of us, but I think Josette took it especially hard. She is a very positive person, so she decided that she would believe that he was somehow still alive.

"We didn't know what to believe because there was no report, specifically, of his being killed or even injured. The battle he was in was intense, and there wasn't much in the way of first-hand reports about casualties." Aurélie stopped and sipped her hot chocolate. She smiled. "I know I said this before, but this hot cocoa reminds me of my *mère*, and it means a lot to be able to have it." She paused and then continued. "Anyway, a couple of years ago, Josette's attitude changed, and while she did not talk about it much, I knew she had resigned herself to the fact that Henri was not coming back."

"It's hard to lose someone you love. As I've said, I lost my wife, and I still have a hole in my heart."

Aurélie nodded her head in understanding. "I suppose it depends on the person, but right now in France, when a woman loses her man, there's not much of a future for her. The last war eliminated a substantial number of our young men, and this war seems to be doing it again. I think Josette became depressed, even with her positive attitude, and felt as though she'd never be able to find someone to love again and perhaps start a family." She turned her head and looked at the supply cabinet. "I think that's why she began to take on the task of helping to bring supplies up here. It wasn't hard for her to develop an attachment to you."

"Your explanation gives me a better understanding of her feelings and the way she behaved, particularly on the last couple of visits. She even wore a dress a couple of times." He smiled at her, and somehow, just looking at her face made him completely at ease with what he was going to say. "She made it difficult not to develop more than just friendly feelings, but I was never completely at ease with those feelings. I felt like there was something more to them, and I think the something more was what you've just explained."

"She is also impulsive and quite stubborn, so when she decides she wants something, she goes after it. I think she decided she wants you." Again, Aurélie smiled—the smile of friendship.

"I've thought about her quite a bit since the visit last week. I had decided to ask her about some of this and tell her that I wouldn't be able to allow my feelings for her to grow, at least until Henri's fate was clear."

"While that's probably for the best, Mark, please do it with gentleness. I believe her feelings for you now are strong."

Mark went over to the cold box and pulled out some leftovers, placing them on the preparation table. "I'd like for you to stay for lunch so we can talk more, if you have time." He looked at her for a response and then before receiving it, he added, "By the way, that is the first time you have called me by my name; it sounded nice."

She hesitated slightly but nodded yes. She knew that she enjoyed being around him, and a few more hours would not mean anything one way or the other.

Mark worked to prepare the leftovers, and Aurélie got up to help. They stood side by side and continued their discussion. "I'm not sure how to address this with Josette, maybe just directly, but as you say, let her know that I do have feelings for her." He looked over as she cut some vegetables. "Any advice?"

"I think that's probably the best way. I wouldn't allow a long discussion concerning your feelings. She will just want to know how deep they go."

Mark stopped and took Aurélie's arm. "They go deep, Aurélie, but not as a romance. I care very much for her but as a good friend or perhaps even a younger sister." He could feel her arm as he put his other hand over hers. "Now I have a question for you. You mentioned a few minutes ago that it wasn't hard to form an attachment to me." He paused and let the unspoken question hang in the air between them.

Aurélie set the knife down and turned to face him. As she looked up, she whispered, "You are kind, considerate, smart, and quite handsome. However, I think you already know this. But because of your wife, you don't allow yourself feelings toward women." She turned and continued preparing the food. "By the way, you mentioned the age difference. Would you mind if I ask how old you are?"

"You seem awfully curious," he said, very much at ease now. "I'll be thirty-nine at the end of this month."

She turned her head briefly and smiled. "Not bad for an old man."

After she left, Mark turned his attention to preparing for the trip to the Butte. He decided on his Sten gun and both his .45 automatic and silenced .22. He also put five pounds of plastic explosive in his pack—the message had suggested, if he was able to get close enough, that he should plant a timed charge underneath one of the pipes. It made no sense to him, but orders were orders. It would just make the Germans mad, and they would quickly replace the tube if they needed it.

CHAPTER 34

◆ ◆ ◆ ◆ ◆

July 14, Butte de Vauquois

Mark left the dugout at a little past midnight on July 12 and arrived at the Butte in some cover about two hundred yards from the facility, just as it was becoming light. A gentle mist was falling, and the overcast sky made the dawn gloomy. He stayed concealed for most of the day, venturing out only briefly to get a feel for the activities around the camp. The next day he continued to gather information, make notes, and take more photographs. The pipes looked much the same as they had during his last visit, but there was a new tube in the middle, pointing almost vertically, that appeared to be elevated slightly higher than the rest. After a closer investigation, he determined that the metal thickness was nearly three times that of the other tubes. *Strange. What are they doing?*

At midday the work crew left to go back to the mess hall for their meal. He was preparing to get a closer look at a couple of the tube sites when a group of five men moved toward one of the tubes on the edge of the site. Mark was only fifty yards from them, so he crouched down to watch and listen. There appeared to be a senior officer with them and a second officer giving orders to the other men. They picked up what seemed to be a large canister or perhaps a shell. A mechanism allowed the round to be lowered into the tube. He decided to take some photographs as they went through their routine.

A wire went to a man positioned about thirty yards from the tube; he was holding a small box with what appeared to be some switches. The junior officer indicated for the men to move away, and within a few minutes, there was a very loud but low-pitched thud as the shell shot out of the tube. Because of its size, it was possible to follow the trajectory. It was clear that it would fall several miles out in the valley.

Pointing the camera and awaiting the impact, Mark was surprised to hear a smaller explosion and see the shell separate into four or five individual projectiles; this occurred approximately three hundred feet above the ground. As the projectiles fell, there was another small pop as each disintegrated, releasing a fog or mist of some kind, immediately followed by a huge fireball and crack. There were six of these explosions, and it appeared each fireball had covered an area approximately one hundred feet in diameter.

He didn't know exactly what it meant, but he instinctively knew that this type of shell would be deadly on ground troops, even on light armored vehicles. He had taken quite a few pictures and realized this new information should go back to London quickly.

He slowly withdrew and waited for dusk before leaving the area to return to the dugout. He wasn't aware that what he had witnessed was a test of a fuel-air explosion that would be lethal to exposed ground troops from the standpoint of removing oxygen from the immediate area, as well as creating a powerful blast wave. He also wasn't aware of the other person observing the test from another angle, just outside the mess hall. The corporal made note of the blast area and visited it later in the evening before making a report back to London. He also added some comments he'd overheard about the vertical tube.

July 15, Berlin

Heinrich Himmler was sitting across from Albert Speer in Speer's office. "So, Albert, when were you going to let the rest of us in on your little secret?" Himmler had received information about the fuel-shell tests and was annoyed that he hadn't known anything about it. He was in the habit of collecting all information concerning any subject in the Reich. He had made a point to Hitler several years earlier that he needed this information to provide comprehensive security. It was nothing more than a power play, and Speer knew it. Many times, Himmler would interfere in programs if he thought it was politically expedient for him to do so. That was the reason why Speer had deliberately kept him in the dark.

"Heinrich, you know I don't send *every* report about *every* weapons program to you, and I never have. However, as you can see, this particular development can be beneficial when the Allies approach eastern France."

"Herr Reich Minister, the Allies won't be getting to eastern France because our troops will keep them bottled up in Normandy. Indeed, this is exactly what has been happening, and there's no reason to expect otherwise."

Speer looked down and carefully considered how to respond to Himmler's obvious politically induced comment. The German general staff expected the Allies to eventually break out, and when they did, progress would likely be rapid across France because of the lack of planning for multiple defense lines. "I'm aware that our troops are fighting well and providing a stiff defense, but it never hurts to have a few contingency plans in place. After all, we certainly don't want them in Germany." He looked directly at Himmler. "Do we?"

Himmler continued to question Speer, which was fine with Albert. He knew Himmler had no idea that most of the shells were destroyed. Even more important, he was ignorant of the Tesla weapons sites as well as the nuclear shells. *Give people a little information, and let them run around chasing their tails while the more significant issues are right in front of them, but they're too busy to investigate.* Still, he grimaced when he realized that the fuel shells, even though very successful, would have a minimal impact on the defense of eastern France. *Just not enough. We are running out of manufacturing capacity.*

Operations Goodwood and Cobra

On July 18, over two thousand heavy and medium bombers from both the RAF and the US Air Force bombed the area around Caen. This was followed up by close air support from No. 83 Group of the RAF. General Montgomery had thrown a considerable portion of the Allied Second Army into this battle, and they succeeded in taking Caen and most of the area around it. This allowed the Allies to finally get in relatively flat terrain, which was more advantageous to their armor. By July 20, they had achieved most of their objectives.

While the British were beginning to advance across northern France, General Bradley had devised a similar plan to carpet-bomb an area north and west of Saint Lo in an attempt to pulverize the German defenses that had dug into the hedgerows there. Eisenhower had activated the Third Army and given Bradley the choice of his commander, strongly suggesting that he choose George Patton. Bradley had willingly agreed. *A dash across open country is custom-made for George.*

On July 6, Patton and his staff arrived at a camp outside of Nehu in Normandy. Bradley met him, and they immediately began formulating plans for a breakthrough after the bombing. On July 25, fighter bombers began to attack German strong points just south of the D900, west of Saint Lo. This was immediately followed by almost three thousand medium and heavy bombers of the Eighth Air Force. They bombed an area six thousand yards wide and over two thousand yards deep. Unfortunately, some of their bombs walked backward and landed on US troops, causing casualties, including the death of Lieutenant General McNair. It was possibly the largest friendly fire incident in US history.

Nonetheless, they continued the operation, and Patton's armored divisions began advancing the next day. There was little or no German resistance, as the ground had been transformed from a serene Normandy countryside into something resembling the surface of the moon. From here, Patton split his forces, some racing westward to the coast and some proceeding south and east across France.

The breakout was finally underway along the entire Allied front despite German attempts to slow the Allies.

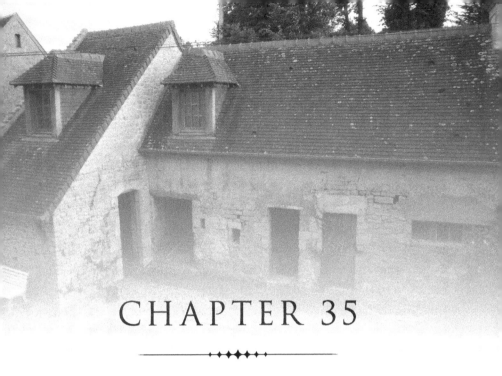

CHAPTER 35

 ◆ ◆◆◆◆ ◆

Midday, July 27, the DeBoy Farm

Alphonse retrieved the message and realized it needed to get to Major Dornier as soon as possible. There had been more German activity in their area in the past several days. In addition, there was a rumor that the Allies had finally broken out of the Normandy area. Obviously, that would make the Germans reevaluate their defensive positions and perhaps strengthen them. All this meant even more German activity.

Alphonse was sitting at the kitchen table, finishing his lunch. Luc had gone back out into the field, and Aurélie and Josette were cleaning up the dishes.

"I need to go up to the dugout to deliver a message," Alphonse said.

Josette turned and looked at her grand-père and then at Aurélie. Henri's parents had received notice the previous week from the Red Cross that Henri was alive and in a prisoner-of-war camp in southern Germany. They said he had been wounded and had lost part of one of his arms. There wasn't much other information, but at least it was a declaration that he was still alive. His parents had visited and shared the notice with Josette. It'd been quite a shock to all of them because they had given up hope of ever hearing from him again. It had shocked Josette even more, particularly because of her recent feelings toward Major Dornier. She was confused, but deep inside, she remembered the feelings she had for Henri. She felt an intense longing to see him again and continue the life they had before the war. That meant, of course, her feelings for Mark would have to be set aside.

She had talked with Aurélie several times, late into the night, trying to make sense of what was going on. Aurélie did not say a lot. Instead, she listened. As Josette explained her feelings, it slowly became evident that she needed to tell this to Mark. Aurélie shared a little of the conversation she had with Mark and how he felt toward Josette. At first, Josette had a small feeling of disappointment, but as she thought more about it, she realized those feelings described their relationship quite well.

Josette dried her hands, went over to the bureau, and picked out a piece of writing paper. "I need to write Mark a note, explaining my news." She didn't attempt to explain further before she began writing. Alphonse looked over at Aurélie and just shrugged slightly.

Aurélie walked over and sat beside Josette as she wrote. "He's a good man. You're making the right decision by telling him of your feelings, but please be gentle. He does care about you."

Josette eyes filled with tears as she looked up at her sister and Grand-père. "I feel like I betrayed Henri, and I think Mark felt that in me. I don't feel like I deserve either one of them."

Alphonse reached over the table and grabbed her hand. "This war has confused the entire world and has mangled many relationships—between people as well as between countries. We all deal with it the best we can and then move on. Your sister's right; you're making the right decision. Major Dornier—Mark—is a good man, and I'm sure he'll understand."

Josette was crying now and leaned on Aurélie's shoulder. Between her sobs, she confessed, "I know this is horrible, but Henri may still never come back, and then I'll be back to no one."

Aurélie smiled and took Josette shoulders with her hands. "Little sister, you will always have me, Luc, and Grand-père, and you will always have Mark's friendship. Besides, you must have faith. If Henri has made it this far, I think he'll come back. You need to be here for him because I suspect your memory has been one of the things that has kept him alive."

"Finish your note, Josette. I should probably leave as soon as I check on Luc."

Aurélie went back to the dishes while Josette finished her note and put it in an envelope. She didn't tell Aurélie, but she suspected her older sister had strong feelings for Major Dornier also. She had included that in her note as well.

She went back to the sink to help her sister finish cleaning up. Putting her arm around Aurélie, she kissed her on the cheek. "I'm lucky to have you as a sister, and thank you for your advice." She hugged Aurélie and then looked into her eyes. "His birthday is in three days. You might think about making him some cookies." She saw the surprise in Aurélie's eyes and smiled. "I saw how you reacted to his name all these months."

Midafternoon, the Dugout

Alphonse slowly sipped his wine while Major Dornier decoded the message. When Mark finished reading it, he realized the part about Operation Goodwood and Operation Cobra was not particularly sensitive. He shared that with Alphonse, adding that the Allies had been bottled up in Normandy, and this could be the start of a major offensive across France.

"I know that there was some concern in London before I left about how to proceed through the German defenses. Evidently, there was a miscalculation about the Normandy countryside because most of their concerns had to do with the defensive positions around and near the rivers."

"It's been over a month since they landed, and they are disappointed that progress has been slow."

"Moving across a country that has been occupied by an enemy who plans as well as the Germans is never easy and certainly not quick. I'm surprised that they were bottled up this long, but I wouldn't have expected them to be much farther than the northern outskirts of Paris or perhaps the Belgium border by now." Mark did not want Alphonse to hear negative things from him because he knew they would get back to the Resistance fighters. Besides, he believed what he was saying.

"Tell your people that there may be more rapid advancement. The Allies have a large number of tanks and other armored vehicles, and the flatter areas south of Normandy are more conducive to an Allied advance. It will also be harder for the Germans to defend because the advance will be so mobile."

Even though Alphonse was not an expert in armored warfare, he remembered in World War I the substantial advantage that even the small French Chennault tanks gave the infantry. He just nodded and cut off another piece of cheese.

They talked for another few minutes, and then Alphonse took Josette's note out of his pocket and passed it across the table. "Last week, Henri Benoit's parents received a notice from the Red Cross that Henri is in a prisoner-of-war camp in southern Germany, and while he was wounded several years ago, he's alive. As you can imagine, this was a shock to all of us and particularly to Josette."

Mark was surprised as well, and his face showed it. However, almost as quickly as the surprise came upon him, he realized that it was best for not only Josette but also for him. After his discussion with Aurélie, he had begun several times to write a letter to Josette, but he tore them all up.

He took Josette's note and read it. A smile came over his face as he read the comment about Aurélie. Alphonse saw it and asked, "I didn't read the note, but I would not think the news would result in a smile."

"I'm sorry; it's just that Aurélie and I discussed this very thing when she was here two weeks ago. I had developed some feelings for Josette, but I also felt strong reservations and didn't know why exactly. Aurélie explained to me about Henri, even though you and Josette had told me about him. I began to better understand her feelings. In fact, I'd decided to tell her, even though I cared for her deeply, that it was not a relationship we should develop any further."

Now it was Alphonse's turn to smile. "I'm just an old man, but I've lived long enough to understand people and particularly my two granddaughters. I suspected this, and I also have come to know you well enough to understand that somehow it would turn out the right way." Alphonse took another sip of his wine. "And besides, I suspect that my other granddaughter wouldn't mind visiting here more often."

Mark smiled again and looked directly at Alphonse. "You're pretty smart for an old French farmer who's never been to the big city. I liked Aurélie the first time I met her, even though she was a bit unfriendly initially. Josette was different, and it's hard not to be drawn to her, but as I said, there was something else there." Mark poured a glass of wine for himself. "I'd like it if Aurélie visited more, but please make sure, as I'm sure you always do, that it's safe."

Just before lunch a couple of days later, on Mark's birthday, he heard Aurélie call from the woods. She had ridden her bicycle to the dugout and had brought him some cookies, made with some of his sugar. He invited her for lunch, and later they walked in the woods. They talked about Josette and Henri, Luc, her grandfather, and Mark's family. He knew there was a risk in sharing this information. He also felt it was time to open up more to the DeBoys; they were beginning to feel like his family as well.

CHAPTER 36

✦✦✦✦✦

August 14, on an LST (Landing Ship Tank) Approaching Vierville-sur-Mer, Omaha Beach

"Slow to one-third, more ballast starboard."

"Slow to one-third, ballast starboard. Aye, sir."

The LST slowed as it approached the beach. It was riding slightly heavy to port. The ballast would help level the ship, allowing its flat bottom to slide onto the beach smoothly. In the hold were M4 Sherman tanks of the Seventh Armored Division. Sergeant Joe Gillis's tank was to be the first one out. Sergeant Gillis was standing in the hatch and turned, motioning to the other tank commanders. There would be three LSTs landing abreast with the remainder of their division landing on Utah Beach. Most of the division had been placed ashore the day before.

Sergeant Gillis stuck his head into the turret and yelled down to his driver, Corporal Gary Elliott. "Gary, get ready. Looks like it's only going to be another couple of minutes." He looked back at the extended engine exhaust and air intake that would allow them to wade through several feet of water, if necessary. His gunner, Sergeant Mike Lloyd, was making the final checks on the waterproofing.

Sergeant Lloyd climbed back on to the turret. "Everything's sealed up, Joe. We should be ready to go. I'll put a round in old Betsy, just in case."

Sergeant Gillis spoke into the intercom. "Don't forget, guys—lock and load but no itchy trigger fingers. There haven't been any recent hostilities, at least not on this beach."

Up on the bridge, the captain received depth soundings from both sides of the ship and gave the order: "Prepare to beach." Sergeant Gillis turned around and looked at the other tank commanders, particularly his friend in the last tank, almost two hundred feet behind him. "Okay, guys, brace." Usually, beaching wasn't that dramatic, but they never could rule out a sandbar that could cause the ship to lurch. Better safe than sorry.

The ship shuddered to a halt about forty feet from the waterline. Since it was low tide, there was another four or five hundred feet of open sand before they could get on the beach road. After the beach master guided them across the sand, they turned west on the road and went up the main draw into Vierville. Their LST had all of the Seventeenth Battalion tanks on it.

When Sergeant Gillis's lead tank got to the top of the draw, they were met by their commanding officer, Lieutenant Colonel John Wemple. Sergeant Gillis took off his earphones and saluted. "Are we still going to Nehu?"

Colonel Wemple climbed up and showed Gillis a map. "Want to take a little different route. Keep going straight on the D30 to Formigny, right on D613 to Chef-du-Pont, and then west to Nehu. Any questions?"

Gillis studied the colonel's map and then made some notations on his. "What speed do you want, sir?"

"This route's about forty miles, so fifteen miles an hour should be enough. Nehu's call sign is 'green forward.' Contact them about five miles out. I'm going to get in the middle of the column. Set a seventy-five-foot gap between vehicles." Wemple climbed down and went back to his half-track.

Gillis radioed everyone the directions. "And make sure we maintain the seventy-five-foot gap, particularly when we get into the hedgerow country."

As they set off, Gillis couldn't help feeling a surge of adrenaline. After all the training, they were finally in France on the way to join up with other elements of the new Third Army, commanded by General Patton. He just hoped they'd be able to keep up with Patton's demands.

CHAPTER 37

◆◆◆◆◆◆

**9:30 p.m., August 28, RAF Squadron No. 617,
Lossiemouth, Scotland**

"Recheck those contacts." The plane captain was worried about the small servomotor that rotated the drum—really just a big bomb—counterclockwise so that when it was dropped, it would skip on the surface of the water.

"Any problems?" The bomb aimer had walked up a couple of minutes earlier and was watching the final checks on the bomb.

"Everything looks okay. I just wanted to make sure that the switch next to the bombsight would close the contacts properly."

The rest of the crew walked out to the plane. The pilots and the navigator had been briefed on Euskirchen—or more specifically, the area around Euskirchen—where the dam was located. The flight would take about four hours because they would change courses several times to avoid flak positions. Tonight, the Lancaster bombers would take off and target two separate dams. Each dam was assigned eight planes. They would approach two abreast, each armed with a special Dambuster, or Upkeep, bomb, developed by Mr. Wallis.

Several months earlier, the British had developed what they termed *skip-bombing*. It utilized a technique that boys had used for years to skip flat stones across the surface of a lake. Dams were tiny targets for aerial bombing, and this technique was developed because absolute accuracy wasn't as important when using this approach. After months of testing, most of it unsuccessful, they developed a bomb that was slightly larger than a standard fifty-five-gallon oil drum. It was mounted on a special brace underneath a Lancaster and contained sixty-six hundred pounds of high explosives. The total weight of the bomb was almost ninety-tree hundred pounds. A servomotor was attached to the brace that would rotate the drum in a counterclockwise direction, which was backward to the direction of the flight. It took months of testing, but they finally determined if the bomb were dropped sixty feet above the surface at a speed of two hundred thirty knots, the backward rotation of five hundred rpms would cause the drum to skip several times before slowing at the dam wall and sinking to its base.

Most of the dams in the German Ruhr Valley had dammed bodies of water that were one to two miles upstream of the dam. If the bombers could level off and drop the bombs four to four hundred and fifty yards upstream, the bombs would skip close enough so that when it detonated, the concussion would damage both the dam structure and the electrical generation gear. The bombs were designed to sink to different predetermined depths, hopefully, close to the dam wall, and then detonate. They utilized both a depth detonation switch and a timer.

Tonight's mission was to the Urft Dam near Euskirchen. The flight crews had not been told any specifics about this dam or a similar dam several miles away. These dams had were dedicated to providing the high-voltage power needed to arm the BR (Tesla) weapons in eastern France. If the dams were destroyed or damaged, it would disable or significantly reduce the effectiveness of the BR weapon.

The eight Lancasters would take off two abreast and keep in formation until a few miles away from the target. They would drop to sixty feet of altitude and assume their attack formation. Five minutes in front of them was a spotter plane that would fly over the reservoir and give them the final green light to proceed.

An hour later, the lead plane assumed its initial heading over the North Sea at an altitude of five hundred feet. The pilot turned to the copilot, "Go check with Martin and have him update our ETA every thirty minutes." The copilot got up and squeezed back to the navigator.

A little over four hours later, the planes dropped below one hundred feet of altitude and started flying two abreast down the broad valley that held the reservoir. The spotter plane had given them the go-ahead, and the partial moon created just enough light on the smooth surface of the lake to allow the pilots to control the altitude, although it took the complete attention of both pilot and copilot to keep the height and speed within the parameters.

"Billy boy, you've got it." The pilot switched over, giving control of the bomb and rotation equipment to the bomb-aimer. They had some crude radar and radio wave equipment to gauge the distance to the dam, as well as a visual display painted on the cockpit windscreen. It was just a white line, scaled so that when the two outside towers on the dam were over the ends of the line, they would know they'd reached the release point. The bomb-aimer switched on the servomotor to begin the rotation while the pilots kept the aircraft at the correct height and speed. It only took ten seconds to obtain the right rpms. The plane beside them was fifty feet off their starboard wing tip and was going through the same drill. The radar panel illuminated the green light; the bomb-aimer checked the visual display, confirming they were ready, and released the bomb. Their wingman released theirs at the same time. The next two planes would arrive in approximately thirty seconds. *I hope Mr. Wallis knows what he's doing.*

The tail gunner reported through the intercom on the bomb. "Looking good; second skip … third skip … fourth … the Marley Gee's bomb looks good also." The plane passed over the dam, clearing its crest by only forty feet. They could see the German antiaircraft crews scrambling to get to their posts. With luck, all four pairs would be able to fly over the dam before the flak became effective.

"The bombs should detonate in approximately one hundred and twenty seconds, and the last flight should have cleared by then." If the plan worked, there would be eight Upkeep bombs setting on the base of the dam—four on the bottom, ninety feet below the surface; two about sixty-five feet down; and two at thirty feet. They would explode at ten-second intervals so the shockwaves wouldn't interfere with each other.

The lead plane climbed to three hundred feet and set a heading due west to escape the flak positions and enemy night-fighter airfields. The tail gunner was charged with the primary observation, even though everyone could see the dam out of the starboard windows. Seconds later, the first two bombs detonated, shooting up towering plumes of water. The second set had a similar result, but the dam was still intact. The third pair of explosions opened a small crack at the base, and the fourth caused water seepage at the bottom. There were also some explosions inside the dam, indicating damage to interior equipment.

Subsequent explosions finally caused the dam to collapse just to the right of center, releasing a tidal wave down the valley. There were similar results at the other dam site, eight miles away. The BR sites would useless for some time.

Early Morning, August 29, German Area Commander Euskirchen

The colonel was awakened at four in the morning to hear the news about his two dams. After assessing the damage and talking to the commanders at the dams, he prepared a report for Berlin, which he sent in a message. He followed that up with a phone call to Speer's office.

"Colonel, your report did not indicate if either of these dams would be able to generate electrical power, even a diminished amount." Speer's chief of staff knew exactly what his boss would want to know.

"No, sir, I just received an update on the dams, and it indicates that both have been destroyed, for all practical purposes, including the hydroelectric equipment. We are looking at how we might be able to tap into the power grids from other dams in the system to provide the high-voltage power requirement."

"Is there any estimate on when the dams might be repaired?"

"I have the engineers working on it now, but a preliminary assessment is a minimum of six to nine months. This includes replacement of all of the electrical equipment."

There was a long silence at the other end of the line. "Do the best you can. I'll report this to the Reich Minister."

Later, the Same Day, a Resistance Cell in Eastern Belgium

Koonrod was reading a message to his group that arrived only a few hours earlier. They were to put together a plan to plant explosive charges on many of the high-voltage towers leading out of Euskirchen.

"Since we'll only get one chance to get near those towers, we'll plant charges above ground to take out several of the towers immediately. We'll also plant charges underground below other tower bases, with timers to detonate days later. Hopefully, the smaller charges above ground will draw attention away from the charges below ground."

It would take three or four days to organize the trip because this was slightly outside of their normal operating area. They had stolen a plan showing the tower locations two months earlier and now used it to determine which towers to destroy. They decided on twenty towers for initial destruction, with charges set on another fifty. Ten days after the initial attack, the charges on twenty-five towers would detonate. Ten days after that, they would blow the rest of the towers.

Between the loss of the dams and the damaged power lines, Speer's Tesla weapon had an uncertain operational future.

CHAPTER 38

August 30, Lower Special Surveillance Office 8, London

General Brawls asked Polly to prepare orders for Lieutenant Ryder to return to France. Colonel Betts decided he needed Lieutenant Ryder's expertise to help Major Dornier collect information on both the site at the Butte de Vauquois and the BR site near Souhesme La Petite.

Polly was in the general's office.

"You can give the orders to him if you would like," he told her. "I know that you have special ties with the DeBoys, and it might be good for you to share that with him."

"I'm glad to hear Alex can be of some help, but"—she paused briefly—"I wish … nothing, I guess,"

Polly left the general's office and found Alex at his desk. She sat down next to his desk and passed the envelope over, quietly whispering, "You're going back to France tonight." She looked at him and could see the concern in his eyes.

"I asked for opportunities outside the office, so I suppose I can't complain." He looked at Polly. "But I'll certainly miss seeing you every day."

She leaned over and put her hand on his. "Go get ready; I'll bring you a sandwich from the cafeteria this evening."

Alex got up and let Lieutenant Boysden know he was leaving, and then he went to his room to pack. The general had sent a field pack over with most of the clothes and items he would need. The orders stated there would be a two-hundred-pound supply bundle accompanying him in the Lysander, with additional things that both he and his contact in France would need. He did not know Major Dornier's name, but he knew there was someone in the general area where he was landing.

He was finishing his preparations when there was a soft knock on the door. He opened it to see Polly standing there. "I brought you a sandwich and a beer." She stood in the doorway and finally smiled. "Are you going to invite me in, or do we have to say goodbye in the hallway?"

Alex was embarrassed. "No, no, I'm sorry, bad manners. Please come in."

Polly handed him the sandwich and closed the door behind her. She walked up and put her hands on his cheeks, kissed him, and then put her arms around him and hugged him tightly. "I miss you terribly when you go away."

Alex put the sandwich down on the desk and then turned back to Polly.

An hour later, he started to eat his food as Polly briefed him from the couch.

"The plane is going land in the same field where our contact initially landed ten months ago. His name is Major Mark Dornier, and he used to work in this office for Colonel Walker in Planning and Logistics. He has been living in a cellar beneath an old artillery dugout, surrounded with tunnels, from World War I. He will meet you when you land and will take you to his camp.

"A French farmer by the name of Alphonse DeBoy supplies him—he is my grandfather. Our family used to visit his farm when I was a young girl. Grand-père's family has gone through great hardships; he has lost his wife, as well as his son and daughter-in-law and then two other sons. He has a daughter named Aurélie, who lost her husband in 1940, and another daughter, Josette, whose fiancé disappeared in

1940 about the same time. They are special people and mean a great deal to me."

Alex looked down, wondering how many other secrets Polly had. "If I get a chance to see him, should I tell him about you?"

"I'd like that. Even if they get caught, the Germans can't do anything with the information." Polly stood up and walked over and kissed Alex again. "Unfortunately, it's time for you to catch a plane."

2:30 a.m., August 31, Forêt Domaniale de Lachalade

The Lysander banked hard to the left and rapidly dropped out of the sky. The small field was marked with four small fires. Alex didn't see how the plane could get into that tight of an area, but the pilot had assured him that he'd landed in smaller fields.

To the north and west, the flashes of light and rumbling had not stopped. Mark estimated that either weather or artillery was probably about twenty miles away. He felt it wouldn't be long until the Allies came through this area.

The plane barely cleared the trees on the east side of the field and then dropped until the wheels hit the ground. The aircraft bounced several times, tipping almost to the point of tearing off a wing. The plane slowed and continued to taxi to the far west side of the field before turning around with its momentum. As soon as it was pointed back east, Alex opened the door and jumped out. He undid the release mechanism for his supply pod, allowing it to drop into the field, pulling it clear. As he did that, the pilot gunned the engine and started his takeoff run, which only lasted about five seconds before the plane was airborne.

Alex heard some rustling at the far end of the field and saw one of the fires go out. He'd been told to stand by his supply pod until his contact approached him.

"Lachalade."

Alex replied with the countersign, "Brooklyn." Out of the darkness, he saw the man approach. Alex had his Sten gun at the ready and saw the other man had one as well.

Mark approached Alex and held out his hand. "Mark Dornier. Welcome to Sherwood Forest. You must be Robin Hood."

Alex could see Mark's smile in the darkness. "So what's next?"

"Follow me. I have some transportation in the trees." They both carried the supply bundle and loaded it. Mark started the engine and gave the scooter a push. "It doesn't go very fast, but it'll get us where we need to go."

Because of the darkness, it took longer than usual to get back to the dugout. They traveled in silence. Mark placed the pod in another nearby dugout, and both men wrestled Alex's supply pod back to the main dugout. By then it was three thirty. Mark told Alex to take the cot in the back of the cellar, near the door to the tunnel complex. Turning the lights on, he asked, "Need anything to drink or eat?"

"No, sir, I'm fine. Probably best if we get some sleep."

"Yeah, good idea. By the way, there's no rank out here. I'm the boss, but no *sir*-ing, please."

They both prepared for sleep. "I'll wake us up about nine o'clock."

Mark woke up a few minutes before nine the next morning. He went over to the stove to heat the coffee he'd made the previous night. Alex began to move and then sat up with a start. Mark looked over at him and smiled. "It happens to everyone, particularly the first night out. You don't know where you are."

"Yeah, I'm not real good at field work."

"Well, someone in London thinks you are. You came with high recommendations."

Mark started preparing a light breakfast. "The sink's over there, so feel free to clean up and shave if you want. I'll make us something to eat and fill you in on the mission."

Over a breakfast of bread and bacon, Mark briefed him on the high-voltage lines running through the forest. "I can't tell you why because I don't know myself, but we need to bring several of these towers down before 9:30 p.m. on September 4. I know they supply the power to a weapon facility just outside Souhesmes la Petite, which is a few miles south. I suspect the Allies are going to be coming through here around that same time."

Alex knew that Patton's Third Army was assigned to this area, and he probably would be close in three or four days.

"So the towers in our woods will need to be destroyed Monday night. We'll go out about 3:00 p.m. and set the charges on four towers to go off by 7:00. Then we'll pick three pairs of towers and set timed charges on two of the legs to go off a few hours before the Allies get here. That should provide enough of an interruption to keep the facility at Souhesmes la Petite out of action during their advance."

CHAPTER 39

◆◆◆◆◆◆

Early Morning, September 4, the Dugout

Aurélie approached the dugout slowly. They all heard the artillery and bombing to the north and knew that the Allies were coming. Her grandfather had received a message about four in the morning for Mark and had asked her to deliver it. Luc and Josette were busy hiding the excess supplies around their farm in case the Germans began to confiscate things.

Mark and Alex awoke about five thirty and made coffee. While Alex was starting breakfast, Mark went outside to finish his coffee to look around. He, of course, heard the truck approaching and immediately pulled the cord that alerted Alex that someone was coming. He realized quickly it was Alphonse's truck, but that didn't mean it wasn't trouble. Kneeling behind a tree and some brush, he readied his Sten gun. He hoped Alex was ready as well, covering the different angles he had shown him yesterday. Mark was concerned that the Germans could use the DeBoys as a decoy and have a platoon surround them.

He watched as the door opened and immediately recognized Aurélie. He still didn't relax because he had created one additional safeguard with her only. She would yell out a challenge of *Kansas* first, if she were under duress. Otherwise, if she waited for Mark to yell out the challenge word, he could assume that she hadn't been followed.

Aurélie looked around as she got out. While she was looking forward to seeing Mark, the war was rapidly approaching, and that meant danger. She stood behind the truck and listened very carefully for a minute or so.

Mark remained concealed but yelled out "Lachalade," to which she replied, "Brooklyn." With that, Mark approached but still held his Sten gun at the ready. He was glad it was Aurélie, but he shared the same concern she did about the approaching war.

"Let's go to the cellar. I have a visitor."

Aurélie fell in beside him, carrying a picnic basket. "Grand-père received a message a couple of hours ago for you. Luc and Josette are busy preparing the farm for the war, and Grand-père had an errand to run, probably to the Resistance."

As they got close to the dugout, Mark yelled to Alex to stand down. Once inside the cellar, Mark introduced Alex and Aurélie. "Alex arrived two nights ago. He's here to help with certain tasks." He looked at Aurélie and then continued. "It's probably better if you don't know all the details, but there's likely to be some activity here in the woods the next couple of nights."

"Bonjour, monsieur, and welcome to Forêt Domaniale de Lachalade. I wish it were under more pleasant circumstances."

"Alex, why don't you warm some milk for our guest; she prefers hot chocolate." He smiled at Aurélie. "I assume, madame. Am I correct?"

"Oui, monsieur. Thank you for remembering. Oh, here's the message."

Alex started heating milk and offered Aurélie some sausage and bread and then started frying some eggs. Mark went over to his desk and began decoding the message. When he finished, he smiled. The first part of the message explained Alex's connection to Polly Berson and then outlined the family connection between Polly and the DeBoys. Finally, it cleared Mark to tell everyone involved.

The second part of the message had three assignments. The first assignment was to meet with an advance party of the Third Army in

Sainte-Menehould that evening at seven o'clock. The advance party wanted a briefing concerning the area and weapons sites. A second assignment was to go to the Butte de Vauquois the following evening and do a final reconnaissance, sending a report back ASAP. Finally, the message confirmed the need to destroy the electric towers in Forêt Domaniale de Lachalade early in the morning on September 5, a revision on the previous instructions.

As Mark approached Alex and Aurélie, Alex looked up. "New orders, boss?"

"Yeah, we have several things to get done in the next few days." Looking at Aurélie and back at Alex, he explained, "There's some personal stuff in here that I'm supposed to share with you two."

Alex and Aurélie looked at each other. "Mark, *s'il vous plaît*, good news only."

Mark smiled at both of them. "It's good news, but it may be a bit confusing, so let me give you a quick summary, and then we can talk. Alex, you work closely with a British captain by the name of Polly Berson." Mark saw the surprise in Aurélie's eyes and watched as Alex nodded. "Well, you should know that Polly and Aurélie are cousins. Polly's mother was a sister to Aurélie's father."

"Polly is … well … I knew she could speak French." He exhaled. "Wow, what a coincidence!"

Aurélie looked at Mark, knowing what was coming next. "So, monsieur, is there something else?"

"As a matter of fact, there is. Alex, you should know that Aurélie lost her husband in 1940, but you also should know that her husband, Sebastian, was Polly's brother."

Alex looked at Aurélie and then back at Mark. He was trying to assimilate everything. Aurélie reached over and put her hand on top of his. "I didn't know of your connection to Poddy—I'm sorry; that was her nickname when she was younger. I meant Polly. Her family used to visit us at our farm when we were younger."

"You and Polly are related." It was more of a statement than a question. "Have you been able to keep in touch with the war and all?"

Aurélie shook her head. "Communications broke down right after the Germans invaded France."

Alex then realized the connection between Polly's statement that she had lost a brother and Aurélie's loss of her husband. Aurélie still had her hand on top of Alex's, and now Alex put his other hand on top of hers. "Polly told me that she lost her brother somewhere in France. I'm sorry, Aurélie. You should know that Polly was very heartbroken for you."

Aurélie smiled at him. "This war has caused losses for many, but I still have my grand-père, a sister, a brother—and I have a cousin and two new friends." She looked up at Mark and then back to Alex again. Aurélie looked at Alex closely. "I'd like to ask you about Polly, if you don't mind."

"Whatever you'd like."

"First, is she doing well?"

"Very well. She works in London and is well respected."

"Second—and you don't have to answer if you don't want to—do you love her?"

That surprised Alex, and it showed, but Aurélie just squeezed his hand. In a soft voice, he replied, "Yes, but how did you know?"

"I'm not sure. Maybe it was the way you mentioned her name. Anyway, I'm glad she's found someone and that she's well."

Major Dornier got up and took the plates. "We should start thinking about what will happen to the DeBoys and our location once the front reaches us. It sounds like Patton's army is approaching, and if that's the case, I suspect that he will sweep through this area rapidly."

"Grand-père thought it would be best if we stayed in the cellar at the farmhouse. There's a small subcellar that goes outside the foundation of the house."

Mark thought for a minute. "It might be better if you split up. Do you happen to have a place out in the fields to take shelter, like a pit or something that would protect you against flying shrapnel?"

"Not really. However, there's a grove of trees in a small ravine where we could dig a pit."

Mark shook his head. "Only as a last resort. A grove of trees out in a field could be an aiming point for artillery. I guess we need to understand where the Germans are going to place their defensive lines. I suspect it will be east of here, and if so, you won't need to be as careful about picking a place for shelter."

Alex nodded in agreement. "We can try to get some information out of the Third Army's advance party, at least from the standpoint of what they would recommend for the local civilians. They won't want to tell us details of their plans, but I suspect they'll want to keep civilians out of harm's way."

They talked for a while and finally decided to wait until Mark and Alex met with the Americans before making any plans. Aurélie wasn't that worried, but she wanted to keep out of sight of any army.

Alex started cleaning up from breakfast and then checked his gear for the trip to Sainte-Menehould. Mark told him it would be about nine miles and should take no longer than four hours.

Mark walked Aurélie back to her truck. Aurélie, for some reason, became worried for Mark and Alex. This was the first time she'd felt concern like this for anyone other than her family. *I like this man, and I don't want anything to happen to him or to Polly's Alex.* Her feelings surprised her, and it surprised her even more when she reached over and took his hand.

Mark felt her hand envelop his and turned to look at her. Suddenly, he felt warmness go through him. He stopped and pulled her toward him. "I hope you know that I have feelings for you and not just as a friend." Aurélie started to reply, but he interrupted her. "They're not like the feelings I have for Josette."

Aurélie looked down at their clasped hands and reached over to take his other hand in hers. Looking up, she whispered, "Would you hold me?"

Mark pulled her up against him, wrapping his arms around her. He whispered into her ear, "We're not supposed to get involved like this, but I can't help it. Please be careful over the next week or so. I don't want anything to happen to you—or your family."

She pulled back and smiled. "I will if you promise me that you and Alex will be careful as well. I've already lost my first love, and I don't want to lose you."

He stroked back of her neck. "I certainly can't let anything happen to Alex. Polly has become quite a dangerous commando, and I wouldn't want to get on her bad side."

Aurélie couldn't help but laugh. "Yeah, Polly always did have a temper, and she *would* get even with you!"

They broke their embrace, and she got into the truck. Mark checked the roads and told her it was clear. She leaned out of the cab and put her arm out. Mark took her hand and kissed it. For some reason, the thought of Josette's coming to visit him in a dress popped in his head. Smiling, he couldn't help but tease her. "Josette sure did look nice when she came here in a dress." Aurélie frowned and started to say something, but Mark said, "I'll bet you'd look even nicer."

She looked forward, smiled, and whispered, "Au revoir. Perhaps … someday." Then she drove off.

Mark went back to the dugout and began helping Alex prepare for their trip.

CHAPTER 40

⋅✦✦✦✦⋅

September 4, Sainte-Menehould

Alex and Mark left the dugout about 2:00 p.m., staying in the woods as they headed south and west. Sainte-Menehould was almost due southwest of the DeBoys' farm. Mark planned to go south as far as they could in the woods before turning west and going across the fields and the D2. They would continue across the fields north of Les Islettes and then west through the woods to Sainte-Menehould.

As they got close to the village, they could see a group of <u>half-tracks</u> with some army trucks on the D3, moving east. "Looks like the advance party."

Mark motioned for Alex to stop while he took a look with his binoculars. As he scanned the village, he could see a large number of vehicles already in Sainte-Menehould. "It looks like most of the advance party has arrived. We're early, but I think we ought to go ahead and see who's there."

They were still almost a mile away and just about out of the woods. Mark was concerned about their approach because he knew the perimeter guards would be jumpy. He had a password, but he might not get close enough to use it, so he had brought a flare gun and would shoot a couple of green flares, if needed.

They continued through a narrow band of trees, almost to the perimeter of the village. After rechecking the village with the binoculars, Mark indicated they should continue. He had just loaded the flare gun when they heard bullets zip over their heads.

They fell on their stomachs in a small depression. "Stay down. I'm going to use the flares." Mark immediately shot one green flare into the air, reloaded, and shot another one. The shooting stopped, and they could hear commands yelled at them, but they were still too far away to make them out.

Looking at Alex, Mark made a decision. "Let's get up and hold our rifles over our heads. We need to get closer to use the password."

They both stood up slowly, holding their rifles above their heads. Several GIs approached them from about seventy-five yards away, spread out in a line. It was clear that other soldiers were covering them. When they finally got close enough, Mark yelled out as loudly as he could, "Victory!" He had to repeat it twice before the lead soldier was able to give him the countersign. As soon as he did, the soldiers lowered their weapons. Mark and Alex continued holding their rifles above their heads.

The lead soldier was a sergeant carrying a Thompson submachine gun. "We've been expecting you guys, but you're early." It was just a few minutes past 6:00 p.m., and the meeting wasn't until seven.

"Yeah, but we had to come on foot since we weren't sure if we'd run into any German patrols. Turns out we didn't see any, and we made good time."

"Well, Colonel Manning said to go ahead and bring you to see him as soon as you showed up. So follow us." He looked back and smiled. "And you can lower your rifles now. We think the Germans are at least five miles to the east."

As they walked into the village, they could see the size of the advance party. In addition to some of the armored vehicles they had seen earlier, there were eight Sherman tanks and eight or ten 81 mm mortars. The advance-party headquarters was in the *mairie*, or city hall.

Alex and Mark were led up to the second floor and shown into a large room. They had just put the rifles down when the colonel walked in. "Welcome, gentlemen. I'm General Patton's chief of staff. I understand you may have some information for us."

Alex and Mark stood at attention and Mark answered, "Yes, sir, information regarding the position of some German units as well as some of the weapon concentrations."

"Stand at ease, gentlemen. Please have a seat." A captain came in. "This is Captain Nevis, my aide, and he'll be taking notes. We should proceed because the general wants to push ahead this evening, if possible."

Mark pulled the notebook out of his pack, which had several sketches of maps and notes on the German positions. He pushed the journal over to the colonel. "I'm not sure from which direction you will approach, but there are some fairly substantial weapon concentrations due east of here. That notebook has some maps with the details, but Alex and I can help you pinpoint the locations on your maps, if you'd like."

Colonel Manning took a look at the maps and passed them over to the captain. "Captain, why don't you get our latest maps. You might also ask Colonel Koch to come in as well. He needs to hear this." The colonel looked up at Mark and Alex as the captain left the room. "Colonel Koch is our G-2, so he needs to integrate this information with the rest of our intelligence."

Within minutes, Colonel Koch arrived, and the captain returned with the maps. After introductions, Mark explained the information he'd gathered over the last several months regarding the German positions and weapons sites.

Colonel Koch listened attentively. "Yes, that agrees with the information we have; actually probably your informationthat you sent back the last several months ."

"Yes, sir, I think the two major obstacles in this local sector would be the BR site at Les Petite Souhesmes and the defensive position at Butte de Vauquois. There's another BR site northeast of Thionville at Fort de Koenigsmacker."

Colonel Koch leaned over the map as Mark explained, "The closest of these sites is just east of Les Petite Souhesmes, here." He pointed to the map. "Alex and I just received orders to destroy the supports for the power lines that pass through Forêt Domaniale de Lachalade, here. That's to happen early tomorrow morning."

Colonel Manning looked at Mark. "Major, it looks like this first BR site is less than twenty miles away. It doesn't look like there's a lot of German resistance between here and there. I suspect we'll be pushing that direction tonight and be in a position to attack tomorrow morning. Mark, if we need the power cut earlier, can you manage it?"

Mark glanced at Alex and then replied, "Yes, sir. We have explosives, and we could blow several towers in the next few hours, if need be."

Colonel Manning looked at Colonel Koch. "What's it look like concerning resistance in front of us?"

"There's not much resistance in front of us in the southern sector, all the way north to Metz. Once you get to the river crossings and the larger towns, you'll get slowed down."

Colonel Manning sighed and smiled. "Well, I'd figure out a way to phrase that a different way because I don't think the general's going to like the thought of being *slowed down*."

A high-pitched but booming voice from the doorway bellowed, "The general is not going to like what, Carlos?"

Mark and Alex, as well as the two colonels, immediately stood at attention as General Patton walked up to the table. *What in the world is Patton doing here?* Mark wondered. *He looks like he stepped out of a magazine—polished riding boots, riding pants, and a tunic with hardly a crease.* Mark couldn't help but notice the two ivory-handled revolvers the general carried. "Stand at ease, gentlemen, and please continue. I'm interested in pushing east as fast as we can. I assume both of you were placed here by MI6–SOE."

For the next several minutes, Major Dornier and Lieutenant Ryder briefed the group on the details of both the site at Butte de Vauquois and Les Petite Souhesmes. It was evident General Patton wanted to push quickly to the BR site east of Les Petite Souhesmes. The general looked at Major Dornier. "So do you think you can take the power lines out early this evening?"

"Yes, sir, as I explained to Colonel Manning, we have the explosives ready. Lieutenant Ryder and I could have the towers ready to blow in about three hours."

Colonel Manning traced the power lines on the map. "How many towers do you plan on blowing?"

"We'll bring four towers down initially and then blow one tower each at the edges of the forest. It will be almost impossible for the Germans to repair that in a day. Further, we're going to put time-charges a foot below ground level on three more towers and set those charges for ninety minutes before your attack."

General Patton thought about this for a minute. "Do you need anything else from us?"

"No, sir, we have everything we need. You just need to tell us when you plan to attack."

Patton looked over at Manning. "What were you thinking?"

"Sunrise is a few minutes past seven, and first light is around 6:10. With clear skies, we should be able to assess the situation properly and plan our attack for approximately six thirty."

Patton looked at his watch. "It's about 7:30 now. Can you blow the towers by two o'clock this morning?"

"Yes, sir. Sounds like we should set the timers around 5:00 a.m. on the last three towers."

"Good luck, Major and Lieutenant." Patton shook each of their hands. "I understand there's going to be an air raid on the site at Butte de Vauquois tonight. Hopefully, they'll knock out most of the defenses there." The general looked at Major Dornier again. "Some more of your valuable information. It's going to save a lot of lives, Major."

Major Dornier looked at Colonel Manning. "Colonel, if you could spare a Jeep, it would help the lieutenant and me to get back to our dugout, giving us more time to start setting up before it gets completely dark."

"No problem. Captain Nevis will find you a Jeep, and good luck."

Mark and Alex walked out and were on their way back in five minutes.

8:30 p.m., September 4, near the Butte de Vauquois

Marie and Thierry were concealed behind some brush about thirty yards from the boundary wire for the site. Eight two-person teams surroundedd the location. They had arrived before dark to find a good hiding spot. The British bombers were scheduled to arrive at 6:15 a.m., with the marking plane coming five minutes earlier. The Resistance would to throw grenades and begin firing, upon receipt of a coded radio message that would arrive between 5:50 a.m. and 6:00. Each team had two ten-pound self-propelled incendiary devices that would travel approximately fifty meters. They would serve as the initial marking of the area to guide the Mosquito marking planes.

Thierry rolled over and whispered in Marie's ear. "I'm going to check the other teams. Stay down and out of sight." He slowly crawled backward until he was in a small depression and then got up and began to move toward the nearest team, about one hundred meters away.

One of the sentries, Private Sender, walked over to a tree to relieve himself. After he finished, he turned around and caught sight of movement about ten meters away. He froze as he watched a Frenchman move slowly outside of the perimeter. He realized there were probably more fighters in the woods, and in fact, they might even be observing him now. He made a quick decision; he had to stop this man and get him back for questioning.

Sender slowly raised his Mauser, clicked off the safety, and aimed for the man's right shoulder. The report of his rifle echoed across the valley.

Thierry felt a blow on his shoulder. It spun him around and knocked him down. He knew he'd been hit and, even worse, he had lost his weapon.

Sender turned around and yelled to his partner, who was about ten meters away. "Tell the sergeant I just shot an intruder and to get some help over here quick."

Fifteen minutes later, Thierry was in the mess tent with the major and several other officers. They had stopped the flow of blood, but Thierry knew the chances for survival were low. One of the officers took out a pocket knife and moved toward Thierry. "You're going to reveal why you're here. The only question is whether you're going to reveal it with or without pain."

Twenty minutes later, the commanding officer finished sending a coded message to Berlin, informing them that they were likely surrounded by Resistance forces and would be attacked tonight or early tomorrow morning.

8:45 p.m., September 4, the Dugout

"Make sure you have the new detonators." Mark was busy loading explosives.

Alex yelled back, "I brought both the old and the new detonators, just in case. We have two hundred rounds each for our Sten guns."

They climbed onto the pod and started moving toward the power lines. They decided to use the scooter pod instead of the Jeep because it was quieter. Each of the towers would take a one-pound charge.

The light was beginning to fade when they arrived at the power line right-of-way. They stopped about fifty yards and split up to check for Germans. Twenty minutes later, they had determined it was clear. They began to dig holes for the charges, set to detonate in the morning. It was just after 10:00 p.m. when they completed the explosives on the three towers. They used their flashlights to make sure that the ground disturbance around the charges was well camouflaged. Mark set the timers for 5:05, 5:08, and 5:10 a.m.

They picked the rest of the towers to set the charges and were finished just after midnight. They had decided to blow the two towers on the edges of the forest at 1:15 a.m. Then they would blow the rest of the towers at 1:45. At 12:50 a.m., they armed the timed fuses and drove back to the dugout. They had just finished concealing the pod when the first towers blew.

"Let's load up on explosives and more ammo and go down the road a bit. The next explosions are going to bring out a lot of Germans, and I don't want to be caught near this dugout."

About thirty minutes later, the other towers came down. By 2:20, several German trucks were coming up the D3 from the east toward the forest.

9:00 p.m., September 4, Albert Speer's Private Quarters, Berlin

Speer got up to answer the door. His aide handed him a message. "We just received this from the commanding officer at the Butte de Vauquois. It appears they've captured a member of the local Resistance and have learned there will be an attack around dawn tomorrow morning. Further, there appears to be evidence that the British will be sending bombers over as well."

Speer invited his aide to sit down as he read the message. "Wake up the colonel and tell him to send a message to all the BR sites. Put them all on high alert, and tell him to prepare for imminent attacks. Then tell him to send a message to Euskirchen and get a status on the repair of the high-voltage lines and the dams."

Speer dismissed his aide and sat back down. This wasn't good because only a small fraction of the BR sites would have access to the power they needed. It was no coincidence that all of this happened in the last several days. He was sure the Allies would attack tomorrow or the next day. He felt sick that the nuclear shells and the napalm were so far below the original goals.

He walked over to his bar and poured himself a large brandy. Holding it up, he said aloud, "To the Third Reich, the Thousand-Year Reich, which probably won't last another six months."

9:00 p.m., Lower Special Surveillance Office 8, London

Lieutenant Boysden picked up the phone and called Colonel Gaffney after decoding the Resistance message. "They're in position, Colonel. You can release the bombers."

Gaffney hung up and called his contact at the RAF airfield. "It's on. Good luck."

2:30 a.m., September 5, Forêt Domaniale de Lachalade

Lt. Colonel Schmidt, riding in his Volkswagen carrier, had a knot in his stomach. He had worried that something like this would happen, and he had put in a request for additional troops to guard the power lines. Even though he had twenty-five men with him, he knew if the demolition was done skillfully, it would be almost impossible to repair the lines in twenty-four hours. He was confident the Americans would attack during that time, which would leave the BR site without power.

He turned to Sergeant Varick. "Do the best you can with repairs. I suspect we're going to be in for a long night."

Mark and Alex had positioned themselves about three hundred yards north of the power lines, just off the access road. They had taken the precaution earlier in the week of planting several mines in the road. Mark indicated for Alex to get lower as the trucks approached the demolition site.

"They're just about on top of the mines. As soon as one of the trucks goes up, shoot any survivors."

Sergeant Varick turned to yell to his squad leader in the back of the truck. "As soon as we stop, set out a defensive perimeter, and help get the wire spools off the truck." They were all exhausted after having traveled from Butte de Vauquois during the day and then checking on the BR site defenses. *I'll be glad when the Americans attack; maybe we can get some sleep before then.*

Just then, they hit a mine. The front of the truck was demolished, killing both the major and the sergeant. The survivors heard machine-gun fire, and the men in the following two vehicles began to take fire. Heinrich Kohler, not officially a soldier, had transferred two weeks before from Arlon, Belgium, to help with the final hook-up at the Souhesmes site. Sitting at the rear of the truck, he realized they all needed to get out and take cover.

"Everyone out and into the ditch!"

Several of the soldiers were hit as they piled out of the truck. Mark and Alex were both into their third clip. The truck that hit the mine was burning and provided enough light to allow them to see. Unfortunately, they didn't realize that both their muzzle blasts and the fire were giving away their position.

The machine-gun crew was setting up the MG 42 while the rest of the soldiers provided covering fire. No one knew how many were shooting at them, but one of the corporals already suspected the force wasn't big.

"When you get the machine gun set up, put short bursts in the area around the muzzle blasts. I don't think there's many out there."

Just as the machine-gun crew was about to return fire, the second truck rolled over a mine and exploded. The flash of light illuminated some soldiers who were grouped, as well as Mark and Alex. One of the soldiers threw a grenade that landed very close to Mark, but he was busy firing in a different direction. Alex ran over and threw it back at them. Mark immediately yelled for him to get down, but it was too late. The machine-gun crew spotted him and put a short burst in his direction.

Alex felt two projectiles hit him, one in the upper left shoulder and the other through his right thigh. He went down in a heap. Mark knew immediately they were in trouble. He took two packets of plastic explosives, quickly inserted a detonator with a short fuse, and threw both charges as far as he could.

"Stay down, Alex!"

Seconds later, the two charges went off and momentarily silenced the Germans. The remaining Germans, deciding discretion was the better part of valor, began to withdraw south to the edge of the woods. Mark waited for a few minutes until he was sure they were leaving and then went over to Alex. He determined quickly that both wounds were fairly clean; the bullets had passed straight through soft tissue. "You're lucky; it didn't hit any bones or major organs." Mark knelt to put a tourniquet on Alex's leg and gave him morphine. "I'm going to get the Jeep and take you down to Alphonse's farm."

The Germans had decided to go back to the BR site and regroup. It took Mark about twenty minutes to get the Jeep back to Alex. After loading him, he took off for the farm, going north and then west to avoid any possible confrontation with the Germans.

CHAPTER 41

3:25 a.m., September 5, Alphonse's Farmhouse

Mark parked the Jeep in front and ran to the house to wake someone. Aurélie and Josette were already up, having heard the explosions and subsequent shooting.

"We need some help. Alex has been shot and needs a place to hide until we can find a doctor."

Aurélie turned to Josette. "Start heating some water and get some rags and disinfectant."

Josette went back to the kitchen, while Aurélie walked with Mark to the Jeep.

The morphine was making Alex groggy. While the wounds were not bleeding profusely, the movement hadn't allowed them to close.

"Mark, drive him over to the front door. We'll take him to the basement."

By now, Alphonse and Luc both were awake. Alphonse immediately knew what had happened and motioned to Luc and Mark to carry Alex into the basement. "Josette, please go down and prepare a mattress, and see if you can get a fire started."

Within an hour, they had Alex resting comfortably on a makeshift bed and a fire going in the basement fireplace. Alphonse had removed Alex's clothes so that they could look at the wounds and begin cleaning them.

"The wounds are clean, so if we can stop the bleeding and keep any infection out, he has a good chance." Alphonse turned to Aurélie. "See if you can pour some brandy in both wounds while he is out, and then bandage both tightly."

Mark went upstairs and sat down at the table. Josette brought him a small glass of brandy. "I received a letter from Henri, and he may be able to return this month."

Mark reached up and squeezed her hand. "I'm glad. The fighting should be through this area in a week or so. I pray your family will get through this without any further losses."

Just then Aurélie came up the stairs. "I think he's beginning to start a fever. Do you have any more penicillin?"

"Nope. I wish I'd saved some or even asked Colonel Manning if he could—" Mark stood up quickly. "I think I'm going to see if I can find the Americans. They shouldn't be more than twelve miles east of here by now." He looked at his watch. "It's four thirty. If I hurry, I should be able to find them by first light."

As he turned to leave, Aurélie grabbed his arm. "I'm going with you."

"No, you need to stay here; besides, this could be dangerous."

"I'm going with you, Mark. We're wasting time arguing!"

Mark opened his mouth to argue but then decided it wouldn't help. "Let's go."

They got in the Jeep, and Mark turned on to the D2. Just as they approached Les Islettes, Mark pulled off on the side of the road.

Aurélie looked over. "Why are we stopping?"

Mark reached over and took her hand. "I just wanted you to know I love you, and I want to spend the rest my life with you."

Aurélie heart jumped. She smiled slightly. "Don't you think that we should wait to see if we are alive after tonight before making such declarations?"

He reached over with his other hand and pulled her closer, kissing her gently. "I wanted to do it in case anything happens. You should know how I feel."

Aurélie put her hand on his cheek and kissed his lips. "I already knew, but thank you. I love you as well."

3:45 a.m., September 5, RAF Airfield, "Hinton in the Hedges"

The flare went up, and three Lancaster bombers increased engine power to full throttle and rolled down the runway. Three Mosquitos had taken off fifteen minutes earlier to mark the target. Eighty Lancasters were in the flight, most of which were carrying 250-pound bombs. The trailing ten bombers would all have ten-pound incendiaries.

The nose of the lead aircraft lifted. "Gear up." The major looked back at his radio operator. "As soon as we get to five thousand feet, send the message to the marking planes."

"Pilot to crew, keep a sharp eye out. We don't want any collisions." He turned to his copilot. "Take over, and get us to the rendezvous point."

The bomb-aimer came on the intercom. "I guess there's nothing to do until the sun comes up. I hope all this is worth it. Seems a waste of resources to send this many bombers to such a small target."

It would take the group about thirty minutes to organize before proceeding southeast almost four hundred miles to the Butte de Vauquois.

5:00 a.m., September 5, Just West of Les Souhesmes-Rampont, Fourth Armored Division HQ

Mark drove dark, with only the soft light of the partial moon to guide them. They skidded through the intersection with the D3 before getting back on the road. Just outside of the small village of Les Souhesmes-Rampont, a spotlight came on, followed quickly by a sharp command of *Halt!*

"Texas league."

Obviously, that was the challenge, but Mark had no idea what the password was.

"I'm Major Mark Dornier; I met with Colonel Manning and General Patton earlier today. A Texas leaguer is a soft fly to the outfield that drops in for a base hit. We have a message for the staff and a request for some medical assistance."

"Get out of the Jeep and lie face down in the road—now!"

Mark looked at Aurélie and nodded. They both lay down while several guards came up and searched them. A large sergeant with a Thompson 45 put his flashlight in their faces. "What is your business? You know you could get killed doing this; there are Germans everywhere."

"I agree about the Germans, and if I could, I'd suggest you turn the flashlight off. I've been here for almost a year gathering intelligence information on some of the German sites that you guys are going to attack tomorrow morning. A British lieutenant and I destroyed several high-voltage towers a few hours ago. As a matter of fact, any time now you're going to hear two more explosions. While I wanted to update Patton's staff that we were successful, we also took a casualty fighting off the German maintenance party. We'd like some medical supplies, if you guys can spare any."

The sergeant turned his flashlight off but still appeared wary. "So what's the French girl doing with you?"

"It's a long story, and I don't have time to explain. She belongs to a family living in a farmhouse on the other side of the forest. She and her family have been furnishing me with supplies since I arrived." Mark was beginning to get exasperated. "So can we please see someone on the staff quickly?"

As if on cue, there were several explosions, indicating that the last two towers had been brought down.

A young lieutenant walked up. "Sergeant, it's okay. Major, I'm going to let you in. Follow this road."

They approached a trailer and were challenged immediately by another set of guards. The lieutenant got them through and took them inside. He found one of the general's aides. "Captain, this is Major Dornier. He claims he's been helping gather information on some of the sites in front of us for the last year. He also says he met with Colonel Manning and the general earlier this evening."

The captain recognized his name. "What do you have for me, Major?"

"We blew the power-transmission towers a few hours ago, and just about five minutes ago the last two towers were brought down. So the defensive position just outside of Les Petite Souhesmes should not have power for the special weapons. Unfortunately, the Germans sent a maintenance party to the area to make repairs. The British lieutenant with me was wounded while we were trying to change their minds about making any repairs. He's starting to run a fever, and I would be grateful if we could get some morphine, perhaps plasma, and any penicillin or other medical supplies you could spare. He saved my life during the fight."

Just then, Colonel Manning and General Patton walked in. Patton immediately recognized Mark. "I'm glad you're still alive. I hope you don't have bad news."

Mark related his story again. Colonel Manning just shook his head and smiled. "You've paved the way for us. We very much appreciate your efforts."

Patton thought for a second and then yelled into the other room. "Charlie, come in here for a second." A gray-haired man walked in. "Charlie, this is Major Mark Dornier. Major, this is my personal physician, Colonel Charles Odom. Charlie, the major and his assistant, Lieutenant Ryder, have taken out some German electrical transmission towers for us, and it's going to save several hundred lives this morning. Lieutenant Ryder's been shot and needs immediate attention. They are in a farmhouse about ten or eleven miles west. Can you go back with some medical supplies and see what you can do for the lieutenant? And then get your ass back up here as quick as possible!" Patton looked at Mark. "Anything else, Major?"

"Do you think you could send this message back to London and get it to MI6-SOE?"

"Done. Now if you'll excuse me, we have to prepare for an attack."

Colonel Odom turned to a medic and gave him instructions for some supplies. They were loaded in fifteen minutes. Colonel Manning had provided a second Jeep with a mounted .30-caliber machine gun, three extra soldiers for security, and several cans of gasoline. They started down the road, with Aurélie in the lead Jeep and Mark following about fifty yards behind with the doctor.

They didn't know that four of the surviving members of the German repair team had walked out of the forest and were currently resting at the intersection of the D21 and the D998, just west of Auzéville en Argonne. One of them was Heinrich Kohler, the electrician, and another was Private Berne Gerhart, who had worked with him at several of the sites. Private Gerhart had suffered a deep cut on one leg from one of the mine explosions.

5:35 a.m., September 5, West of Auzéville en Argonne at the Intersection of the D21 and the D998

Berne Gerhart was moaning because his leg throbbed. Heinrich had pulled a small piece of metal out of the bottom of his thigh, and one of his friends had fashioned a tourniquet to stop the bleeding. Heinrich Kohler had taken one of the Schmeisser submachine guns and was standing about ten feet away from the others. Heinrich, while technically a sergeant, was a master electrician. He had been allowed to dress in civilian clothes, which was more suited to electrical work. Both of the repair-party trucks had hit mines, and he knew for sure the major was dead. After the tremendous explosion in the ditch, they had found only eleven men alive, and four of them had severe wounds.

Heinrich looked at his watch and noted that it was getting close to 6:00 a.m. The eastern sky was already showing signs of the coming dawn. Heinrich had heard the movement of troops all through the night and knew the Americans were planning to attack this morning somewhere close. He was sick of the war and what it had done to his family and this country. Now he knew Germany was doomed, and further, that the Allies' frontline was close. If they could survive the next several days, there was a good chance they would get to see their families again.

One of the others murmured, "Don't we need to get moving? Berne is not doing well, and I suspect that our site is going to need us back."

Heinrich didn't bother turning as he replied softly, "First, keep your voice down. All the vehicle noise we heard a few hours ago was the Allies. Look at the tracks on the side of the road." He bent down and pointed out both tire and tank tracks in the dim light. "I'm pretty sure we're behind the front lines now, and I don't think there's anything more we can do for our base. When the transmission lines came down, it severed the high-voltage power that our weapons need. I suspect all they have left is conventional weapons, which won't stand up long to tanks."

The young man turned to walk back to his friend. "Surely there's something we can do."

"Yeah, be quiet, stay hidden, and try to survive the next couple of days. The war may be over for us."

The distinct noise of an American Jeep suddenly increased in volume, indicating that someone was coming toward them. "Get back to the others, and make sure Berne stays quiet!"

In the Jeep, Aurélie leaned over to the driver. "How can you see well enough to go this fast?"

"Don't worry, ma'am; it's getting light, and we've been making night runs for the last couple of months."

Just then the driver slammed hard on the brakes. Two fence posts were lying in the middle of the road, and the driver didn't want to go into the ditch to avoid them. As soon as the Jeep came to a stop, the soldier on the machine gun flipped off the safety, as did the other soldier. Unfortunately, it was too late.

"Don't move, and get your hands up!" The command was loud, clear, and with a heavy German accent.

The soldiers had no choice and surrendered their weapons, as Heinrich and his two associates guided the Jeep on to a small dirt road where it could be hidden from the D21 by dense brush.

No sooner was that accomplished than the sound of a second Jeep announced its approach. The three Germans leveled their weapons at the three American soldiers and Aurélie. As soon as the Jeep passed, Heinrich approached. "Do you have any medical supplies? We have a wounded man."

The man on the machine gun replied quickly, "No, we were on a trip to the rear to get some additional ammunition." It was not true, but was reasonable since they were traveling to the rear.

The soldier next to Heinrich pointed his Mauser at Aurélie. "Why do you have the girl with you?"

None of the Americans replied quickly, so Aurélie spoke up. "I live in the area and was asked to guide them along the roads."

The sergeant who had been riding in the back seat spoke up. "You guys realize you're behind our lines now. In fact, in just a few minutes, we're going to begin an all-out assault in this sector."

The knot in Heinrich's stomach grew tighter, but in some ways, he was pleased. However, the two soldiers with him seem irritated by the disclosure. "You Americans think you can always have your way. You may defeat a few defensive positions here, but we have weapons waiting for you with destructive power you can't imagine."

6:00 a.m., Butte de Vauquois

"The marker planes should be here in ten minutes and we'll mark in five minutes." They had received the coded radio message confirming the arrival of the British bombers. The French commander spoke softly into his walkie-talkie. "Mark the targets at 6:05 a.m."

Each of the six two-man teams prepared their bazooka tubes and pulled the safety pins from the projectiles. As soon as they fired their rounds, they would begin shooting in a predetermined direction while their 60 mm mortars would drop shells inside the German perimeter.

6:05 a.m., Butte de Vauquois

The French teams fired their incendiary rockets and simultaneously began to rake the area with automatic fire. Within seconds, the mortar shells began impacting. All of the rockets exploded, spreading a sheet of flame in a two-meter circle, clearly marking the perimeter that included the German weapon tubes. Two separate teams were busy designating the suspected ammunition dumps as well.

6:07 a.m., Twenty-Eight Thousand Feet, British Lancaster Flight Leader

"Pilot to navigator, time to target, please."

"Nine minutes, on my mark."

6:12 a.m., Five Thousand Feet, British Mosquito Marker Flight Leader, Approaching from the East

The copilot pointed to the fires that were visible. The pilot went on the intercom. "Prepare to descend to two thousand feet." The first two planes would drop five incendiary bombs each, and one marker plane at ten thousand feet would follow up with marker flares.

Pilot Officer Kearney followed the instructions of his bomb-aimer and corrected slightly to the left, slowing his speed to one hundred and fifty miles per hour. As soon as he felt his payload release, he closed the bomb-bay doors and began to climb. Suddenly, his right engine exploded, and Kearney felt the impact of multiple shells hitting the fuselage.

"Bail out!" Kearney knew it wasn't likely that any of them would survive. He fought with the controls to keep the plane level. Seconds later, the right wing collapsed, and the plane went into a violent vertical spin downward. It impacted about a mile from the German perimeter. One parachute slowly floated to the ground.

6:16 a.m., inside the German Perimeter, Butte de Vauquois

"Are the rockets ready?"

"Yes, sir, and we have the altitude and speed of the flight computed."

"Fire two rockets." The colonel wished that he had more of the rockets from headquarters. However, instead of the fifteen he had been promised, only three had arrived. He would keep one as a reserve.

Both rockets lifted off, heading for a point in the sky where the bombers would be in about thirty-five seconds.

6:16 a.m., Twenty-Eight Thousand Feet, inside One of the British Lancasters

Captain Billingsly corrected his course slightly to follow the lead plane. Their formation was called a *combat box*. His aircraft was located on the far left. The bomb-bay doors opened as they prepared to drop bombs and incendiary devices onto a tiny target area. *I hope they know what they're doing because this is like threading a needle.*

"Nose gunner to pilot: two rockets approaching from the right!"

A split second later the first rocket passed just behind the right wing and knocked the plane slightly off course with its backwash. The warhead had malfunctioned, and the rocket continued for another one thousand feet before the motor cut off, and it began plunging back to earth.

The second warhead did not malfunction. It passed about thirty yards in front of the lead plane, slightly to the left. It detonated about eight hundred feet above the left edge of the formation. All Captain Billingsly saw was a bright light, followed by darkness.

Sergeant Johnson was a bomb-aimer in the rear of the formation about three hundred yards from the detonation. The bright light was followed by a shockwave that swallowed seven or eight planes, disintegrating them. The shockwave then knocked several planes off course, causing three collisions.

"Secondary flight leader taking over; everyone hold course. Fifteen seconds to drop." After he got off the radio, he called to his bomb-aimer. "Do you have the target?"

"Yes, sir, we're on target."

"Drop when ready."

Once the lead plane released their bombs, the other planes followed in unison. The rocket that had malfunctioned impacted just northeast of the Butte, and the impact caused the warhead to detonate with an enormus explosion. It was near an intersection filled with German vehicles that were rushing reinforcements to the Butte. Most of the troop transports were damaged or destroyed.

At approximately 6:20 a.m., the bombs began to impact. The French Resistance had retreated four hundred yards from their previous positions. The first bombs fell outside the perimeter, but the next set hit directly on the weapons sites, as well as on the surrounding facilities. The colonel had just given the order to fire the last rocket as the bombs dropped on his position. A split second later, bombs obliterated his headquarters, burying the third rocket under debris.

Three of the Lancasters near the rocket explosion were falling out of the sky, trailed by a few parachutes. The French Resistance saw them and sent people to rescue the survivors.

CHAPTER 42

6:20 a.m., Just Outside Clermont-en-Argonne

It was getting light enough that Mark should've been able to see to see the lead Jeep. He was becoming more concerned with each passing moment. He turned to Colonel Odom. "Have you seen anything of the first Jeep in the last several minutes?"

"No, but they may have gotten farther ahead of us. Let's keep going; there's a wounded man that needs our help."

The rumbling of the air raid at the Butte was lighting up the horizon to the north. While Mark had not been told any of the details, he suspected either the British or Americans were bombing the site.

6:32 a.m., at the Intersection of the D21 and the D998

Kohler was unaware, but for several minutes, the two German soldiers were whispering between themselves. Aurélie had the feeling they were talking about her. They turned and started walking toward Heinrich, the Americans, and Aurélie. As Heinrich turned, he became concerned with the looks in their eyes. Just then, the rumble of thunder exploded only a few miles east as the American attack began. It was apparent they were using artillery, as the horizon lit up in sharp, bright flashes, followed by rumbling explosions. The horizon north was illuminated in thunder as well. None of them realized that the British were bombing the Butte de Vauquois.

The taller of the two Germans indicated the Americans were to remain in place. The other man smiled and walked over to Aurélie, pushing her down. In an instant, he was on top of her and had his legs between hers. Heinrich suddenly realized he intended to rape her and moved to try to stop his attack.

The taller German yelled at Heinrich, "She's just a French whore, and she'll likely be dead by evening anyway."

"German soldiers don't behave this way. Don't do this!"

The man on top of Aurélie continued to pull at her clothes. It was clear he wasn't going to stop. Heinrich raised his Schmeisser, but the other German used his gun like a club and knocked Heinrich over.

Aurélie was scared as she struggled to free herself, but the man was too strong. He slapped her hard, stunning her. As she relaxed, he reached up underneath her dress and ripped at her undergarments. In a flash, she felt the man force himself inside her. She tried one more time to push him off but was unsuccessful. She could hear two other German voices arguing, and she knew enough German to realize they were trying to stop what was happening.

Indeed, Berne had found his Mauser and was trying to shoot the taller German, but the soldier was too fast and kicked the gun out Berne's hand and clubbed him with it. Aurélie saw stars, and finally, everything went black.

6:50 a.m., West of Auzéville en Argonne

Aurélie regained consciousness and heard the two Germans laughing. It was obvious they both had raped her and were now bragging about it. She looked over and saw the two Americans and the other two Germans. She controlled her rage and decided to take a chance. She rolled over and got to her feet and then walked over to the two Germans, who were sitting down.

She tried to put a calm look on her face. "You didn't need to do it that way. If you would've just asked, we all could've enjoyed it." They both looked up at her with a surprised look on their faces, and their hesitation was all Aurélie needed. She quickly reached down, grabbed the Schmeisser out of the nearest man's lap, flipped off the safety, and shot both men multiple times.

Then she turned to the other two Germans. Speaking in broken German, she asked, "Which one of you is named Heinrich?"

"I am."

"You tried to stop them; thank you." Walking over to the two Americans, she untied them. "We need to keep going to my home. We should take the wounded soldier and Heinrich with us."

7:10 a.m., the DeBoy Farm

Colonel Odom cleaned Alex's wounds with Alphonse's and Josette's help. "You're lucky, Lieutenant. These were clean wounds. Infection would've set in, but I think you're going to be fine now."

Mark looked down at Alex. "How are you doing?"

"I'm fine, but I'm worried something has happened to Aurélie."

"I am too. Somehow we lost her Jeep a few miles back." He turned to Colonel Odom. "If you can spare me, I'd like to go back and see if I can find her and the other Jeep."

"Go ahead, Major. I'm going to be another forty-five minutes or so. When I'm done, I probably should get back."

"I'll be back soon as I can." Mark ran out, got in the Jeep, and started down the road, retracing their route.

It took him only a few minutes to get on the D21. Just as he turned east, he saw the other Jeep approaching. He pulled over, and the second Jeep stopped. He could see the two Germans in the Jeep and that Aurélie seemed shaken up.

"What happened? You guys okay?" Aurélie was sitting in the front seat, and Mark went over to her. "Are you okay?"

Aurélie glanced at him briefly. "We ran into some Germans. We shot two of them, but these two helped us. Let's just get back to the farm."

They arrived at the farm a few minutes later. They carried Private Gerhart down to the basement. Mark motioned to Colonel Odom. "We have a few more injuries to deal with."

Colonel Odom turned his attention to the leg wound and began cleaning it. He asked Alphonse if he would look at Heinrich's forehead. Aurélie jumped in and started dressing the cut. Heinrich looked at her. "Why are you helping me after what my friends did?"

"You tried to stop them, and besides, I don't think they were your friends."

For the next twenty minutes or so, they worked on the two Germans and then finally took a break. Mark knew something was bothering Aurélie, but he wasn't sure what it was. She walked over to Colonel Odom and said something in a low voice. Mark turned his attention back to the two Germans to make sure they weren't a threat. When he turned again, he saw Colonel Odom giving Aurélie a shot of penicillin.

The colonel whispered to Aurélie "Perhaps we could go to your bedroom so that I could take a look?"

As they went up the stairs, Mark looked at Josette and Alphonse. "What's going on?"

Josette wasn't sure, but she thought something might have happened with the two Germans on their way back to the farmhouse. She followed Aurélie and the colonel upstairs. Alphonse stayed in the basement with Mark. Alphonse too was suspicious, and he knew Mark would be worried. "Let the colonel examine her. We need to stay down here. Aurélie will be fine; she's a strong woman."

7:30 a.m., Seventh Armored Division, Seventeenth Tank Battalion, Charpentry, North of Butte de Vauquois

Sergeant Joe Gillis stood in the turret hatch. His platoon of four tanks was on a small, unnamed road, turning south into the village of Charpentry. "Gary, slow down, and Mike, load up. You never know what's going to be up ahead."

He switched to the radio to talk to the other three tanks. "We're going to slow here for a minute. Michael, make sure you've got a round in your gun, and turn the turret to the rear."

Sergeant Michael Gillett commanded the fourth tank in their platoon and covered their rear. "You two middle guys, go right and left." They had practiced this for the past several months. The middle two tanks positioned their turrets thirty degrees to the right and left, so the column had all directions covered—not that it mattered. If there was a German tank out there or one of their high-velocity antitank guns, they'd probably get one or two of them.

Sergeant Gillett replied, "Done. What's all that smoke to the south?" They'd all been focused on the ridge that was pounded about an hour earlier by a flight of bombers.

"I don't know, but I suspect it was a German position—emphasis on *was*." They had been on the move all night and would need to be refueled shortly. "The old man just called a few minutes ago and wants us to head northeast out of here on the D998. We're supposed to go on to Montfaucon and wait outside the village for the fuel trucks."

Patton had told the commanding officer, Lieutenant Colonel Wemple, to wait at Montfaucon until the rest of the Seventeenth caught up. Then they were to join the attack on Thionville and cross the Meuse River near an old World War I battleground. There was a German strongpoint called Fort de Koenigsmacker about two miles northeast of Thionville on the east side of the river that had to be taken out. The Ninetieth Division was assigned to lead the attack, and they needed some help from the Seventh Armored Division. They didn't know, however, that this particular location had an active BR weapon and the electrical power to use it.

7:45 a.m., on the D163 at Souhesme-la-Grande, a Half Mile South of the BR Site

The tanks and infantry were finishing mopping up the area. Without electrical power, the BR site was an easy target for Patton's thrust. They had lost a few tanks to mines, but casualties overall were light.

General Patton was standing in his Jeep with his binoculars. "By God, Alex and Mark's information was exactly right. If I could find them, I'd give Mark command of one of our infantry companies!" He turned to one of his staff officers. "Bill, did that message to London go out before we attacked?"

"Yes, sir, about two hours ago."

"Did my comments go as well?" He had added a recommendation. Patton had fought with Captain William Berson in World War I and had kept in touch with him with the occasional letter. He knew Polly as well. *I hope Ike will let her come.*

CHAPTER 43

✦✦✦✦✦

7:30 a.m., War Cabinet Rooms, St. Charles Street, London

Polly's hands shook as she read the message. "We don't know anything more than this?"

General Brawls shook his head. "Apparently, Major Dornier is okay, but Alex has been shot and is at the DeBoy farmhouse."

The message indicated that Alex's wounds were not necessarily life-threatening but serious and that Mark had managed to wrangle medical assistance from elements of the Third Army.

Polly looked up. "I'm going to go."

General Brawls just sighed. "I thought you would say that, so I approved a flight for you, leaving at ten in the morning. Normally, this would be impossible, but somehow General Eisenhower was persuaded and approved it."

A lot was going through Polly's mind, including what things she would have to pack before she was ready to travel. General Brawls interrupted her thought. "Linda packed some of your things; you'll also find a combat pack with clothes at the airstrip. All you need to do is go and catch the car that's outside the office. You should be in France before lunch."

Polly ran around the general's desk, hugging him, and then ran out of the office.

8:30 a.m., the DeBoy Farm

Colonel Odom came downstairs. "Alphonse, could I have a quick word with you, please?"

Alphonse walked over, and they went through to the wine cellar. Colonel Odom got right to the point. "Aurélie was raped this morning by the two Germans who were killed. My examination showed that physically she's okay, but obviously, this has a serious psychological impact."

Alphonse looked at the ground and let out a large breath. He paused for a minute and then whispered, "What about disease or pregnancy?"

"It's too early to determine either of those. I took some tissue samples and will have those tested. I'm not exactly sure how I will communicate the results back to you, but I can assure you if the results are positive, I will find a way, and I'm sure that General Patton will support it. I've left several doses of penicillin for her to take, should we find out further treatment is necessary. For the time being, I think you should keep talking with her and encouraging her to remain positive. While I'm not much of a romantic, I think she and Major Dornier care about each other. You should consider his feelings in this as well."

"We will, and thank you for your help."

"I need to spend a few more minutes here with the wounded. After that, I'll need to go."

Alphonse nodded and left the wine cellar to talk with Aurélie and Josette. "Mark, can you and Luc stay down here and help Colonel Odom? I'll be back in a few minutes." Alphonse knocked on Aurélie's door. "May I come in?"

Josette opened the door. Her eyes were red. She had obviously been crying. "Oh, Grand-père, we're glad you're here."

After hugging Josette, he walked over to Aurélie, who was sitting on her bed. He sat down beside her, and Josette joined them. Hugging his granddaughter, he stroked her hair. "We love you." He pulled her head to his chest as she began to sob.

"I tried to fight them off, Grand-père, but I couldn't. I didn't … want …"

"I know that. I know you and your heart. I couldn't ask for two better granddaughters. You've both grown into beautiful, strong women." He put his arm around Josette and pulled both of his granddaughters to him.

They sat for a while in silence until Aurélie spoke. "The two that survived tried to stop it. I'm grateful to them, and I hope they both recover." She slowly pulled herself to a sitting position, staring at the wall, and whispered, "Does Mark know?"

Alphonse took his arm from Josette and held Aurélie's face in his hands. "He doesn't yet, but it's clear he loves you. You should probably be the one to tell him."

Aurélie started sobbing again, and Josette knelt in front of her, holding her hand. "How could he ever look at me again after this?" Her sobbing grew in intensity. "He would … what if I have a baby? He will always remember when he looks at me."

Josette stroked her hand and looked up at her sister, speaking forcefully. "Aurélie, that is nonsense! I know he loves you. He has a good heart, and you can build a happy life with him."

Aurélie was still sobbing. Alphonse stroked her hair lightly. "You rest up here for a while. The doctor is looking after the wounded, but then he has to return. We'll tell Mark you're upset about shooting the Germans, so don't worry. When you're ready to explain, he'll be here for you."

9:00 a.m., September 5, Albert Speer's Private Quarters, Berlin

The Reich Minister looked at a preliminary report on the status of the defenses in eastern France. A German reconnaissance aircraft had been near the Butte de Vauquois and had flown over the site after the bombers left. It'd landed shortly before eight in the morning and sent its film to the photo lab, along with a hasty report to Berlin.

Speer stared at the report:

> Approximately sixty minutes after the attack, fires were still burning, and there were several explosions. Despite the smoke covering the site, it was apparent that many of the bombs had fallen inside the perimeter and had caused extensive damage to the facilities. Some ground fire in the surrounding area was evident, probably from the Resistance units. Eight or ten potential crash sites were spotted, indicating their antiaircraft defense had been sporadically effective.

Speer picked up the phone and called his chief of staff. "I want a staff meeting in fifteen minutes. Prepare messages to all of the major defense sites in eastern France, reinforcing that they need to be on high alert, especially around the high-voltage lines leading to the BR sites."

At least the main lines from the dams that were damaged had were restored last night, he thought. *Even though some were on the ground, it was better than nothing. Some of the BR sites will have enough power to allow them to be operational.*

Speer put the report in his briefcase and walked downstairs, where his car was waiting to take him on the short drive to his offices. *I'm sure when Himmler finds out, he'll tell the Führer. I think I can put this in a better perspective.*

9:30 a.m., the DeBoy Farm

Colonel Odom started packing up. "Lieutenant, you're going to be fine. You've lost a lot of blood, but I'm leaving you several units of whole blood as well as plasma. It's going to take several months to heal. Just make sure that you don't try to get up too soon." Turning to Gerhart, he said in German, "Private, your shrapnel wound should heal just fine. I've given you some penicillin and have left several doses. It would be best if you did as I've indicated to Lieutenant Ryder; take it slow. I wouldn't worry too much about a prisoner-of-war camp. I'm going to talk to General Patton about you."

Upstairs, Josette had prepared a bath for Aurélie. Alphonse came down and asked about the wounded. "Are they going to be okay?"

"I was just explaining to them that I think they'll heal fine; they just need rest and are not to be moved around much for the next few weeks."

Mark was worried about Aurélie. The two US soldiers who had been with her had not said much. "Colonel, how is Aurélie?"

"She's fine for the time being. She had a tussle with the Germans before she shot them."

"I suppose you need to be getting back." Mark thought for a minute and then turned to Alphonse. "Do you have some writing paper? I'd like to send a message back with the colonel."

"Come upstairs. We have some in our desk."

Colonel Odom and the three US soldiers prepared to return while Mark wrote a note.

General Patton,

Thank you for your assistance. Dr. Odom has been extremely helpful, and our wounded should recover.

I want to draw your attention to the fact that the lady I was with is part of the DeBoy family who have been supporting me in the field for almost a year. She, her sister, her brother, and her grandfather have been of great assistance to me and have done this, knowing they were risking their lives and property. I don't know what type of citations or awards you might be authorized to provide to French civilians, but I think it would be much appreciated if you could send them a note of appreciation. Lieutenant Ryder saved my life last night and was a crucial factor in our successful attack on the power facilities that disabled the BR site your forces faced this morning. I believe he is worthy of a citation. I will leave that for you to decide.

Finally, I ask something personal. The lady with me last night is Aurélie Berson. Her husband was killed in 1940 when the Germans invaded. I love her and intend to ask her to marry me before I leave France. I respectfully request your permission to do so.

I wish you and your army Godspeed and good hunting.

Very respectfully,
Major Mark Dornier

Mark put the message in an envelope and walked back down to the cellar. The colonel and his soldiers were just about ready to leave. "Would you give this to General Patton when things quiet down a little?"

"Of course. I wish you good luck here, and thank you again for all of your hard work over the last year."

As they carried some of the gear out to the spare Jeep, the colonel turned to Mark, "There should be enough in the way of medical supplies to see those two through to a full recovery. You may want to keep the blood and plasma as cool as you can. Fifty degrees or cooler would be best." He got in the Jeep and then looked at Mark one last time. "I wouldn't worry about Aurélie. She'll be fine." He turned to the driver and said, "Let's go find the general. Just follow the shooting."

Approximately 11:00 a.m., a Lysander at Eight Thousand Feet over Compiègne

Polly was nervous and anxious to see Alex. The message had revealed few details of his wounds. In her supply pod were fifty pounds of medical supplies and another three hundred pounds of food and clothing. She had no idea how General Brawls had managed all of it, but she was grateful.

She leaned over to the pilot and pointed to the map strapped to his thigh. He indicated their position. She estimated it would take sixty minutes or so to reach the DeBoy farm. She would have to wait and hope that Alex was doing okay. The message also didn't indicate who was taking care of him, but the fact he was at the farm indicated that some of the family members still lived there. Evidently, Major Dornier had survived because he'd sent the message.

CHAPTER 44

✦✦✦✦✦

11:30 a.m., Seventh Armored Division, Seventeenth Tank Battalion, Montfaucon

Sergeant Gillis's tank platoon made it to Montfaucon by ten o'clock. They met up with a platoon of infantry that helped clear out the small town. They were waiting for the rest of the Seventeenth Tank Battalion to arrive, along with the fuel trucks.

"Hey, Joe, see that tall tower on the hill?" Corporal Gary Elliott was somewhat of an amateur historian and was interested in all the landmarks as they passed through France.

"Yeah, but I don't know what it is."

Sergeant Mike Floyd, their gunner, spoke up. "It's a monument commemorating the American victory in the Meuse-Argonne Offensive during World War I. There should be a large American cemetery somewhere around here. This area saw a great deal of heavy fighting in the last month of that war."

A sergeant from the infantry came over and yelled up at Gillis. "Have you guys got any way to heat our rations? Some of the boys found chickens as well as a few dozen eggs. If we could find some cooking gear, we might be able to have a hot meal for a change."

Gillis stuck his head in the turret. "What do you think, Mike? Should we share our stove?"

"Hell, yes. I'd do anything to quit eating these C rats,[7] especially cold."

Gillis smiled and yelled down to the sergeant, "Yeah, we got a stove and some cooking utensils. We even have some flour. We might be able to fry up some chicken!"

Noon, the DeBoy Farm

Josette had come down to the kitchen after helping Aurélie with her bath and started preparing some food. Mark climbed the cellar stairs to help her. Heinrich went up as well, even though his head still hurt from the clubbing that morning.

Heinrich asked Mark in English, "May I help as well? I know how to cook."

Mark turned around, surprised at the comment. "I guess it's okay but depends on the DeBoys." He turned to Josette and asked her in French if it was okay. Aurélie had already given her a bit more detail about her ordeal with the Germans, so she knew that Heinrich had attempted to stop what had happened.

"Tell him he's welcome to help."

They worked for the next several minutes—using a combination of French, German, and English and hand signal— before Mark heard the low hum of a small plane. He went outside and immediately realized it was a British Lysander. *Why would a Lysander fly here in broad daylight?*

Just as the plane flew over the farm, it banked to the left and began to circle overhead. Mark saw a supply pod drop, and then a person jumped out. Mark ran back to the house, grabbed his Sten gun, and

---

7. C rations, developed in 1940. The "combat" meal was known officially as Field Ration, Type C. There were three individually boxed meals for breakfast, dinner (i.e., lunch), and supper. Soldiers quickly tired of these meat-and-hash meals.

yelled a warning to Alphonse. Running back out, he looked up and saw the pod was on the ground behind the barn, and the jumper was going to land in the plowed field just beyond.

He decided to remain concealed inside the barn while the jumper removed the parachute and began walking toward the house. The jumper produced a Sten gun as well and started running toward the barn. Mark backed into one of the milking stalls as the jumper came through the back barn doors a moment later. The jumper was continuing through the barn to the front when Mark stepped out. "Halt! Don't go any further!"

The jumper stopped, with raised hands, "I'm British. I'm Polly Berson, and I came to see Lieutenant Ryder."

Mark smiled, but he still kept his Sten gun on her. "Turn around, Polly." As she did, he recognized her face and her hair that fell to her shoulders when she removed her helmet. "What are you doing here?"

"We received a message early this morning that you and Alex had met resistance, and Alex had was wounded. General Brawls allowed me to come down to see what I could do to help."

Mark had to smile again. "I doubt if the general *allowed* you; it was probably more like you told him you were coming, regardless."

This time Polly smiled, but it quickly faded. "Where's Alex?"

"He's in the basement with Luc and your grand-père. Follow me."

As they went through the front door, Josette saw Polly and couldn't believe her eyes. "Poddy!" She ran and embraced her. "I'm so glad you're here. We've had a busy twenty-four hours." Polly broke the embrace, and Josette immediately added, "Your lieutenant is down in the basement. General Patton sent his doctor. Alex is doing fine, although he's not going to be up running around any time soon."

Josette took her downstairs, and as soon as Polly saw Alex, she ran over to him. He was waking up, opening his eyes. He could barely believe what he saw.

"Polly, how ... why?"

Polly leaned over and pressed against his side, kissing him on the cheek and giggling. "I'm glad to see you too!" She ran her hands over his face and chest, being careful not to disturb the bandages. "We got a message early this morning that you and Mark had been in a fight, and you were shot. General Brawls let me come down to help and bring extra supplies."

Alex managed to smile and was able to put his left arm around her back to hug her. He kissed her and whispered, "I love you."

Polly sighed as she enjoyed feeling the warmth of his body. "I hear that you were shot twice, but the doctor thinks you'll be okay."

Luc got up and walked over to Polly. She stood up and hugged him and then saw Alphonse and went over to hug him as well. Switching to French, she said, "Grand-père, thank you for helping Alex."

He shrugged. "He and Mark did a lot in the woods to help the Americans. It was only right."

Mark walked up and introduced her to Private Gerhart. "This is Berne Gerhart. He and Heinrich Kohler were part of the German force last night that surprised us on the road. Berne was injured when his vehicle hit a mine. He and Heinrich and two others captured the Jeep that Aurélie and our soldiers were in this morning, but these guys helped protect Aurélie."

Josette walked over to Polly, realizing Mark didn't understand what had happened. "Aurélie is upstairs resting. She'll be down in a few minutes, I'm sure."

Alphonse went over to Josette. "Let's go upstairs and help with the food, and let Polly and Alex talk."

Polly sat down in a chair next to Alex's bed and took his hand in hers. "I'm so glad your wounds weren't life-threatening." She leaned down and kissed him gently. "You rest now. I'm staying with you."

Alphonse, Mark, Luc, and Josette climbed the staircase and went to the kitchen. Heinrich was cutting vegetables for the stew. Mark saw that they had used some of the wild boar meat that he had given them the week before. Heinrich turned around. "This should be ready in a couple of hours or so."

As Mark turned around, he saw Aurélie coming down the stairs. It was the first time he had seen her since early this morning. He smiled and went over to her. "Are you okay? You had me worried."

She looked him in the eyes and smiled briefly before looking down.

"I'm fine, thank you. I think I'll sit for a while. I got hit on my head when they captured us, and I'm still a little dizzy."

There was a noticeable bruise on her right temple. Mark reached over with his hand to stroke her head, but she abruptly moved back. "It's sore, Mark, so maybe don't touch."

Mark withdrew his hand, but he sensed something was wrong.

Aurélie went into the kitchen. She needed to get away from Mark, even though she felt guilty in doing so. Her emotions were in turmoil. Even though she cared about him deeply, what had happened earlier that morning completely threw her mind into a state of disarray. She wanted to reach out to him but was terrified that he would reject her when he found out.

4:00 p.m., Paris, Eisenhower's Temporary HQ

Colonel Betts took the message across the hall to Eisenhower's suite of rooms. He was still trying to get used to his new duties, as Eisenhower had temporarily taken him away from working with MI6. They had decided to set up headquarters in a hotel near the ring road, northwest of Paris. He looked at the corporal busily typing something and then nodded toward the door.

"He's in there, Colonel; go on in."

Eisenhower was getting ready to lift the phone when he saw Colonel Betts enter. "What's up, Dave?"

"We just got this message in from Montgomery's headquarters. Evidently they encountered some sort kind of new weapon last night in the area between Brussels and Ghent." He handed the message over.

Eisenhower studied it for a minute before looking up. "Napalm shells? I didn't know they had any. I know we've been using them in the Pacific." He kept reading. "It looks like there was a large salvo of these things, and they slowed his advance."

"Yes, sir, and we're digging up a report from a French Resistance cell about the use of a similar type of shell around the Butte de Vauquois.

Moreover, it looks like they have a powerful new antiaircraft missile as well. I'll bring the report to you in a few minutes."

Colonel Betts left the room, and Eisenhower walked over to the window. *How can they keep coming up with stuff like this? In the end, we're going to win, and all this does is increase casualties on both sides.*

A few minutes later, Colonel Betts came in with two messages. "General, here's the report from the French Resistance cell on the Butte de Vauquois attack. The air raid appears to have been successful in knocking out most of the German defensive capabilities, but they did encounter occasional napalm explosions." Colonel Betts paused and looked down at the message again. "The troubling thing is that they saw two missiles fired at the bomber formation. There was only one explosion—a massive one that took out ten or more aircraft. They described the explosion differently than you would a conventional flak shell. It was an extremely bright light followed by a huge shock wave."

Eisenhower looked up and took the report, and Betts continued with the second report. "This is a report from a British formation returning from bombing Munich this morning. They were attacked by a similar type of missile that exploded just outside the formation. There was considerable damage to multiple planes. The eyewitnesses reported an extremely bright light followed by a shock wave and deafening blast. It destroyed fourteen planes. A second similar explosion was noted four miles to the right of the formation."

"What is going on? Have we heard anything from London on new Nazi weapons?"

"No, sir, but based on these two reports—and especially since they're in different areas of the front—I think the Germans have developed something very powerful. With your permission, sir, I'll see if I can find out what's going on."

Eisenhower paused to think for a moment. "No radio. Get on a plane and take copies of these messages back. Get your people working on it ASAP, and stop back here before you leave. I have a message for General Brawls and the PM." Eisenhower looked up at Betts. "Pack an overnight bag and get out to the airfield. If there's anything to worry about, send me a message using the code word *Halloween*. Nothing else, and then get your tail back here."

7:00 p.m., the Dugout

Mark had decided to go back to the dugout after eating a second meal and satisfying himself that Polly, Alphonse, and Luc could handle the situation. Berne was in no shape to threaten anyone, and Mark knew Heinrich was happy to be "captured."

He was also glad Polly had arrived, as her presence lifted everyone's spirits. Her supply pod contained not only medical supplies but clothes and food items that were scarce in France. Despite the happiness in the air, Mark had a knot in his stomach. He hadn't been able to say more than a few words to Aurélie, and it was plain to see that she was bothered by something. Josette had made it a point to talk with him, and Alphonse had asked for his help in the barn to bring in some cheese and fresh milk. He got the feeling that they were hiding something and wanted to keep him busy. So after eating the evening meal, he excused himself, saying he needed to go back and check on the dugout.

As he pulled up, he decided to conceal the Jeep in the clump of trees where they hid Alphonse's truck so many times. *No use in being careless at this point; there still may be Germans roaming around.*

He went through a routine check of the area around the dugout and saw no signs of recent activity. Then he went down into the cellar to check the various tunnels. After being satisfied his "home" was still secure, he sat down and put on some coffee. While that was boiling, he laid out some fresh clothes for an early rise tomorrow morning.

When he finished his coffee, he decided to have a drink. Alphonse had given him several bottles of a French liquor called Calvados. He took a glass outside and walked around for a while. He turned the coffee off and went upstairs. The last slivers of light were fighting their way through the trees from the west. *At least the weather is good.*

He walked down the small dirt road to the south as he sipped on the Calvados. He thought about the meeting with General Patton and sabotaging the power lines with Alex. *Was there something I missed that could've avoided the firefight? Probably not, but I still feel bad. At least Alex will recover, and with Polly down here … exactly how did all that happen?*

He kept going over what had happened to Aurélie. He remembered the kiss, what he said in the Jeep on the way to Patton's position, and her response. She had even put her hand on his forearm as he was driving. What happened? When the Jeep she was riding in had started back, it got ahead of his and then just disappeared. It must've been very traumatic to be stopped by the Germans. *Something happened, but what? I still love her.* He took another drink. *This stuff is potent! I think I'd better get back while I can find my way.*

CHAPTER 45

+ ◆ ◆ ◆ ◆ ◆ +

9:00 a.m., September 6, German High Command in Berlin

S peer had spent most of the previous day communicating with Kurt Diebner and the head of production at Ploesti. Despite their best efforts, Ploesti wouldn't be able to manufacture the raw materials for additional napalm shells for at least another two months. The damage to the facilities had been too severe, and sabotage in the interim slowed repair efforts.

Diebner's news was better. They had received a fresh team of skilled operators to use in the contaminated reactor area. They also developed protective suits that should keep the laborers productive for three to four months. With these developments, he projected that he could have one to two kilograms of U-235 ready in twelve weeks. Unfortunately, the purity would be down from the 92 percent they'd achieved previously to around 40 percent. It was the purification process that took so much time. This drop in purity would mean a loss of explosive yield—a considerable loss.

Speer walked into the conference room. Alfred Jodl was already there. "Good morning, Albert. I see we have a few positive reports from the front. Patton is still an issue in eastern France, but as we expected, Montgomery is moving cautiously in the north."

Wilhelm Keitel, the head of the OKW, came in looking fresh. "Gentlemen, let's make this quick. I have another meeting to go to."

Speer smiled and rolled his eyes. "Wilhelm, you always have another meeting to go to. Sometimes I think you just want to avoid me."

Keitel smiled back. "Now why would I want to avoid such bright shining faces like yours and Alfred's, there?"

"Enough with pleasantries. Albert, why don't you give us your report?" Jodl didn't have much patience these days.

Speer gave each man a folder with a summary of the production in the Reich, as well as the goals that had been met in the last week and those that had not. "As you can see, our overall production is doing quite well. Moving the factories to underground tunnels, despite the expense and effort, is beginning to pay off. You can also see that we have made considerable progress on several new weapons while continuing the production of the V2 rocket."

Keitel interrupted. "What's this section about experimental weapons?"

Speer had listed five or six weapons programs that included the napalm shells, as well as the nuclear-tipped missiles. "Those are the top programs that have shown promise and are continuing. The gasoline-shell program, or napalm, as the Allies refer to it, has been deployed to several defensive sites in France and has been successfully utilized in the last three or four days in several actions against massed Allied infantry and even some of the armored divisions. The only issue right now is the inventory, which is about 30 percent of what we would like it to be.

"The nuclear-tipped missiles are small antiaircraft missiles designed by Dr. von Braun's team and have shown great potential in disrupting large bomber formations. Several of the missiles were fired in the last week, with the destruction of fifteen or twenty aircraft and damage to twenty or thirty more."

Just then, Heinrich Himmler came through the door. "Reich Minister, can you explain why these weapons are deployed only on the Western Front and not the Eastern Front?" It was obvious that

Himmler was annoyed that he was not kept in the loop. And for this reason only, he intended to criticize.

"Yes, sir, damage to the refining facilities in the east, as well as radiation poisoning of key individuals has slowed both programs. We have decided to use a small amount of our petroleum reserves to manufacture additional napalm shells. The reactor at Haigerloch is now back at full capacity and will deliver several kilograms of nuclear material within the month." Speer was well aware that he was exaggerating, but Himmler had no way of verifying these figures.

"Reich Minister, you did not go through me and proper channels for these programs. If you had, we would've been able to prioritize supplies and provide the proper protection, guaranteeing they would not be behind schedule. I may have to go to the Führer with this troubling news."

Speer looked down to get control of his emotions. Then he slowly looked Himmler directly in the eyes. "Reich Minister, you can do as you please, and, in the presence of these generals, I would encourage you to do so. However, you must understand that I will have my weekly meeting with our Führer about production tomorrow, and he has been very supportive of our efforts."

Later, in the car back to his office, Speer formulated his thoughts in case he was asked to the Führer's office before his scheduled meeting. *It's too bad there are people like Himmler wanting only praise and power for himself. If only the Führer could see that.*

8:30 a.m., September 7, the Dugout and the DeBoy Farm

Mark got up early and walked around the forest with his morning coffee. At this time of year, the sun came up later, so much of his walk was in the dim light of dawn. The weather was holding, although there was a hint of fall in the air now. Yesterday he had driven down to the farm to check on Alex and the family. Actually, he had gone down to see Aurélie, but she still kept her distance from him. After the noon meal, he made an excuse to return to the dugout.

After making breakfast, he checked his weapons and backpack and slowly started southwest toward the village and the DeBoy farm. He felt ill at ease but wasn't able to attach any reason to it. As he exited the forest, the bright sunlight made him squint. There were a couple of farmers out in their fields, chasing what appeared to be stray cattle. He waved, and they waved back. *What a beautiful place to live.*

A few minutes later he pulled in to the farmyard. Alphonse was coming out of the barn, carrying a pail of milk. "Bonjour. There's another pail in the barn, if you'd like to get it."

Mark walked over to the barn and went around to the last stall that housed the milk cow. He was surprised to see Aurélie just finishing the milking. He smiled and squatted down in front of her. In spite of herself, she smiled back. "Glad to see you're feeling better." Aurélie looked down, not knowing what to say next. Mark put his hand on her shoulder. "I can't help but feel something is wrong."

Aurélie squeezed the pail handle, and Mark could see she was nervous. She knew she should tell him, but she dreaded a reply that might exclude her from his life. Despite herself, tears began to roll down her cheeks.

Mark gently took her hand off the pail and knelt in front of her. "I love you, Aurélie. I know that something has happened, but I want you to know that all I care about is you."

Aurélie started sobbing and stood up to leave. Mark put his arm around her from the back and pulled her into him. She began to push back but then gave in, turned around, and put her arms around him, holding him tightly as her body jerked with sobs. Mark stroked the back of her head and kept silent as she continued to cry. It was then Mark suddenly realized that the Germans had probably raped her. *I don't know why I didn't figure it out sooner.*

It took several minutes before she was able to get control of her emotions. *I'm going to tell him. Please, God, don't let him leave me.* It felt so good to be in his arms. She hadn't had feelings this deep for anyone since Sebastian.

"Mark, when we got separated coming back from the American

headquarters, Heinrich and Berne were with two other Germans and …" Aurélie didn't know how to continue. She looked away.

Mark turned her head back toward him and lightly kissed her forehead. "Forgive me for not realizing this sooner. The bastards raped you, didn't they?"

She looked up at him. "I tried to stop them, but I couldn't. Heinrich and Berne both tried to stop them, but they clubbed them with guns." As she looked at him, she could see nothing but love in his eyes. "Mark, I … it's … so …" She started sobbing again.

Mark put his arms around her again and held her tightly. Hearing her cry broke his heart. He whispered in her ear, "Sh-h-h, it's over; the important thing is that you're okay." Putting his hand behind her head, he guided it into the crook of his neck. "I love you, and the only thing that matters right now is that you're alive, and we're together."

She started sobbing even harder. They sat down on the barn floor, leaning against each other. She could feel Mark's strong arms around her, and it made her feel safe and loved. He reached over with his other hand and closed it over hers, gently kissing her cheek. "I meant what I said a few days ago. I want to spend the rest of my life with you." Tears were now running down his cheeks as well.

"But after what happened, are you sure that you—"

He put two fingers over her lips. "I love you, and nothing will ever change that. You're a beautiful woman. I can't imagine being with someone else or feeling like this ever again."

Aurélie leaned into him and lay her head on his chest. In a soft voice, she whispered, "I don't deserve you. I love you so dearly."

"Aurélie, you don't earn love; it's a gift, and you have mine forever."

She put both arms around him, closed her eyes, and held him tightly. She never wanted to let go. *Thank you for bringing me a man like him.*

"I'm not interrupting, am I?" Alphonse said. "I came out to the barn to see why the second bucket of milk disappeared." He squatted in front of them and spoke to Aurélie. "Did you tell him?"

"Yes."

He picked up the pail of milk. "When you are ready, come in have breakfast. Josette and Polly have prepared something special for you."

Aurélie looked over at Mark. "I guess I should tell Luc as well?"

Alphonse agreed. "Yes, but I would get him alone first. Everyone is aware, but there's no use in making that kind of thing public."

She put her other arm around Mark and tucked her head into the base of his neck. "Let's go in and eat something."

Heinrich ate with them, while Polly stayed downstairs with Alex and Berne. After they finished eating, Aurélie took Luc outside and explained what had happened to her. At first, Luc wanted to punish both Berne and Heinrich, but Aurélie insisted they had both tried to prevent it.

Polly and Josette took care of Alex and Berne while Heinrich helped Alphonse and Luc with the chores. Mark and Aurélie took a walk in the fields behind the farm and talked. Toward the end of the day, Mark started back to the dugout, not because he wanted to leave but because there wasn't enough room for him at the farm.

7:30 p.m., September 7, the Dugout

Mark parked the Jeep in an old trench that was part of a large shell hole, twenty-five yards from the dugout. He went down to the cellar to make sure everything was okay and then took out some boar so it could defrost. He would start a pot of stew tomorrow.

He decided to take a shower, change clothes, and then take a walk around the area to check up on things. He walked up the path to the road and then decided to cross and take the trail going northeast into the woods. He couldn't get Aurélie out of his mind. There was no doubt that he loved her and wanted to marry her, but he was hesitant how best to make it happen.

If I try to stay in France, it won't work. I suspect the army will want to send me back to the United States once the war is over. If that happens, it could take a year or more before I could come back. Probably the best solution is to get married while I'm still here, and maybe they'll let me take her back to the States with me when I leave. But that means she would be separated from her family for a while.

All he knew was he couldn't leave her. As he walked, daylight faded fast. There was a light breeze blowing, but apart from that, there was no sound. He inhaled the fragrance of the woods and felt the stress of the last several days begin to leave him. *It's so peaceful here. I can't imagine wanting to live anywhere else.*

9:30 p.m., September 7, the DeBoy Farm

Josette, Polly, and Aurélie finished cleaning up Alex's and Berne's area and then helped Heinrich. Alphonse and Luc were out in the barn when the girls came up for tea.

Polly looked tired but happy. Josette set the mugs for tea on the table and then went over to Polly and hugged her. "Alex is going to be just fine, and we're so glad you're here."

Polly smiled and held Josette's arms. "I'm glad I'm here too. I thought about you guys so many times in the past several years. I'm glad to see you all in such good health—Josi."

Aurélie smiled. "We've been lucky, even though we have lost family members."

"You've got Alex, and Aurélie has Mark, and hopefully I will get my Henri back soon."

Polly took a sip of tea. "Speaking of Mark, I can tell you two have feelings for each other. I didn't have the chance to get to know him well in London, but I know that he is a very good man."

"Aurélie always takes things slow." Josette poked at her older sister. "But I think this time she should make sure he knows how she feels."

Aurélie looked down, thinking about the last several days. "He knows."

"How do you know?"

"Because I told him."

"Well, it wouldn't hurt you to go up there to see him and spend the day—or even the night."

Aurélie looked at her sister. "I'm not going to go up there and spend the night!"

Polly smiled, and Josette giggled. "You've already spent one night up there. Remember last winter? Besides, he wouldn't take it that way. You know it. Use it as a chance to get to know each other a little better, that's all."

Aurélie looked over at Polly and saw her smile and nod. "I think it's a good idea."

5:00 a.m., September 8, the Dugout

Mark woke up, shaved, and began to prepare the stew. He browned the meat for a few minutes while he cut up the vegetables. Then he added in a couple of cans of beef stock and tomatoes before putting the pot on the heat. While that was cooking, he fried sausage to eat for breakfast with cheese and bread.

He decided to take a walk around outside with his coffee. It was a little past six o'clock but still dark. He put on his survival pack and took his Sten gun. There could still be Germans around.

Down at the DeBoy farm, Aurélie had woken early and decided to spend the day and probably the night at the dugout. She was packing her bag when Josette came in. "You should take a dress along. You would look good, and I think you should show Mark how much of a woman you are."

"It's not a very good environment for a dress."

"It's perfect." Josette smiled. "Especially the ladder to the cellar."

"Josette!"

She laughed. "Just be sure to wear something nice underneath."

"Josette DeBoy, shame on you!"

Daylight was beginning to show through the trees when Mark started walking back. As he got close to the road from the north side, he heard a truck approaching. He moved up behind a group of large trees, set his coffee cup down, and readied his Sten gun. He didn't think it would be Germans because they likely wouldn't be driving on the main roads, but he wanted to be careful.

He saw the truck come around the corner with its small lights on and recognized it immediately as Alphonse's. He watched as it made the turn down the road toward the dugout. It pulled into the small space that hid it from the road. He was surprised to see a woman get out, but hoped it was Aurélie.

"Brooklyn."

Aurélie turned around and yelled the countersign and added, "It's just me, and I'm alone."

He crossed the road and took her in his arms. "I'm glad to see you, but what are you doing here?"

"I wanted to come up and spend some time with you. You don't mind, do you?"

Mark suddenly got nervous, but knew he was happy she'd come. "I'm just surprised that's all." He moved to the back of the truck instinctively and saw that she had brought some additional food and a suitcase. He picked up both and started to the dugout. "I just started some stew. I was going to bring it down to the house."

"We can take it down later and come back in the Jeep. If you can set up the extra bed, I'd like to stay the night as well."

Mark was still a little confused but glad that she had made the trip to see him.

CHAPTER 46

＋✦✦✦✦＋

8:00 a.m., September 8, Fort de Koenigsmacker, Northeast of Thionville

Oberleutnant Borne was nervous, realizing an attack was imminent. "Be certain all the equipment is working. The Americans have crossed the Moselle south of here and may be in this area by noon. We should have enough electrical power to fire the beam weapons."

The young lieutenant saluted and went back to his control booth. He went out to the floor and started questioning all of the technicians, making sure everything was in working order, especially the ability to draw electrical power. After satisfying himself that the weapon systems were ready, he returned to the control booth and checked the targeting mechanisms. *I hope the heavy-weapons platoon has enough ammunition because there's no way we're going to stop even eight or ten tanks with this stupid weapon. It takes too long to charge.*

8:30 a.m., Seventh Armored Division, Seventeenth Tank Battalion, Florange, Two Miles Outside Thionville on the West Side of the Moselle

In the last two days, they had made good time. Some of the division had crossed the Moselle at Dornot, but their battalion had stayed on the west side. They pulled up outside of a small village called Florange. Gillis had received orders from Battalion HQ late last night. They were going to assault the German strongpoint built up around Fort de Koenigsmacker, an old fort from the previous century. Three tank battalions were going to attack from the south and southeast on the east side of the river, while their group would stay on the west side and provide covering fire for the infantry.

Gillis examined the village with his binoculars. He asked one of the two squads attached to their group to work their way around to the west and see if there was any threat from the village.

Lloyd's head bumped into Gillis's leg. "Want to load old Betsy?"

Gillis crouched down and saw that Lloyd had a HE, or high-explosive, round in his arms. "Hold off for a few minutes until Smitty gets back. If there's a Kraut tank in there, we're going to need an AP [armor piercing]. Otherwise, the HE will work." They were almost a half a mile from the village in a small depression, so he wasn't too worried about someone taking a potshot at them. Besides, they had to wait there until the fuel trucks caught up with them.

9:00 a.m., SHAEF Headquarters, Southeast of Paris

"Find out where George is, and tell him to slow down until we can get Monty further east. A gap is starting to form." General Omar Bradley knew his friend would cuss a blue streak when he got the message, but he had to slow him down, or the Germans might exploit the weak point forming in their front. The communications officer took the message downstairs to the radio room. The entire Allied line was approaching the area where the BR weapons had first been discovered, and nobody knew whether they were operational.

Midmorning, Field Marshal Montgomery's Field Headquarters, Belgium

Field Marshal Montgomery, General Brian Horrocks, and Prince Bernhard of the Netherlands stood in a field as Montgomery briefed the prince on the upcoming Operation Market Garden. The field marshal had just relinquished command of the Allied armies back to Eisenhower and had been promoted to field marshal by Churchill the same day.

"The plan entails dropping three airborne divisions here, just outside of Arnhem." He indicated the positions on the map he was holding. "We have several bridges to secure, but we're confident that we'll be able to do it quickly. German resistance in this area is relatively weak. In addition, we will be dropping in daylight."

The prince, while not a military strategist, was concerned. "It looks like quite a long way along the highway. I should think it requires close coordination between all of the units involved."

General Horrocks quickly replied, "General Eisenhower has given us complete operational control over all of these units, and we have discussed precisely what you've mentioned for the past week. Besides, the field marshal has made certain we've considered each detail that could cause a problem." Like all staff members, he was very loyal to his boss. "Ike has redirected supplies to support this operation. If we get across the Rhine at Arnhem, we can be into the industrial heart of Germany quickly, giving us a chance to end this war by the end of the year."

11:00 a.m., the DeBoy Farm

Alex woke up and groaned as he tried to move. Heinrich was in the basement, watching both his friend and Alex, while Polly and Josette were upstairs. Polly had been with Alex almost nonstop for the past couple of days and had gone upstairs to take a bath, while Josette prepared the noon meal.

Heinrich walked over slowly, realizing that Alex might not recognize him. He tried to remember the small amount of English that he knew and then realized that Polly had written some phrases on a piece of paper. He picked up the paper and walked over to Alex, pointing to the words that read, "This is Heinrich Kohler. He is a friend. I will be back in a few minutes. I love you."

Alex nodded and then groaned again. Heinrich checked his wounds and saw that he was not bleeding and then checked the medication record. It had been five hours since his last dose of pain medicine. He gave Alex two pills and held his head up slightly while he swallowed some water.

A few minutes later, Polly returned, and Heinrich used his broken English and sign language to explain to Polly the medication he had given Alex. She immediately went over and checked on Alex, who was dozing again, and then checked on Berne. Berne was running a fever. Following Colonel Odom's instructions, she gave him another shot of penicillin.

"I didn't realize you were a nurse." Alex had turned his head and smiled.

Polly turned around and smiled back, continuing to clean the wound area. "You'd better be a good boy, or I'll use this needle on you next."

Alex smiled and then closed his eyes briefly. He whispered, "I've been dreaming about you. It seems like all I could think about for the last few hours is you."

Polly sat by his bed and took his hand. "You haven't been very coherent since you were shot, but it looks like you're starting to get better."

He coughed as he tried to say something, and Polly held his head as he sipped some water. "When did you get here?" Closing his eyes, he then added, "What happened? All I remember is shooting at the Germans in the woods, and then everything went black."

"You shot a couple of Germans who were going to fire at Mark, but unfortunately, others shot you—once in the leg and once in the shoulder. Mark and Aurélie got a doctor from General Patton's group, and he fixed you up. Apart from the pain, you should heal fine."

"But how did you get—"

"We had a message in London, probably sent by the Third Army, that you'd been shot. Mark asked them to send it. General Brawls got hold of it and called me. There was no way I was at not coming down here." She held his hand in both of hers. "Besides, the DeBoys are my cousins, and a visit was long overdue."

Alex stared at her and gently squeezed her hand as he closed his eyes. The pain medicine was starting to take hold, and he knew he would not stay awake for long. "Love you … and so glad … you're here."

CHAPTER 47

Noon, Seventeenth Tank Battalion, Northwest of Thionville on the West Side of the Moselle

They finished refueling and joined up with two companies of infantry that had four assault boats. Gillis wasn't very confident of the plan they'd put together, as it had the infantry crossing the river in broad daylight. It called for artillery to lay down a smoke barrage, and then the tanks and infantry on the east side of the river would attack to draw fire away from the river.

Gillis turned the intercom on. "Mike, start with HE, but have a couple of AP rounds ready. Gary, when the artillery starts, get ready to move up." He switched to the intercom phone on the rear of the tank, where Lieutenant Roberts had a squad of his platoon. "Lieutenant, the artillery should start anytime, and we'll move up at walking speed. Be ready to unload the boats as soon as the smoke rounds start." Each tank was towing a small trailer with four small assault boats.

They heard rumbling to the east, and shortly after that, they could hear the artillery rounds passing overhead. There were twenty to twenty-five explosions in and around the walls of the fort. "Gary, let's go." The tank lurched forward, and they started moving toward the riverbank. There were a few mortar explosions nearby from the fort, but most of the firepower focused on the force attacking from the other side of the river.

Inside the BR Building, Fort de Koenigsmacker

Hauptmann Veld saw the attack through the periscope and spoke to his *Feldwebel*. "Inform Oberleutnant Borne the Americans are approaching from the south and southwest on this side of the river, as well as a smaller force crossing the river from the west. We are tracking the force from the west and south. Also, inform the power room to begin raising the voltage in preparation for firing both weapons." This was one of the facilities with two beam weapons.

He could hear the generators as they came up to full speed. The needles on the control panels indicated charging of both weapons. It would just be another two or three minutes before they were ready to fire.

"Control to position one and two. Position one: target one of the lead tanks from the south. Begin tracking and engage in two minutes. Position two: go to wide-angle and target the largest concentration of assault boats. Report when you have a suitable target.

Inside Sergeant Michael Hanson's Sherman Tank, South of Fort de Koenigsmacker

The smoke rounds began to shield the assault craft in the river. "Bob, let's keep moving, and Ray, make sure we have an AP loaded. There's a pillbox to our right at five hundred yards. Prepare to engage."

Inside Gillis's Sherman Tank

The tank was at the river's edge. They were waiting for the infantry to offload the assault boats. Smoke rounds were reducing visibility. The German machine-gun positions were raking the shore.

"Mike, machine-gun position, two hundred fifty yards, five degrees to the left. Use HE." Mike rotated the turret slightly to the left and sighted in the target. The 75 mm gun fired, rocking the tank. The round landed short and to the left. "Correct three degrees right, plus ten." Seconds later, the gun roared again, and the machine-gun position disappeared. "Good shooting. Another machine-gun position three hundred yards on the bluff, ten degrees to the right."

Infantry was moving the assault boats into the river and beginning to cross. Above the noise of the artillery, there was a high-pitched whine, followed by a bright flash that shot out from an opening in the fort's south wall, toward the attacking force.

What was that?

Almost instantly there was a bright-red glow, followed by an explosion, as one of the tanks disintegrated. Gillis yelled down to Mike, "Did you see that?"

"All I saw was a bright flash."

"It looked like a light beam or ray—and one of the tanks on the other side blew up."

Inside Sergeant Michael Hanson's Sherman Tank

Hanson's gunner Ray had been looking through his sight when the beam flashed by and hit the tank next to them. He groaned and held his eye; the brightness had temporarily blinded him. Hanson had been looking through the periscope but missed directly looking at the beam. He knew something was wrong.

"Anybody see what happened? What was that?"

Inside Fort de Koenigsmacker

Oberleutnant Borne targeted four assault boats that were closely bunched together. "Hauptmann Veld, I have a target, and I'm on wide-angle. Four assault craft."

Veld looked in his periscope and immediately spotted the craft, partially covered with smoke. "I see them; engage."

Borne flipped a switch and pressed the fire button. He heard the high-pitched whine and flipped the dark shade down on his sighting device. A bright flash followed. He flipped his shade up and was amazed to see wreckage and body parts floating in the river.

"Begin recharging." Recharging was their only weakness. It took too long.

Inside Gillis's Sherman Tank

"What the—" Gillis couldn't believe that he'd just witnessed three or four assault craft disintegrate before his eyes. A bright flash—and then nothing. *What kind of weapon do they have?*

"Mike, see the bunker structure about four hundred yards slightly to the left of the fort? That's where the flash came from. Put several rounds of AP on it. Gary, wait till he fires two rounds and then take us back and to the left as quickly as you can." Gillis wasn't about to have his tank be a sitting duck for that weapon.

Well to the North, a Small Resistance Force Outside Dippach, Belgium

Koonrod had led his small band of saboteurs through the woods. They had already attached charges to three of the high-voltage towers. They hadn't been told why but were informed this was a high-priority mission. The electric transmission lines going south were to be brought down as soon as possible. Once that was achieved, they were to retreat into the woods a couple of miles and move south to target several more transmission towers.

"Set the timers for ten minutes, and let's get moving."

Inside Fort de Koenigsmacker

"Hauptmann, both weapons are ready for discharge again. We have targeted a tank to the south and a tank to the west. There's no suitable target on the river because of the smoke."

Veld responded quickly, "Engage when ready, and recharge immediately. We have the mortars, and the machine guns are targeting the assault force on the river. And our artillery is starting to find the range to the south."

Borne looked at the American tank to the southeast, flipped the shade down, and pressed the fire button. He heard the whine, followed by the bright flash. This time the beam was slightly off and hit the tank on the right-front tread. He felt the concussion of shells impact his bunker. *It's going to take more than a tank gun to get through our walls.* He immediately switched his attention to the second tank across the river, recharged, and fired.

Inside Sergeant Hanson's Sherman Tank

Hanson had seen the bright flash out of the corner of his eye. They were moving northwest and had just turned. He felt the heat before he heard the high-pitched hum, and then he heard his bow gunner scream. He looked down to see a dull red glow to the front right side of the tank. He had no idea what had just happened, but he wanted everyone out before the ammunition exploded.

"Everyone out, immediately! Get away from the tank!"

Inside Gillis's Sherman Tank

They had put four rounds on the bunker. He was just beginning to tell Gary to go back toward the river when he heard the high-pitched whine and saw a flash. For some reason, he had a sickening feeling that they were targeting his tank. That was his last thought before his world lit up in a bright flash. His tank exploded, and they were all dead before they could even feel the heat or realize what had happened.

Inside Fort de Koenigsmacker

Borne continued to target tanks, and at one point, he went to a wide-angle beam dispersion and was able to eliminate a group of infantrymen who were foolish enough to congregate together. He didn't know, however, that the timers on the high-voltage towers outside Dippach had reached zero, and the small charges set by the Resistance force immediately interrupted the power supply to his weapons. Borne saw the dials on the control panel drop.

"Hauptmann, we've lost our power!"

"Stand by your posts. I will ask our exterior force to determine if the damage is anywhere near our location."

3:30 p.m., Outside Fort de Koenigsmacker

A flight of P-47 Thunderbolts had attacked at 2:00 p.m. and had pummeled the fort with rockets and five-hundred-pound bombs. The bombs opened several breaches in the exterior walls, and the tanks and infantry had pushed inside to mop up any resistance. The river assault had been a surprising success, in large part because of the smoke cover and the aggressive fighting of Lieutenant Colonel Wemple's tanks. He had lost five tanks to the BR weapon.

Wemple radioed a squad standing by. "Sergeant, take your squad over to that bunker, and let Colonel Reedy examine the machinery inside. Any information on these weapons should be sent back to SHAEF as soon as possible."

4:00 p.m., on the D931, Outside Suippes, about Twenty-Five Miles West of Lachalade

Henri Benoit had been walking for days. He escaped from a POW camp in southern Germany and had reached Switzerland. From there, the Swiss put him on a plane to Paris, even though they were supposed to remain neutral. Usually, repatriated French soldiers were reassigned to duty. However, Henri had a considerable amount of shrapnel in his left arm. While healed, he hadn't regained full use of the arm. He was discharged and provided transport to Rheims. From there, he was able to catch a few rides from French citizens, but he was still a long way away from Lachalade.

He was anxious to get home and see his family, particularly Josette. Because of his many camps while captured, he knew she had no way to contact him. He wasn't even sure if the letter concerning his whereabouts and his condition ever got to his family and her.

Earlier in the Day, the Dugout

Mark and Aurélie had taken the stew to the farm together, driving both the Jeep and Alphonse's truck. That way, Alphonse would have his vehicle.

Mark went downstairs to check on Alex and wasn't surprised to see Polly by his side. "So how is our patient doing?"

Polly was holding his hand. "He's still in quite a bit of pain but doing better." She stroked his hand and then looked over toward Berne. "I think Berne is doing a lot better too and has developed an appetite. I'm glad that Heinrich is here to help."

Mark went over to Berne's bed and sat down. He changed to German and asked, "How is your leg?"

"It's better. These people are so nice to take care of an enemy soldier."

"I want to thank you for what you did. I know that you and Heinrich tried to prevent what happened. It means a lot to me, and I'm sure Aurélie is grateful also."

"I wish we could've done something more. Those two guys were not good."

"Well, rest and try to get better. You and Heinrich are welcome to stay here for a while. There's no reason for us to turn you over to the authorities now, and besides, the Allies have their hands full."

Upstairs, Josette had taken the stew from Aurélie. "So are you going to stay tonight?" Josette's eyes sparkled. "Did you take a dress?"

"Yes, and yes, as if it's any of your business."

Josette giggled. "Well, I hope you have a good time. You two need to spend more time alone."

"Just so you know, little sister, we set up the extra bed."

Josette rolled her eyes. "I wonder when Henri will get back?"

Mark and Aurélie returned to the dugout midday and walked around the woods. Mark enjoyed showing her some of the trails he'd developed over the last eleven months. They got in the pod with some food and drove to the landing field, where they enjoyed a late lunch.

They were sitting on the ground together, looking east into the valley, when Aurélie reached out and took Mark's hand. "Thank you for what you said in the barn yesterday. It meant a lot to me."

"I mean it. Over the past several months, my feelings for you have grown. I meant what I said the morning we went to see General Patton. I want to spend the rest of my life with you."

Warmth swept over Aurélie. She felt unconditionally loved. Her feelings for him had developed as well, and she wanted nothing more than to be with him. "I feel the same way, but what are we going to do when you have to leave?"

Mark smiled because of her practicality and openness. "Part of the reason I love you is you think ahead. I've thought about it, and while I don't have everything worked out yet, I will before too much longer. I would be willing to live in France, if that's what it takes, or somehow take you back to America. I don't care which, as long as we are together."

When Aurélie's face betrayed her feelings, Mark said, "Yes, I know, there are obstacles in our way. We'll work it out—together." He leaned over, took her face in his hands, and gently kissed her, whispering, "I love you."

They enjoyed their time together for another hour and then decided to head back to the dugout. Mark dropped her off and then drove the pod to its parking space in a nearby shelter. Aurélie took the picnic basket down to the cellar and then decided to start cooking for the evening meal. She had brought a venison roast from the farm that was actually some of the meat Mark had shared with them.

Mark returned and saw her working on dinner. He came up behind her and put both arms around her. "What are you doing, Mrs. Berson?"

"I'm going to cook for you. I know you do a pretty good job yourself, but I'm not too bad around the kitchen either." She lay her head back on his shoulder, stopping her preparations momentarily. "And you should know that I'm not used to being called Mrs. Berson."

Mark squeezed her a little. "I know, but that's who you are. It is the name of the woman I love."

"If you keep your arms around me like this, we're never going to have dinner."

Mark sighed. "It's a difficult decision. Keep holding you, or eat." He kissed the base of her neck and quickly said, "I guess I'm not going to eat!"

For the first time in a long time, Aurélie squealed in delight and then giggled. "I know I'm beautiful, but I think you're going to need some nourishment, so release me. Please sit down over there and talk to me while I prepare our dinner."

She worked on the roast and then started preparing the side dishes. She and Mark kept up a constant conversation, and he occasionally helped her. Mark watched her cut up potatoes and other vegetables and put them in the oven next to the roast. Whatever she was doing, it was much more than he typically did.

"What are you fixing with the vegetables?"

"It's a surprise." She turned around. "And speaking of surprises, I have another one for you, but you'll have to go outside for just a short time while I get myself ready for dinner."

"Suppose I don't want to go outside."

"Then I guess I'll just have to take all my clothes off and shower in front of you."

Mark laughed. "I don't doubt that you would, and I'm sure I would enjoy the show, but I think I'll give you some privacy."

5:00 p.m., SHAEF Headquarters, Southeast of Paris

Eisenhower was on the phone with Montgomery, while "Beetle" Smith was just outside, listening. He knew that Eisenhower didn't yell very much, but he could tell his boss was aggravated. Montgomery had been planning an offensive for several weeks that he promised would win the war early—although very few people believed it outside of Monty's own staff.

"All right, we'll give you the resources, but you better make sure about this because we're making good progress in the south of France."

Eisenhower came out of his office. "Beetle, where are those action reports from earlier in the day concerning the Seventh Armored?"

"They're on your desk, sir. The BR weapons are devastating, but apparently, they take a long time to recharge. It's based on a principle that Nikola Tesla developed years ago. We need to take out the high-voltage power lines that feed them, and they'll be out of business. We have a good start because we've been bombing the dams, and the French Resistance groups are in the countryside, continually bringing down transmission towers."

"It's just one thing after another with the Nazis. I don't understand how they find the resources to create technology like this."

CHAPTER 48

7:00 p.m., the Dugout

Aurélie finished her shower and put on her dress. It was dark blue with a full skirt that dropped below her knees. She had also brought some of her mother's perfume. Mark finally yelled from the dugout, "Can I come down now?"

Aurélie suddenly got a fluttering sensation in her stomach. She hadn't dressed up for a man since Sebastian. As nervous as she was, she was looking forward to spending time with Mark. "Come on down. I'm done trying to pretty myself up."

Mark came down the ladder. His first glance took his breath away. "Wow, you're beautiful!"

Aurélie blushed. "Thank you." She could tell he was really pleased. She had put several candles around and had brought a tablecloth and a small centerpiece. It looked nice, at least for a cellar

"I like the candles and everything." He paused slightly and then looked back at her. "But the best thing is you. You are beautiful."

Aurélie blushed again. "Why don't you get cleaned up, and then we can enjoy a glass of wine."

They had put a rope across the room and hung a sheet over it to cordon off the back side of the room so they each could have some privacy. Mark went back, took off his dungarees, and unpacked a pair of civilian slacks, a dress shirt, and his civilian shoes. Putting on shorts, he went to the shower, looking over at Aurélie as she set the table. *It's nice to have her here.*

He showered, dressed, and then stepped out. It was Aurélie's turn to be impressed. "Well, Major, don't you look nice—and so civilian."

"It's the first time I've worn civilian clothes since I got here. It feels good."

"Well, you certainly look nice. Why don't we have a glass of wine?"

"I have a bottle that I brought with me—a Bordeaux I believe is ready to be enjoyed." Mark went over behind the stores and picked a bottle out of the rack and opened it.

They sipped the wine and talked a bit about the events of the last four or five days.

"It's hard to believe that in such a short time, we've gone from being behind enemy lines to being behind the Allied lines. It's a good feeling."

Aurélie passed a plate with some small pieces of bread and cheese. "Try these. The cheese will go well with the wine." She stared at Mark and felt a warmth rush over her again. It was a powerful feeling after all these years.

Mark picked up the wine and poured another glass for each of them. "What are you thinking about? You know you're staring at me?"

She looked up and smiled. "I was just thinking how nice it is to have this time with you." She reached over and put her hand over his and squeezed.

They continued talking for another half hour. and then Aurélie got up and removed the roast and vegetables from the oven. She made a plate for both of them and took it to the table. "This is your meat. Major, so if it turns out to be bad, it's your fault." She looked over at him, her eyes twinkling.

Mark took a bite; it was delicious. She had added spices and seasoning he didn't know he had. The vegetables that she roasted were excellent—potatoes, carrots, brussels sprouts, and broccoli, all seasoned with garlic and covered with grated cheese and butter.

They ate in relative silence, enjoying the food and each other's presence. Mark and Aurélie shared the cleanup and then went upstairs to sit on the bench in the dugout.

"The meal was delicious, Aurélie. You're not only beautiful but a great cook."

"Thank you. I learned a lot from my mère, and we also had my grand-mère's recipes."

Mark noticed it was cool and went back down to get his heavy coat. "Put this on. Maybe it will ward off the chill a little."

"Thank you." She paused for a second. "Have you ever thought about what would have happened if you had not accepted this mission to come here and live with us?"

Mark looked at the little path in front of the dugout. In fact, he *had* thought about it but only once or twice. "I did some, particularly in the last several weeks. All I can say is I'm glad I came and was able to help your family." He paused as he turned to her and put his arm around her. "Of course, mostly I'm glad that I got to meet you."

"You make me blush, Mark. I'm glad you came also. I didn't think I would ever feel this way again after Sebastian disappeared."

"It must've been very hard for you, and Josette, and your grandfather. We don't have to worry about that kind of thing in America. We're fortunate in that regard."

She turned to look at him and found his eyes locked on hers. His other hand reached up and gently touched her cheek and pulled her head toward his. They kissed, tightening their arms around each other. Aurélie could feel her resolve melt away. Mark sensed it and pulled back.

"If we went back down to the cellar, would you dance with me?"

She smiled. "We don't have any music, so how would we dance?"

"I can hum, and besides, I don't need music with you."

He helped her down the ladder, putting his hands around her waist; he helped her down off the last step. He put his arms around her and smiled. "I like your dress."

She couldn't suppress a giggle. "Josette warned me about you—the ladder and dresses."

Mark felt his face redden, but he tightened his arms on her back.

"Josette—I should've known." He took a deep breath. "That was an honest mistake, but I still like your dress."

Aurélie laughed. "Josette's like that." Her eyes twinkled as she added, "She told me to make sure I wore something pretty underneath."

Mark could feel his face heat up more. He was just about to say something when he decided that there was no way out. So he began to hum and took one of her hands while placing the other on the small of her back. They moved slowly around the room, enjoying being close to each. Aurélie looked into his eyes at one point and was almost overcome by her feelings. She put her head at the base of his neck and breathed in his scent.

Mark could hardly believe he had this beautiful woman in his arms. He hadn't danced with anyone since Joanne died. He pulled her closer, enjoying the feel of her breath on his neck and her softness as they molded themselves to each other. Time passed, and they continued dancing until Mark could not resist.

He kissed the side of her hair. "I love you so much. I'm never going to let you go."

She looked up and kissed his cheek. "I don't want you to—ever."

He let go of her hand and put both arms around her back as his lips met hers. It was like he was falling, but he had her love to protect him. Aurélie put one hand on the back of his neck and pulled him toward her. She wanted to get as close as she possibly could.

After several minutes, they looked at each other. Aurélie was the first to speak. "My feelings for you are so strong that it scares me. I don't know what I'd do if I didn't have you."

"I know. It's strange because we come from such different backgrounds, but I feel the same way." He pulled her close again and rubbed the back of her neck with his fingers. "I enjoy being with you so much. I especially like having you in my arms, but perhaps we should call it a night."

Aurélie pulled back slightly and looked at him with a smile. "Probably, but I hate to separate." Reaching up to caress his cheek, she said, "Besides, I think can feel how much you like having me in your arms."

Mark could feel his face getting red again and leaned his forehead against hers. "I apologize. I didn't realize—"

"Don't apologize. I enjoyed you just as much."

Mark went behind the sheet and undressed, getting ready for bed, as Aurélie did the same on her side. Just before he went to sleep, he heard her whisper, "I'm cooking breakfast for you." Somehow it just seemed … normal.

7:30 a.m., September 9, the DeBoy Farm

Alphonse and Luc were coming back from the barn, where they'd finished milking and collecting eggs. Luc was curious about what his grand-père thought of Aurélie and Major Dornier. "So what's going on with them?"

Alphonse looked at his grandson. "I think they've both found someone special. For this to work, they'll have obstacles to overcome, but I believe they'll find a way." He shifted the milk pail slightly. "It takes love and patience. You'll see someday."

Josette and Polly were in the kitchen, preparing breakfast, as the two came in. Josette told Luc to put the milk in the icebox and took several eggs and handed them to Polly.

Alphonse went over and stood behind Polly as she began to prepare the omelets. "So how are our patients this morning?"

"Berne is doing much better, but Alex didn't have a very pleasant night. His leg wound gives him a great deal of pain."

Alphonse put his gnarled hands on her shoulders and gently squeezed. "It's not easy to see someone you love suffer, but he's going to get better soon. This I know, and I want you to believe it." He paused. "I can finish the omelets if you'd like to take a break."

She leaned back and turned her head. "Thank you, but I like doing something different for a while."

Josette came over. "Why don't you go for a walk this morning after breakfast, and let me clean up. I can change the guys' dressings, and besides, Heinrich is a big help. That way you can get a break."

Polly smiled, and Josette nodded.

I do need to get away for a little while, Polly thought. She felt better after what Alphonse said.

CHAPTER 49

✦✦✦✦✦

11:00 a.m., September 9, Albert Speer's Office, Berlin

The Allies were continuing to advance all along the front in eastern France. The reports indicated that the napalm shells were effective; unfortunately, there wasn't a large inventory. The nuclear shells were another matter. One had exploded near an Allied infantry formation and caused extensive casualties. The antiaircraft missiles, however, were malfunctioning. Several of the rockets detonated in flight, and some of the warheads malfunctioned. Apart from the one that exploded over the Butte de Vauquois, only a few of the shells had been effective.

Speer reached over and buzzed his assistant. "Have the reports from Fort de Koenigsmacker arrived yet?"

"Yes, Reich Minister. They arrived via courier a few minutes ago." He walked in and laid a folder on Speer's desk.

Speer looked at the reports and noted that the weapons had evidently performed as designed, but the power lines had been sabotaged somewhere in Belgium. *It's just one thing after another. Deploying anything is difficult. The Allies control the air as well as the local population.*

He called his assistant. "Send a copy to OKW headquarters, and file our copies."

"Yes, sir." He turned to leave and then turned back to face his boss. "The weapons helped. It's not your fault the infrastructure can't provide proper support."

Speer looked out the window and then back to his assistant. "I'm sure Himmler will take that into consideration before he goes to the Führer." *If I didn't have to fight our bureaucracy, I might be able to slow the Allies down. Unfortunately, it's too late for that.*

9:30 a.m., September 10, the Dugout and the DeBoy Farm

Aurélie finished packing, and Mark carried her suitcase upstairs. He had a knot in his stomach, and she did as well. They'd spent three extraordinary days together. The time cemented their feelings for one another.

"It's going to feel empty without you here."

"It's foolish, but I'm going to miss you as well. I'm only going to be a short distance away at the farm, and we'll get to see each other every day."

"There was just something special about having you around and knowing you didn't have to leave." He helped her into the Jeep. "But I guess if we continued to do that, eventually something would happen."

Aurélie put her hand behind his head and kissed him. "I wouldn't care, you know."

"I know, but we can wait."

Mark took the road south, which meant he had to loop back to the farm, but he didn't care.

They pulled into the farmyard as Alphonse was walking toward the barn. "Bonjour. Everyone is in the house."

Mark followed Aurélie down to the basement. Polly was feeding Alex some soup, and Josette was helping Berne change his clothes. "So, ladies, how are the patients today?"

Polly looked up and smiled. "Alex has finally gotten his appetite back, and I think Berne is ready to get out of bed and walk a little."

Heinrich was helping Josette with Berne. "I think Berne enjoys the nursing." Both Polly and Josette laughed when Mark translated.

Josette started up the stairs, "I need to take the bed linens upstairs. I'll be right back."

She walked from the kitchen to the washroom, left the dirty linen, and as she started back down, she happened to look out the kitchen window toward the main road. There was a man just stepping off the D2, walking toward their house. There was something about him that looked familiar. Suddenly, she realized it was Henri. She squealed, covering her mouth, and then started yelling, "Henri is here! He's come back!"

She ran through the door and across the yard. She didn't stop until she threw herself into his arms. "Oh, Henri, I thought I'd never see you again." They kissed, and then she pushed back to look at him.

"There were times when I wasn't sure I would get back, but all I could think about was you." He smiled and pulled her up close. "I dreamed for so long about holding you."

"I'm never letting you out of my sight again." She began to sob, and then she heard something behind her.

Alphonse, Luc, Aurélie, and Polly all came out. Alphonse shook his hand with tears in his eyes. "Welcome home, boy; welcome home." So many young boys didn't come back from Alphonse's war.

Luc hugged him, and then Aurélie and Polly did as well. Then Josette inserted herself into his embrace again. "He's my fiancé, and I'm the one who ought to be hugging him," she said, half teasingly.

Aurélie led them back to the house. "Let's go inside, and we can talk. Much has happened to us all."

They spent the rest of the morning talking about what had happened to Henri as well as to their family. Josette introduced Henri to Alex, Berne, and Heinrich. At first, he was baffled about the two German boys but understood once Josette explained.

Mark was introduced as well. "They've all missed you, especially

Josette. When I first got here, I think she had almost lost hope. She's an exceptional woman, though."

They continued talking through the noon meal, finding out about how Henri's unit had been overrun and the various prisoner-of-war camps where he'd been held. He showed Josette his scars from the shrapnel in his left arm and explained that he wasn't able to fully extend it. All the while, Josette didn't leave his side.

About four o'clock, an American Jeep pulled into the yard, and a young lieutenant got out. Mark went out to meet him. The lieutenant saluted Mark and then handed him a letter. "This is from General Patton. He asked me to deliver this to you and to extend his sincere gratitude to you, the DeBoy family, and the British lieutenant. He also asked me to give you this." He handed Mark a box.

Mark invited him inside for a few moments and offered a cup of coffee. "You might as well drink it; it's ours. They keep me pretty well supplied here."

The lieutenant related how fast the Third Army was progressing and how many German strongpoints they had overrun. "I've heard the general and his staff mention your name several times. The information you provided was very valuable."

The lieutenant finished his coffee and then excused himself. Mark walked him to his Jeep and then sat down on the front steps to read the letter. As he was opening it, Aurélie came out and sat down beside him. She put one of her arms through his and leaned up against him. "Can I read it along with you, or do you think it's secret?"

"I don't think there's too much secret at this point. Let's see what the general has to say."

Dear Major Dornier,

We have progressed rapidly, in large part due to Lieutenant Ryder's and your efforts. We overran the first strongpoint outside Les Petite Souhesmes in less than an hour and then proceeded further east, guided by your information. I asked London to provide me with a few details of your mission and received a reply yesterday. I want to offer my sincere thanks to you, Lieutenant Ryder, the DeBoy family, and the team back in London. You've already allowed us to save countless lives and steered our advance, allowing us to penetrate the weak areas of the German lines. Seventh Armored Division attacked a German stronghold north of Thionville, and while we had some casualties, we were able to take the position quickly, thanks to your input. You might also be interested to know a group of Belgian Resistance fighters cut the power lines to that entire sector, which took those terrible beam weapons out of service.

As to your specific requests, enclosed is a certificate of appreciation from the Third Army to the DeBoy family. Also, I've submitted paperwork for an official citation from either the French government or SHAEF. I've enclosed a citation, along with a Silver Star and Purple Heart for Lieutenant Ryder for his efforts on September 4. Finally, and probably most important to you, is a letter granting you permission to marry Aurélie Berson. Since I am not aware if you've asked her yet, I have worded the consent for a wide range of dates, as well as a French civilian ceremony, or, if you prefer, a military wedding. I have asked London to extend your stay in France. I should also mention that Colonel Odom explained to me what happened to Mrs. Berson. If I can be of any additional assistance, please don't hesitate to contact me. In addition, I would like to do something to ensure your two German soldiers aren't punished too harshly, and somehow possibly rewarded for what they attempted to do.

To conclude, I've enclosed a citation as well as the Distinguished Service Cross for your efforts over the last eleven months. Your service to your country has been exemplary.

I extend my blessings to Mrs. Berson's and your marriage, the DeBoy family, and to Lieutenant Ryder. I can't express how personally grateful I am for your service.

George Patton

George S. Patton, Lieutenant General
Commanding, US Third Army

Mark was a little surprised at his citation and was also embarrassed about the reference in granting his permission to marry Aurélie.

She squeezed his arm and kissed his cheek. "Thank you for asking him to thank us. It will mean a lot to grand-père." She paused briefly, "What is the Distinguished Service Cross?"

Mark felt relieved that perhaps she had missed the mention of the marriage permission, but a moment later, he realized he was wrong.

Aurélie whispered in his ear. "I don't remember being asked." She snuggled up against him.

Mark put his chin on the top of her head. "I told you I was working on something. It is just one of the obstacles I had to get past."

"*We* have to get past."

"Okay, *we*. I also wanted to talk to your grandfather."

She couldn't help teasing just a little. "How do you know I will say yes?"

7:00 a.m., September 11, the Dugout

Mark slept until six thirty. He couldn't go to sleep at first because the cellar seemed so empty. He got up and started some coffee. He could still smell her perfume. Somehow, it just didn't feel right to be apart. He took his coffee outside, walking down the path toward the other dugouts. A dense fog had formed, and it enveloped the forest. It made him feel completely alone and safe. It was relaxing—even more so now that the Allies had come through.

After thinking about it more, he decided to approach Alphonse about Aurélie. He hoped Alphonse would give his blessing. He turned back toward the dugout to eat breakfast before he went down to the farm.

10:00 a.m., the DeBoy Farm

Alphonse was busy fixing a harness in the barn when Mark found him. Alphonse guessed why he had come, so he pulled up a stool and let Mark stammer through his request. Smiling at him, he said, "I was wondering when you would get around to asking." He took Mark's hand. "Absolutely you have my blessing, but I do need to ask one thing."

"Anything."

"Are you okay with what happened to Aurélie? I think you probably are, but it's going to be something in the back of her mind, and you need to be prepared to deal with it. Stuff like this can come out today, tomorrow, or years from now."

"I love her, and I told her in the barn that day that I realized what had happened. I've made sure she knows that each time we're together."

Alphonse looked at him and nodded. "I just want you to know it's something that she'll probably never forget completely."

"I realize that, but I will do my best to make sure that she does forget, or at least that she's so sure of our relationship that it will never be an issue." Mark thought for a minute. "I'm not exactly sure how we will organize our lives. I wouldn't mind staying in France and raising a family here, but going back to the States might be a reasonable alternative as well."

"Mark, just let's get past the marriage first, and then we'll all think about what comes next."

Mark got up and started to walk back to the house when he remembered General Patton's letter. "I almost forgot. The letter I received from the Third Army included some things for you and Alex. Maybe we could all get together after lunch, and I could present those."

After lunch, Mark asked everybody to go down to the basement since Alex couldn't come upstairs yet. Mark had written a short citation and read it before presenting Alex with his medals. He then read the letter of appreciation that General Patton had written for the DeBoys. Mark then shook both Alphonse's and Luc's hands and gave Aurélie and Josette a hug.

Polly was so proud of Alex that she beamed. Josette wanted to find Henri and show him the letter. Mark looked over at Aurélie and held out his hand. "Why don't you and I take a walk?"

They walked out to the yard and then behind the barn into the field, finally stopping at a little copse of trees. Mark turned around and looked at Aurélie. She knew there was something on his mind. "So why are we out here, and why are you so quiet?"

Mark couldn't help but laugh. "Are all French girls as pushy as you?"

She scowled. "Okay, why?"

"How is this going to work out if you're always asking me questions?"

"How is *what* going to work out?"

Mark took her hands and looked into her eyes. "Our marriage."

Her eyes got wide when she realized what he was saying. Without letting go of either hand, he got down on his knee and looked up at her. "I don't want to live without you, Aurélie, and I love you more than I thought was possible. Would you please do me the honor of becoming my wife so that we can spend the rest of our lives together?"

Aurélie had a hard time believing what she was hearing, even though she suspected that this moment was coming. She just looked at him trying to adjust to the moment before she realized she was holding her breath. Tears welled up in her eyes as she caressed the sides of his head. She could barely whisper her answer. "Yes, positively, without a doubt, yes. I will be your wife, and I will love you for the rest of our lives."

Josette had walked out the front door, intending to see Henri was at his family's farm down the road. Her curiosity got the best of her, and she looked out into the field and saw Mark in front of her sister on one knee. Her heart fluttered, and she took in a deep breath as she realized what he was doing. She began to jump up and down and squeal and ran out into the field.

Aurélie and Mark were still too engrossed with each other to realize Josette was running to join them. Once she got closer, Aurélie turned and knew her sister had guessed what was happening.

"Did he just ask …"

Aurélie wiped the tears from her cheeks, smiling, and caught Josette as she flung herself into her arms. "Yes" was all she could get out because Josette wouldn't stop squealing.

After hugging her sister for a moment, she turned to Mark and hugged him. "I'm so happy for you both." She turned back to Aurélie and hugged her again. "I'm going over to tell Henri. Mark, will you stay for dinner tonight, so we all can celebrate?"

They all went inside and told everybody, and then Mark drove Josette over to pick up Henri. The women started preparing a large meal. Both Berne and Alex were awake enough to congratulate him, as did Luc and Heinrich. Mark looked at Alex and smiled. "You might want to consider asking Polly while she's here; that is, if you're so inclined."

"It's funny you should say that because I was thinking about doing exactly that if I can get out from the fog of all of this medication."

CHAPTER 50

------ ✦✦✦✦✦ ------

11:30 a.m., September 13, War Cabinet Rooms, St. Charles Street, London

Colonel Gaffney was at his desk, going over the latest reports regarding the Allied advances. He was getting more and more concerned about Montgomery's Market Garden plan. It required quite a few assets and would mean they would have to slow General Bradley to divert resources. *That's a gamble that might not be worth it.*

There was a knock at his door, and Colonel Walker came in. He hadn't seen Jeremy in several months and suspected he was visiting to ask about Major Dornier's status.

"I haven't seen you around for a while," Colonel Gaffney said. "Sit down."

"How are you doing, Johnny? I've been busy like everyone else. Finally got a break, and I thought I'd come over and see what was going on."

"Well, things are going better than they were a few years back. Looks like we're pushing the Germans back." Colonel Walker shifted in his seat.

"Actually, what I came by for was to find out about Mark Dornier," Colonel Walker said. "I knew about the original mission, of course, but I was curious if you could tell me anything about what's going to happen to him now."

"Right now, he's holding tight where he is. General Patton was happy with the information concerning the German defenses generated by Mark and several other teams. It looks like it made a big difference in terms of lives spared, as well as the speed of our advance. Pardon me—would you like to have some coffee or tea?"

"Tea would be fine."

Colonel Gaffney got up and asked his assistant to bring them tea. Returning to his desk, he said, "I wouldn't expect him back any time soon. I just got word this morning that we want to send him over to the Butte de Vauquois to do a first-hand evaluation of the damage, as well as get a look at some of the weapons up close."

"Yeah, I heard that the Germans had an antiaircraft shell that made quite a bang."

Colonel Gaffney smiled. "Of course, I can't tell you anything other than there were explosions all along the front that woke people up for miles around. We want to see what's left, if anything. Mark is as well qualified as anyone we have. Then there seem to be some other issues that are going on that require his presence in France for several more months."

"Can you share anything about that?" Colonel Walker asked.

"If I knew anything, I couldn't share it, but I don't know anything. It came down through SHAEF that he's going to stay put for a while. We are to put resupply missions in motion as early as next week. I guess your major likes France."

9:00 a.m., September 14, the Dugout

Mark was busy cleaning up and checking equipment. He needed to finish the weapons and ammunition inventory. After he completed that, he planned to go down to the farm for lunch. Just then, he heard the rumble of a truck approaching, and while he wasn't worried about Germans, it still didn't pay to be careless. He grabbed his Sten gun and his pack and quickly climbed the ladder into the dugout. He breathed a sigh of relief when he spotted Alphonse's truck. Mark was glad to see Aurélie get out but also wondered why she had come up here this morning. Was something wrong? By force of habit, he remained concealed as she walked toward the dugout. It certainly looked as though she was alone.

Aurélie was carrying a message that had been delivered around midnight. Her grandfather had received it and then suggested that she might want to take it to Mark. She enjoyed coming to the dugout, and it wasn't just because of Mark. She enjoyed the forest as much as he did. It was calming, and she liked walking on the paths. Since the occupation, the whole family had stayed away from the woods.

Her eyes scanned the area, as Mark had taught her. The dugout looked deserted, and there was no sign of him anywhere. *He may have gone for a walk*, she thought. Just then she heard the challenge sign: "Brooklyn!" She smiled and replied, "Lachalade!" Mark was always cautious, and she appreciated it.

Mark stepped out of the dugout. "To what do I owe the pleasure of this visit?"

Aurélie approached and put her arms around him. "I needed a hug, and besides, this message came for you last night late. Grand-père thought I should bring it to you this morning."

As he squeezed her, he kissed her. "Remind me to thank your grand-père." He took the message and looked at the coding. "Come on down and have some coffee while I decode this."

They wanted him to go to Butte de Vauquois and perform an evaluation of the site. He was a little surprised he was asked to do it, but they probably didn't have any other American officers available in the area who were familiar with this site. It would be a two-day exercise.

He looked over to Aurélie. "They want me to evaluate a site close to here. Evidently, there were different types of weapons used during the battle, and they are asking me to see what I can find out about them."

A worried expression came across Aurélie's face. "Why can't someone else do this? I don't want you getting hurt, especially now, since the war is mostly over in this area."

He went over to her from behind and put his arms around her shoulders. Resting his chin on the top of her head, he said, "I'll be fine. I suspect I'll be accompanied by some Resistance fighters as well. So I doubt it's anything more than a few days' work."

She put her hands on his arms and leaned her cheek up against his arm. "Please be careful. I've lost one husband, and I don't want to lose another."

Mark couldn't resist teasing just a little. "Well, I'm not your husband yet. I'm only a prospect!"

At that, she turned around. "You know what I mean. You're going to be, and you'd better not get yourself injured." She put her arms around him and squeezed. "Now why don't you figure out what you need for your new assignment and then come down to the farm for lunch. I'm sure you can leave tomorrow or later today, if necessary."

After Aurélie left, Mark checked the supplies he would need. Besides weapons, he would need food for at least two days. Mark decided to take the pod since he would need a dry place to sleep. He also needed to check his film supply. He made a mental note to send a request for additional film with his next report.

CHAPTER 51

◆ ◆◆◆◆ ◆

4:00 a.m., September 15, the Dugout

Mark woke up early and had coffee and then breakfast. He had gone down to the farm yesterday for lunch, returning in the late afternoon to pack his supplies. He definitely would need more gasoline if they continued sending him on missions like this.

He quietly told Alex that he had to be gone for a couple of days on surveillance but didn't mention the destination. Even though he trusted Heinrich and Berne, they were still the enemy. As he was leaving to go back to the dugout, Polly came out to ask him where he was going. He told her and also mentioned he was going to meet three Resistance fighters near the site. Aurélie drove him back to the dugout so she could take the Jeep back down to the farm.

He started down the road, leading south out of the forest, and then turned east on an unnamed road that would go into Boureuilles. His route crossed the D946 there, and then he would take the D212 to the Butte. This would keep him off the main roads.

He was to make contact with the Resistance fighters at the top of the Butte at 8:00 a.m., which meant he would have to push the scooter to its maximum.

The road out of the forest went downhill, and he saw the light fog across the valley. It was just beginning to get light but was still chilly from the clear evening sky. This was one of the parts of the assignment he enjoyed. He liked traveling through the countryside, especially when he knew that he would be alone—although lately, he found himself wanting to share it with Aurélie more and more.

The darkness was surrendering to daylight as Mark pulled through Boureuilles and started up the D212 toward Vauquois. He hadn't seen anyone in the village and hadn't expected to this early. Nonetheless, he put his hand near his pistol and his Sten gun. He had also packed his sniper rifle with a few rounds, just in case.

7:45 a.m., September 15, Butte De Vauquois

When he got to Vauquois, he turned at the church and started on the road up to the Butte. Near the top, he passed the large craters from the heavy shelling in World War I, interspersed with fresh holes, probably from the recent air raids. As he turned the corner, he could see a vehicle up ahead near the site perimeter. This was always a tense moment—meeting his contacts. He was to pull up next to their truck and then get out and yell the challenge, and they would answer with the countersign.

Thankfully, everything went fine with the sign/countersign exchange. He recognized one of the Frenchmen from his first trip to Thionville almost a year ago as he approached. "We are supposed to assist you. What's the plan?"

"Let's find out where the main headquarters buildings or bunkers were, and look around for plans or any other paperwork that might have survived. Then we'll split up and walk concentric circles around the area, looking for anything that might be of interest."

They walked over to what looked like a collapsed tent and saw the remains of a large bunker about thirty yards to the left. "Let's go over there. I want to take some photographs of this area, and then we can search the remains of this tent." Mark started taking overlapping photographs, rotating his camera in a 360-degree pattern. They started moving toward the tent but didn't find anything of interest. Most of it was destroyed mess gear.

They walked over to the bunker and went down inside. Half of it had collapsed as a result of a bomb hit to the rear. There was quite a bit of information in filing cabinets that were still intact, and they spent time going through them.

One of the Frenchmen brought a folder over to Mark. "I can read enough German to see that this is an inventory of weapons. There appears to be a section titled 'Proprietary.' This might be of interest."

Mark took the folder and scanned it quickly. It was indeed an inventory of ordnance, and there was mention of several new types of weapons. He decided to photograph several pages. "It appears as though the Germans deployed a new type of shell to be used both as artillery and antiaircraft weapons. We'll get to the launch tubes over there later, but I think we ought to stay here for a while and see what else we can dig up."

They finally decided to take most of the papers that were readable back with them. Mark photographed the pages he thought were significant, and then he let the Resistance guys take the remainder. They had a truck and also the means to arrange for priority air transportation.

They continued to work through the day, concentrating on the bunker. As the sun was setting, they went over and examined the "mystery tubes"—the tubes used to launch the antiaircraft missiles. They had found enough references to these weapons to understand their use.

As Mark and the two men walked among the launch tubes, he was struck by the thought of how lucky the Allies were that only three or four of these weapons were operable. He had seen two bright flashes followed by two huge explosions the morning of the air raid, and he suspected these weapons were responsible. He took additional photographs, and then the men decided to set up their camp and get some rest. They had another busy day tomorrow.

They pulled their vehicles into the woods and picked a spot that would be easy to defend. They weren't expecting any problems, but it had only been a week or so since the Germans had retreated. The Frenchmen had enough food for everyone, but Mark decided to share some of the pork he had brought, and they appreciated the gesture. After they ate, they set up a schedule for one standing watch while the other two slept.

The next morning they started walking the site perimeter, noting the extensive damage done by the air raid. Even though Mark knew better than to ask the question, he was curious. "Were you guys nearby when the raid started?"

The men looked at each other, and one finally said, "I was. We were over there in the trees about two thousand meters away. Why do you ask?"

"I was just wondering."

The man paused before saying, "They had missiles mounted with some sort of special warhead. I saw one explosion near the planes. It was enormous, and many of the planes just disappeared. A second one went up, but it evidently malfunctioned because there was no aerial explosion. It exploded when it impacted in the valley."

The other man turned and said, "There may be an unexploded missile here. I suspect they had more than two."

Mark nodded. "Let's keep going. Pick up anything out of the ordinary." He kept taking pictures and making notes. He was interested in what the one man said about the explosion as well as the possibility of an unexploded warhead. He made a note of it.

They continued working until about three o'clock. Mark then shook their hands. "Thanks for your help. Please file your report as soon as you can. I will finish mine when I get back and send it and the photos to London. I think it's particularly important that we try to find that unexploded warhead."

They started back down the road toward Vauquois. The men let Mark lead the way in the pod; they turned and went toward Boureuilles. About a quarter mile outside of Vauquois, there was a small grouping of trees to the left of the road. As they pulled even with it, rifle fire erupted.

Mark instinctively pulled toward the ditch. He felt a blow to his left shoulder. He almost fell out of the pod but managed to right himself.

The two Resistance fighters behind him put their truck into the ditch and moved toward the muzzle flashes. Mark looked up and figured maybe two or three snipers were shooting at them. He was bleeding from his wound, but he was fairly sure the bullet didn't hit bone. There was an exit wound several inches below his shoulder. While the two French guys attempted to overpower the ambushers, Mark got his first-aid kit and put sulfa powder on his wound. He couldn't get anything on the entry wound, but he took some sterile gauze and plugged both the entrance and exit holes. *It burns like a hot poker!*

It didn't take the Resistance fighters long to corner the snipers. The Germans were Waffen SS and refused to surrender, so the Frenchmen killed them with grenades. They came over and started working on Mark's wounds. Once they had bandaged him, they loaded the pod in the back of the truck. Mark was put on the seat between the two, so they could keep him upright. Before they started traveling, Mark pulled out a morphine syringe. The Frenchmen administered it. Before Mark lost consciousness, he muttered something about the DeBoy farm and Les Petites Islettes.

8:15 p.m., September 16, the DeBoy Farm

Mark vaguely heard several voices and felt himself being carried. He thought he recognized some of the sounds and smells but wasn't sure. He passed out again.

10:30 a.m., September 17, the DeBoy Farm Cellar

Mark opened his eyes slowly and tried to focus. He was lying down, and when he attempted to sit up, the pain in his shoulder reminded him of what had happened. He moaned.

"I thought I told you to be careful and not to get hurt."

Mark opened his eyes again and focused. Aurélie was bending over him. She kissed his forehead and put her hand on his head.

He tried to smile, but even that was an effort. His shoulder really hurt. "Sorry." His voice was raspy and barely above a whisper. "Ambush on the road."

She stroked his head and face. "I know. The men you were with told us what happened. They are going to send a report back today to London. I have your notes, and I'll write up the report for you as soon as you feel you can talk."

"But it needs to—" He grimaced with pain.

"Sh-h-h, rest, please, and don't move. Your wound is also a clean one. The bullet didn't strike a bone. So all we have to do is watch for infection and make sure you don't start bleeding again."

Thanks to Colonel Odom, they had plenty of medical supplies. Alex was already beginning to move around and would be up and about soon. Mark felt Aurélie press up against him. As he took in her familiar scent, he relaxed and fell back to sleep.

CHAPTER 52

◆◆◆◆◆

**7:00 p.m., September 20, German High Command
in Berlin, Oberkommando der Wehrmacht**

Reichsführer Himmler had been monopolizing the meeting for the past forty-five minutes. Jodl was annoyed but knew it was better to allow Himmler to say his peace without interruption. That way he felt like he was being heard, although Jodl hadn't paid any attention, and he suspected that few of the staff had either.

"Finally, I'd like to point out that significant resources of the Reich were diverted by Reich Minister Speer for his personal projects—projects that I would say have proven to be failures."

Speer had been waiting for him to make his move. Even though Himmler was well aware that most of the project failed for reasons that were beyond Speer's control, he knew that Himmler was unable to stop himself from throwing blame toward someone else.

"Reichsführer, if I may, I would like to point out that while some of the projects that I have sponsored were not successful, our total industrial output this year has significantly exceeded previous years, even in the face of the massive Allied air raids." He paused briefly before continuing. "One of the most successful, as I'm sure the Reichsführer is well aware, is the V2 program. That also has 'diverted' a large volume of our resources but has resulted in a reign of terror on London, the likes of which the British have never experienced."

Speer was well aware that the V2 rockets, even though each one individually was significant on the whole, were merely a pinprick or an irritant that resulted in an even more determined Allied war effort.

Jodl was just about to interrupt when Himmler decided to challenge Speer. "While I agree the V2 program has been very successful, some of your other programs, including the nuclear program, have been a disaster."

Before he could continue, Speer interrupted. "Thank you, Reichsführer, for your kind words, but I would like to point out, specifically about the nuclear program, that a large part of the reason for the failure of nuclear production rests squarely on the shoulders of the SS. Not only did they fail to secure our production sites, but they also failed to protect key facilities from numerous Allied attacks."

The SS had been in charge of security for most of the critical Nazi projects. Even though Speer knew that the Allies would've been able to slow production, he wanted to make sure that Himmler knew he wasn't going to accept his verbal attacks without reprisal.

Himmler stood up. "The SS's record over the last ten years has been without blemish. I will not stand for this ... this unsubstantiated gossip. I will go to the—"

"With respect, Reichsführer," Jodl said, "please sit down and allow us to continue our meeting. If you think that the Führer needs to hear your thoughts on this subject, that is your prerogative. However, the staff has heard quite enough. Let us continue."

Speer suppressed a smile. *Old Alfred can sometimes show what he's made of. Too bad he doesn't do it more often. I wonder if the Reichsführer knows that some of his precious SS are wasting their lives in small guerrilla battles behind the Allied advance.* He had read the report regarding the action near the Butte de Vauquois. He doubted Himmler would mention this to anyone. *The SS are fools. We can still force the Allies to a negotiated peace,* if *we can keep focused on industrial production.*

CHAPTER 53

✦✦✦✦✦✦

7:30 a.m., September 21, the DeBoy Farm

Mark's pain had decreased significantly over the past several days, and he was anxious to complete his report. Aurélie was at his bedside, helping him to eat breakfast. She ran her hand over the stubble on his face. "I think you need a shave. You'd never pass inspection."

"If you could help me sit up, I could do it."

"I'll help you up, but I'm going shave you. I not only know how to cut hair, but I also know how to use a razor." She smiled at him. "Besides, my lips are getting sore kissing you."

Polly had helped Alex into the cellar bathroom. They were returning as Heinrich came down the stairs. "Why don't I get Berne up, and let him take a shower?"

Polly looked up and smiled. "That would be nice. It seems like we're running a hospital here, doesn't it?"

All three men were healing, thanks to the Third Army medical supplies. Aurélie walked over to Berne. "If you would like, I can shave you as well." Mark translated for her, and Berne smiled, clearly happy with the attention.

While Heinrich helped Berne into the shower, Aurélie helped Mark to sit up and started shaving him. "I'm glad I haven't done anything to make you mad. A woman with a razor on my neck could be a bad thing."

"Please be quiet, monsieur." She moved over to his left side to finish the shave.

Mark couldn't help putting his good arm around her and hugging her. "I know I don't smell very nice, but I like having you close to me."

She smiled at him and took his arm from her back. "After the shave, you can take a shower, and then maybe I should test my shaving skills with a few kisses."

A few hours later, all the men had been cleaned up. Mark and Aurélie were busy working on his report. He was dictating to Aurélie from his notes.

Josette came down the stairs, with Henri right behind her. "Henri came over to help Grand-père and Luc with the chores, and he brought Marie over to help take care of our patients." She walked over to the three beds. "We seem to have an epidemic of our men being shot."

Marie was Henri's younger sister. She was short with light-brown hair. Her personality was similar to Josette's, bubbly and optimistic.

Josette introduced the men to Marie. "These are our 'patients.' This is Major Mark Dornier. He and Aurélie got engaged a few days ago, and then he went out and got himself shot."

Marie reached down to take his hand. "Henri told me a little about what happened. I'm so sorry that you got hurt, but we're glad you were here to help."

"And this is Lieutenant Alex Ryder. He was wounded about three weeks ago. Polly came from London to help take care of him." Marie smiled at him. "Finally, this is Private Berne Gerhart. He was stationed at one of the German positions just east of here, and he was also wounded the same night as Alex. He and Heinrich helped protect Aurélie from two other German soldiers, so we're very grateful to them."

Marie sat on the side of Berne's bed and said in perfect German, "You know we French don't like Germans very much, but I've never really met one. You look like a nice person, and you probably would like to go home. So we'll take good care of you."

Berne, who didn't understand much French, sat up, smiled, and spontaneously took Marie's hand. "Thank you, mademoiselle, it's nice to have another person to speak with. Maybe you can help me learn some French."

Aurélie looked at Mark and suppressed a smile.

Mark finished reading the report and motioned for Aurélie to come over. "I'd like to add a couple of sentences to the paragraph, describing those unusual rockets. I want to make sure they understand that it's possible they could have made the missile tips with napalm."

Aurélie took his dictation and added those remarks to the report. Then she asked, "What's napalm?"

CHAPTER 54

1:30 p.m., September 21, General Eisenhower's Field Headquarters, France

General Eisenhower was looking at the reports detailing the progress of Market Garden, which had started on the seventeenth, and also the tank battle around Arracourt. The Market Garden advance had slowed when the bridge over the Son River was destroyed before the 101st Airborne could secure it. It also didn't help there was only one two-lane highway to move the massive numbers of soldiers and heavy equipment. He remembered some of the briefings three weeks ago, in which these very issues were brought up as concerns.

General Horrocks had been quite forceful in his denunciation of all the apprehension. "The element of surprise, which we certainly will have, along with the fact that rear-line troops lightly defend the area, will allow us the momentum we need."

Ike murmured, "Momentum, indeed!" While he realized he wasn't as good of a field general as some of the others, he could recognize a failure in the making. Adding to Montgomery's difficulties, the Allies had found resting, frontline, battle-hardened soldiers and panzers. *You always have to make plans for contingencies.*

Ironically, Patton was winning the battle to the south near Arracourt, where his Sherman tanks were facing the superior German Panzer V Panthers. *All of this on short supplies!* Ike knew he would have to tell Brad to have George pull up because resupply wasn't going to happen due to Monty and Market Garden. He didn't want to be there when Brad gave him the news. *I don't blame him one bit. Montgomery's plan was a long shot, and George told us so.* Managing the Allied advance and at the same time dealing with the political egos of his subordinates was, indeed, a delicate give-and-take. He snorted to himself. "I think I know what George will say."

10:00 a.m., September 24, War Cabinet Rooms, St. Charles Street, London; Lower Special Surveillance Office 8

Recently promoted, Captain Boysden finished reading Mark's report. *Now we have Major Dornier down as well as Alex, and we're taking care of two German prisoners on top of that! At least it looks like they have enough medical supplies.* He got up and walked to Major Stone's office. Stone also had been recently promoted. Boysden knocked on the major's door and then went in.

The major looked up. "Good morning, William. I hear we have another report from our 'French' major."

"Yes, sir, some interesting information regarding the Butte de Vauquois site and some of the armament the Germans deployed there." He laid the folder on the major's desk. "It appears they were able to develop a small nuclear device and mount it on missiles for antiaircraft defense. It's probably what they used against our Lancasters three weeks ago. You'll recall that there was a huge explosion reported that destroyed or crippled twelve aircraft."

Stone continued turning the pages until he got to the part about

Dornier's wound. "So now we have both of our field agents hurt. Dash it all, but at least it appears they are on the mend."

"My summary notes are on the first page. The lab is making copies of the report and photos to send over to the scientists so they can review them. We should have something to take to the colonel late this afternoon."

"Well, make sure we get something, even if it's preliminary. The colonel is already under pressure to report to the PM." Closing the folder, he said, "I suppose we should see if we can get another Purple Heart from our American friends for the major. We can probably send it along with some additional supplies. They may be down there for another couple of months or so."

1:00 p.m., September 25, General Patton's Field Headquarters, Southwest of Metz

General Patton was pacing. His friend Brad had asked for a quick meeting. He knew what was coming because he had access to the reports coming in from Market Garden. *I told Ike not to try it. They didn't plan for all of the unknowns. Dammit. Now the Third Army's going to pay.*

A few minutes later, General Bradley's Jeep pulled up. Patton went outside to greet him and saluted. "Hello, Brad. To what do I owe the honor of this visit? Does Ike think I'm moving too fast again?"

"Let's go inside, George."

The two men went inside and faced each other. General Bradley had a grim look on his face. "George, there's no way to sugarcoat this, so I'll just say it. Ike wants you to slow down. He's going to divert all supplies—gasoline, ordnance, spare parts, and whatever else they need for Market Garden—to Monty." Patton started to reply, but Brad cut him off. "George, I don't want to hear it. I know they didn't plan the attack like they should have, and you knew it as well. Now Monty's got himself in a fix, and we're going to have to do what we can to get them out of it."

"I knew that SOB would figure out a way to slow me down!"

Bradley stared at his friend. He had to get back to his headquarters near Verdun, so he didn't have time to go through the full litany of what George might want to say. He raised his hand and put the other one on Patton's shoulder. "Your march across France has been brilliant, but sometimes you need to shut up. Your mouth is your biggest liability. I'm your friend, and sometimes"—he paused for a second—"sometimes, George, you're just a big pain in the ass!"

Patton stopped and looked at his friend. It wasn't like him to talk like that. *He must be in a corner. I owe him.* "I'm sorry, Brad. I know I'm hard to control, but at least I admit it. I'll do as you ask." He too paused for a second. "Besides, you're my commanding officer, and we've been through a lot together. More important, you're a good friend."

Bradley exhaled slowly. "Thanks, George. I appreciate it."

A small smile sneaked across Patton's face. "You wouldn't mind if ... well, you know, we might need to send out patrols to probe the Krauts. You wouldn't want them surprising us, would you?"

Bradley couldn't help laughing. "I couldn't stop you if I tried, but just remember, you're not getting any more supplies for a while, so don't use up all your gasoline."

CHAPTER 55

9:00 a.m., September 26, the DeBoy Farm

Aurélie had come down to help Mark eat his breakfast. Berne and Alex were mobile enough to go upstairs to eat. Mark thought it seemed like something was bothering her, and despite his questions, she avoided any answers. In the middle of breakfast, he realized someone needed to go to the dugout to get clothes and other supplies. He had plenty of meat in his freezer, and with five extra people to feed, he was sure they could use some extra food.

When he mentioned it, Aurélie nodded and said, "I'll go." As she got up, she leaned over and kissed his forehead. "I love you."

The way she said it confused him, but he took her hand and said, "I love you too. Maybe you should ask Luc or Henri to go with you."

She shook her head and went up the stairs.

It left Mark with a sick feeling, even a knot in his stomach. There was something wrong—again.

11:00 a.m., September 26, the Dugout

Aurélie had put Mark's extra clothes and his rifle with ammunition into the truck. She also had retrieved two boxes of canned goods. She deliberately left the food in the freezer until last.

She had been walking around in a daze, doing things automatically. She sat down on the bed and finally couldn't hold her emotions in check anymore. She started sobbing, and the more she cried, the worse she felt.

I was afraid of this, and now I'll lose Mark as well. When she had awakened earlier that morning and went to get dressed, she saw the heavy pads in her dresser that she used every month for her menstrual cycle. It was then that it hit her: *I should've started several days ago or yesterday at the latest!* She had felt strange over the last several days and even had some tenderness around her breasts. She knew enough about pregnancy to recognize the signs. The main symptom was no cycle. She was pregnant; she was carrying a German baby!

Why, oh why? Why now, when I've finally found someone to love? She continued to sob. She didn't know what to do. How could she tell anyone? She couldn't bear to see the look in Mark's eyes when he found out. *Why a German? Why now?*

Time passed, and she continued to cry until she looked at the clock. It was almost two o'clock. The family would've expected her back by noon. She dried her eyes and loaded up the frozen food. As she drove back, she decided that after helping to unload the supplies, she would take a walk through the field and up the ridge to the west of the farmhouse. She wanted to be alone.

2:20 p.m., the DeBoy Farm

Josette came out the front door as soon as Aurélie pulled into the yard. "Where have you been? We were worried and started thinking maybe something happened to you."

Aurélie jumped out of the truck and went to the back. "Why don't you ask Luc and Heinrich to come out and help unload this?"

Josette followed her to the back of the truck. When she looked at Aurélie, she knew her sister had been crying. "What's wrong?"

"Nothing. Just ask the boys to come out and unload. I'm going to take a walk."

Josette reached out and grabbed her arm. "Please tell me—whatever it is."

Aurélie took her arm back and looked at her sister. "Some things can't be fixed so easily. I won't be gone long." She started across the field.

Josette stood there shocked, not knowing what to do. Alphonse came out and saw Aurélie walking out through the field. "Is something wrong with Aurélie?"

"Yes, but she wouldn't tell me. Would you get Luc and Heinrich to help unload the truck?"

Josette went in and ran into Henri coming up the stairs. "Is Aurélie back? Mark was worried about her."

Josette just nodded and went downstairs. She walked over to Mark's bed. "Something is troubling Aurélie. Would you happen to know what it might be?"

"I've been worried about her all day. She wasn't acting like herself this morning. Something was bothering her."

"Well, when she got back from the dugout, I could tell she had been crying. Then she just walked out in the field west of the house. I couldn't stop her, and she wouldn't tell me anything. I'm worried."

The look on Mark's face showed his concern. "I know there's something wrong, and somehow I think it has to do with what happened to her. I thought she might have been getting over the worst part. We had a great time at the dugout. I know she's happy about our engagement, so I don't understand what could've upset her. I hope it wasn't something I did."

Some thoughts started stirring in Josette's mind. She put her hand on Mark's arm gently. "No, I'm sure you didn't do anything. Rape, however, is an awful thing for a woman. It could just be that some bad memories are coming back. Let me go upstairs. I have to help to put the food away, but I have some ideas. Please don't worry. I will talk with her when she's back."

Josette went upstairs and then to the second floor. She thought for a few minutes and then went into Aurélie's room. She pulled open the second drawer of the dresser where she knew Aurélie kept her underclothes. Her heart caught in her throat at what she saw. There in the middle of the drawer, in disarray, were Aurélie's menstrual pads. *Oh God, she hasn't started her cycle.*

Josette thought for a second. *Should I tell anyone, or should I go after her myself?* She finally decided she needed to tell Polly and Grand-père. They could go after her together. She felt they would be able to talk with her better as a family.

She went to the basement and found Polly. "I need to talk to you for a minute." They both went upstairs and found Alphonse, Luc, and Heinrich sitting at the kitchen table. She went over to her grand-père and whispered, "Can I talk with you for a second?"

They went into the next room, and Josette turned her back to the kitchen to make sure no one heard. "Did either of you notice that Aurélie was acting strange this morning?"

Alphonse nodded, and Polly replied, "Yes, it was like she didn't want to be around anyone. I tried to get her to talk, but she wouldn't say much."

"Well, when she came back from the dugout, she had been crying, and she didn't want to help unload. That's not like her. Then she told me that she was going for a walk up to the western ridge. I went down and talked with Mark, and he told me he felt something was wrong too." She paused to get control of her emotions. "I don't know why this idea came to me, but I suddenly realized that it was probably time for her menstrual cycle to begin. Sometimes she acts funny, but I just checked and noticed her menstrual pads have not been used." Tears started running down her cheek. "I think she believes she's pregnant, and she may very well be. We need to go find her before Mark figures some of this out and tries to go out on his own."

Alphonse didn't say anything. He went to get his coat, as did Polly. He looked back at Luc and Heinrich. "We're to be out for a few minutes, so can you watch the guys?"

Aurélie had crossed over the field and went into the woods. She found a small clearing and sat down on an old log. A wave of discouragement swept over her. *How can I face anyone? Especially Mark. It's bad enough that this happened in the first place, but to be pregnant. Why? What am I going to do? Just when I found somebody to love!* She started sobbing again, and she didn't hear them approach.

Josette took one look at her sister and fell to her knees in front of her. She grabbed her hand as Polly sat down beside her and then put her arm around her. Josette looked at her sister and said, "I'm guessing, but you didn't start on time, did you?"

Aurélie just nodded and sobbed more. Josette got up and sat on the other side of her while her grandfather knelt in front. Polly and Josette both hugged her, and Alphonse held her hands.

Polly was the first one to speak. "I'm so sorry. You certainly don't deserve this, but you're not alone. No one's going anywhere. We're all here as a family to support you, and that includes Mark. We all love you dearly."

Josette kissed her sister's cheek and pulled her head to her chest. "Polly's right. We all love you so much. It's not your fault. As a family, we'll face these challenges, as we always have, and together we'll be strong."

Her grandfather looked up at her. Between her sobs, she said, "I'm … I'm … carrying another man's child. I'm so ashamed. I won't be able to … face anybody." The sobs deepened.

Alphonse kissed her hands. "Airi, this is not your fault. I know this is a bad situation. Remember that God presents us with challenges in our lives, knowing that we can grow stronger because of them. We all thank God that you are still with us today. It could have been different. You are also blessed with the love of a great man, whom you love deeply. Please know we will find the strength to get through this."

Aurélie stood up in anger. "But I don't want a German baby!"

Alphonse stood up with her and encircled her with his arms, pulling her to him. Polly and Josette stood up as well and hugged her from the back. "You are precious to all of us, and we are a strong family," he said. "Together we're going to make things better; you will see."

Aurélie was shaking and sobbing hard. "Why? Mark will … never …"

Alphonse stroked her head and neck. "Sh-h-h, Airi, don't do that to yourself. Of all the things that you might worry about, Mark's love isn't one of them."

Josette added, "Grand-père is right. Don't worry about Mark. He loves you too much ever to consider giving you up, no matter what." She kissed Aurélie's ear. "You're stuck with each other for the rest of your lives, big sister."

Alphonse and the two women continued to console Aurélie until she finally calmed down a little. They all sat down with her on the log, and Alphonse took her hand again. "You need to tell Mark. He has to know."

Aurélie almost started crying again. "How can I do that? Just walk up to him and say, 'Oh, by the way, I'm having a German baby.' I'm sure he'll be delighted."

Alphonse took her face in both of his callused hands, "Make it simple, but make it clear." He kissed her cheek and smiled slightly. "Besides, you forget your baby will be half French too."

For some reason that struck her as funny, and she started laughing. Polly smiled as she put her arm around her cousin. "We'll be there. You need to tell him alone, but we can all share the news."

Josette got up, and with her typical optimism, she took her sister's hand, pulling her up. "In fact, he already knows there's something wrong, and he thinks he did something to upset you. I think you should go down right now and tell him."

They talked for fifteen or twenty more minutes before Aurélie decided she would do as Josette suggested. They would get Mark upstairs in the parlor and then leave them alone.

4:00 p.m., the DeBoy Farm

Mark was talking with Berne and Alex. Marie had come over an hour earlier. She had become a regular visitor for the last four days, spending most of her time with Berne. She had already started teaching him French, and it was evident that while he wanted to learn French, he would've been happy doing anything with her.

Even though he was trying to keep his mind off Aurélie's behavior, Mark knew down deep there was something very wrong. He was also sure it had something to do with what had happened to her that night with the German soldiers. *It was almost three weeks ago, and I thought she and I were happy. I didn't talk about it much because I thought she preferred it that way. I can't understand how she feels, but I tried to make her know that it didn't matter to me.* For some reason, he suddenly focused on the date. *Three weeks ... oh ... surely not.* He started to move off his bed. *I have to get to her.*

"Marie, will you and Henri help me up the stairs, please? I need to find Aurélie."

Marie came over quickly. "Mr. Mark, you can't do that. You'll start bleeding again."

"I need to find her. It's very important."

Henri helped his sister, and they just got Mark to the kitchen just as Josette returned. She went over to Mark, and he could see in her eyes that his guess was probably right. She pointed to the parlor, and Henri, and Marie helped Mark get comfortable on the main couch.

Josette sat down next to him. "Aurélie is coming in, and she needs to talk with you." She took his hand. "Please promise to make sure she knows that you love her—no matter what."

Mark kissed her hand. "I promise, and I think I know what it is. Please ask her to come in."

Josette went out and got Aurélie. "He's waiting in the parlor. I think he already knows; he must've guessed." She hugged her sister. "Just tell him; he loves you."

Mark was sitting on the couch, feeling a little lightheaded from exertion. He heard a small noise and looked up and saw Aurélie in the doorway. For the first time that day, the knot in his stomach disappeared. Standing there, she was so beautiful. "Please come over and sit down. Josette said you had something you wanted to talk about."

She walked over and sat beside him.

"Why don't you move over to my other side?" he suggested.

Looking confused, she got up and sat down on his good side. "Why?"

"Because I want to hug my future wife, and I can't do it with a lame arm. Whatever you have to tell me, you'll tell me with both arms around me, and my one good arm around you." Aurélie relaxed as they embraced. He whispered into her ear, "I love you, and I don't care."

She pulled her head back slightly and looked straight into his eyes and could tell he meant it. Her eyes began to fill with tears as he kissed her and pulled her tighter. "It'll be okay. We love each other."

She was barely able to whisper in his ear, "Oh, I'm so ashamed. I'm pregnant from the rape."

He hugged her even tighter. "It's nothing for you to be ashamed about. I guessed it just a little while ago. I can't imagine what you've had to go through these last three weeks, but I'll tell you this." He pulled his head back slightly so he could look at her. "There is nothing in this world that can keep me from marrying you *and* loving you for the rest of my life." He let her absorb what he had just said before continuing. "While I didn't think about it earlier, it's not so bad. We'll start our family a little sooner than expected."

Tears blurred her vision, but she continued looking at him and hugged him again. "I love you, Mark. I don't deserve you, but I love you so much."

He kissed her lightly. "I've told you that you don't earn love. You can't do anything ever to make me stop loving you." He looked at her and smiled. "Maybe we should begin to make our plans for a wedding. I was getting impatient anyway. I can't wait to get my hands on you!"

Aurélie smiled and then giggled through her tears. "Just like a man, only thinking about one thing."

"Oh, I think about other things, but right now that's at the top of my list."

They continued to hold each other for several more minutes before Aurélie decided to get up and tell her grand-père, Polly, and her sister. They decided to get everyone together and announce that Aurélie and Mark would have a baby, and there would be a wedding very soon.

9:00 p.m., Walking from the DeBoy Farm to the Benoit Farm

Henri was thinking about what he and Josette had discussed. The announcement about Aurélie's baby had upset him more than he thought. However, it appeared that Mark was going to marry her and evidently as soon as possible. He and Josette had walked around the yard after dinner, and Josette mentioned they should set a date for their wedding too. She was a little unsure and had asked if Henri still wanted to get married. Just as Mark had indicated earlier that evening to Aurélie, Henri couldn't imagine living the rest of his life without Josette.

Josette squealed and threw her arms around Henri's neck. "I think we should get married with Mark and Aurélie."

He laughed. "I guess I won't have to worry about making decisions anymore!" Henri had no objections, as long as Aurélie and Mark didn't care.

Life with Josette was going to be interesting, no doubt about it. Moreover, his sister had found a new gentleman friend in the young German soldier. He just hoped if their relationship went any further, it wouldn't cause trouble.

6:30 a.m., September 27, the DeBoy Farm

Mark realized late last night that he didn't have a ring for Aurélie. He had left his wedding band with his personal effects in London. He realized Aurélie wouldn't mind, but it still bothered him.

He had risen early and began slowly exercising his right arm. He felt it was getting better rapidly. Marie had already arrived and was checking on all three of the patients, obviously spending a little more time with Berne. When she saw Mark was awake, she came over and sat on his bed. "How's the arm? Does it feel better today?"

Mark slowly moved his arm. "Yeah. It still hurts, but at least I'm getting more movement."

"Josette and Polly are making breakfast. I'll tell them you're awake."

Mark reached over and took her arm. "You like Berne, don't you?" he whispered.

Marie blushed slightly and nodded. "I know he's German, but I think he's a good person."

"He is, but just be careful because people can be unforgiving at times, especially toward Germans."

A few minutes later, Aurélie brought Mark a small tray. "*Petit dejeuner*, monsieur." She sat down on the bed and leaned over to kiss him. "How are you?"

He ate the bread, cheese, and homemade yogurt. When he finished, he asked Aurélie if she would have her grandfather come down. She looked at him questioningly. "Don't worry; I'm not having second thoughts, if that's what you're thinking. By the way, we need to come up with a date."

She smiled and then hesitated slightly. "Suppose Josette and Henri wanted to get married soon also. Would you object if we had a double wedding?"

He took her hand. "I don't object, but I hope they aren't rushing things just because of us."

"I don't think so, but nothing has been decided yet. I think Josette mentioned it to Henri last night before he went home. They're anxious to get married."

"Well, 'the more, the merrier,' as we say in the States."

Later in the morning, Alphonse came down. "Aurélie said you wanted to talk with me."

Mark was sitting on the edge of his bed. In a low voice, he said, "I don't have a ring for Aurélie. I don't think it's a problem for her, but I thought I'd mention it to you. I don't suppose there is somewhere around here where I could buy a wedding band?"

Alphonse thought for a moment. "There might be, but it probably would have to be made, and I think it would take too long." He paused for a second. "However, I do have my Maria's ring and also Monique's and Oliver's rings. They took them off when they left for the war. I would think one of those should fit. Something else we should discuss is where you think you might want to live."

"I can be happy here in France, but I'm not sure that's going to be possible without a long separation. I'm going to contact London at some point and find out what plans they might have for me."

"Well, one thing I thought about was perhaps having the boys help me clean up the old farmhouse with the garden in the woods. It would make a good place to start your lives."

Mark considered that for a moment. Alphonse was right. It would be a good place. "That sounds like a good idea, but I think Josette and Henri may be thinking about a double wedding, and they don't have a place either."

"Henri's père owns a small farmhouse north of Lachalade. I suspect that's where they would end up, but if not, it's something we can work out."

There was a lot of talk throughout the day about the upcoming weddings. By the end of the day, it was clear that Josette and Henri—at least Josette and the girls—wanted to make it a double ceremony. Saturday, October 14, was the date selected. The men had little input except to agree.

Aurélie came down and knelt by Mark's bed. She appeared anxious. "Is it okay for the ladies to make all these decisions? I know things are happening fast, but ... well ... we want things to be as good as they can be."

Mark took her hand and chuckled. "The same thing as the States—the women take over for weddings." He paused to catch his breath. "I'm not particular about the details; I just want to marry the woman I love."

October 14 was only two and a half weeks away, so there was a great deal of work to complete in a short time. Mark suggested that Henri, Alphonse, and Aurélie or Josette should go up to the dugout to get supplies, like flour and sugar and anything else that would be helpful for the preparations. He also told the two ladies he had several parachutes from the pod and some other supply drops that could be utilized for wedding dresses. And there were always Polly's parachutes as well.

CHAPTER 56

————— ✦✦✦✦✦ —————

October 1, Peenemünde

Dr. von Braun had traveled from central Germany to visit with Dr. Walter Dornberger. The V2 rockets had been falling on London for almost a month now. While it had not done any strategic damage, it did negatively affect the morale of the British civilians—at least that was everyone's hope. They didn't know, as most of their information coming from Britain was compromised.[8]

Dr. von Braun had been busy supervising the manufacture of the rockets in underground caves in central Germany. Reich Minister Speer contacted Dr. Dornberger about additional antiaircraft rockets to carry his nuclear shells. Von Braun wanted to nip that in the bud. There were precious little resources to go around, and those that were available needed to go toward the V2s.

"The Reich Minister was very specific. He wants improvements made quickly and testing to begin right away."

"I'm sure he does," Von Braun said, "but our first priority is the big

8. Early in the war, MI6 (British intelligence) discovered all the German Abwehr agents and either executed them or convinced them to work for the British as double agents.

rocket. Have your team continue working on the gyros, as we planned, and I'll talk to the Reich Minister myself."

I doubt if these rockets are making any real difference, but we might as well work as hard as we can to perfect what we have while we have the chance. The Führer will support me because, at the very least, it confronts the British with a weapon that they are powerless to defend against.

1:00 p.m., Thursday, October 5, the DeBoy Farm

Marie, Josette, Polly, and Aurélie were taking the brunt of the pressure. They had made good progress in the last week. The parachutes had indeed provided them with the ideal material for the dresses, and Henri's mother had volunteered to make them, with the help of another lady from Lachalade. The girls were trying to plan the food as well as take care of their wounded men—a tall order, to say the least. On Monday, several of the women from the area volunteered to help with the food, which reduced the workload on the four ladies.

Happily, Heinrich and Henri were there to help Luc and Alphonse with the chores. Alphonse had solved the issue with the rings when he realized he still had his wedding band. He was willing to donate that, so they now had all four rings, albeit with some crude sizing.

Alphonse was busy with fixing up the old farmhouse with Heinrich and either Henri or Luc, depending on how busy they were with their chores. Marie also helped with the cleaning.

After lunch, Henri came down to talk with Mark. Alex listened as Henri complained about all the activity. "Sometimes I think it would be better to go to the mairie and have it done in fifteen minutes."

"No. There's no way either of them would agree to that." Mark looked over to Alex. "What do you think?"

Alex just smiled. He had healed a lot in the past month and was moving around, although his strength had not fully returned. "Josette and Aurélie are going to have a wedding if it kills them. Although I don't think it will. Marie and Polly are tremendous helpers, so I'm sure it will all come together."

Mark looked at Alex, remembering that Polly had shown up right after he was wounded and hardly had left his side until the wedding-planning panic began. "You realize if you asked Polly right now, she'd say yes."

Alex nodded and replied. "I know. I hinted at that the other day. I think we'll wait for a while."

"You might want to think again about jumping in," Mark said. "The water's fine, you know. You're both here, and I doubt if one more couple will make any difference."

Alex thought about it. He'd already decided he wanted to ask her after his first mission to France. *There's just too much going on to add one more wedding.*

11:00 a.m., October 10, War Cabinet Rooms, St. Charles Street, London

General Brawls yelled out to his secretary, "Linda, get Colonel Betts on the line! And while you're at it, get Colonel Gaffney as well."

The Germans had been less aggressive in the past week. He wanted to see what Betts had in the way of information. Some people thought it was the result of their "victory" at Arnhem, but he wasn't so sure. It's true that Montgomery had run into some crack units on the way to Arnhem, but it seemed a little too easy. *I'll bet Patton is more than a little upset.* Third Army had slowed their advance across eastern France to allow additional supplies to be sent for Operation Market Garden.

Linda Schmidt came in a few minutes later. "They're both available in thirty minutes if you'd like to meet with them."

He looked up. "Ask them to come to my office, please."

7:00 p.m., Wednesday, October 11, the DeBoy Farm; Dinner

There was quite a gathering at the dinner table. All of the wounded men had mended well enough to eat upstairs, and Marie was invited to join them. The wedding preparations were progressing, and the women even had begun to relax a little.

Mark sat next to Aurélie and couldn't help whispering in her ear. "I think Alex is going to ask Polly."

Aurélie turned her head and looked at him. After a moment, she allowed a smile to come across her face, and she reached over and squeezed his hand.

Just after Alphonse said the blessing, Alex got up. "I have something to say. First, I would like to thank the DeBoys, Marie, and of course Polly for all of the hard work and the care they have provided. It's meant a lot to me, and I know that Major Dornier, Heinrich, and Berne are grateful as well." He stopped for a moment and looked around the table, finally letting his gaze fall upon Polly. He put his hand on her shoulder. "I answered a question in my own mind on my first trip to France many months ago. While I realize this may not be the best timing, this war has taught me to take advantage of opportunities."

He caressed Polly's neck, and she looked up at him. He looked down, and slowly knelt on one knee—his good one. He took Polly's hand and saw the surprise and shock in her eyes as she realized what he was doing. "Polly Berson, I love you, so would you be my wife? Will you marry me?"

Polly's mouth opened, but no sound would come out.

Aurélie, sitting next to her, leaned over. "Poddy, give the man an answer."

Polly squealed and kissed Alex. "Yes … yes, I'll marry you. You are right; it's horrible timing, but I don't care."

Alphonse sighed and helped Alex get up. "Somehow, I'm not surprised," Alphonse said, "but I have run out of rings!"

2:00 a.m., Friday, October 13, North of Arlon, Belgium, in the Ardennes

Koonrod led his four-man group through the dense forest and the steep hills of the Ardennes. He had sent reports back to London, indicating the Germans were beginning to withdraw. He knew this was just the first of many exploratory missions. Something was going on, and it was up to them and the other Resistance groups to provide the Allies with information.

The message from London had been rather strange. In addition to the typical information, such as strongpoint locations and approximate enemy strength, they had requested an incursion into the facility located on top of a small knoll between two much larger hills. Koonrod remembered this was the place where large steel tubes had been installed last year. Their mission was to find the ammunition storage point for this location, and photograph it, if possible.

Trying to get close to an ammunition dump without being discovered was almost impossible. Besides, the message specifically requested that any ammunition or ordnance that looked out of place was to be taken, if at all possible, and sent back to London. Failing that, he was to take photos.

Koonrod had been doing this for five years, and he knew his business. He also knew that sooner or later, he would either be captured or killed. This mission certainly seemed like it could end up with either of those unpleasant possibilities. That's why he decided to go in himself. He and a colleague had sneaked within thirty meters of the installation's perimeter, and then he continued alone.

He was relieved to see there was no barbed wire or other physical obstacles between the guards and the facilities. He slowly penetrated the installation, crawling toward where he thought the tubes would be. He guessed that the ammunition storage would be within ten meters of the pipes. After crawling around for almost thirty minutes, he literally fell into a ditch and found himself face-to-face with all sorts of ordnance.

He spent a few minutes very carefully looking through the stacks of shells with a muted red light. He was about ready to grab one of the larger mortar shells when he saw a box in the corner. It looked like it might be large enough to house one or two mortar shells, but it was built much thicker than required for two shells. *That qualifies as something unusual, and if I stay around much longer, London isn't going to get anything.*

He lifted up the box and slowly retraced his steps. It was difficult because the box weighed twenty or twenty-five kilograms. *If these are mortar shells, they're the heaviest ones I've ever handled!*

Thirty minutes later, he joined his colleague just outside the perimeter. Another thirty minutes, and the group was carefully withdrawing. He dragged the heavy box out of the installation, sure that London would be very interested. The container certainly contained something that wasn't ordinary.

1:10 p.m., Saturday, October 14, the Church in Lachalade

The entire village had helped decorate the church. The sanctuary was covered in flowers, greenery, and bows. It wasn't often that three couples got married at the same time. All of the DeBoy and Benoit friends had contributed food, wine, and even some champagne for the celebration. Henri's mother had found her mother's wedding ring for Josette, and Aurélie gave her first wedding ring to Polly. So the problem of the rings was solved, except for the men.

Polly, Aurélie, and Josette were all in a room completing their final preparations. Two of the women in the village were seamstresses and had been able to fashion three beautiful and different gowns from the parachute silks. They even found some lace to complete the veils. They'd also made nightgowns for the girls to help make their wedding nights special.

Mark, Alex, Alphonse, Heinrich, Berne, Luc, and Henri were in a separate room. It was apparent that Henri was very nervous. Mark walked over to him. "I was just as nervous as you when I married my first wife. I think it's just the ceremony. I knew that I loved her, but I was still nervous."

"I love her, but I wish this would just be over quickly."

"Take a deep breath because you are going to want to remember every moment of this day and especially the moment you see her coming down the aisle."

Alphonse motioned for all seven of the men to join hands. "I don't pray as much as I should, but there is a God, and he has protected and blessed us. Let's say a prayer of thanks and blessings for these three unions."

3:00 p.m., Albert Speer's Quarters, Berlin

I hope Werner keeps his word about those upgrades. Speer had been able to convince von Braun to work on some of the improvements for the antiaircraft rockets after he finished the next phase of the V2 gyros. Even though neither man had mentioned it, it was apparent they both shared the same sentiment: very little, if anything, they accomplished now would affect the outcome of the war.

Even though the number of the nuclear shells had been severely limited by an air raid on the Luftwaffe base near the reactor, there had been thoughts of placing the napalm warheads on the missiles. In fact, several missile tips with napalm had been fabricated. It would create a vacuum and a shock wave that could cause more damage than single flak shells. If the improvements in the guidance system of the rockets were successful, they would be more accurate.

9:00 p.m., the Dugout

After Mark and Aurélie dropped Polly and Alex at the old farmhouse, they drove to the dugout. Josette and Henri were going to spend their wedding night at the small house on his parents' farm, and Mark and Aurélie decided on the dugout. Of the three locations, the dugout was probably the least desirable, but Aurélie had been insistent.

"So, Madame Dornier, shall we retire to our boudoir?" He extended his hand, and she slipped her hand into his.

"Let's put our bags in the cellar, and take a walk."

When they went down to the cellar, what they saw surprised them. Sometime in the last couple of days, someone—probably led by Alphonse and Luc—had put down additional rugs, cleaned up, and, most important, replaced the old straw bed with a larger frame and a feather mattress.

Mark put his arm around Aurélie. "Wow, someone did an awful lot of work."

"Look at this." Aurélie walked over to the counter and pulled a bottle of champagne out of the ice. "They thought of everything."

Aurélie started crying, and Mark walked over and hugged her. "Why don't we take the ice and champagne up to the dugout and enjoy it there?"

The Old Farmhouse

Polly and Alex were also surprised when they got inside. They both had worked on cleaning it, along with several other people, but someone had made several improvements over the last couple of days. Someone had stocked the house with food, made up the bed with fresh linen, and even had a fire in the stove that was heating several gallons of water. This last gesture was particularly thoughtful since the house only had frigid well water.

"I wonder who left the champagne."

Alex walked over and started working on the cork. "I suspect Alphonse had something to do with it. I would guess they left similar presents for all of us."

"I hope Aurélie and Mark are okay in the dugout. I felt bad about making them spend their wedding night in an old dirt cave."

Alex handed her a glass of champagne and then hugged her. "I spent some time there, and it's not bad. Besides, Alphonse had Luc and Heinrich working to spruce it up yesterday."

Polly kissed Alex on the cheek. "I think it's special for Aurélie because that's where she first met Mark."

Alex took her glass and put it on the table. "Enough talking about Aurélie and Mark. I would like to find out what it's like to have a beautiful wife on my wedding night."

CHAPTER 57

+ + + + +

1:30 p.m., October 16, War Cabinet Rooms, St. Charles Street, London

General Brawls was finishing the report on the shell collected by the Resistance near Arlon, Belgium. *The Nazis just keep coming up with new things.* He got up and went out to his secretary. "Linda, convene the usual suspects. See if you can get them here in the next fifteen or twenty minutes."

In less than thirty minutes, Colonels Betts and Gaffney, along with Major Stone and Captain Boysden and several others, were in the general's office. The general looked around. "So what do you gentlemen think of all of this?"

Betts looked over to Captain Boysden. "The captain and his people developed a theory, and I agree with it. Perhaps he would be the best one to explain it."

Boysden got up and distributed several briefing sheets. "We've taken information gathered from several different sources over the last month. The latest raid near Arlon yielded a nuclear shell, quite intact. We also received a second warhead the Resistance recovered from the

386

Butte de Vauquois three weeks ago. The science team is still looking at them, but they reported just after lunch that the shells would be able to create a blast consistent with what was reported in the air raid on Butte de Vauquois last month."

Colonel Gaffney said, "I don't see a notation here about the possible interruption in the production of these shells or missile tips, including the ones filled with napalm."

"That's right sir. The colonel is correct that even though there is an unknown quantity of both types of shells or missile tips already fabricated, we believe that their ability to create additional nuclear material has been destroyed or at least severely set back, due to an air raid on a Luftwaffe base near Haigerloch. It was actually a mistake because the intended target was the air base. We got reports of large explosions—much larger than would be associated with a munitions dump—followed by many individuals in the area becoming sick. The scientists think it was probably due to a significant release of radiation from the reactor. In any case, that particular reactor is probably out of commission."

Boysden went over to a chart that he'd prepared earlier. "We think they may have fabricated forty to fifty of these shells. We don't know, however, how many have been distributed and to where. If they are used, they will be dangerous, not only from their explosive potential but also from possible radiation poisoning."

General Brawls had already deduced some of this. "If they concentrated their efforts installing these shells on a missile, what would that do to advancing troops."

"The scientists are still working on better estimates, but it's probable the blast would be equivalent to a four-thousand-pound bomb. The radiation would likely affect everyone within a half-mile radius."

General Brawls just shook his head. "Why don't we move on to the napalm issue? Hopefully, we can hear a little bit of good news."

Captain Boysden frowned. "Perhaps. Apparently, the gasoline being used to produce the napalm came from the refineries in Romania. Most of that production was slowed or completely stopped as a result of the air raids in July. The refineries were damaged sufficiently, so all of the gasoline and diesel production was allocated for fuel."

This time Colonel Betts motioned to Boysden. "The general already knows this, but we're uncertain how many of the shells were fabricated prior to July. We know that these shells were used in isolated cases, and they have been very effective. We suspect the Germans concentrated most of these shells around the BR sites. Perhaps as many as seventy to eighty have been allocated to each site."

General Brawls chuckled. "So for both of these new weapons, we don't know how many are out there or where?" He sighed. "I thought we were winning this war."

Captain Boysden turned to face him. "I'm afraid there's one more thing you should know, General. Based on a report from early August, we heard from a source inside Germany that some of the napalm shells were redesigned to go on small missiles. This was also confirmed by Major Dornier's report and some of the information gathered at the Vauquois site." Boysden could see the general was getting ready to interrupt him, so he quickly added, "We also confirmed a report from a missile facility that the Germans are making some improvements to the guidance system for the small missiles. It's likely they are going to use them in an antiaircraft role as well. Our people think that they may be much more effective in that role."

Brawls was amazed—just one piece of good news after another. The briefing went on for another thirty minutes before the he went back to his office and put a call into SHAEF headquarters.

2:00 p.m., the DeBoy Farm

Luc, Heinrich, and Alphonse were working on the fence behind the barn where they kept the milk cows. Josette and Henri were walking up the drive and waved.

Luc couldn't help but make a crack. "Well, they finally decided to get outside."

Alphonse just chuckled. "That's how it is when you first get married. Don't tease them."

Josette found Marie cleaning up the dishes from lunch. Marie looked up and smiled. "I'm so glad you visited. With everyone gone, it's been a little lonely."

Henri went downstairs to check on Berne. Josette went over and hugged Marie. "We wanted to get outside and thought we would come over and see if you could use some help."

"It's a full-time job taking care of all these men."

Josette elbowed her. "But you get Berne all to yourself, don't you?" When Marie blushed, Josette added, "It's no secret. We all can tell you two care for each other."

"I hope we can manage somehow. It won't be easy with him being German."

"Polly, Mark, and I talked about that. Mark is pretty certain that he can get permission for both Berne and Heinrich to stay here in France, at least until the war ends. Mark already sent a letter back to London and also to General Patton, asking for permission."

Henri came upstairs. "Our patient could use some water." He went out to the well and pumped half a pail. As he came back in, he went over and kissed Josette. He put his arm around Marie. "He's healing very nicely. I think he likes his nurse."

Marie blushed again. "Does everyone in the whole world know about us?"

CHAPTER 58

◆◆◆◆◆◆

6 a.m., November 19, Western Hurtgen Forest

L ieutenant Pyle had just returned from the briefing about the obstacles ahead. His platoon was dug in on a ridge just east of a dirt road. A patrol last night had located a bunker with secondary defensive positions. They noticed there were a considerable number of power lines running through the area. Pyle was to take his platoon, along with three tank destroyers from the 703rd Tank Destroyer Battalion and neutralize the position[9].

He walked over to the three tanks. "Sergeant Gibbs, why don't you and the other tank commanders come over here?" He spread a map out and began to explain his plan. "There are two bunkers, here and here, and between the bunkers, there are at least three machine-gun positions with mortar positions in the rear. We didn't spot any antitank weapons, but we have to assume they have some. I'll have a squad flank from either side, and I'd like to have one of your destroyers with them."

"What about artillery?"

---

9. The M-10 tank destroyer was developed to counter the Nazi armor advantage. It was based on the Shernam tank body with a 3 inch main gun mounted in a topless turret. While lightly armormered, it boasted speed over armor.

"We're going to get a twelve-minute barrage from the 105s, but they're not going to start until we are in position. We'll pull up to within seventy-five yards of the perimeter and radio back for the 105s to begin. We'll have to be ready to move fast. After eight minutes they will start walking the barrage toward the bunkers and drop some smoke."

Sergeant Gibbs started to speak when one of the other destroyer commanders interrupted him. "Are those 105 boys going to be careful they don't drop their shells on top of our heads?"

Pyle just smiled. "I've already talked to their targeting people. They're only a mile back and shouldn't have any trouble hitting their target. Our job is to move fast as soon as the barrage lets up."

They all returned to their positions and began to prepare. There was a lot of griping because it was cold, and everybody had been cold and wet for weeks now. The Hurtgen Forest, or wherever they were, had been a cold, damp, and very sloppy place to be.

An hour later, they were in position—one squad each on the left and right flank, with a tank destroyer twenty yards to their rear. Pyle had one squad just off center to the right. The artillery barrage started right on schedule, and the 105 howitzers laid their twenty-five-pound shells right on target, ripping up the barbed wire and exploding the mines. The first shells had landed twenty-five yards in front of their positions and, after a few minutes, began walking up toward the bunkers.

The barrage went on for about ten minutes, gradually zeroing in on the bunkers.

Pyle spoke into his walkie-talkie. "Stand by to advance in two minutes."

The last shells were smoke. As soon as Pyle saw those, he gave the order to advance. Inside the bunker, the high-pitched whine of the generators went unheard because of the artillery. The German commander knew they would be overrun, but he was determined to take as many of the enemy as possible. He had four of the new gasoline-type mortar shells and, of course, the beam weapon. He gave the order to load the gasoline mortar shells.

Once the smoke shells began exploding, Pyle gave the order to attack. The tank destroyers on either flank fired into the bunkers while the infantry began to advance. Inside the main bunker, the targeting officer finalized the coordinates on the tank destroyer to the left and gave the order to fire. There was a high-pitched whining sound, followed by a flash of light. The tank destroyer immediately glowed red hot and exploded as the ammunition inside overheated.

The tank destroyer on the right immediately backed up and moved to the left—and just in time, as the second beam cut through the trees and set the woods on fire where the tank had been seconds before. The infantry squad pressed ahead as their machine-gun positions laid down covering fire. The Germans returned fire with both mortars and machine guns.

The first of the gasoline mortar shells was fired. One of the soldiers looked up and saw a black object falling from the sky toward their position. About one hundred feet above him, the shell exploded in a ball of fire, raining burning fuel down over an area covering half the squad. The fire stopped just a few feet from him. He watched as his buddies turned into burning heaps. He was carrying a twenty-pound satchel charge. He realized if he didn't get the charge into one of the bunkers, they were all going to die. He got up and ran the fifty yards to the pillbox. He fell down in front of the main bunker, miraculously unhurt, trying to catch his breath. He could hear the whine of the electrical gear inside and decided to start the fuse on the charge. Since the fuse was twenty seconds, he counted carefully to fourteen and slung the satchel through the bunker's embrasure. The electrical noise increased, and he smelled a strange sweetness in the air. Then the charge went off.

There was a secondary explosion as one of the generator fuel tanks ignited. The remaining two tank destroyers opened up on the other bunker, and the machine-gun positions quickly neutralized them. One additional gasoline mortar shell exploded harmlessly to the rear of their lines, causing an impressive fireball.

By 9:00 a.m., the platoon had secured all of their positions. As Pyle was preparing his report, he called for trucks to gather up the wounded and dead. *Whatever this weapon was, I hope they don't have many.*

CHAPTER 59

❖ ◆ ◆ ◆ ❖

7:00 a.m., November 23, the Dugout

Mark woke up early to take a walk around the area. He quietly dressed, not wanting to wake Aurélie. After the walk, Mark went down and looked at Aurélie. It made him realize how happy he was that she was his wife. He went over, knelt beside the bed, and kissed her gently on the neck.

Aurélie had been in a deep sleep but was drawn back into the waking world by gentle pressure on her cheek. She opened her eyes and realized that Mark was stroking her cheek and kissing her neck. She looked up and smiled. "You're up early this morning."

He leaned over and pressed up against her, but she gently pushed him back. "I love you, but I have to use the toilet."

Mark laughed. "I forgot."

He went over and began to boil some water for oatmeal while Aurélie took a shower. A few weeks back, she had started becoming slightly nauseated in the mornings, so they decided to switch to cereal, bread, and cheese for breakfast.

Aurélie came out of the shower, drying her hair. "Why don't we walk over and see Polly and Alex today? We haven't seen them since we had dinner at the farm last week."

"Sure. Are you feeling better this morning?"

She went over and hugged his back. "Not as bad; hopefully, it will get better soon."

Mark turned around and hugged her as he nuzzled her neck. She started giggling and squealed, "Stop it! We have so many things to do today. I don't think we should be going back to bed right now."

"I know. I just like to make you squeal." He knelt in front of her, opened her robe, and kissed her belly. Talking to the baby, he said, "You're making my wife ignore me!"

Aurélie pulled him close to her and kissed him. "I will never ignore you."

10:00 a.m., the DeBoy Farm

Most of the routine chores were finished, so Luc, Heinrich, and Berne sat down to play some cards. Marie was upstairs, changing bedding, and Alphonse was in the barn.

Josette and Henri walked over with Claudine, one of Josette's friends. Heinrich had related he'd been married for a year before he had to leave for army service. His home was in Dresden, unfortunately in an area ravaged by the firebombing raids. He hadn't received any letters from his wife or any of his family since then. One of his friends had gone back on leave and snapped some photographs of their old neighborhood. It was clear the chances that his family had made it out alive were almost nonexistent. About a week ago, Josette approached Henri about perhaps introducing Claudine to Heinrich. At first, Henri was not very supportive, but Josette finally won him over. There weren't many French men left of marrying age, and both Heinrich and Claudine were lonely.

As they were walking down the driveway, Marie and Berne were coming outside. Berne's wounds had finally healed after a short reoccurrence of infection, and he seemed to enjoy getting out, particularly with Marie. They were holding hands.

Josette walked up and hugged Marie. "We thought we'd walk over and give you a little bit of a break." She turned and introduced her friend to Berne. "This is Claudine. She lives in Lachalade, and we have been friends since childhood."

Claudine looked at Berne and nodded.

"Bonjour, mademoiselle," he said. "It is good to make your acquaintance." He'd obviously been practicing some basic phrases.

Marie beamed and kissed Claudine on her cheeks.

"Where is everyone?" Claudine asked.

Marie nodded toward the house. "Luc and Heinrich are in there, and Grand-père is out in the barn."

Josette motioned for Claudine and Henri to follow her into the house. She was eager to introduce Claudine to Heinrich.

2:00 p.m., War Cabinet Rooms, St. Charles Street, London

Colonel Gaffney finished reading the reports from eastern France. They weren't good. The entire front was stalled. The Americans had sent several divisions that were beaten up over the past several months, particularly in the Hurtgen Forest, to rest in the hilly Ardennes region. No one was expecting any action in that area, particularly in the middle of winter and with this type of weather.

The colonel and the entire general staff were bothered by not knowing how many more of the BR sites and other nonconventional weapons the Germans possessed. They had become uncharacteristically quiet except for a few areas, and it was concerning. General Brawls even mentioned that Patton had cautioned General Bradley to be careful. Patton had suggested the Germans might be planning a counterattack. In the winter that seemed unlikely, but it was clear the German army was far from defeated.

1:00 p.m., November 28, the Dugout and Forêt Domaniale de Lachalade

Aurélie had asked Mark to load some things in the Jeep while she packed some food to take to Alex and Polly. He came back down the ladder just as she was finishing. On the spur of the moment, Aurélie walked over and put her arms around him. He slipped his arms around the small of her back and pulled her close.

"To what do I owe the honor of this particular hug, Mrs. Dornier?"

Aurélie kissed him gently and then pulled back, smiling. "It seems that I felt something pressing up against my back this morning. I just wondered if perhaps you would enjoy some attention. I know I would."

He smiled and sat down on the edge of the bed, pulling her onto his lap. "That's just something you need to get used to in the morning. It just happens and doesn't necessarily mean anything."

She kissed him and whispered, "It means something to me. I want to make sure my husband is happy."

He looked at her eyes and felt like he was falling into her. She felt warm, soft, and very much alive. "I thought we had a lot to do today."

She gently pushed him back on the bed and then began to loosen his clothes. "We do—in a little while."

A while later, they pulled up at the old farmhouse. Alex and Polly were sitting on the front porch in heavy coats. Polly came bounding down the stairs. "I'm so glad you guys came over. We were thinking of taking a short walk."

Mark carried the box of food, following Aurélie into the house.

"Why don't we all take a walk together?" Aurélie suggested. "We brought some extra food because Mark thinks we may get some heavy snow."

Once Mark set the box down, he turned to Alex. "You feeling okay?"

"Yeah, I think I'm mended, except for some stiffness."

"Are you getting enough exercise?"

Polly walked up and put her arm around his waist. Alex looked at her and smiled. "It seems like all I'm getting is exercise."

Polly blushed and elbowed him in the side. "I haven't heard you complaining about it."

Aurélie couldn't help giggling. "Perhaps we could get some fresh air along with our exercise this time."

Both couples joined hands as they started their walk. No one talked much; they were enjoying the sound of the wind coming through the trees. Every once in a while, there would be the rustle of an animal in the brush or the odd bird singing.

They walked down the small road that led to the old landing field. They spent several minutes taking in the beautiful view of the valley to the east before turning back to the main country road. They walked on the road for a while, then went cross-country to the west, and then north back toward the farmhouse.

As they approached a small creek, Polly noticed some movement in the thicket. They all stopped, and Polly and Alex both leveled their Sten guns. Mark motioned to them to stay back as he leveled his 30-06. He mouthed the word *boar* as he took aim. They could use the additional meat. A second later, the boar was dead on the ground.

Mark sent the other three back to get the Jeep while he began the process of field dressing the carcass. It took him about fifty minutes to start quartering the animal, and by that time, Alex was back with the Jeep and a saw.

"I left the girls back at the house," Alex said. "They were going to start preparing some other things to go along with our roast boar for dinner tonight."

Mark continued cleaning the boar "You know we're lucky to have wives like Polly and Aurélie."

Alex knelt and started helping Mark to cut up the carcass. He had thought the same thing every day since they were married.

CHAPTER 60

✦✦✦✦✦

9:30 a.m., December 10, General Patton's Headquarters

Colonel Koch, Patton's intelligence officer, had just brought in a report from the Twelfth Army Group.

"So there's no activity whatsoever along our entire front?" Patton didn't think much of Bradley's intelligence staff.

"No, sir, and what's even more unusual, patrols aren't able to locate much in the way of troop movements. General Bradley has sent night probes five miles east, and they've reported sounds of traffic, mostly truck movements."

Patton put the report down and walked over to the window, staring out on the soggy streets of Nancy. *This is not good. They aren't beaten, despite what Ike's people are telling him. Something is going on, but right now, there's no way to be sure.*

"Oscar, come over here, and show me on the map where our probes have been."

Colonel Koch walked over to the map. "Mainly in this area, General. It's difficult to conceive any large build-up here—the terrain is just too difficult to maneuver, particularly in this weather." He was pointing to the area in the Ardennes from Neuerburg, south to Wallendorf.

Patton stared at the map for a few more minutes. Suddenly, he visualized several paths the Germans might be planning to take—right through the 99th, 106th, and the 28th Divisions—all untested soldiers and full of new recruits. He recalled his history. The Germans hadn't mounted a major winter offensive since the Franco-Prussian War.

Suddenly, Patton punched the map with his fist. "They're sitting there, Oscar; they're sitting there right in front of our three divisions, and we're about to get the crap beat out of us." He turned and went out to his aide. "Captain, get Colonel Manning in here on the double."

Colonel Manning came running from his office, having overheard his boss. "What is it, General?"

Patton explained his thought process briefly. "I don't know exactly *where* just yet, but I expect the Germans to mount a major offensive, probably around Christmas. Get our staff and every one of our division staffs working on a plan to pivot Third Army to move north and attack here. We'll need to leave some people in positions here to keep the Germans honest, but most of us should proceed north. Tell them we'll need a regimental combat team and the Seventh Armored ready to move on twenty-four-hour notice. The rest of the Third Army will follow twenty-four hours later."

Carlos Manning was shocked at the orders. No one had ever turned the axis of attack of an entire army ninety degrees in such a short period and in this kind of weather, but Manning knew his boss well enough to know that his ideas were not fiction. *We'll have to make sure we have enough supplies. It's over one hundred miles in the middle of winter!*

11:00 p.m., December 11, East of Wallendorf, Germany

Koonrod's small group was on patrol again. They had been transported thirty miles east of Arlon through the Ardennes to the border with

Germany. There, they had slipped through the lines twice in the last three days. His group was chosen because it was one of the best in the Belgian Resistance. While he didn't know for sure, he suspected the Allies were concerned about a German buildup somewhere in western Germany.

They had slipped through the Allied lines around noon that day. The line in this area was held by the Second Infantry Division. The Second had taken a beating in November, so they were pulled back and replaced with the newly formed 106th Division. Koonrod wanted to make sure the 106th had the correct password. He didn't want to get shot by rookies when he came back across the lines later that night.

"So which outfit is going to be here?"

The sergeant from the Second shouldered his pack and said, "Do I look like Ike? I don't know, but I heard the 422nd may be replacing us." The 106th Division was composed of the 422nd, 423rd, and 424th Regiments. The sergeant's platoon leader yelled for him to muster their troops. Turning, he yelled back at Koonrod, "I don't care, as long as we get out of here and get some hot chow. Just don't forget the password 'cause the new guys will be jumpy."

Koonrod led his men up to the Schnee Eifel[10] and then down the other side. After traveling about seven miles into Germany, they came across a grouping of tanks sitting in the forest, just off the road. They carefully approached until they were close enough to hear talking. They made notes on the markings on the tanks and the remarks they heard coming from the soldiers.

They retreated slowly until trees and darkness completely concealed them. Then they started trotting back toward the Allied lines. Hundreds of tanks, thousands of men, food, and supplies—they had to get this information back and fast!

Three hours later, they were climbing back up the slope of the

---

10. A heavily wooded landscape in Germany's Central Uplands that forms part of the western Eifel in the area of the German-Belgian border. Its highest elevation is on the Schneifel ridge, about 2,800 feet, and historically forms one of several natural obstacles from foreign invasion.

Eifel when they were challenged. They gave the countersign and were allowed through the lines.

Corporal Norris came up to Koonrod as he was passing through. "What have you guys been doing? Intelligence says there aren't any Germans out there, at least not anywhere close."

Koonrod glanced at him as he walked past. "I wouldn't know, but I'd suggest you guys make sure you check everyone who comes through this area and keep people on guard." He didn't want to set off a general alarm, but he also felt he should at least remind these guys they were on the front lines. Norris just looked at him.

10:30 a.m., December 12, the Old Farmhouse

Polly was outside, splitting wood, and Alex had gone back to the garden to harvest the last of the root vegetables before they were ruined by the colder weather. He went down to the basement from the rear entrance and put the vegetables in storage containers with dry sand. When he returned, Polly had finished splitting some additional kindling, which he loaded in the wood boxes in both the kitchen and the main room.

Polly sat down while Alex arranged the wood. It was already getting colder outside. "I thought it was going to warm up after it snowed," Polly wondered.

"It did, and now it's going to snow again—its winter."

Alex walked over and sat down beside her. Polly leaned her head on his chest. One of the things she liked best about domestic life so far was being able to sit down next to Alex.

"What are you thinking about?" Alex asked.

"How nice it is to be here alone with you."

"I wonder what Aurélie and Mark are doing."

Polly raised her head and kissed his neck. "I suspect Mark is making sure that their little cave is ready for the snow."

Alex thought for a second. "I feel kind of bad that they have to live in that old cellar, especially with Aurélie expecting."

Polly put her arms around his middle. "I told you Aurélie likes the place." After thinking for just a second, she said, "Maybe we could offer to switch places in a couple of weeks."

"Maybe, but I think we all may be moving back to Alphonse's if it gets too much colder." Alex pulled Polly closer. "Besides, I'd like to go back upstairs."

Polly feigned ignorance. "Why would you want to take a nap now?"

Alex pulled her off the couch and into an embrace. "I wasn't thinking of a nap, Mrs. Ryder."

Late Afternoon, the DeBoy Farm

Luc and Heinrich were in the barn, putting down hay and feed for the livestock and especially making sure the milk cows were comfortable. It would get cold that night, and Luc didn't want to go out to feed them again until morning.

Heinrich went to the other side of the barn to check on the chickens. They had all come in to roost. He made one last check for fresh eggs and then went back to help Luc. He had mentioned more than one time that he was very grateful Luc's grandfather had allowed Berne and him to stay. Berne was almost completely healed and had developed a relationship with Marie.

Heinrich thought she was pretty, but early on, he could see she liked his friend better. *I guess I can't blame her. Berne is a good man, just a little young.* His disappointment had been blunted somewhat a few weeks back when Josette introduced him to her friend Claudine.

Luc came up behind Heinrich. "Haven't seen much of Claudine lately. I always liked her."

"I was just thinking about her. I wouldn't mind seeing her again. I guess she has work of her own, taking care of her parents."

"Her dad can't do a lot, but she has two brothers who help out." Luc kind of nudged Heinrich. "I think maybe she likes you, although I can't imagine why. You're ugly, and on top of that, you're German!"

Heinrich shot Luc a scornful look. "I'm not ugly, and I can't help where I was born. Besides, you're one to talk about ugly."

The two boys had become good friends over the last several months. Heinrich thought, *Who would ever think that I would be in France on a farm surrounded by the French and Americans and two British—and enjoying it!*

6:30 a.m., December 15, the Dugout

Aurélie opened her eyes. It was still dark outside, and she could hear the wind blowing. It had started snowing hard the night before, but so far, their propane stove and heater were keeping them warm. The cellar, for all its drawbacks, was insulated reasonably well by the earth.

She turned on her side and snuggled up against Mark. She felt movement in her tummy. It wasn't much, but it was definitely there. She thought she'd felt something three or four days ago.

She put her arm around Mark's chest and allowed his body to warm her. He moved slightly and opened his eyes, smiling at her.

"Good morning, beautiful. Sounds like a good day to stay down here," he said, listening to the wind. "I was going to start heating some water. What do you feel like?"

She kissed his temple and snuggled closer. "Maybe coffee. I think I'm feeling better this morning." She smiled at him, took his hand, and put it on her stomach. "I felt the baby move a few minutes ago. I can't believe I have a little person inside me."

Mark moved his hand around on her midsection and kissed her briefly. "Our family is growing." Just then, Mark felt the movement. He smiled again. "I can't believe it."

He started to get out of bed, but Aurélie pulled him back. He looked at her for a second, and then she smiled. "Let's just lie here a few more minutes. It's warm." She started running her fingers on his stomach. "Besides, I told you I was feeling better."

An hour later, the coffee was ready, and they both were dressed. Aurélie and Mark decided to go up to the dugout to drink their coffee.

Mark had set up the wood for a fire the night before in the front of the dugout, just under the cover. After lighting it, he came back down and took their covered porcelain mugs up.

The woods had been transformed into a winter wonderland. There'd been some freezing precipitation before the snow, so icicles were covering a lot of the trees. While the wind was gusting, the dugout walls offered a cozy place to sit, especially with the fire.

Aurélie slipped her arm around Mark's as she sipped her coffee. "I guess we'll have to go down to the farm in a couple of months. I'll be so fat that I won't be able to go up and down the ladder."

Mark looked at her. "Your grandfather suggested that we might want to do more work on the farmhouse—install some water drums up in the attic, and run some electric lines from the mainline or even from here. That would give us a place to stay if we wanted some privacy."

"What about Polly and Alex?"

"They can stay as long as they're here, but I suspect they'll be ordered back to England in a month or so."

That made Aurélie sad. She had enjoyed Polly's company, particularly with the pregnancy. She just hoped they wouldn't send Alex toward the frontlines. Mark could tell she was concerned, and he squeezed her arm. "I suspect they'll both go back to London and work in the intelligence section. Unless there's a special mission somewhere, I don't think they'll send Alex out again."

Looking up at him, she asked, "When did you talk to Grand-père?"

"Couple of nights ago, when we had dinner with them."

Everyone had attended the dinner and then enjoyed a long afternoon and evening of each other's company. Polly and Aurélie had suggested it because they didn't get to see the rest of the family much. "I think Marie and Berne are going to work out just fine as a couple. It's hard to think that he was an enemy soldier just a few months ago."

"War does strange things," Mark said. "I think there might be a second Franco-Prussian partnership forming up as well—Claudine and Heinrich."

Aurélie smiled but then shivered. "I'm going back down to make breakfast."

He kissed the top of her head. "I'm going to get some more firewood from the other dugout, just in case we need it."

"After we eat, why don't we drive over and see Polly and Alex?"

CHAPTER 61

◆ ◆ ◆ ◆ ◆ ◆

**3:30 a.m., December 16, Five Miles East of the Allied
Lines on the Schnee Eifel**

Private Dieter Brandt heard their sergeant bellowing. "Get up, you
lazy pigs! It's time we go push the Allies back." Dieter knew the
sergeant was joking, but he also knew it was time to get up. He elbowed
his friend Reinhardt. "We better get up. I suspect we'll be moving out
soon."

They both groaned from the cold. Dieter and Reinhart had to break
down their small tent and load supplies, especially the machine-gun
ammo belts. The mess runners were already returning from the galley
tent with pots of hot broth and bread.

They ate in silence, thinking about the day ahead. They hoped
their commanders were correct—that the American lines were lightly
manned, and their attack would cause a great deal of confusion. As
Dieter chewed on a piece of sausage from his broth, he wondered if
he'd be alive at the end of the day.

Dieter and Reinhardt joined the rest of their squad and helped the armored vehicles with their final preparations. They could hear the rumble of the diesel engines as they turned over and started to warm up.

An officer walked in front of their company. "Remember the artillery barrage starts, as usual, at 5:30 a.m., but this time it will last only for ten minutes. When you hear the whistle, move forward. We will turn the searchlights on. Shoot everyone in front of you. We will not take prisoners."

5:30 a.m., Schnee Eifel, 422nd Infantry Regiment, 106th Division

Corporal Fred Norris and his foxhole-buddy Calvin heard the low rumble of diesel engines in the woods, east of their position. That was nothing unusual, as the same thing had happened for the last several days. Right on time at five thirty, German artillery began to shell their positions. It usually didn't do very much damage. The worst part was if a shell exploded in the treetops; it rained both shrapnel and wood splinters down on them, even in their foxholes. They quickly learned to drag logs from the downed trees and cover their foxholes to give them a little protection.

Norris hated the shelling and immediately began to shake. Calvin put his hand on Norris's shoulder. "We're fine here. Unless a shell lands right on top of us, nothing is going to happen to us."

"Yeah, it's that shell that lands right on top of us that I'm worried about."

Calvin laughed. "Don't worry; if it does, you'll never know it."

Suddenly, the barrage stopped. Norris stuck his head up. *That's strange. Normally, it lasts for half an hour or more.* He looked over at Calvin. "Maybe they ran out of ammo."

Just then, the woods were illuminated with an eerie light. The early morning fog was diffusing the Germans' searchlights. Soldiers all up and down the line were looking up, wondering what was going on. They didn't have to wonder long, as the first white-clad stormtroopers started walking through their lines, shooting anyone outside of their foxhole.

In less than five minutes, the front line of their battalion had been overrun, and the Americans were either shot where they were or as they ran to the rear in panic. Fred and Calvin were about fifty yards behind the most forward position. Fred didn't know exactly what was going on, but he knew it wasn't good. "We better start moving to the rear right now. This looks bad."

They both got out of their hole and began to move back, crouching as low as they could while still running. The situation was surreal; between the strange light and the white-clad soldiers, everyone seemed to be in a state of confusion. Norris looked to his left and saw one of the attacking soldiers, and he sent a burst from his grease gun in that direction. The soldier went down, but another one materialized, shooting at them. Fred and Calvin could hear bullets whizzing around their heads.

We need to get back to the company HQ, and maybe we can regroup and stop this, Fred thought. Just then, he felt two solid impacts on his back and was thrown to the ground. When he tried to get up, he found his arms wouldn't work. He tried to yell to Calvin and then realized that Calvin was lying next to him with a glassy stare. *If we can just get back to HQ ...* and then he felt very cold.

Fred and Calvin had no way of knowing that the battle, later referred to as the Battle of the Bulge, had just begun, and the 106th Infantry Division would lose two of its three regiments in the next two days. The Germans would capture almost six thousand American soldiers in the largest surrender in American military history.

7:00 p.m., December 16, General Patton's Headquarters

Patton's aide was standing in front of him as he read the report. Patton looked up. "Have the staff assemble in twenty minutes."

He walked down to Colonel Manning's office. "The Germans have attacked in the Ardennes, and so far, it looks like they're pushing several of our divisions back. Staff will convene in a few minutes. We need to implement our plans to pivot and go north immediately."

CHAPTER 62

—— ✦✦✦✦✦ ——

10:00 a.m., December 17, the Old Farmhouse

Alphonse had been checking his drop point in Les Petites Islettes regularly, even though the frontlines had moved farther east. Today there was a message for Mark, and Alphonse was on his way to the dugout in the old truck. Even though they had not heard much for several months, Alphonse had a bad feeling about this. Aurélie and Mark were not in the dugout, so he decided to drive over to the old farmhouse.

Alex and Mark were standing near the well in the back of the house, trying to figure out how best to run a water line into the house. Polly and Aurélie were in the kitchen, preparing a stew. Alex heard the truck first and ran back to the house to get their Sten guns. By the time they ran around the house, they could see it was Alphonse's truck.

Polly had heard it as well and had grabbed her Sten gun, telling Aurélie to stay in the kitchen.

Alphonse got out of the truck and held his hands up in mock surrender. "I'm not armed, so hold your fire."

Alex laughed and walked up to him. "What brings you out here?"

"A message for Mark, and it may have something to do with you as well."

Mark took it and saw that it was in code. Turning to Alex, he said, "Why don't you stay here with the girls, and I'll drive back to the dugout and decode this." He started toward the Jeep but then turned back. "You might show Alphonse what we're thinking about on the water line. Maybe he has some ideas."

Mark was back at the dugout in less than ten minutes, even with the icy conditions. He decoded the message and saw that his stay here had been extended until summer. He also read that there would be a plane drop with some additional medical supplies and even a small medical kit to help take care of Aurélie. Alex and Polly were mentioned only briefly, with the implication that they could stay in France for a while as well.

As Mark drove back, he felt relieved that he would be able to be here when the baby came in early June. He was also glad to have Alex and Polly stay, and he was confident everyone else would feel the same.

He walked into the farmhouse and found everyone talking in the main room. He announced, "It was routine but good news. I get to stay until next summer, and Polly and Alex apparently get to stay a little longer as well."

Aurélie brightened up and hugged Polly. "I get to have my husband here for the baby!"

After lunch, Alphonse went out back with Alex and Mark and talked about the best way to run a water line into the cellar. Placing the drums in the cellar would provide more freeze protection than the attic "I know where we can get four or five more drums for storage. I think I can find a small electric pump as well. Now, all we have to do is figure out the best way to get electricity here.

3:00 p.m., December 19, the Dugout

Mark and Aurélie were walking on the road about half a mile from the dugout when they saw Alphonse's truck come around the corner.

"I wonder why Grand-père's up here again so soon. I hope everything is all right."

Alphonse stopped and held the message out for Mark. "I had a bad feeling about the message the other day, but this time I think it is bad news. The butcher in Lachalade said he heard the Germans had amassed a large counterattack in the Ardennes."

Mark and Aurélie got in with him and rode back to the dugout. Alphonse and Aurélie had some hot chocolate while Mark decoded the message.

Aurélie could tell he was tense. "Not good?" She tensed up as well because she desperately didn't want Mark called back now.

"I get to stay here, but the rumor you heard about a counterattack is true. Evidently, the Germans pushed several of our divisions back and have taken many prisoners. It doesn't look good, and on top of that, Polly and Alex have to report back to London in a few days."

Luckily, they had received the resupply drop right after sunrise yesterday. *It may be a while before we get another one*, Mark thought. "One other thing, although it doesn't mean much—I've been promoted to lieutenant colonel."

Aurélie smiled and hugged him. "It means something to me."

They went over to the old farmhouse and told Polly and Alex the news. They started packing, and Aurélie and Mark went back to the dugout to inventory their supplies.

Mark could tell that Aurélie was upset. "I don't know for sure, but I think they're going to work in London, at least for the short term. Things are too confusing right now to send Alex into this."

11:00 p.m., December 19, General Patton's Headquarters

Patton just returned from a Verdun meeting with Eisenhower and the Allied commanders. Walking into his office, he yelled at Colonel Manning, "Carlos, where do we stand?" He had called back several hours earlier when it was clear from the conference with Ike that he needed the Third Army to try to relieve Bastogne.

"We're awaiting some additional supplies, and we should be able to start moving in four or five hours."

"Keep the pressure on. We've got to get up there." *I knew those Krauts were up to something. I hope we can get there in time.*

Noon, December 21, the DeBoy Farm

Since Alex and Polly would have to leave on the twenty-third, the family decided to have one last day together. Mark and Aurélie drove down to Alphonse's farmhouse with Alex and Polly and would spend the night. Josette and Henri had brought a ham from the Benoit farm. Marie showed up, along with Claudine. All the women were busy in the kitchen, putting the meal together.

They decided that since everyone was there, they should celebrate Christmas. Alex brought a large roast from the wild boar Mark had shot, and Mark contributed a large venison roast. They all provided vegetables, and Aurélie raided some of the supplies from the dugout for sugar and some of the other dry goods that were in short supply in France.

Alphonse came in the door with several bottles of wine, followed by Luc and Berne, carrying cheese. "It smells great!" He stood behind Aurélie and Marie, looking around the room and realizing his entire family was all there. "It's good to have everyone in the house again."

Aurélie looked over at Luc. "Would you get some wine glasses, please. We might as well have some wine and snack on the cheese."

Heinrich was sitting at the kitchen table, cleaning some vegetables and stealing glances at Claudine whenever he could. He had grown up on a farm outside Dresden and could remember his extended family gathering, very much like this, for a large meal. His memory went back to the loss of his wife and parents, but then he remembered that many people throughout Europe had nothing or no one left in their lives. He was fortunate to be alive and in the company of such people.

Josette saw the look on Heinrich's face. She leaned over and whispered to Claudine, "Why don't you talk to Heinrich? I think his memories may be making him sad."

Berne walked up behind Marie, placing his hands on the back of her shoulders and gently massaging.

Marie leaned back, sighing. "Merci."

Alphonse went over to Heinrich and engaged both Claudine and him in conversation. After a few minutes, he decided he should leave the two of them alone. As he got up, he placed his hand on Heinrich's shoulder. "I'm glad you're here, my friend."

Several hours later, the table in the main room was loaded with all sorts of food, and everyone sat down. Alphonse, seated at the head of the table, looked at each one and bowed his head. "Father, thank you for our blessings, keep us safe until this war ends, and thank you for bringing us all together this day."

They ate, drank, laughed, and shared stories well into the evening. The women had managed to make pies and tarts for dessert. They exchanged homemade gifts and just enjoyed each other's company. Each one realized how memorable this time was.

As the evening wore on, they started cleaning up. The married couples allowed Marie and Bern and Heinrich and Claudine to have some time together. Josette, always the matchmaker, walked over to her little brother. It had not gone unnoticed that Luc didn't have a girlfriend, and of course, Josette knew precisely the right person to solve that problem.

"Have you seen any girls who interest you?"

Luc turned his head. "I guess, but it's been difficult with everything that's been going on the last few months."

"I saw you looking at Francine a couple of weeks ago."

"Yes, she's pretty, but I don't think she's noticed me."

Josette smiled and put her arm around him. "Well, I happened to see her last week, and I mentioned you." Luc looked up, about to say something, but Josette started laughing. "She's noticed you. She's just waiting for you to speak to her."

8:00 p.m., December 22, SHAEF Headquarters, Luxembourg City

Ike and General Bradley were in Ike's office. Bradley sat down across from his boss. "I'm sure Monty enjoys finally having some Americans under his command."

Eisenhower took a drag on his cigarette. "He's already taking credit for stopping the advance in the north."

"Well, he's correct, but he's not doing much with impeding their progress west."

"How's George doing?" Ike was anxious to have Patton get to the 101st.

Bradley got up and pointed to the map. "He's about three-quarters of the way to Bastogne, but I suspect things are going to slow considerably. The weather has taken a turn for the worse, and the Germans are dynamiting roads and anything else they can to slow him. I'd be surprised if he makes it by Christmas."

Ike lit a cigarette. "You know, George is just about the only commander in the world who could do this. He was firmly engaged in fighting on our Eastern Front, and within twenty-four hours, he's asked his men to turn ninety degrees, travel more than one hundred miles in the snow, and go into another battle without any rest. Remarkable, to say the least!"

Ike looked out the window at the blowing snow. "You know, Brad, he was right about one thing; he's pulled my ass out of the fire more than once."

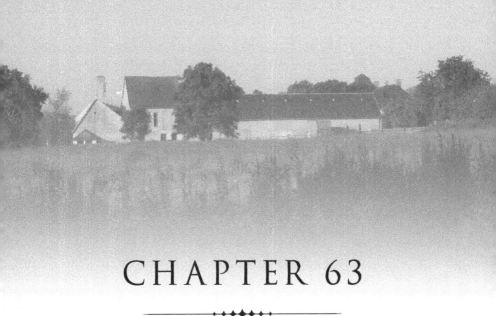

CHAPTER 63

9:00 a.m., December 23, the DeBoy Farm

The Lysander was circling the farm. It started a steep descent over Les Islettes and set down on the D2, stopping just in front of the farmhouse. Alex and Polly were standing by their gear as the plane slowed and shut its engine. Alphonse and Heinrich began loading the equipment into the aircraft.

Polly hugged Aurélie. "You make sure to have Mark take a picture of the baby." She went to each of the men and said goodbye, especially thanking Berne and Heinrich for what they'd done to protect Aurélie. She then hugged Marie and reminded her to take good care of Berne.

Mark and Alex shook hands. "Give my regards to General Brawls, and please make sure Colonel Walker gets these," Mark said. He had written a letter to Colonel Walker relating what had happened in the intervening fifteen months. He also had written a letter to his sister, with an insert for his son William, and his daughter, Darlene. While the children had received monthly updates from Colonel Walker, they knew little about what their dad was doing because of the need for secrecy. While he had not named this location, he did mention that he had married a woman in France and they were going to have a child. *I wish I could be there in person to tell them. I hope they take this well.*

Finally, it was time to leave. The Lysander pilot didn't want to stay on the ground any longer than necessary. Polly and Alex got in the plane, and everyone moved back to watch them taxi down the road and then turn back into the wind for takeoff.

Polly and Alex were crowded in the plane, but both waved as they left the ground. Tears ran down Polly's face. Alex reached over to wipe them away. "They'll be fine," he assured her. "They're why we'll beat the Nazis into submission."

7:00 p.m., December 26, War Cabinet Rooms, St. Charles Street, London

The main conference room was crowded. The briefing had been going on for over an hour. The Prime Minister got up. "Gentlemen, I have to relieve myself. When I return, please make sure you've figured out how to stop Jerry and return the momentum to us."

Polly and Alex had been invited to squeeze into one corner. They were waiting for their turn to discuss their experiences. Polly had read the report concerning Patton and his advance. She'd just been handed a wireless transmission indicating that forward elements of the Third Army had made contact with the 101st Airborne Division just outside of Bastogne.

January 15, the Old Farmhouse

Heinrich, Berne, Luc, Alphonse, and Mark were putting the finishing touches on the new water system. Alphonse had found a pump, but they still had to finish the last couple of poles and string the wire to the house. They had used a few German poles and lines. They also had found five large drums to store water, and Luc had been able to convince one of their neighbors to donate an old boiler for hot water. To complete their remodel, they had salvaged an old propane tank from an abandoned farm and added a propane-powered stove to the kitchen, a heater in the main room, and a heater upstairs in the hallway. The new heaters, added to the three fireplaces and the thick stone walls, kept the interior reasonably warm.

Josette, Aurélie, Marie, and Claudine were all in the kitchen preparing a meal for the men. Aurélie was now four months along and beginning to have back pains. The baby was very active, and Mark and Aurélie continually discussed how parenthood would change their lives

6:00 a.m., April 3, a Small Flat on Gloucester Road, London

Polly woke up and slipped out of bed quietly. Alex had been up late, and she wanted to let him sleep. She went into the bathroom and closed the door. Her stomach was queasy, but she managed to calm it down. She suspected last week she might be pregnant, but now she knew for sure. Her menstrual cycle should have begun three days ago, and she was very seldom late.

She went into the kitchen and made some tea. She and Alex had been working long hours, keeping up with the flow of information, and it was taking a physical toll on both of them. *At least this war should be coming to a close soon—unless the Nazis come up with another wonder weapon.* There had been one surprise after another over the past five months. The biggest was the deployment of the ME-262 jet. Luckily, the Allied bombing campaign had finally started taking a toll on German production. It was amazing how resilient German manufacturing capacity had been throughout the war.

She sat down at the kitchen table and reread Aurélie's letter. Polly had written four times since they left, but it was difficult to get letters delivered to France. Aurélie said she had written three times, but they'd only received two letters. The letters were included with the supply drops, but those were becoming few and far between.

Alex had argued with Major Boysden on several occasions about keeping Mark in place and supplied. There had been little opposition to this until the Allies finally pushed back to the original December frontlines about eight weeks ago. He had also lobbied General Brawls about Mark's value as a crucial asset, with regard to his being a backup in case of another counterattack, as well as someone who could help coordinate rebuilding of the area.

Polly had to share her news, so she sat down to write a letter.

Dear Aurélie, Mark, and family,

Alex and I both hope everyone is in good health and that, indeed, the entire family, as well as Heinrich and Berne, are also doing well. We miss your company daily and will do our best to visit as soon as this horrible war is over. Mark, please take care of Aurélie in these next several months, as she will become more and more uncomfortable as the big day approaches.

I need to wake Alex, as we both have to go back to the office today. Before I leave, I want to mention that I am reasonably certain that I am expecting—still very early days. If I'm right, we should have a baby by Christmas.

Please take care, and make sure nothing happens to you or any of the family. We love you all.

Polly and Alex

PS—I'm curious as to how Marie and Berne are getting along, also Claudine and Heinrich.

She addressed an envelope and sealed it and then got up and went to the bedroom. Alex was starting to stir. She smiled; she liked the way he looked when he was asleep. She took her gown off and slipped under the covers. *If we're late by a few minutes, it'll be worth it.* She rolled over on top of Alex and began to kiss his neck lightly.

April 23, the Führer Bunker beneath the Reich Chancellery

Speer was waiting for the Führer to call him in. Speer had been quite disappointed with the reports of the last two months about their manufacturing capabilities. The Allies had been very effective in bombing the facilities and interdicting the transport of products. He had run out of ideas. Most important, he'd lost faith in the Führer's cause. He'd even thought at one time about introducing gas into the bunker's air-filtration system as a way to be rid of the madman. It would've been relatively easy to do, given his knowledge of the system.

However, Adolf Hitler's personal charisma still had a powerful influence on Speer, and in meetings last month he'd decided not to oppose any further. He had reflected over the past several weeks how his abilities had probably prolonged the war to no constructive objective. More and more soldiers and civilians, both German and Allied, were losing their lives. *It's time this war came to an end and we start the rebuilding process.*

The SS guard came in. "Reich Minister, the Führer will see you now."

Speer went back to the main conference room. He had been shocked over the past several months by how much Hitler's appearance had degraded. Even since the last time he'd met with him, his complexion had grown paler, and he appeared to have difficulty walking without shuffling his feet.

"Albert, we will speak candidly. We are close to the end, and I wanted to thank you for your efforts. History will see your contributions positively"—he paused and sat down heavily in a chair—"even though I'm sure I will be vilified."

Speer had not expected Hitler to recognize the end was near and had trouble formulating a response that he felt was appropriate. Even now, the man exuded an aura that could still control people.

"My Führer, I must tell you I think you are wise to see the end coming. I also must tell you that our manufacturing and industrial capabilities are almost completely destroyed."

"Albert, you did all you could. I think it is time for you to leave. I will stay here until the end."

Speer again was surprised. Hitler had finally accepted his fate. Speer was confused, but he was also moved. The one thing he remembered for the rest of his life was how lifeless Hitler's movements were.

April 30, the Old Farmhouse

Mark finished packing clothes and other things to take down to Alphonse's house. He and Aurélie had agreed last week that it was time to move down where they would be closer to the rest of the family. The improvements on the house were completed by the end of January, so it became a comfortable home. They had moved over from the dugout in February, since it was easier for Aurélie. Mark was impressed with Aurélie's eye for decorating. It reminded him of how Joanne could always take a house and make it a home.

Aurélie was walking through the house, checking to see if they'd left anything. She went back to the bedroom as Mark was closing the suitcases. She sat down on the bed, feeling fat. She had been, however, remarkably free of discomfort up to this point.

Mark leaned over and kissed her. "What are you thinking about?"

"I'm sad to leave, even if it's only for a little while. I like it here; I even like the dugout."

He sat down next to her. "I think you might have a little bit of a problem going up and down the ladder."

"I know, but it's special there. I can see why you enjoyed being there."

He put his arm around her and put his other hand on her stomach. "It was nice but lonely. I didn't realize how lonely until you started coming up." He kissed her again.

Aurélie shifted and sat on his lap. The bed sagged down, and both of them noticed it and started laughing. "I guess you just have a fat wife."

He was still laughing but managed to say, "I love every pound."

Aurélie poked him with her elbow. "Calling your wife *fat* is not the best way to get any attention. By the way, we may be getting close to your becoming celibate."

Mark frowned but then smiled. "Yeah, I figured that was coming. It's okay."

She took his face in her hands and kissed him. "Oh, maybe we can figure out something to keep you relaxed."

After a few minutes, they got up, and Mark loaded the Jeep. He made sure the heat was regulated so that nothing would freeze, and then they drove down to the farm.

May 3, the DeBoy Farm

Aurélie and Mark had moved into her old bedroom. Heinrich and Berne still lived in the basement, and they had made significant improvements down there to make it more comfortable.

Alphonse walked through the door after coming back from the village. "A message." He handed it to Mark.

Mark went upstairs to get his codebooks. When he read it, his heart leaped. *So Hitler finally ended it.*

He went downstairs. "Let's get everybody in the main room. The war is over." In a few minutes, everyone had gathered around, and he made the announcement. "I received a message this morning that Hitler committed suicide in Berlin four days ago. The German High Command has already approached the Allies for peace terms and has tacitly accepted unconditional surrender. I don't know when, but I would expect that the official surrender will take place at any time now."

There was a considerable release of tension by everyone, including Berne and Heinrich. Heinrich looked at Berne and then turned to the rest of them. "He was evil, and the Nazis were evil as well. I'm glad this is finally over."

May 8, War Cabinet Rooms, St. Charles Street, London

Churchill was leading the meeting. "Gentlemen, this will be our last meeting here. From now on, we'll either meet at Number 10 or at the old staff headquarters."

After the meeting was dismissed, Colonel Walker came up to General Brawls. "What have you gentlemen decided about Major Dornier?"

"We've extended his stay to the end of the year. I believe his new wife is going to give birth any day, and since he's not needed here, we've decided to have him oversee any rebuilding and reconstruction in that area of France."

Colonel Walker nodded. "I'd like to get a letter to him about his children, if that's possible."

"Just give it to me when you're ready, and I'll make sure it's delivered."

Colonel Walker had heard from Mark's sister and his two children. His son, William, had married in January, and Darlene had graduated high school early and with honors. They both expressed their happiness at the news of their father's marriage. Darlene even commented that she was looking forward to being an older sister.

CHAPTER 64

-◆◆◆◆◆-

6:00 p.m., June 4, the Midwife's Delivery Room, Lachalade

ark was pacing back and forth. Josette was in the room with her
sister, while Marie and Claudine were doing their best to keep
the men calm. Aurélie had gone into labor right after breakfast, and
they had taken her into Lachalade immediately.

A small high-pitched cry rang through the house. Mark immediately
stopped, and Marie and Claudine got up. Claudine took his hand. "I
think you're a father."

The midwife came out and went over to Mark. "It's a girl, and
Aurélie and your daughter are both doing fine." She took him back
into the room.

Mark went over to Aurélie. She looked beautiful and not even a bit
tired. She was holding their daughter on her chest.

Mark knelt down. "Are you okay?"

Aurélie nodded. "Is Chantal still okay for a name?"

Mark leaned over and looked at his daughter. "She's beautiful, and
Chantal is exactly the right name."

Aurélie looked up, and Mark leaned down and kissed her. Aurélie put her hand on his cheek. "Am I imagining things, or does she look like you?"

They both smiled.

July 25, 1945, the Old Farmhouse, Forêt Domaniale De Lachalade

Mark, Aurélie, and Chantal had returned to the old farmhouse in the first part of July. Polly and Alex had managed to get some leave and arrived about a week later. They stayed at the farmhouse to help out. For the next two weeks, Alphonse had all of his family, both the old and new, in the same area again. Everything was as it should have been. They quickly fell into their old routine.

Mark and Alex were out back in the garden, harvesting vegetables. They also discovered some apple and pear trees and were experimenting with making cider.

Polly was holding Chantal. Her own pregnancy was starting to show. "I can't wait for our baby to arrive. It's still five months away."

"It's amazing. They grow inside you and then come out and have everything they need—hair, fingernails, and certainly an appetite."

Polly asked, "Do you enjoy nursing, or is it uncomfortable?"

"I love it. It's like we're one person. You'll like the entire experience—well, labor can be a little bit intense, but once it's over, the rest is like nothing you could ever experience."

Polly looked at Chantal's little face. She did resemble Mark a little. "Is Mark still … I mean, is he still okay with all this?"

"Several times, waves of guilt or even panic have come over me. Each time, Mark has been there for me." Aurélie's eyes watered. "I couldn't have asked for a better husband."

Alex and Mark walked in and went over to their wives. Mark put his arms around Aurélie's middle. "You're getting back to normal," he said and kissed the small of her neck.

Aurélie squealed. He knew she was ticklish there, and besides, it made her want to turn around and hug him to death.

Polly laughed and then turned to Chantal. "You're going to have to keep an eye on your parents when you get bigger. Otherwise, you're going to have a house full of brothers and sisters!"

EPILOGUE

✦✦✦✦✦

World War II was the most destructive war in human history. Depending on the area of the world, it lasted for six to twelve years and resulted, conservatively, in fifty-five million deaths. It uprooted families and caused unmeasurable heartache all over the world. The Nazis and the Japanese military were held accountable for starting wars of aggression and other unspeakable atrocities. While Hitler escaped judgment, most of the remaining Axis leadership was held accountable.

Albert Speer was sentenced to twenty years in Spandau Prison. When he was released, he wrote several books about the Third Reich and his role during the war. He made a lot of money with them, partially because he was candid about his part and the blame associated with it. He died in 1981 in London at age seventy-six.

Winston Churchill was voted out of office two months after VE Day. While he became Prime Minister one last time in the 1950s, it was clear that Great Britain thought more of him as a wartime leader. It was he who coined the term *Iron Curtain*, and he also warned the West about the Soviet intent.

Stalin continued his rule of the Soviet Union and was successful at stealing a number of designs and other intelligence from the West. The most important may have been the design of the Nagasaki plutonium bomb, nicknamed "Fat Man." They exploded their first nuclear device only a few years after World War II ended. They also stole the design of the B-29 from one of the planes they had confiscated toward the end of the war. The Soviet version was called the Backfire bomber.

Mark was awarded the British Military Cross and the French Croix de Guerre, in addition to the Distinguished Service Cross, and he received another letter of thanks from General Patton shortly before his accident,[11] congratulating him on the medals and his marriage. While there were many agents at work in eastern France, there were only two other agents similar to Mark, and one of those in northern Belgium was killed in late 1943. The Belgium Resistance stepped in to fill the gap. Mark's willingness to carry out orders and his detailed notes were invaluable.

Mark and Aurélie were able to stay in France until the end of 1945. They went to London in early 1946, and Mark was offered a position in the American diplomatic corps. They settled near Bletchley Park, north of London, where Mark helped work on developing new code sequences. They had a second child in 1947, a boy they named Jean. They traveled to the US to be reunited with Mark's family—William and his wife and Darlene, as well as Mark's sister and her family. Darlene was smitten with both Chantal and Jean. They were able to visit each other often.

Josette and Henri continued living in Lachalade and had three children, one of which they named Maria after Josette's grandmother. Josette was one of those women who just bounced from one thing to another and whom everyone loved. Henri sometimes felt as though he was being pulled through life by her energy.

Marie and Berne had two children and made their home in Les Islettes. Berne learned French and never had a desire to return to Germany. His family had been in Berlin, but despite several attempts

---

11. George Patton was injured and paralyzed in a minor traffic accident near Speyer in southwest Germany on December 8, 1945, and died twelve days later.

to make contact, he was never able to get in touch with them. He found out in 1949 that his mother, father, and older sister had all been killed when the Soviets shelled the city during their final assault. Berne was grateful his entire life for the kindness of the DeBoys.

Luc got married in 1948 and made his home with Alphonse until Alphonse's death in 1956. It took a while, but he finally married Francine, the girl whom Josette had picked out for him. Josette turned out to be quite a matchmaker.

Heinrich and Claudine married in January 1946 and made their home in the old farmhouse in the woods. Heinrich always thought it was strange that he felt so much peace in a place only a half mile from where he had once participated in a battle as the enemy. They traveled back to Germany several times, starting in late 1946, to help in rebuilding. They had three children. The oldest, a son, they named Marc after both Aurélie and Josette's brother and Mark Dornier.

Mark, Aurélie, Josette, Henri, Luc, Francine, Heinrich, Claudine, Marie, and Berne all got together at least once a year in the old DeBoy farmhouse. Luc and Berne made sure the dugout was kept in good repair.

Today, the dugout is still there, as is the tunnel system. People have restored some of the dugouts and made improvements. Mark and Aurélie stayed in theirs several times. Although Chantal and Jean were too young to appreciate it fully, Mark and Aurélie took them on walks in the forest. It's a special place that is cool in the summer, warm in the winter, full of trees, and surrounded by the scars of two world wars.

One time, Mark explained to Aurélie what it was like to fly over the Forêt Domaniale De Lachalade—it was like coming home.

July 2010, the Dugout

The wind gently moved the leaves in the tree tops. Mark stared at the dugout, now restored by some unknown person or organization. He looked over to his older sister, Josette, and took her hand. "I wonder how grandpa felt living here."

Josette took a deep breathe smelling the forest. "Remember what

Uncle Jean said. He enjoyed it, but grandma and her family made it special."

They walked down the road and then through the trees just like their grandparents had almost sixty-five years earlier.

Mark whispered, "It *is* just like home."

ABOUT THE AUTHOR

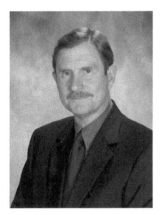

Chris is a retired engineer, husband, father, and grandfather. He has always had an interest in history and especially World War I and World War II. He has traveled widely over the course of his career and to all the locales mentioned in this book. He currently lives in Texas with his wife.

CPSIA information can be obtained
at www.ICGtesting.com
Printed in the USA
LVHW041515040122
707834LV00001B/54